The Seeding Seven's Vision

Allen Dionne

Books by Allen Dionne
FICTION

The Seeding Seven's Vision
The Seeding II Virgin Landfall
Duhcat, Mystery and Legend Unfold
A Summer in Mussel Shoals

Cover art: Dave Archer painting, *Spirit City*, Copyright ©1992
Spine Art: Allen Dionne ©2012
Copyright ©2012 AD by Allen Dionne

Book Design by www.integrativeink.com
My warmest thanks to:
Stephanee Killen, Project Manager at Integrative Ink

ISBN: 978-0-9853979-0-6

The Seeding, Seven's Vision is entirely a work of fiction. Names, characters, places and incidents are a product of the Authors imagination and dreams. Any similarities to the real world are purely coincidental.

Printed in the United States of America by Lightning Source

For Myhrlyn, because of his encouragement.

One

ANDAREAN had never before entered the normally sequestered domain of Seven Galaxies hierarchy. Few were allowed, and he pondered the reasons that his presence had been required. Walking towards the seven azure columns standing before the Dome of Wisdom, he was stricken by their forms. Andarean understood the art of growing crystals, yet he had never seen any so massive; they appeared flawless and perfectly matched—seven translucent, sapphire-blue sentinels, sparkling against the early morning's crimson sunrise.

On the opposite edge of the courtyard, seven falls of water merged into one glistening pool. The crystal columns were mirror-like, creating a color-filled kaleidoscope reflecting falling water. In all his travels, throughout his many years of life, Andarean had seen nothing so breathtaking. He could hear birdsong from several species, but there were no birds to be seen. No guards were present either. He was alone. Stopping between the falls and the azure columns, Andarean absorbed a new day's light unfolding upon the scene: a transition of astonishing wonder, surreal and mesmerizing.

Desiring to stay longer, yet also feeling anxious, he walked through the courtyard and up seven steps. A black-onyx door slid open silently.

Andarean continued through the archway into an outer chamber. Although no plants could be seen, he was immediately taken with the scent of wild roses, sweetly stimulating, as though mixed with winter mint.

There was no receptionist, only an area with chairs, a couple of floor mats, two long benches, and immense double doors. Preferring to stand, he waited.

A soft, flowing voice called his name. The two giant doors auto-opened. Andarean walked through, and they closed silently behind him.

Before him was a young woman clad in a long silken gown of the same stunning blue as the columns outside. Andarean's breath became short. The woman was something from a dream. He had seen her before, only he knew not where.

Her hair was long and had been braided and wrapped above her head in the form of an ancient water vessel. It showed colors of ebony and redwood, two distinctly contrasting shades. Her eyes were luminous and immense. Andarean took in their overpowering sea-green. Other colors flickered—violet, rose, and jade, as if her eyes had been cut from a thin curl of cresting ocean wave at sunset. The flashing colors reminded him of the seven crystal columns from which he had departed only moments ago.

I could die this moment, he thought, *and I would not care in the least, for I am the happiest I have ever been.*

The woman moved fluidly. Her eyes pulled at his soul.

She said, "A splendid morning to you, Andarean. I am Estellene. I'm pleased and honored to finally soul-meet you after so many years."

"And I you, Estellene," said Andarean, smiling graciously.

Her voice soothed him; she exuded tranquility and set him immediately at ease.

He wondered how it could be that she knew of him.

"They are ready for you," she said. As though timed to her voice, another set of twin doors swung open, and Estellene motioned him forward. She walked beside him to the archway, lightly grasping his left elbow. At her slight touch, Andarean's skin became warm all over. He felt himself flush a faint shade of pink.

She stopped at the opening, and he walked through alone. The doors closed quietly behind him. He heard the shush of air displaced by their enormous size.

Before him was a crescent-shaped table of an iridescent stone that was unfamiliar to him. The Fifteen were seated around it, facing the one empty chair that waited in the concave arc created by the immense stone slab.

One spoke. "Please sit down," said the Ancient, motioning to the open chair.

Andarean had seen an Ancient only once in his eighty-five years, at a memorial service for his mother's great uncle, a diplomat of some renown who had passed at the age of six hundred and twenty.

The wise one who had spoken appeared much older. She hailed him with no pretext of ceremony or pomp; her demeanor was that of an old friend, not anything like he had expected.

"Andarean, I bid you a gracious morning. Thank you for coming."

Andarean settled into the offered chair with well-masked relief, stifling an involuntary tremble in his legs.

Before him was the governing body that ruled not only the planet of his birth but also the Seven Galaxies—a vast portion of the known universe.

"We have watched with great interest your work these past sixty years," the Ancient began. "The progress you have achieved with regards to genetic flaws within the human race has kept our attention. I do not only speak of physical weaknesses and those of the intellect, but of morality as well."

The moral correlations in his genetic research were a part of Andarean's privately held theory, not one he had documented in writing.

"We chose to keep your work quiet and observe you all these years because we believe self-importance and arrogance to be flaws in the human entity. We did not want your work affected by emphasis or by praise, so we have kept the advances you have achieved secret for reasons we will impart to you this day.

"Although you are now aware that we have kept abreast of your work, public acknowledgement will not be possible. Do you understand?"

"Not entirely," Andarean said, puzzling over the meaning of this meeting. "However, I do not question your methods or intent. I wish to understand all that you are willing to share, and I will do my absolute best to study and abide by any precepts you impart. Likewise, I will implement your desires with all of my physical, mental, and financial resources."

"We appreciate your dedication. We require your mind and body, but your unwavering willingness to cooperate with all belief, energy, and intellect—and a positive frame of mind—are most important to our designs. By allowing you within our presence, you have been honored and commended." The Ancient paused before continuing, studying Andarean's reaction.

"This is a strictly private acknowledgement, for reasons we are about to explain. There can be no other way.

"This meeting will change your life forever, if you accept our proposal. Financial resources in this matter are unlimited. We cannot, in mere words, express the utmost importance this has to Seven Galaxies; our very survival over the next six millennia may depend upon your mission."

Andarean's mind flew, racing through the words just spoken. What could they mean? How could his work or his intellect possibly be so important? Calming his thoughts, Andarean spoke: "I am deeply and spiritually moved by your belief in me and in my work. I give thanks and offer all that I am and all that I possess to the needs of service within Seven Galaxies."

"What we are about to impart will require that you leave the jurisdiction of Seven Galaxies. Do you understand?"

Andarean shook his head. "Not entirely, your imminence."

"We do not stand on ceremony here," the Ancient said. "Put simply, we are only people, much like you, who have dedicated our lives to upholding the certain fundamental truths we hold sacred; therefore, much responsibility has been heaped upon us. Our work may seem glorious to those who seek power, yet our entire group has only sought truth. We have attained much wisdom along our journey. Our search for truth has brought us here today. There are many more like us—people like you, who are the threads that weave our vast society together, the stitching that keeps the great quilt of our influence from coming apart at the seams.

"Andarean, in the past thirty-five years, you have isolated certain renegade genes that affect the mental, physical, and moral character of humankind. You have been successful in your experiments, effectively removing the negatives and replacing them with a closer-to-perfect nature, and we have been patiently observing the small group of three hundred you successfully cloned from your selections of unflawed genes and then introduced into our society. In this, we are truly astounded. They are exemplary! All healthy, extremely intelligent, peaceful, yet not lacking in courage. Most importantly, we have observed a total lack of interest when we expose them to temptations of greed, or corruption in lieu of power, or moral debasement, or any such tendencies as prevail among low-minded people. They are not attracted to those activities which, when followed, lead towards a more serious criminal nature.

"In other words, they all seem to be more perfect humans. Where others of our race are consumed with the Achilles heel of human kind, your people are filled with generosity, hard work, love, and honesty.

"In light of all we have just enumerated, would you like to add anything to our observations and comments?"

"Yes," Andarean said. "I have found certain patterns within the criminal element. They were associated with deviate behavior for millennia by the school of psychoanalysis.

"Throughout our history, we have acknowledged that an impressionable young child can be influenced by such things as mental, physical, and sexual abuse when they happen during the developing years, or by chemical abuses while in the womb. Even abject poverty in youth can drive a weaker person to justify crime in order to attain material things that were absent in their youngest years.

"However, my studies have also proven that many of the most vicious criminals had excellent upbringings, good childhoods, and much parental love. What began my quest for knowledge on this very engrossing subject is the mirror image of these ancient and unfalteringly accepted psychiatric theories, which have permeated our culture for thousands of years. Irrefutable fact shows that many very moral, respectable, hardworking adults came from . . . shall I say, grievous childhoods." Andarean paused, looking to the Fifteen, wondering if they were seriously interested. He was also allowing time for what he had just said to sink in, before continuing.

"A question then arises within an enquiring mind: why do some take the dark path yet many take the path of light? Hence, my quest began, and I must say I am still traveling it. Everything I have just imparted prompted me to embark on a journey into exploring the minds, genetic correlations, habits, and diets—and a host of other things—within the criminal element itself. It was fascinating indeed.

"I began to develop certain correlations and cross-references to a diverse gene-pool within the criminal element. Isolating the DNA was the key. You see, our race was built from a limited . . . shall I say, foundation. Dominant genes are reinforced by the same dominants. I began to explore this, and before I knew it, I was onto something exciting, intriguing, and extremely frightening, all at the same time."

"You say 'frightening,'" a man said. He was not an Ancient. He looked as though he might be a commander of high authority. "May I ask why you use that word?"

"I use the word because there is not one among us who doesn't possess within his or her DNA threads of the criminal element," answered Andarean.

"You, dear Admiral Ty, have the mind of a bright, enquiring child, a trait which endears you to me, but please hold it in check for the moment. We must all concentrate upon the data Andarean is sharing. This will speed the process; our unified focus will enable Andarean to articulate his thoughts more precisely." The Ancient's reprimand was affectionate, and quiet laughter emanated from the fourteen. The admiral smiled at the warm rebuff.

"As you wish, Leandra," he said.

"Please continue, Andarean," she said.

Andarean, who had been taken a bit off guard, felt himself relaxing. *The Dome of Wisdom has a sense of humor,* he thought. *How refreshing.*

"As I was saying," he continued, to more muffled chuckles, "it is frightening when you think that any of us in this room has had the dark side of our personality speak to us on occasion. Is this not true?"

Andarean could not believe he had just posed such a question to the Fifteen, but subdued nods of assent came from most of the group.

He continued. "We have all debated with or even fought the voice of darkness when it has spoken. When this happens, we have made a conscious choice to continue our journey and travel the path of light—that path brought us to this meeting today. Why, then, does so large a portion of our society choose to go in the other direction? I say 'choose' because it is my belief that the choice is conscious, even to the unenlightened. I have asked myself this question repeatedly over the past thirty years. My answer, or what I believe to be the answer, finally came in the form of the genetic information imbedded in each person's DNA.

"The interesting—and I must add, enlightening—discovery, was that those with a history of violent, criminal, or socially unacceptable behavior also had DNA with ever-increasing concentrations of certain genes, which I have been fortunate enough to identify and isolate.

"Can you imagine?" Pausing for emphasis once more he let silence reign for a brief moment before continuing. "If the common person were to become conscious of these findings, they might begin to test any future mate or breeding partner in an attempt to find a mate with few negative gene characteristics. Who would mate with the undesirables?

"Would a criminal mind then set out to find a diabolical breeding partner so as to perpetuate his or her precepts? Would the theory be taught in school? What would the impact of this knowledge be in the average person's education?

"I could not possibly consider all of the future implications; therefore, I was loath to place the unproven thought-process on paper. Am I making any sense? I seem to be rambling. The words are flowing out without my usual careful consideration."

"You are making perfect sense, Andarean. Please go on," Leandra said. She seemed to chair this meeting. He felt camaraderie with her, as if she were his advocate within the Fifteen. *Who is Leandra?* he found himself asking.

"Rather than placing theories on paper, I applied them in laboratory. I began with animals." Andarean had never before had such an interested audience when explaining his experiments and theories. Each of the Fifteen seemed to be hanging upon his every word. It was surreal—something from a dream. He continued, attempting to quell his internal dialogue.

"It has long been accepted within equestrian circles that a good stud horse will, many times, pass on its temperament—"

Andarean paused as Estellene entered the hall. Her fluid stride took her briskly to the Ancient's side.

Leandra listened intently to Estellene's words, which were spoken softly into one ear so that no others in the room could discern the message.

Leandra looked up, began gathering her papers, and said curtly, "There is an urgent need for my presence. We will take a recess until tomorrow morning—same time as today." She looked over at the admiral. "Ty, will you be so kind as to show Andarean the gardens?"

With that, she left the hall swiftly, without a backward glance.

TWO

Andarean and the admiral left the crescent hall and walked along a vast corridor.

"Andarean," the admiral began, "you will find in your time here with us that we do not stand on formalities. As I call you by first name instead of your official title, you may do the same with me. It would be my preference that you call me Ty, which is short for TyGor. All my close friends use the shortened version."

As they approached the corridor's end, a single, unadorned door opened. A warm breeze carried in the sound of birdsong and the scent of herbs and flowers. Foremost were the scents of wild roses and winter mint. Golden sunlight shone through the opening.

The admiral stopped short of the archway, saying, "After you."

Andarean stepped through the portal and was immediately overcome by the sensation that he had been transported to another place in time, long ago—back into some ancient culture's lost world of beauty, the likes of which he had only seen in archives. Ancient Greece and the art of Maxfield Parrish came to mind.

The land sloped downward, away from the structure they had just exited. In the distance, he saw a sparkling, crystal-blue lake. Behind the lake, mountains rose high above the shimmering water. Precipices and cliffs of stone fell to shore, while green slopes were evident wherever any soil could be held. The lower mountains were cast in violet-blue haze. Above, the rugged cliff faces were draped in aquamarine crevasses and pure white from the fresh snowfall.

The land running downhill, away towards the shore, was steep in places, but terraced levels created giant steps that led to the water's edge. On more gentle slopes were rolling meadows of tall, golden grass that waved in summer's breezes. Other areas were manicured short and green. Trees dotted the landscape, many bearing fruit, and Andarean could also see fields of berries and gardens abundant with herbs and vegetables.

Andarean embraced the scene, breathing deeply, soaking in the sun's rays and feeling instantly renewed. He turned towards Ty and was surprised to find no building or structure of any kind. "Ty, is the landscape real or holographic?" Andarean asked.

"It is real, my friend. The Ancient took on this project some four hundred years ago. She is a botanist—or was, before the Dome claimed her."

"Before this, I didn't know much of anything about you or the Fifteen."

"It may seem reclusive to you, yet that is the way. Most of us do not leave here. I am one who does," he said, smiling. "Andarean, I will never have the privilege of seeing the Virgin, yet in my mind's eye this is how I imagine she will be."

"What do you mean, the Virgin?" asked Andarean, befuddled.

The admiral smiled again but ignored the question. He gazed out across the panorama before them, a wistful look in his eyes. He then turned his attention once more toward the conversation at hand. "I am sorry, Andarean. What were you saying?"

"Until today, only in my dreams had I seen such a place, or in reproductions kept in the planetary archives."

"I know. I have visited most of our worlds worth seeing, and many more that were not. Here, I experience something I find nowhere else. It's not just the way it strikes my eyes, ears, and nose. It's the way this place affects the heart, making it extraordinary and special to me—and to many others who come here."

"Andarean, I wish to speak with you about many things; however, today is not the time. Your first day in the gardens must be absorbed without worries or cares. We will discuss the details of the great adventure that is before you later. Promise me that you will spend your time today relaxing and enjoying the company and overwhelming beauty you will find here."

"If you insist, Admiral."

"I do insist," he said.

"I'm sorry, I meant to call you Ty.... It's difficult for me to cast off protocols ingrained over a lifetime," Andarean added, looking at the ground.

"I understand and take no offense, but try and work on it, will you?" Ty smiled and then warmly placed a hand on Andarean's back.

"There is a cabin waiting for you. It is tucked away amongst the gardens. Stay on the stone walkway and keep to the right. There you will find the one reserved for you."

"How will I know which cabin?"

"Oh! Did you think I was saying the *cabin* was reserved? I was speaking of Estellene." Ty smiled again, even larger than before. "Enjoy yourself," he said. "I will see you at the same time and in the same place as today."

"Thank you, Ty."

"Estellene will show you the gardens. Go to her first, or you may get lost out there; it is vast and overwhelming, to say the least. She was raised here and knows this place as though it were her own. You have an adventure before you like none in our history," he added. "Believe my words: my spirit and heart will be with you always."

"Please, tell me, where will I be going?"

Ty looked at Andarean, appreciating his curiosity. "Not just yet. Until the morrow, then." The admiral turned, walked half a dozen paces, and suddenly was there no more.

THREE

ANDAREAN was unsettled, having heard and seen things that morning, which seemed better suited to fantasy. He walked a few meters and sat down upon a carpet of green, not sure that this wasn't all a dream.

He grabbed two handfuls of grass and pulled the fibers between his fingers. Putting both hands up and over his head, he could smell the freshly broken pieces. He opened his hands, and the grass cascaded down upon him. Surely this was no dream. He thought about pinching himself but decided it could be construed as mental instability to anyone watching.

Laughing at his obvious foolishness, he stood and went in search of Estellene.

Could it be true? That most amazing young woman could not possibly be interested in him, he thought. Certainly Andarean did not look old—more mature than Estellene, but not old. Could she see him in that light? The very thought excited him.

Many people these days lived past five hundred years. Surely, judged by ancient standards, he would be considered a fossil; back then, people had died at an average

age of seventy years. Perhaps there was a chance that she had seen something in him he did not see in himself.

Andarean felt lighter. Instead of shuffling along, preoccupied with his concerns, he remembered Admiral Gor's words. Today, he must relax and enjoy the gardens; there would be the morrow for sorting out loose ends.

Walking around a bend in the stone path, he saw her, seated beneath an avocado tree. In an opening between the trees was a small meadow of wild flowers. Estellene sat braiding a ring of blossoms together. An enchanting sight, Andarean thought.

Absorbed in her task, she did not notice him at first. He stood still, leaning against the trunk of a tree, and watched her. She was softly singing a melody that brought to mind a choir of angels.

She finished what looked like a small wreath, and then quit her melody as she carefully inspected the work. She must have felt his presence, for suddenly she looked up and, without searching the area with her eyes, gazed straight at him. It was as if she had connected with him telepathically and had known exactly where he stood.

Her smile brought out his own. She jumped up and began walking towards him. Staying in the shade of the trees, Andarean took her in as she walked. Her hair was no longer fixed above her head; it hung about the waist and swung gently with her swaying hips. Andarean was rooted to the spot. He could only watch her come. No words were forthcoming between the two, but their eyes held one another's.

She stopped short of the tree's shade. "Do not be shy," she said. "Will you come out and play?"

Andarean laughed like a child, and Estellene laughed along with him. *I feel like a child*, Andarean thought. *How is it that this woman and this place can make me feel so alive, so young?*

He walked out of the shade, moving within arms-reach of her.

She raised the wreath of flowers and adorned his head with it. "I made this for you while I was waiting." She stepped back a pace and looked him over, sizing up both him and her handiwork. "Perfect. Just perfect. I chose colors to match your eyes, and it is just right! Follow me, please. I have a picnic lunch ready on a blanket by the canal. And hurry; I'm famished."

She began to run—not fast, just a graceful lope. Andarean found himself trotting behind her. He caught her fragrant scent and ran a little faster to be beside her.

Having difficulty looking at both Estellene and the path while running, he stumbled and almost fell. She grabbed him in an instant. Andarean was impressed by her strength and speed. They stopped and looked into each other's eyes. He could see only affection, and the warm love of friendship beginning.

"I'm sorry. I just couldn't keep my eyes off of you. I'm not normally so clumsy. It's just that I wasn't watching where I was going. You have a profile that strikes me to the soul."

"Perhaps," she began, "we have known one another before."

"I am not sure I follow you," said Andarean.

"When you entered the Dome today, I had never seen you—no picture, nothing—and yet I had seen you before.

"The Fifteen have kept you very secret, for I have tried on many occasions to find out something about you. All my attempts met a wall solid as brick, until today. I can't believe I have the good fortune of being with you."

"I had that same exact feeling when I saw you. How could that be?" Andarean asked.

"The Ancient says we all have lived before and that we retain certain memories from our past lives. What do you think about that, Andarean?"

"Well, I must say, after what I have experienced today I might believe most anything."

"That is not an answer. Do you avoid my question?" Estellene asked, teasing him.

"Not intentionally, I assure you." He laughed, and she joined in naturally with him.

They continued walking down slope towards the picnic spot.

Nearing the canal, Andarean noticed two massive columns made of what appeared to be pink granite. They were carved in the tradition of ancient Greece and were standing alone. They did not appear to be part of any previous structure—just a planned focal point along the walkway.

"We will stop here," Estellene said. She took his hand and led him between the pillars.

Beyond was a courtyard of stone, with fountains and a waterfall. Andarean stopped, taking it all in. In the distance lay the canal, back-dropped by snow-draped mountains. Grapes grew on trellises, shedding flickering light, pale, moving, fluttering green-gold and shading a large area. Sunlight reflected off the water, casting golden patterns like shifting, flickering jewels. Magical, was all he could think.

"Do you like the spot I chose?" she asked.

"Estellene, I am enthralled. I feel I am in the Garden of Melody."

"What do you mean?"

"The Parrish painting."

"You must mean the one titled Daybreak."

"With the pillars and water before mountains cast in blue light? With the two young women on the terrace between the pillars?"

"Of course. So you *are* familiar with it? Why would you call it the Garden of Melody when that is not its name?"

"I don't know," he said, smiling a bit. "The painting gave me a sense of déjà vu, and I always thought Garden of Melody was its title."

"My favorite painting in the whole archive, actually," she said.

"Are you serious?" Andarean asked.

"Even when I'm joking, I am serious," she said, laughing. "Are you an admirer of Parrish as well?"

"I believe Parrish rivals the Great Renaissance artists, like da Vinci and Michelangelo, although he chose a different theme for his work. He is no less a master, in my opinion."

"Oh! I agree completely. All those church scenes and cherubs and Satan with horns—a little redundant, don't you think?" Playfully, Estellene drew him in.

"Well, of course, yet surely you understand who was paying the great da Vinci's keep."

"Don't you think it creatively arresting to have your art dictated to you?"

"Of course. If I were an artist, but truly I am only a casual admirer."

"Can you admire this?" She posed by the fountain, dipped her cupped hands in the flow, and then raised them to her lips to drink. The backdrop was perfect: the mountains; the columns drenched in golden sunlight; trellised grape leaves waving in the breeze; and sea-green estuary. Droplets of water spilled through her fingers, sunlight playing off them.

I am in love, Andarean thought. *She has captured my heart in a moment. All other days pale by comparison. My entire life has been empty of the beauty I find in this woman. Why not add this scene to it—to my life?* In that moment, he was falling for her, head above heels, completely at her mercy.

"Are you showing off?" he asked.

"Absolutely! I must make you understand better the medium in which you have worked. I also wish you to fall in love with me; if that could not happen here, in my most favorite place, then where?

"You must believe"—her expression changed to a seriousness he had not yet seen—"that today and every day thereafter, we are one; where you go, I will follow."

Andarean became serious, too. "Estellene, I cannot dare believe that you could honestly be happy with me. How could it be so? I am much older than you. You could choose from any young men. All would gladly kneel before you."

"I do not want them," she said, shaking her head. "I want only you."

"How can you be so sure?" he asked, in utter disbelief.

"I like the way you look. You are, to my way of thinking, very handsome. I have had love for you since I gained the concept, many years ago."

"Love for me. How so?" He was astounded.

"As a child loves a father, yet you are not my father. All my life, I have wanted to meet you, to know you and to thank you."

"Thank me for what?"

"For my life. Without your hard work and research, I would not be. I love this place. My life has been one joy flowing into another. Beauty, happiness, fulfillment: all have been mine. Yet today, I yearn for something I have not experienced. No longer am I fulfilled."

"Of what do you speak, Estellene? How are you so suddenly unfulfilled? And what do you mean about my work?" His mind reeled, cluttered with unanswered questions.

"You are all I need."

Andarean was stunned and speechless.

She trembled, near tears. "Please, promise you will not refuse me. I desire to share life with you. I have dreamed of meeting you someday. When the Ancient came and informed me that I was to be your mate, butterflies took over my stomach. I could not sleep for two days and could only wonder when you would come. Then today it happened. You arrived, and we are here, knowing one another."

Andarean was completely and utterly shocked to find that this delightfully compelling creature could have grown so fond of him. He again considered pinching himself but found himself laughing instead.

The sound of his laugh was a bit unnatural. He had never been a social animal, and yet today he was feeling gregarious.

"Where, my dear Estellene, is our lunch? I find that your wonderful company creates a great thirst and even larger hunger within myself."

She smiled and let out a huge sigh, which could only be one of relief, and then she took his hand. "This way," she said.

They walked slowly, her hip bumping against his along the way.

FOUR

Nesdia, the sworn enemy of Seven Galaxies, thrives on conflict like an aboriginal wolf pack. The strong dominate the weak or submissive, and the alpha position is constantly fending off direct challenge. The women of Nesdia are subservient to men, save for the few who learned to use their scent and feminine rewards to subtly dominate their males from behind closed doors. Unless a Nesdian woman learned and used the art of love/conflict—the art of arousing not only a man's desire but also his adrenalin at the same time—she would simply be one of the masses, a slave to her man.

Xeries Tenth of Nesdia, commander of Nesdia's aggressive new Navy, had not experienced war before—unlike his grandfather, who had sustained a twenty-seven-year running battle with the realm that later, upon his destruction, became Seven Galaxies. The only battles Xeries Tenth had ever experienced were the constant struggle to be a man of power in the eyes of the populace, and—of course—the ever-present war going on with Zuzahna behind the closed doors of the bedchamber.

Xeries might have convinced the populace of his power and prestige, but Zuzahna knew well that appearances were not always reality.

Zuzahna had been selected as a young, homeless waif and then brought into the Duhcat Foundation, an elite family that, over past millenniums, had effectively mastered the art of Nesdian love conflict.

To be Queen, and not just of some backward planets but of a greater world, was her goal. To live in pomp and splendor, and to have the masses bow at her feet as Xeries often did, was what occupied her thoughts. She believed, without doubt, that she was born to rule, and so she used the power of her talents relentlessly.

As commander of the Nesdian Navy, Xeries Tenth had engineered attacks on settlements of Seven Galaxies. Now he sat in the command chair and waited—waited for the obvious response to his belligerent, ruthless attacks against the innocent women and children, as well as against the simple men who were not warriors but who tilled the ground to seed crops.

Xeries felt that such aggression was not what his ancestors had called him to accomplish, but Zuzahna, the Zorra, Nesdia's religious leader, and the Book of Prophesy had all convinced him the path was true.

Therefore, he waited. Zuzahna had said that any Seven Galaxies commander would respond at once, rushing to be swallowed by the set trap; but anxious days had passed and still no one had come. In Sector-G, there was nothing but silence.

Xeries was confounded. "Cowards!" he said. "Cowards and women commanding the fleet of Seven Galaxies!" Repeating the words often made him feel better.

Zuzahna was never wrong, he told himself. She had made him admit she was never wrong many times.

Yet, in the silence, the voice that spoke within Xeries' head asked, *What have you done?!*

Ahdujen, the first mate, approached. "Your Imminence, if I may have a word with you?"

"What is it!"

"Imminence, what shall I instruct the crew to do now? We have transferred all prisoners to the ships that will transport them to the slave colonies. I have no orders after the ones I have fulfilled. Imminence, I am waiting to fulfill your next wish. Please share it with me."

"Set course for Sector-I. We will destroy all Seven Galaxies settlements there as well!"

"Imminence, if I may have your gentle ear for one moment?"

"Of course! Make it quick."

"My Dear Lord, we have wreaked havoc enough to draw the despised enemy into our trap. If we set sail for Sector-I, all of our carefully laid plans to ambush the Seven Galaxies' Fleet will come to naught."

"Zu . . . ahem. . . . I feel we should be on the offensive. Destroy more settlements; provoke a response!"

"Your Imminence, it is a bold approach and much honor would come if it were successful. May I have your gracious consent to impart my views on the subject?"

Xeries waved his hand. "Very well—speak!"

"Imminence, we should wait. We have baited and set the trap. They will come; it is assured. They cannot let the slaughter go on unaddressed."

"Then where are they?"

"I cannot say, yet it is assured and written in the Book of Prophesy that if we slight their innocents, they must come. Imminence, we must wait—wait for the scriptures to be fulfilled." The first mate paused.

"Now, to change the theme—with your benevolent permission—I have not been able to share the recent news since you returned from resting in chambers."

"What is it? Do you play a game of suspense with me?"

"Imminence, swearing upon my mother's blood, I would never play a game with you!"

"Then spit it out!"

"Intelligence gathered by one of our moles inside a Seven Galaxie newspa—"

"Must we rely on newspapers for our intelligence?"

"No! No! Of course not, Your Imminence! Their newspapers are only a convenience to understand what lies the Seven Galaxies are disseminating to their populace.

"We have learned through our diligent deciphering of *all* forms of information that the reigning admiral of the Seven Galaxies Fleet has retired and will serve no more!"

"His name was Vestige, was it not?"

"Yes, Imminence; an admirable memory you have!"

"An admiral with no genetic predisposition to command, yet he was appointed by the notorious Fifteen; am I mistaken?"

"No, Imminence, you are never mistaken!"

Xeries puffed at the obvious flattery. A first mate in Nesdia's Navy was ever preoccupied, more with the commander's bloated ego than true and relevant issues. "So! Do you wait for me to beg for the name of the new admiral?"

"Imminence! No! I was only taking a small breath so it would be possible for me to impart our most recent intelligence!"

"Go on," commanded Xeries.

"It seems the notorious Fifteen have appointed a seasoned commander, one with experience in Nesdia's Twenty-Seven Years War, for purification of the universe."

"He fought against the Great Xeries Eight?"

"Yes, Imminence."

"What is his name? What was his participation in the Twenty-Seven Years War?"

"Your Imminence, as a young graduate of the Galaxy Academy, he is a veteran of the entire conflict: the entire twenty-seven years."

"What is his name?"

"Admiral Gor."

"This TyGor was responsible for the destruction of the Nesdian Navy, commanded by my ancestor Xeries Eight."

"You are correct, as always, Imminence."

"Under Gor's directives, all surviving Nesdians were transported to the penal colonies where we have spent the last two hundred years training and praying to God—our God! The Only God of the universe—for this chance to defeat Gor and bring forth the retribution and cleansing of our universe."

"Yes, Imminence!"

"This TyGor, when does he come?"

"Your Imminence, it is not within my power to see his arrival."

"Then what do I do? How shall I avenge my ancestors?"

"Imminence, you are the Supreme Commander of Nesdia's Navy. My opinion in this matter is of no importance."

"Then I shall retire to my bedchamber and meditate upon the subject at hand."

"Yes, Imminence."

After their exchange, Xeries Tenth went in search of Zuzahna.

Entering her chamber, he could smell her scent as the auto-door slid open. He was aroused and called out, "Where are you, Zuzahna?"

"In the bedchamber, dear Xeries."

He felt adrenalin rush into his veins; she awaited him!

Striding forward with haste, he opened the bedchamber door.

It was as if she had known he was looking for her; she was waiting for him, dressed in next to nothing. The nothing consisted of a silken material that resembled black gauze.

She was lying on the sleeping mat, legs open, writhing and enjoying his response to her show. "Do you desire me?" she asked, knowing the answer.

"I always desire you!"

"If you always desire me, by what title did you forget to address me?" She changed her pose, no longer provocative.

Xeries answered without delay.

"My Queen!"

"Yes, you are right. You forgot! Do you not wish to feel the heaven of my love?"

"I cannot survive without feeling the heaven of your love!"

"Then you shall address me again in the appropriate manner."

"Yes, I will! My Queen, my master! My sweet dream! May I lie with you?"

"I suppose, for a few moments," she said, sounding bored. "But if you do not answer my questions appropriately, I will send you away."

"No! No! Please! Do not send me away!"

"I will not, if you agree with the strategy imparted while you share the bed with me."

"Always, my Queen. I agree! I am your humble servant. I will fulfill your desires; they are my agenda to fulfill! So you will allow me to share your bed tonight?"

She nodded, then held up her hand. "Only if you agree to my terms."

"I agree! I agree! I would gladly die for you!"

"Come to me, then." Zuzahna repositioned herself into the pose she had held when Xeries first arrived. "Come to me, I said!"

When he entered her, she said, "Repeat your last sentence again," as she squeezed.

"I would gladly die for you!"

Zuzahna thought, wickedly, *You, my poor Xeries, may have to.*

Xeries finished quickly and lay back on the cushions, panting, his canine teeth exposed. Beads of perspiration rose on his forehead. His scent—the overpowering smell of sweat, new and old, mixed with his cologne—made Zuzahna despise him more.

Why do Nesdian men shun the bath? she wondered. Ancient tradition spoke that bathing weakened a man, so the ship outside her chamber smelled of a locker room: rancid sweat covered by a variety of perfumes, which the men believed excited the opposite sex. Zuzahna shook off the thought. She had work to do.

"Dear Xeries," she said, "since the enemy are too cowardly to show themselves, when do we depart for Sector-I?" She rolled onto her side and reached towards him, smiling enchantingly while while stroking the deep coarse hair on his chest. She did not want to, but knew how Xeries lapped up such adoration, even if it was feigned.

"Ahdujen believes we should follow the original plan. He believes we should wait for the Seven Galaxies Fleet to arrive, spring the trap, and destroy them."

"Xeries, have we not already spoken of this?"

"Yes, Zuzahna."

"What did you call me?"

"Forgive me, my Queen, I am distracted by the decision I must make."

"Dearest Xeries, we have already decided. Have you forgotten?"

"No! No, of course not! It is just, well . . . I want to be sure the next move is correct. New information has just arrived."

"Tell me at once! What is the news?"

"The Seven's Fleet has a new commander: a veteran of the Twenty-Seven Years War. He is responsible for the destruction of my grandfather, Xeries Eight."

"This is a good omen," she said, sitting up. "God will deliver the infidel so that you may destroy him. With that accomplished, who would dare question your ascension to the throne?"

"It is true; the omen speaks of God's divine plan for our civilizations."

Xeries spoke boldly, yet in the back of his mind doubt nagged at him. His skills in battle had never been proven in the field. This human was a seasoned and War-hardened veteran. Xeries had studied the tactical applications of Deep Space war, yet he was still unsure of himself. All of this passed through his mind.

"Xeries, you are distracted. You are not focusing on my beauty. Bring your eyes upon me and feast."

He returned his focus to Zuzahna. She was panting, her tongue gliding lightly across her lips while she writhed. The sight was, to Xeries, as Opium is to an addict.

"I must have you again," he said, responding to the sight.

"And you will have me, when we arrive in Sector-I. You may come share my bed."

"But Sector-I is over a moon from our present position at break-ship speed!"

"Do not debate with me! The discussion is over. We made the decision yesterday!" She rolled away, turning her back to him.

"I could take you physically, without your consent," Xeries said. "It is my Nesdian right!"

"Little satisfaction you would gain with me lying beneath you like a limp, dead fish!"

"There are others who would lie with me!"

"Yes, but as you have told me *so* many times, none with my natural born talent or beauty."

She looked over her shoulder, fluttering her long black eyelashes and doing her best to look demure.

"We will depart for Sector-I within the hour!" Xeries announced quickly, hoping to regain Zuzahna's favor.

"I may relent and let you lie with me before we arrive ...*if* you promise to erase your subordination and bend to my will."

"I have other obligations to consider!" Xeries eyes darkened from gold to black, and Zuzahna knew he was angry.

"Consider this, servant!" she said, raising her voice. "Your cousin, Xrisen, has the golden eyes! Xrisen covets my beauty almost as much as he covets the Royal Crown!"

"I will not consider your last comment," Xeries shouted, quaking in rage. "I alone carry the great name Xeries!"

"Make sure you don't forget this little conversation, or you will be extremely distressed to find I have chosen another," Zuzahna replied, taunting him.

"You wouldn't!"

"Are you so sure, Xeries?" she asked, her voice calm. "Do you wish to take the chance?"

Xeries turned and stormed from the bedchamber and apartment. When Zuzahna heard the outer door to the apartment glide closed, she began to laugh.

FIVE

The Ancient sat waiting, gazing out upon the courtyard of the seven falls. Normally she was always busy at her duties, but this moment found her in quiet contemplation.

Many changes were afoot, although there was nothing upon which she could place her finger. Energy unlike anything she had felt in the past two centuries was flowing. Leandra's senses were prickling; war was coming, yet the adversary had not exposed himself. The thought chilled her.

To live in peace had been her strongest desire . . . her life had been dedicated to that end. Seven Galaxies had lived for over two centuries without war—the accomplishment was monumental. Peace had been her most honorable achievement.

No rumors had been forthcoming. No aggressive moves by other cultures clouded her mind. It was feeling—her natural born instincts and her years of mental training—that brought the news. The Ancient had lived long enough to trust her sixth sense and know its inherent truth. She listened to it now and began mental preparations.

A knock came at her apartment door.

"Yes?"

"It is Ty."

"Come in, please."

He opened the door, walked in, and closed it softly behind him.

"It is a fine day outside; shall we talk out on the terrace?" he asked.

"Ty, what I want to speak of is only for you to hear," she replied. "Soon enough others will be informed, but for now, I would like to speak in the privacy of this room. Please, sit down with me. I wish to speak on an informal level as friends, old friends, for that is what we have become. I must admit that I watched you long before you were out of the Academy. You were the one who stood out from all others."

"Respectfully, I was not the top of my class," Ty said humbly.

"No, you were not, yet other qualities were evident to me and to others—qualities which are not always judged by academic accomplishments or standards. These are what I wish to speak about."

"This conversation is to be about me?"

She nodded. "About you, but more importantly about another whom I have been watching and whom I feel possesses a similar temperament and character to you. You heard Andarean's presentation today. What do you think?"

"I think it necessary to acquire more information from the good doctor before I can analyze and determine for myself how much is fact and how much is simply theories and logic. Therefore, I must hold my judgment—or shall

I say more appropriately, my opinions of his work—until then."

"I appreciate your non-commitment to the information you received today. It was so abbreviated and quickly imparted that you are surely disseminating at the moment, and will be for some time to come." Leandra smiled at TyGor. "I did not really bring you here to discuss Doctor—I mean, Andarean's work. I had in mind something of a more personal nature."

"That is well, for I would much prefer to consider a subject on which I am somewhat informed."

"Then let us discuss your genetic makeup. If you wish," said Leandra. "Understand your duties are first to the Dome and then to all else. Because you are the most recent addition to the Fifteen and must depart shortly, I will move to the point quickly. I have followed Andarean's work with diligence and great interest over the past sixty years. In fact, the interest I had in his theories even before that period were responsible for granting his first lab. Within Andarean's work, we began to document the worst of the criminal element, but also we began another parallel study, isolating the best of the human persona as well. The same theories Andarean has applied to the criminal element, we applied to the most forward-thinking, positively moral portion of our society, and do you know, dear Admiral, what we found?"

"Please don't make me guess. I'll save that for strategic decisions, where no data exists to support anything else." He smiled.

"We found the mirror image of Andarean's theories about the criminal element. The larger the proportion of negative genealogy—or radicals, as he refers to them—

found within a humanoid, the more magnified the negative traits; but it has also been proven that the reverse is true. For some reason, certain families and genetic groupings have considerably fewer of the radical genes. Whether this is through centuries of choosing mates with kind dispositions and benevolent natures or for some other reasons, we do not know; but the numbers speak for themselves, and we have been running those numbers in computer simulation for over thirty years."

"How does this relate to me?" asked TyGor.

"It's simple, Ty. You are one of the few in our society who has experienced only a minimal impact, genetically speaking, from the criminal element."

"Are you saying that for some reason I have escaped the plague Andarean spoke of—the plague of compounded negative genes?"

"Yes! And quite the reverse is true; you have within your DNA a preponderance of dominant genes, which have been found to carry characteristics that are the mirror image of those found in the criminal element."

"What you say is interesting, but why are we discussing my gene pool?" asked TyGor. "Have I not proven my character during service to Seven Galaxies during the past two centuries?"

"But of course, Ty. Your proven character, intellect, genetics, and experience are the reasons you have been selected as Admiral and honored by appointment as one of the Fifteen," Leandra answered.

"I appreciate the Dome's view on this very interesting subject, yet I would rather not dwell on my *theoretical* merits, but on the physical manifestation of my work, and the works of other prominent persons, past and present."

"Point taken."

"Shall we move on?" he asked.

"Certainly! Many of the command responsible for victory in the Twenty-Seven Years War are no longer with us on the physical plane, or they are retired and no longer mentally or physically able to serve Seven Galaxies.

"You were a young man straight out of the Academy when the conflict arose; it was a brutal time in our civilization's history. I still shudder sometimes when I think of those dark periods.

"The old guard—as I enjoy thinking of them—many dear friends and other irreplaceable people have all but disappeared. Among the young officers who experienced the Nesdian conflict firsthand, none possess the tactical knowledge, sixth sense, and unfailing determination to succeed against the most dire odds, not as you do. Rarely in our culture's history have we found a human who has sacrificed so much for unselfish gains. Leandra picked up a small pillow from where it rested on an end table and repositioned herself, placing the pillow behind her lower back, sighing lightly with more comfort.

"In my personal opinion, many brilliant commanders from the past were, unfortunately, striving for power, riches, and notoriety—they desired History's acknowledgement of their accomplishments. A few come to mind who were not; for example, George Washington, General of the ancient North American revolution; Mahatma Gandhi, leader of ancient India; William Wallace of Scotland; Poncho Villa, revered hero of ancient Mexico; General Quan of China; and, of course, Jesus Christ of Nazareth.

Some of the men just mentioned were not military leaders but guardians of the common man. I am sure you have knowledge of their lives and accomplishments."

"Yes, of course!" he answered.

"On the reverse parallel, some brilliant military tacticians and leaders of men were General Mao of China, Napoleon Bonaparte of France, Hitler of Germany, Stalin of Russia, Alexander the Great, and Genghis Khan, not to mention our more recent Xeries of Nesdia. All brilliant, all temporarily successful, and yet of their conquests little or none remain. There are subtle threads, possibly, and many dark memories, but lasting accomplishments? Do you see any?"

"Few indeed, Leandra," Ty admitted.

It was the first time Ty had used her birth name; he was obviously becoming more comfortable, Leandra thought. She smiled.

"Shall we have a bite to eat on the terrace and resume this conversation indoors afterwards?" Ty asked.

"Certainly. I am hungry."

They both rose. He could see the old woman was having some difficulty, yet he knew her independence meant that she would not appreciate physical help. They walked towards a window that rose from the floor to the ceiling some ten meters above. The glass slid open silently, and they walked out onto a stone terrace. On the south side, marble pillars formed a pergola, which was covered in a flowering vine Ty had never seen before. The small white flowers smelled like jasmine. "Is this trailing vine jasmine?" he asked.

"It is a genetic modification of that plant from Ancient Earth. The genetic alteration allows it to bloom all year and to withstand the freezing temperatures that often fall upon us here in the winter months. It is enchanting both in beauty and fragrance."

"It is breathtaking."

"Thank you. Some of the accomplishments I take the most happiness from are the advances in horticulture. This was my own creation, and I simply love the effect it has on me, and on others."

Ty sincerely liked the old woman. Her taking enjoyment from such a simple thing as flora created a picture of her that he had not previously possessed.

The food arrived: an assortment of fresh fruit, obviously from the gardens, along with smoked salmon, barbecued chicken, and fresh whole-grain bread, still hot from the oven. They ate, enjoying the view and comfortable silence, occasionally commenting on the weather, the colors of the flowers, and the blue-hazed mountains.

After they had finished, they sat gazing out over the colorful and fragrant gardens. The blue water shimmering in the sunlight brought back fond memories of earlier carefree days to them both. Leandra took in a long breath, held it for a few moments, and let it out. With a resigned yet peaceful look on her face, she said, "I wish our days, dear Ty, could be spent in such fulfilling pursuits as horticulture and farming, yet reality calls us back to duties at hand, doesn't it?"

"As always, Leandra. As always."

Occasionally they heard laughter, and now and then a woman's giggles, echoing in the distance.

"It sounds as if Andarean and Estellene have hit it off!" Leandra said. She smiled knowingly, appreciating, it seemed, the happiness of others.

Ty contemplated for a few moments. "Andarean was quite overwhelmed. I must say, we dropped quite a lot on the good doctor today."

"I am sure he will accept it all in stride. I have spent a good deal of time considering his work ethic: extraordinary, and yet a man cannot possibly be fulfilled with work alone, can he, Ty?" she asked, with the slightest smirk.

"Well, there are many different types of men. Generally, I find generalizations to be in error," Ty said, playing into her humor.

"And what about you, if I were to ask of your personal experiences?"

"As you know, I was once married, with a family. In that time, so long ago, I did not believe I could live without her. Losing my soul mate gave my heart a calloused edge, and those sentiments of old have never been renewed. As for the company of a kind or beautiful woman, I know of no normal men who do not crave—or in some way, *need*—that companionship."

"Are you saying that our Andarean is not normal?" Leandra asked, with a humorous glance.

"Absolutely! Absorbed by his work all these years, with no thought for personal desires, only for the final accomplishment: this, in my opinion, is not what most people would call normal, yet few of us are."

"Bravo, Ty! You have just hit the nail on the head." Leandra laughed heartily, and Ty joined her, thinking that life could be absurd.

"Let us go back inside and resume our previous discussion," she said. "This conversation brings us then rather abruptly to the real reason I asked you here."

"And what, may I ask, would that be?" he asked, as they left the terrace and walked back indoors.

"Your grandson, TayGor."

"Tay! What need is there to mention his name within the Dome?"

"The Dome requires his Service."

"What do you mean?"

"You will be visiting both the valley of your birth and your grandson when we finish our strategic planning here, is that not true?"

"Yes," he said, nodding. "I plan to go home and spend whatever days I have remaining on-planet with my daughter and grandson."

"I wish you to convince him to come back and to board *Independence* with you, to be a special liaison of sorts: your personal advisor and confidant."

"Tay is not yet eighteen," Ty said, surprised. "He has not attended Academy and would need consent from the special twenty-four."

"The consent of the twenty-four has already been forthcoming. All that is left is for you to convince him to come."

"And why would I do that, Leandra?"

"You trust him as no other, don't you?"

"Of course!"

"Where you are going, dear Admiral, you will need an advisor who will look out for you, be in tune with all the shipboard nuances, know the five common languages, and have skill in the art of diplomacy—a skill, I am sorry to say, Ty, you have in short and intermittent supply."

"Where *am* I going, Leandra?"

"We will talk of that before you go home. At this moment, I am only gathering information. I cannot answer your question at this time. Soon though, very soon."

"So it is a mystery then?"

"Yes, one I am working to sort out."

"Any assistance I can offer, know that I am at your service."

"Yes, I know. Thank you, Ty. I *can* tell you the main reason he has been chosen by me and the other fourteen."

"Do tell!"

Your grandson's genetics mirror your own to within a ninety-nine and one half percentage. We need a person like you to learn all that you know, including the sixth sense you have for strategy and for the creative application of textbook learning to the battlefield."

"Leandra, I will think on what you have said. If you don't mind, I must leave you and meditate upon all I have heard today."

"Surely you are free to go. Thank you for coming."

"Thank you, Leandra, for speaking your heart." Ty bowed out of customary respect for the Ancient. She acknowledged his bow, and Ty took his leave.

SIX

THE Ancient left her apartment, walked down a long corridor lit by overhead skylights, and entered her office. Her assistant, a middle-aged woman with extraordinarily large and piercing blue eyes, greeted her.

"Leandra, I thought you had gone for the day! I was about to send away your visitors until tomorrow, as I didn't want to bother you. I contacted the Keeper of Dreams and Telepathy Master earlier and told them that you urgently wished to speak to them. They are both in your ante foyer waiting."

"Serene, thank you for your diligence. You know how much I appreciate you, do you not?"

"You are gracious enough that I feel appreciated every day," answered Serene.

"By the way," Leandra said, with a mischievous smile on her weathered face, "have you met the new addition to the Fifteen?"

"Admiral Gor? No, I have not."

"Well, I do hope you are not scheduled this evening; I would like you to share dinner in the garden with him. And please, by all means, call him Ty—not Admiral. He is so tense; it seems that we need to loosen him up just a bit. Could you help us with that?"

"I assure you, Leandra, it wouldn't matter if I had something to do; I would cancel in a heartbeat to spend an evening with Ad—I mean, Ty."

"Good. I will advise him to see you in the Garden of Melody at, say, seven this evening?"

"That would be perfect! Thank you, Leandra!"

"Always, my pleasure. Only one thing: promise me you will help him to relax."

"I can assure you, Leandra; that is exactly what I have in mind."

The Ancient passed through the outer office and into the ante foyer where a woman and a man waited. "I must apologize for keeping you waiting," she said. "I hope it hasn't been long. Will you both please follow me?"

Twin doors auto-opened, and the three walked into an immense room. The ceiling was a raised arc of glass supported by huge wooden timbers. Inside, hundreds of species of trees and flowers abounded, and butterflies of many colors fluttered at endless varieties of flora. The Ancient continued walking, stopping now and then to pluck a dead leaf or to smell the many wonderful fragrances.

"I do hope you both will relax and enjoy the atrium," Leandra said. "Few come here, and I sometimes feel selfish that it can't be shared with more people."

They wandered a bit and finally arrived in a cozy alcove of stone. A large fire was burning in a corner, under a brass hood that protruded from the rock wall. It was surrounded by several soft chairs and a large, overstuffed sofa.

"Please, sit." Leandra dropped into a chair facing the sofa and motioned for the two to sit there.

She began. "I have called upon you two for reasons that are not completely clear to me, and I need you to assist me in determining where the energy is emanating from and what it means."

The man spoke first. "What type of emotions are being brought about by this energy you feel?"

"A subtle uneasiness...anxiety and dread. I don't want to say fear, for I have lived much too long to fear anything. I have been expecting the reaper for over a hundred years. He may visit me at any time, and I'll have no regrets."

"Fear for the wellbeing of others, could it be? As subtle as the feeling might be, your life has been a work for others; it makes sense that concern for the wellbeing of our people would bring about such feelings."

Leandra thought for a moment, a perplexed look in her eyes. "I will consider what you have just imparted."

"You speak of uneasiness," the woman said. "A dream came to me last night that left me feeling the same way. I woke thinking to call for a meeting, but when I arrived at my studio, your request for my presence was on the message base."

"What happened in the dream, and where did it take place?" Leandra asked.

"It was land I had never seen: three moons graced the evening sky, and the people there lived by farming the land and hunting wild game. Their lives seemed peacefully simple, uncomplicated by modern ways. The children were well taken care of, and the houses were small, made of wood from the local forests. Fires burned in the homes for warmth. It seemed as though I had gone back in time. The place was similar to archived pictures I have seen of ancient Earth."

"Tell me more please," the Ancient requested.

"There were horses in the field, some bred for riding and others for work. There were cattle as well."

"The people, they were humanoids?" Leandra asked, her intuition pounding.

"Yes! In the first segment, in the happy part of the dream, but then it changed. The homes were burning, and I saw men's bodies, some lying on the ground and others tied to posts and mutilated; no *nailed* to the posts, not tied. They were nailed by the flesh of their arms with spikes that were not round, the shafts were three sided… triangular." Lenore stopped, obviously distraught from recalling the visions.

"How many nails were used?" asked Leandra.

The Dream Keeper sat silent for a moment, thinking, remembering. "Seven. Seven in each arm—I can see them clearly. It is a horrible sight. The mutilations."

"What else was done?"

"The skin of the men's torsos was slashed with a blade of some sort, slashed diagonally in lines that started at each nail and then converged like the lines of a fan at the center of their abdomens. The men were being burned at the solar plexus with an iron tool. It was reheated for each use in a fire of red-hot coals. I could not see the ones inflicting the torture, only the results."

"Branding!" the Ancient exclaimed.

"Yes, Leandra. I had forgotten the term used for that type of torture. It was awful to witness."

"And the mark left by the burn, what did it appear to be?"

The Keeper of Dreams was silent a moment, obviously straining to remember. "It was like the letter E, yet not one used in our languages. It was backwards and curved, like the fork of a Trident on its side, if you will. The three legs of the letter were pointed and barbed, like fishhooks, and above the letter was a crown with what looked like an eye in the center."

"Thank you. Only one more question: the moons of this planet, were they all the same size?"

"No, one was huge, larger than any moon I have seen in person or in photographs. In the dream, it was in the center of the night sky, with the two smaller moons one on either side, yet riding much higher above the larger moon."

"The small moons, were they similar in size?"

"No, the one on the right was smaller, and they both cast shadows upon a portion of the larger moon. The shadows were not black but a beautiful blue. I had never seen moons like that. I was awestruck—until the violence started."

"Did you see any of the violent ones?"

"No, only the bodies of the men."

"You saw no women or children?"

"In the beginning of the dream there were women and children, but I saw none after the destruction of the civilization."

"You say destruction of the civilization. Why?"

"Because, Leandra, in the dream I was flying, and I saw many villages all along the shores and inlets of a pristine saltwater sea. Every village contained the same scene, many times repeated."

"Lenore, I wish you to immediately go and have the memory of this cleansed. Do as I say; my directive will be followed. Visit the spa; I will send the Dome's healer. Have a few drinks and a hot mineral soak, and when the healer is finished, a long massage and volcanic mud wrap. Speak of this dream to no one. Do you understand?"

"Yes, Leandra!"

"Thank you for all your help. I am truly sorry this has been so painful for you."

"Each of one of us has a burden to carry. The Dome would not have claimed us otherwise."

Lenore shared a glance of understanding with the old woman, her mentor. "I will see you in the morning," she said. "Good afternoon, Intras, Leandra."

"I look forward to our meeting tomorrow. It is my hope that the dream will come to you no more."

"It is my wish as well."

"Take some flowers on your way through the atrium and have the spa attendant fashion a ring for your neck and another for your crown. Good day, Lenore."

After Lenore left, Leandra turned to her other visitor. "Now, my old friend, what do you think?"

"It was a good choice sending her to the spa," Intras said. "She carries a tremendous stress from the experience. The dream is not a casual working of some subconscious trauma, nor was it merely brought on by eating the wrong food; it carries a distinct message. I know this for I have experienced another form of the same message. Early this morning, I woke in a cold sweat. I could feel the cries of thousands of innocents. I could feel the pain of fourteen nails—seven in each arm—and the burning of the red-hot iron. I also felt the destitution and disbelief of the women and children as they were kidnapped and teleported to the invaders' ships." Intras looked at Leandra, his mouth turned down in a frown.

"You understand, of course, that the attackers are the Nesdians," Leandra said. "Intras, you must speak of this to no one! The thought of Nesdia attacking a settled colony would create chaos!"

"Yes, I agree, but how could it be possible?"

"I don't know. You have been called in order that we—you, me, and Lenore—may delve into the mystery and make sense of it. We must work quickly."

"How is this possible?" Intras asked. "After the Nesdians were defeated over two centuries ago, we relegated what remained of their race to several planets in an unexplored sector so distant they could never again be a threat. The planets could easily support their race in multiplied numbers, but they were chosen specifically for their distance from any anticipated future settlements of ours, and because they lacked the raw materials, minerals, and metallic ores necessary to build a complicated technology-based culture. Remember, we sent many unmanned probes to those worlds to be *sure* that the strategic raw materials needed to build ships of war were not present. So how is it possible they have gained the ability to travel Deep Space?"

"Perhaps an alliance of some sort has been made, enabling them to obtain the missing materials," Leandra said. "Perhaps an ally has established them on other planets endowed with the necessary and missing elements."

"But who, and why?"

"Intras, that is what we are burdened with determining. There is not a moment to waste. I will contact High

Command and see if any of our patrol cruisers are missing or have failed to report on time. In the meantime, you must sequester yourself. Think of no other matters. Monitor, to the best of your ability, the thoughts and mental energy emanating from G-sector."

"Why G-sector, Leandra?"

"The moons in the dream…I believe they belong to a planet in that sector. These are our people! I feel it. We have only settled one place with a trio of moons. The size and shadowing Lenore described matches what I remember from the exploration probe's original research photos.

"Come to me, day or night, as soon as you obtain any pertinent information, whether it seems important or not. I will call a meeting of the Fifteen. Fortunately, we are all present and will assemble tomorrow, mid-afternoon. Hopefully by then, you and I will have obtained some evidence, and not what some of the more analytically skeptical of the Fifteen would call hocus pocus."

Intras smiled. "You, Leandra, have lived long enough to know that those who disbelieve certain methods lack understanding. Out of this dire situation may grow a tree whose fruit will be just that: understanding."

"I agree. Within every crisis lies opportunity."

SEVEN

No sooner had Intras departed the atrium than Leandra was on the secure com to High Command.

"General Voltrans. Urgent!"

A moment passed and a voice came through. "General Voltrans speaking."

"Good day, General. I need you to check the log for G-sector, to see if any of the patrols are late reporting in. Monitor all communication with our best systems held in reserve for strategic intelligence gathering Sectors-G, -H, and -I. I want to know of anything moving out there, down to dust in the nap. These orders are to be carried out as a red-level directive covered in black. Do you understand, General?"

"Yes, sir! Red under Black directive. May I ask what all of this is about?"

"I am asking you, dear General, to tell *me* what this is all about. Spare no cost and get back to me with any abnormalities in those sectors. I don't care if it appears to be a vapor shadow against the surface of a moon, I want the reports. Do you understand?"

"Yes, sir! Immediately!"

"Thank you, General."

Normally the Ancient treated everyone with a maternal courtesy. As of today, things had changed. Two centuries of peace could lull a governing body into dangerous complacency. It was time to build the fire, to place people in the hot seat and demand both diligence and attention to the minutest of details. The Ancient hoped that by the time the meeting of Fifteen convened tomorrow, she would possess some concrete facts to present.

Less than seven minutes had passed before Voltrans was back on the secure com. "Sir, I have something—it is very abnormal: two cruisers, one passing Sector-G and another in Sector-H, have failed to send their daily reports."

"When were the reports due in?" Leandra asked.

"Every afternoon between the fifteenth and sixteenth hour, sir."

"What time was it when I called you?"

"Sixteen-forty, sir!"

"Did it take my call for you to be concerned?" Leandra asked, applying pressure.

"No, sir. Normally we would not yet be concerned. Certain physical mediums, like asteroid dust and debris, can drastically weaken a signal, and it would then bounce from another transmission enhancer, effectively delaying its arrival."

"Sector-G and Sector-H, how many light years are they apart, Voltrans?"

"In round numbers, sir, about ten thousand."

"What are the odds that this type of disruption of signal could happen at the same time, affecting two signals ten thousand, three hundred and forty light years apart?"

"I would have to run digital simulation to tell you. As I said, I was speaking in round numbers."

"Well, I can tell you within an error percentage of .00653 that you would more easily win the Seven Galaxies lottery. Voltrans, in the future, I do not want round numbers; confine yourself to the actual data without any sort of modification. Do you understand?"

The reprimand was subtle; Voltrans got the message clearly.

"Yes, sir, as you wish."

"Has there been anything else?" Leandra enquired.

"We are effectively blind in those sectors. Shall I send in a few of our closest warships?"

"Absolutely not! That decision will be left to the admiral. The Fifteen will convene tomorrow at the Fifteenth hour, and by then I would like to have your full report of the incident, including—but not limited to—all anomalies found by our intel sweep of the sectors I mentioned."

"Yes, sir."

"Two other things: inform the entire fleet to use Full Stealth Cloak immediately. Shields are to be dropped for no reason, with no exceptions. Voltrans, are we clear on that last point?"

"Yes, but sir, the energy used to maintain Full Stealth Cloak is astronomical. The Fleet can only keep that system engaged seventy-two percent of the time, and only if energy designated for full shield is diverted and shields are kept at minimum safety level."

"With a Full Stealth Cloak, how many days can the ships keep it up before re-energizing the reserves?"

"It varies on the different vessels." Voltrans was becoming short of breath, nervous about being interrogated by the Old one. "But on average only one hundred and forty-five hours."

"Compile the details," Leandra commanded, "including the length of time each and every ship in the Fleet can sustain. I want the exact location, plot, and speed of each as well. Send all this by secure courier, without delay!"

"Yes, sir."

"Next, send two unmanned probes under Full Stealth to the planet we settled in Sector-G, the planet with three moons—I have forgotten its official designation on the charts. Forward all of the data they collect to my office ASAP. That will be all, General."

"Yes, sir."

Voltrans was sweating when he hung up the phone. *What is going on?* he thought. Surely the messages had been delayed for some technical reason. Why did the Ancient have a bur under her saddle?

Voltrans was determined to follow the orders flawlessly, without delay. The chair of Fifteen was the absolute commander, outranking even the admiral. He dispatched two probes immediately. They left at speed and with an estimated arrival time of the sixth hour of the following morning. He then presented a special team with the task of identifying location, speed, and plot of each ship in the fleet, as well as the maximum time allowable in Full Stealth Cloak. He had activated rarely used security and intelligence-gathering systems, which were usually reserved for breaches or suspected breaches of Seven Galaxies' security. The buzz in the War Office was more than humming. Everyone involved in the investigation and data gathering was wondering what the hell was up. Up until that point, not a single one of them had ever, in their entire careers, acted upon an order classed Red under Black.

EIGHT

Serene walked through the gardens on her way to the Garden of Melody, named such because of the waterfall. It was not just a waterfall but a sounding fall as well. Serene had often stood in the water, reconfiguring the many stacked stones that tuned the water's melody as it fell. It never ceased to amaze her how the music could be altered by the varied alignment of the stones. Many of the rocks were flat, but even two stones of the same shape and size would produce a different sound if they were different types. She felt like playing in the water this evening and had arrived early with that very thought in mind.

She hesitated for a moment before removing her dress and stripping down to nothing but skin. She hoped the admiral would not be offended. Serene was sure that in his two hundred forty-seven years, he had seen most everything. A naked woman standing in a waterfall shouldn't startle him in the least.

The voice of the falls was much too pronounced this evening. She had in mind a soothing, swirling current and knew from past experience which particular arrangement would bring about the desired effect. Absorbed in the task, she quickly lost track of time.

When she finished creating the melody of her choice, Serene turned towards the granite columns, wondering what was keeping Ty.

The admiral was leaning against one of the massive pillars, watching her.

"I didn't know you were here. Welcome," she said.

"I didn't want to disturb your concentration," he said. "I was very interested in hearing your changes in the melody. I must say, I was also enjoying the view; quite lovely."

"Are you speaking of me, or of the falls?" Serene asked.

"A combination of the two, actually. This is my very favorite spot in the gardens, yet you have never been part of the picture. Today, it is more special than ever before."

"Are you flattering me, Ty?"

"Possibly. Will flattery help win your affections?"

"Dear Ty, coming from you, flattery could be the key to unlocking yearnings I have kept to myself for years."

"Then I shall practice the art of complimentary comment as never before."

"We have never met, but I have heard much about you. I am Serene." She walked towards him without bothering to dress. He was enraptured before she even spoke to him. Now, as she walked towards him, hips swaying in a rhythm old as time, he took her in anew. Her eyes were a striking blue, extra-large and piercing. He thought she might be middle age in years, although at that moment, she looked like a young girl, a bit of mischief in her eyes and that lovely fluidity in her step.

Serene paused before him and offered her hand.

"I am in awe…I assure you," Ty said, full of wonder as he took the offering, bowed, and kissed her hand lightly.

"Ah! A true gentleman is so difficult to find these days!"

"Dearest Serene, I must say that the social graces I am forced to perform with others, you bring out in me naturally."

"Go ahead, keep on; flattery will get you everywhere. Shall I dress?" she asked, tossing back her hair and exposing her neck more fully.

"A difficult choice for me. I would love nothing more than to admire your nakedness all evening, but the sun is down and a chill rides the evening air. My selfish desires should not weigh more than my absolute concern for your good health and wellbeing."

Ty picked up her towel from the chair and began drying her. She swayed into his movements, the toweling evolving into a subtle massage.

"Ty, you said you enjoyed admiring my nakedness, did you not?"

"My hunger for food pales in comparison."

"Then perhaps after we eat, you would accompany me to my quarters. I keep it very warm there."

"Are you saying I would be able to see the graceful curves and melody of your movements unbridled by cloth once more?"

She smiled. "That is exactly what I am saying."

"Then the sorrow my heart feels seeing you dress is temporary."

Serene was silent, sliding her dress over her head and giving her body a light shake until it settled in place. She took two steps towards him until their chests were touching, then placed one hand on his lower back and the other flat over his heart. Looking into his eyes, she said, "Very temporary."

NINE

Leandra woke early. It was not yet four hours. Checking the secure delivery box, she found reports detailing the Fleet's plotted positions and coordinates. Breezing through the documents, she made copies for Admiral Gor. Reports from the Stealth drones would arrive before noon. The Ancient dispatched a summons for the admiral to meet in her quarters at the noon hour for lunch, but she did not share her uneasy feelings with him.

Intras had texted her requesting a sit-down in the early morning. Leandra went through her normal Tai Chi without the usual concentration; she could not help being distracted. Seeing the silent, blinking notice appear on her communication system did nothing to relax her. Abandoning her morning workout to the rigors of the day, she checked the notice: Lenore was requesting a meeting in the early part of the day also.

She called both Lenore and Intras and scheduled them together for the hour of seven. Afterward, she took a quick shower and then consumed some fresh green juice, all the while formulating her thoughts. She, purposely, had not laid out her concerns for the admiral. He was one who, through proven habits, believed in intuition and the sixth sense, but Leandra first wanted some facts to corroborate what she was feeling.

Just as importantly, Leandra wanted the admiral to have one night, if only one, without cares and concerns of a military nature. She sincerely hoped that Serene had done her duty on that score. Thinking of Ty and Serene together, she picked up her brief and left the atrium for her office.

Upon entering the outer office, Serene's domain, she noticed something: Serene looked ten years younger and was absolutely radiant.

"My dear Serene, you look positively beautiful this morning. Did the evening treat you well?"

"I must thank you, Leandra, for your thoughtfulness in arranging my meeting with Ty," she said, smiling. "He was wonderful. I shall say no more."

"Dear Serene, you don't have to say any more; your countenance tells the story. I only hope the admiral shows as well as you!"

"Will you be seeing him today?" Serene asked, attempting to ignore Leandra's humor.

"Yes, in my quarters for lunch."

"Please, Leandra, do no more to encourage him towards me. I wish to know if he is truly interested or just following orders."

"What a horrid thought that I would order him to seduce you!"

"Well, the thought did cross my mind."

"Erase it at once!" Leandra exclaimed.

"Yes, ma'am."

"I am happy you two hit it off. Was he stiff and formal?" Leandra asked.

"Oh! My no! He was charming, funny, and very intellectually stimulating, in a steamy sort of way."

"Amazing. I had never thought of the admiral as a steamy intellectual!"

"See, that's exactly what I was afraid of!" Serene looked embarrassed.

"Your secrets are safe with me, Serene." Leandra grabbed the incoming papers from her mail slot and looked again at her assistant, sly humor showing in her eyes. "My dear, you are a very beautiful shade of red!"

"Go on, Leandra; you have work to do!"

Leandra left Serene's office, chuckling to herself. She didn't think she had ever seen the normally cool and collected woman blush.

Intras and Lenore arrived on schedule. She seated them as before, in the stone alcove. "I bid good morning to you both. What news do you carry?"

Lenore and Intras began to speak at the same time.

"Clearly you both have information that is important," Leandra said, interrupting. "Lenore, would you be so kind as to impart yours first."

"An important dream came to me this morning. I woke at its end and called you immediately. The place was foreign to me, but it appeared to be a ship because of how the rooms were configured. All the men aboard the vessel were skinny—no...skinny isn't the right word: lean and sinewy. The odor exuding from the men frankly reminded me of a wet dog sprayed with perfume.

"There was a man and a woman, humanoid, yet unfamiliar; however, there were physical characteristics in both of them that reminded me of a wolf. Their eyes were calculating, always searching for weakness. The man had golden eyes, which were quite spooky. When he became agitated or his ego was threatened, the color changed dramatically—to *black*. It was as if adrenalin affected the color.

"The dream took place in bedchambers. The woman was writhing, seducing the man. The man was helpless to withstand her wiles; he was her complete and utter slave. She spoke of Sector-I, and their need to depart their present position and journey there. The man questioned the decision; the woman rebuked him. In the end, it was decided that the ship would quit waiting to ambush Seven's Fleet. They would instead make way to Sector-I and attack more of our settlements there.

"Is what I'm dreaming really happening, Leandra?"

"Calm yourself, Lenore. In fact, we do not know. Your visions have been helpful, as always, but I cannot say more. Were the names of the man and women used?"

Lenore thought for a moment. "Yes! The woman called the man Xeries, and he called her several names: his Queen, master, and also Zuzahna."

"Thank you, Lenore, you may depart."

The Dream Keeper rose gracefully from the sofa and walked from the alcove.

As Lenore crossed the atrium, the Ancient began speaking with Intras, her brow furrowed in contemplation. "I can only presume the Xeries of whom she speaks is a son, or possibly a grandson, of Xeries Eight. Intras, if a new Nesdian Navy exists, and this Xeries is the appointed commander, it is important to remember that his father or grandfather was the Nesdian's Navy commander in the Twenty-Seven Years War. Xeries Eight was destroyed in the final conflict by TyGor's battle group.

"The Nesdians have a long history of seeking revenge and holding fallen leaders up as martyrs, slain by foreign infidels. In this way, they perpetuate their religion—if one can call it that—of secularism, hate, and retribution against all peoples of different faiths. Unless a foreign race is to help the Nesdians gain material and or military worth, then all the often boasted dogma of the infidel is forgotten, their memories conveniently washed clear by their greed, power-lust, and a twisted desire to dominate the universe."

"Based on the telepathic information I have received in my meditations over the past fifteen hours, I believe that a new Nesdian Navy is not a presumption but an actual fact," Intras said, his brow furrowed.

"What details convince you?"

"As you know, Leandra, what I am about to share with you I cannot prove factually; it is only that I have been successful in intercepting certain emanations from Sector-G and beyond."

"Intras, while I do not consider myself a telepath, I understand the Art. I have experienced limited success applying its principles myself. You do not need to explain. It has always been obvious to me that we humans underuse our brains. Using less than eight percent of the brain's mass shows there are many unknown, or little-known, uses for this mysterious organ. We humans have many possible functions that the average citizen does not understand. This is why, under my direction, the Fifteen began programs under the Prodigy designation. Most of them are highly classified, as is your work. Please, go on."

"The Nesdians have begun aggression against Seven Galaxies and our most distant settled worlds. The seven nails in each of the victim's arms and the branding of the abdomen are rituals of religious affiliation, condemning Seven Galaxies to death through the power of Xeries and the royal crown."

"I garnered as much. I have studied their culture extensively. The facts fit their race's, shall I say, genetic psychosis. What more do you have?"

"Much! They move as Lenore dreamed. They are, as we speak, in Deep Space drive, intending to attack more settlements and provoke our Fleet. Xeries and the Nesdian Navy have set sail for Sector-I. Also in my meditations, I received extremely powerful emanations from a culture with superior mental abilities—mental proficiencies that enable them to communicate as one. It is as though the culture's highest leaders are not a combination of different separate minds but of one mind: a mind that speaks the thoughts of the group as one—a body of brains working in utter concert, omniscient, with a perfect assimilation of thoughts. It appears to be an intellect so advanced...I have never experienced anything like it before."

"Do you feel this mind is a threat to our worlds?" asked Leandra.

"Not directly, but for some reason the culture has enabled the Nesdians. It is confusing."

"Why would a super-advanced race ally themselves with such a brutal and primitive culture?" Leandra asked, clearly astounded.

"Exactly! That is what I pondered, because I lacked understanding. What could the Unknowns have to gain by enabling the Nesdians to make war?" The question had been nagging in the back of his mind.

"Perhaps it is no alliance," Leandra said. "Perhaps the Unknown ones are using the Nesdians for some reason we do not yet comprehend."

"It is possible."

"Intras, as I instructed yesterday, you are to focus on nothing but the mystery of the Unknowns and anything new from Nesdia. We must understand them. And one more thing: the emanations from this combined mind, is there any clue as to where in the universe they originate?"

"That I can tell you: Deep Space, farther and deeper than Nesdia's reservation planets, and far beyond those. They exist in, and are of, the universe never explored by outsiders. This I feel to be the case."

"Could it be that this Unknown race feels some threat by our ever-expanding settlements?"

"That, and possibly the population explosion over the past two hundred years on Nesdia One, Two, and Three.

I understand that the Nesdian's spiritual dogma was altered drastically after their defeat in the Twenty-Seven Years War. One of the many changes being the mandatory birth of at least one baby per year from all adult females, regardless of marital status. The law of the Nesdian realm allows for the execution of adult females who shun childbirth or who do not make the quota for voluntary reasons. In essence, all three reservation planets occupied by the Nesdian culture have seen the population of their race explode exponentially.

"Perhaps the Unknown ones realized that any wayward star traveler could land a ship on a Nesdian planet and then be persuaded to transport some Nesdians to planets with the necessary minerals and metals to support a technological society. Once the Nesdians gained the ability to travel in Deep Space again, their astounding numbers would create a Diaspora of epic proportions, and their aggressive and backward gene pool would spread like a plague through the entire universe. Perhaps the Unknown ones have set the Nesdians against us, so that each of our cultures will be weakened by conflict. It is inevitable in War.

"What I have shared with you is in part intuition and mostly thoughts cast into the great energy of the universe. I am fortunate to possess the talent or capacity to be, simply put, a receiver."

"Why then would the Unknown ones enable the Nesdians, as we believe has happened?" Leandra was blindly searching for understanding, seeking clues with which to piece the puzzle together.

"I believe any alliance between two cultures would be conditional on certain things."

"Such as?"

"Such as instigating war on a third culture—in this case, Seven Galaxies. It's an age-old tactic when three potentially powerful opponents fear and distrust each other. The most intelligent and manipulative of the cultures can set out to encourage or enable conflict between the other two. This allows the catalyst culture to wait, watch, and assess the morals, intelligence, tactical skills, and ultimately the combined consciousness of a people, a world, or a race. In this way, they may minimize damage to themselves, while seeing which of the other two cultures prevails. Once there has been a victory and the vanquished have been placed in a position where they are no longer a threat, the more intelligent or advanced culture, observing and not involved in the conflict, can easily make peace with a society weakened and exhausted by war."

"You are correct. This is an age-old and proven strategy. Is it possible we are experiencing such calculations and manipulation at this time?"

Intras only shrugged his shoulders. Whether he was right, they could not know, and yet Leandra wondered how true his hypothesis might be.

TEN

The admiral came to Leandra's personal quarters for lunch. She waited until after the very pleasant conversation and meal to talk of conflict. "Ty, I must say, I have enjoyed your presence here. The time we've spent together has been short, yet in that time I feel we have come closer to understanding each other's minds."

"I feel the same way."

"You are different from the other fourteen; while we sequester ourselves here, you have accepted your duty and taken on the responsibility of being the Protector of Seven Galaxies, and of all our settlements in Deep Space."

"A responsibility, yes; but more importantly an honor, one that I hold dear above all other official duties."

"It is well that we see eye to eye on this very important subject. My position, as you know, compliments your own. With our minds, strategies, and moral agendas traveling on parallel paths, much will be accomplished."

"Leandra, I must speak plainly."

"Please do!"

"In the youngest years of my time as an officer, when I was straight out of Academy and had no actual battlefield experience, I was thrown into the leanest and most horrific military conflict experienced in five millenniums of our history. I witnessed it all: back-fighting for position, egos affecting strategy, as well as greed, lust for power, and a host of other human conditions I prefer to forget. In the end, you were still standing, unscathed despite the entire ordeal. I looked up to your honor, your unselfishness, your work ethic and military ability, and most of all to your belief that we, as a moral and tolerant people, would survive the worst.

"When the dust settled and the enemy was vanquished, you remained as an inspiration to us all. I never thought I would have the opportunity to speak these words directly to you, but I swear, through the entire twenty-seven years, I prayed for your safety and your wisdom, and most of all that in the performance of my duties, I would never disappoint you."

Leandra looked upon the man she had observed as a boy, had watched with curiosity, interest, and hope. He had fulfilled her aspirations, in his career, in his command of the battlefield, and in the simple and unselfish way he gave of himself to serve and protect the common man.

"Dearest TyGor, in all the years of service to Seven Galaxies and the preceding realm, I can say unequivocally, you have never disappointed me."

"It is well that we have spoken of these things."

"Yes," Leandra said. "It is well!"

"What other subjects are on your mind, Leandra? I feel that there is much you wish to discuss."

"You are correct, Ty. I have many pressing concerns, and I will share them all with you. First of all, I would like to hear your thoughts on the possibility of TayGor serving with you on *Independence*."

"As you know, my acceptance of Admiral Vestige's command was conditional upon certain terms."

"Yes, you mentioned you had terms to submit and that the interim appointment may be temporarily permanent—forgive the oxymoron."

"The condition I wished to put forth is just what you asked: to have my grandson aboard *Independence* with me."

"Wonderful. We are of like mind."

"Not so quickly, if you please, Leandra. First, I must be assured that his time aboard will count as Academy study and that if we are to be in active service, credit for such would reduce the normal four-year time requirement at Academy by one half."

"Agreed," she said, nodding.

"Good. Then, with his consent, I will consent to accepting the permanent position.

"When shall I depart the Dome to visit him? It has been a very long three years. Although he is my grandson, I have always thought of him as the son I never had."

"I am afraid that first we have some important complications to discuss, which could delay your trip to home."

"What sort of complications?"

"Nesdia has burned two of our patrol vessels in Sector-G and has landed and destroyed all settlements on planet."

Ty leaned forward in his seat, alarmed. "How is this possible?"

"I will share all I know. The first concrete evidence, collected by Full Stealth drones, arrived only a few minutes before you. I speed-read them, and the facts appear indisputable. The reports lay in front of you. Admiral, before you disseminate the information, you must understand that until a few minutes ago, I have been relying on my sixth sense, and on the talents and expertise of the Dream Keeper and the Telepathy Master. In the past eighteen hours, the three of us determined that the attacks had taken place, yet we were without actual proof, so I was hesitant to call upon you."

"You may call upon me for a hunch, even if it is just an uneasy feeling in the stomach that is later determined to be gas. Do not withhold from me the voice of your sixth sense!"

"I had, also, a selfish desire to fulfill."

"You, Leandra?" Ty said, smiling. "I hardly believe my ears!"

"I wished you to have one evening before being engaged in conflict again—one evening that would stand undiminished in your memory…. Did you have a pleasant time last night with Serene?"

"At your age! Matchmaking! You should be ashamed, Leandra, asking me such questions."

"At *your* age, Admiral, I am surprised to see you blush!"

"I am *not* blushing!" Ty said, continuing to blush.

"You are, I assure you. Would you like a mirror?"

"I can see bantering with you is useless! Shall we concentrate on a *real* war instead of a battle of wits?" He smiled, that ever-rare article that revealed his enjoyment and affection.

"Yes, unfortunately, Admiral, we must." She sighed. "The stealth reconnaissance drones have picked up readings of debris in Sector-G. The debris has been positively identified by its chemical and alloy compounds to be from our vessels. The drones have also ferreted out a trap. No less than nine enemy warships were waiting in full cloak for us to respond.

"Furthermore, I received information from the Keeper of Dreams this morning, and her most recent dream makes me believe their Navy is moving towards our settlements in Sector-I. The Telepathy Master concurs with this. I believe they have tired of waiting to spring the trap and are moving to destroy more of our people. Leandra fell silent and looked towards the tall window wall. Gor thought he noticed a longing or wistfulness in her eyes. Then she picked up her words where she had left them and continued.

"In your opinion, Admiral, what do you think has happened? How could they have surprised and destroyed our patrol craft without them ever having sent distress signal?"

"In the past war, I have seen this .sort of ambush pulled off numerous times," the admiral said. "We precipitated attacks on the Nesdians during the Twenty-Seven Years War using tactics they have obviously not forgotten. As you know, a ship must drop shield in order to transport cargo or persons to and from the vessel using particle acceleration, or to dispatch a drone or smaller manned exploratory craft. It is not a complicated matter for an enemy to stalk a target under full cloak, at least no more than it is for a lion to stalk his next quarry. Many opportunities to strike will be lost, but if the predator is hungry, stealthy, and determined, sooner or later the quarry will make a mistake or drop its guard for a split second. Then the predator can strike. In that minute opening created by lack of diligence, all is lost." He shook his head, then said, "How many crew were aboard our ships?"

"Two hundred thirty-two, Admiral."

TyGor reflected for a somber moment. "Such waste! Peace for our society has lasted for over two centuries. Our commanders have had no threats to fine-tune their instincts and sixth sense. Thus, the commanders and intelligence officers aboard failed in one simple task."

"What would that be?" Leandra asked, attempting to follow the admiral's thoughts.

"They failed to listen to their inner voice when it spoke. When hunted, any highly evolved animal has an antennae that warns of impending danger. It is only when the inner voice is ignored that the sixth sense abates. Then we are blind, but for our mechanical and electronic abilities. Where there is a weapon or a cloak, there is also a way around that defense. History has repeatedly taught us this brutal fact. Peace has brought complacency to many commanders in the Fleet. We must correct this deficiency immediately!"

"I agree, Admiral."

"First, we must order Full Stealth Cloak and maintain it until such time as we have briefed the entire command down to the lowest rank of the dangers we face and the losses already sustained. No dropped shields, no exceptions, until we sort out our plan. You will, I hope, approve?"

She nodded. "I have given those exact orders to the entire Fleet command, much to the consternation of certain diplomats who were aboard some of the vessels when the orders were implemented."

"Very good, Leandra. Diplomats have no real sense of war. Their discomfort brings me just a small fleeting pleasure. I guarantee you, if we do not drop our guard, attacks cannot be so easily pulled off. The predator will become hungry. It is then that *he* may blunder. When were the Full Stealth Cloak orders implemented?"

"Eighteen hours ago, after my meeting with the Telepathy Master and the Keeper of Dreams. The information imparted to me by those two made me uneasy and convinced me to act."

"It is well that you did or we may have been receiving similar reports of losses in other sectors. We must make provisions for a rotation of craft into full security curtain protecting them from threat while reserves are reenergized…. If the Nesdians have dedicated nine ships of war to the trap, they would have at least that many somewhere in safe reserve.

"Experience has taught me that Nesdia is not an unintelligent enemy. They are brutal and merciless but in no way stupid; they are a cunning race, bred through millenniums of the alpha-pack control system. This has created a ruthless mindset and imbedded it deep within their gene pool."

"Ty, you are sounding quite a lot like Andarean right now."

He was taken aback. He considered the Ancient's thoughts and then smiled. "Leandra, your words have merit."

"I have called a meeting of the Fifteen for the hour of fifteen today."

"Good," Ty said, nodding his approval. "We have our work cut out for us in the meantime. Foremost, I must explain that I will accept appointment as Admiral and see this conflict extinguished, but only on my terms. I must have full control of the Fleet, no exceptions. You, and only you, Leandra, must be my liaison within the Fifteen while I am away from the Dome. These conditions are not negotiable. I will not be hamstrung by waiting on orders in desperate situations. I must also have full complement of supply and the budget for this war approved as an open, unfettered grant.

"We must act rapidly, for if the Nesdians possess twenty or more ships of war, as I am convinced they do, they will have twenty more complete within the year. Send Full Stealth Cloak drones into sectors settled by the Nesdians and into the surrounding sectors as well. I want to know immediately what they have moving and where the armament planets are located. They could not possibly have built this fleet on one planet; they must have several planets producing military hardware and Deep Space vessels. Gor paused and closed his eyes for a moment as if seeing the future or his plan in formation.

"First, we must meet them in Sector-I, protect our people there, and destroy as many craft as possible. Next, I must go to their nests and destroy any capability to produce more warships as well as any supply lines enabling that production. They must be producing components underground, else we would have had some clues long before now. If they are underground, our task may entail burning entire planets to cinders. If this is the case, many innocents will die."

"Admiral, the group consciousness of this race is inherently evil. How could there be innocents?"

"I speak of the children."

"Admiral, do not let sympathy for the little ones affect your judgment or decisions. That is an order! You must remove any and all emotion from your being. We were attacked! As you know, war is ruthless and many innocents have already died or been carried off to who knows where to become slaves, possibly to be tortured daily or to live as beasts of burden.

"When we kill a rattlesnake that threatens our child, we do not carry the nest of baby snakes home to make sure they are safe. We kill the baby rattlesnakes as well, so that they do not grow to adulthood and multiply in numbers. Leandra paused for effect. She reached for a glass of water on an end table next to her, watching the admiral's reacton to her words as she drank.

"Many of our society believed when the Nedsians were defeated in the Twenty-Seven Years War that we should exterminate them completely. Ethics and morals imbedded in our beliefs prevailed, and we allowed the survivors to begin anew, on planets that would comfortably support a simple life of farming and food gathering.

"Instead of appreciating a new beginning, the Nesdian Zorah modified the religious teachings in their Book of Prophesy to promote intolerance of other religions, sectarianism, and hate. The Zorah's amended version contains prophesy that teaches the Nesdians to smite the innocents of all other faiths, setting the stage for us to respond in defense of our people and to be defeated; this absurdity would create a new realm of power and glory for the Nesdian king. Make no mistake, for two hundred years the Nesdian Zorah, their supreme religious leader, has been brainwashing their entire populace! What we are facing is a form of unified religious fanaticism, unbridled and rampant in their culture. Now they possess technology, enabling their leaders to attempt at making the fanatical prophesy reality."

"Leandra, you speak for the Ancients and their wisdom, and I listen with an open mind," Ty said. "When it comes to destroying entire planets, my conscience speaks to me as well; however, I will carry out the protection of our society and the second defeat of Nesdia with diligence and thought only for our people, no matter the cost to Nesdia!"

"Very well. We are of like mind then?" Leandra waited for confirmation.

Ty nodded. "We are."

"We have two hours before the Fifteen meet. We must formulate a sensible reaction to this Nesdian aggression without giving away your complete strategy. Even within the confines of the Dome, we sometimes have unauthorized information leaked to the press; we must be careful."

"I agree, Leandra."

"Before we begin strategizing, I want to make something clear. You will depart early tomorrow morning. Before you leave for your beloved valley, the Fifteen will meet again with Andarean to share our plans for the Virgin with him. After this meeting, you will go home and convince your grandson to join you. You have twenty-four hours leave. Upon your return, you will both board *Independence* and make speed to Sector-I."

"All is clear. We will prevail against the dark onslaught quickly, I am sure."

ELEVEN

The Ancient began the meeting. "Andarean, I apologize for my abrupt departure from our previous meeting. Please, if you could pick up the pieces and begin at the point where you were interrupted. We have little time, as Ty is departing within the hour."

"I believe I had just begun speaking about my work with the genetics of animals, so if it is acceptable to the Fifteen, I would begin there today."

All of the Fifteen nodded assent.

"It is an accepted fact that an excellent stud is one that passes a good conformation to his offspring. It is also accepted that to be a truly excellent stallion, the horse should be of a gentle disposition and be intelligent, and these traits should be carried through to the foals.

Andarean felt a bit naked. Without his vid display, flow charts and algorithms he could tune and caress. He was simply standing with no props before the Fifteen.

"Horses can be very dangerous animals, especially when we consider a person riding, performing dressage, jumping, herding, roping livestock, or trail riding, which may take riders along a precipitous route. A gentle, reliable, and willing disposition is extremely important.

"Now, if we consider that this understanding of equestrian breeding goes back thousands of years, why should it not relate to other animals and possibly to humankind as well?

"My lab at the time I was studying this was very small, and I did not have room for a stable, so I chose canines as my subject matter. Besides, they have much shorter gestation periods and mature into adulthood much faster than equines. I acquired two groups of breeds: The first group was made up of breeds known for being unpredictable, independent, incorrigible, and ruthless fighters, prone to attacking humans. The second group consisted of breeds known to be of gentle, obedient, and faithful temperaments, with the courage and urge to protect their masters, even in the direst circumstances. I categorized these two groups as A, for alpha, and B, for benevolent.

"I tested their DNA, found some common denominators, and then began breeding and observing them over a period of seventeen years. The results were astounding.

"Certain genes only appeared within the gene pool of the A group that were almost completely absent in the gene pool of the B's, and vice versa. Thus, I was able to identify the genes responsible for each group's particular temperamental traits.

"After years of observation, in which I crossbred the A's and B's, disturbing yet very interesting data presented itself, and the pattern became irrefutable. Whenever a pup was born that had more than fifty percent of A's gene pool, the result was, in most cases, personality characteristics and tendencies that matched the A group. However, I must make it very clear that even before the ancestry of a pup reached the 50/50 point in genetic balance, ugly traits reared their head.

"You see, one of the breeds I selected for the A group was *canis lupus*, more commonly known as the wolf. I had a difficult time procuring a certified wolf that had never been in contact with civilization or captive breeding and was, therefore, completely wild. This task caused me no small trouble, but I suspected such an animal would have many inherent qualities, which, through natural selection would be imbedded deep within its genetic make-up.

"Good fortune shone, and I obtained two perfect examples of *canis lupus*. Several planets we had recently settled still had aboriginal wolf packs that had not been hunted to extinction. With a little finagling and a great amount of squeeze, I was able to obtain not only an adolescent male but a mature female as well. Andarean felt a twinge of pain remembered and shuddered ever so slightly. His mental fit went unnoticed.

"The female, for the most part, was very sweet, and yet every time I began to turn my back on her, the hair on the back of my neck would prickle and stand up—an eerie feeling, I can tell you. The male, even as a young dog, was different. He seemed always to be sizing me up. I was told by persons very familiar with the breed that, in the presence of a wolf, I should never make direct eye contact or turn my back, and most of all I should always stand up straight and retain the alpha position, even though I was human. I took good notes and practiced daily what I had been taught.

"When the male reached adulthood, the tenuous situation became worse. Instead of bowing his head and being submissive when I brought food, he began trying to look me straight in the eyes. I avoided direct eye contact as instructed, yet I began to feel uneasy around the animal. The more uneasy I felt, the bolder he became. It was as though he had telepathic ability.

"One day, I had a minor accident: I slipped on some icy steps and twisted my ankle. The next day, preoccupied with my duties and not really thinking about my limp, I went to feed the male wolf. Fortunately, I had an assistant accompany me into the enclosure that day, for as soon as I began to pour food into his dish—something I had done every day for over two years—he attacked, lunging straight for my throat.

"I had sense enough to spin my body in a circle and deflect his momentum; however, he turned and went for my throat again. I managed to get my arm up to protect myself—I still carry the scars to this day. My assistant picked the wolf's rear legs high off the ground and the dog let go.

"I share this experience with you in order that you may relate to the mental process I went through afterwards; that wolf would have killed me to gain the alpha position. He spotted my weakness, and attacked. I believe, from all that I have learned and observed, that the criminal element is, at its worst, no different in behavior to that wolf. A school bully preys upon the weak; he sniffs them out, knowing they will not stand against him but instead will cringe and suffer the abuse he delivers. The school bully is striving for position, hunting weakness and creating enemies in the process, which will no doubt haunt him later. Pausing, Andarean swept a glance across the Fifteens face's. He wondered again what they were thinking.

"We have come to understand organized crime to be similar: some underling in the organization is always seeking to take the kingpin's place. Feudal or autocratic governments through the ages are no different. In all these examples, a ruthlessness and dissatisfaction with the present position exists, driving certain persons—but not others—to aspire for the alpha position. Why?" Andarean paused and then said, "I must apologize; I have gone on much too long."

"We have asked to hear of your work firsthand," the Ancient said. "Do not apologize; we appreciate your analogies and the edification brought with your experiences. You have much more to share with us; however, Ty must depart from us shortly. We will carry on this discussion after he leaves. Before we adjourn, we must share with you the reasons we requested your presence. You will be able to stay the night here again, will you not?"

"But of course, if I am invited. I would be honored beyond measure."

"Good, it is settled then. The Fifteen have already extended the invitation to you. You will sleep here, and for the rest of the day you may wander the gardens between meals and relax. But for now, please just absorb what we are anxiously waiting to impart."

"You have my undivided attention," Andarean said, altogether curious of what would be imparted.

Leandra looked to the admiral, as if giving him a silent cue.

The admiral began, "The reason we have called you here is a very complicated matter. The subject, and its inception, go back to our previous realm and its view of the future. Please do not forget that the majority of the

Dome's wisdom does not come from the Fifteen; it began as knowledge and truth passed down by the Ancients, who no longer reside with us on the physical plane.

"Over three Millenniums ago, an Explorer from our former realm, searching the universe for inhabitable planets not occupied by humanoids, came upon a priceless gem: a planet in the last throes of its molten beginnings—a planet with oxygen, water, gravity, and a climate without severe extremes, perfect for the support of human life. The discovery was mostly useless at the time for the simple reason that while this planet could support a diversity of life, it had none: no trees or grass, no fish in its many freshwater and saltwater seas, and no mammals walking the surface. For all intents, it was completely sterile.

"The ship's captain responsible for the discovery diligently reported it and forgot about it, but some did not forget. They erased all records of its location and surface mapping, and it became a secret project for our previous realm. Only a few were aware of it as, over time, an immense biodiversity was nourished there: trees, plants, fish, mammals, insects, and so on, but no humanoids.

"Upon the change, from our previous government and the fusion of Seven Galaxies into the present union and the Dome of Wisdom's rule, the secret was passed in trust to be held by the Fifteen. We have told no one, not until this day when we brought you into our confidence. We ask that you swear an oath of secrecy before we share any more information with you. Will you agree?"

Andarean was willing, yet a bit confused. What did this planet have to do with him? he wondered. "In all honesty, I am completely at your service. I swear that

I will not speak of anything I hear or learn while I am under the Fifteen's hospitality. However, I must admit, I am befuddled as to my participation in this meeting."

"Since you have agreed and sworn an oath of secrecy with the Fifteen as witnesses, we now wish to enlighten you," said the admiral. "Before us lies the opportunity to settle and inhabit a Virgin planet. Our society has done this many times in the past, most often with very unsettling results. Many of the planets onto which portions of our society have migrated have devolved confrontational factions and have split on lines of religion, race, politics, or lust for power. The strong have preyed on the weak, and those of higher intellect have used the strong to pursue their selfish personal goals. The greedy despoil pristine waters, forests, and farmlands and hold agendas that are not for the betterment of mankind but for the perpetuation of their interests, often inherently evil; and all this despite careful screening by the best scientific data available in those time periods.

"I have painted a harsh picture of our past migrations. Not all have been as terrible as I have shared, but most. To see paradise lost once more would be, to my way of thinking, unthinkable, a crime against the ages. So, Andarean, we have called upon you. Are you willing to serve humankind, to attempt once again that which has eluded us?"

"Dear sir, I pray, do not keep me in suspense any longer. Share with me the plan, and I will dedicate myself to it."

"The World of which we speak is waiting—waiting for *you*. It waits there, unblemished by the ugly side of man. It waits with tall golden wheat, pristine waters teeming with sea life, and savannas covered in an abundance of animal life. It contains biodiversity the likes of which none in this room have ever personally witnessed. An unspoiled heaven, many would say. We wish to send you as the Virgin's steward and protector. You will board a science vessel that is being provisioned for the settling migration. However, unlike previous migratory voyages, only two people will depart with the ship; all others will be cloned in transit.

"The journey is one of twelve years. You and your mate will be mother and father to the shipboard children. You will teach them survival skills, horticulture, fishing, hunting, animal husbandry, math, reading, literature, and love for fellows and family, for you will all be family. The gentle, honest, loving race you have engineered will have an opportunity to thrive, and to live in true harmony and peace."

"Sir...Admiral," Andarean began, in shock. Never in his wildest dreams could he ever have conceived such a plan, yet here he was in front of the Fifteen, chosen to carry it through. He could think of only one glitch. "It is an inspiring and intellectually challenging opportunity. I see only one problem: I have no mate. My work has been my love, and it has left meager time for romantic pursuits."

"Andarean, did you not swear to uphold the duties we lay upon you?" the admiral asked loudly, as if in reprimand.

"Yes! Yes of course," Andarean answered immediately.

"We have analyzed the entire test group living among our society, but we feel their exposure to our worlds may have an adverse effect upon the mission," the admiral said. "Of the three hundred you have raised, only one has been sequestered and not exposed. She is the only intelligent and logical choice. Do you have any objections to Estellene?"

"Estellene?" Andarean asked, once again feeling shock. The admiral could not possibly be serious—that divine creature, that angel of mercy, that flowing feminine form could not possibly be the one, he thought. "Why... this is all so sudden. It's as though I'm dreaming. I am dreaming, aren't I? Did you say *Estellene*?"

"Yes, Estellene!" the admiral answered again, struggling to be patient.

"Who could object to such grace, such beauty, such harmony. She is one of the three hundred?"

"Yes," the admiral said.

Andarean took in the faces of the Fifteen before him slowly, settling his gaze upon each for a second or two. In most, he detected a trace of humor; in others, only the enquiring mind.

"I accept!" he said. "I am honored! I believe I will wake shortly and be desperately disappointed to find this has all been a very vivid dream sequence. Yet, I must believe! It is the ultimate objective. Thank you for your trust." Andarean bowed lightly. "Thank you for this unbelievable opportunity. With your help and support, the migration and settling will be a complete success."

"We will adjourn, if there are no objections," Leandra said, standing.

No objections were forthcoming.

"Ty, will you show Andarean the entrance to the gardens, and then return to my private quarters? There is a subject on which I would appreciate your opinion."

"Certainly, I will be there shortly," said the admiral.

The remaining fourteen stood, as did Andarean.

The admiral came forward. "Andarean, it has been a pleasure. Will you be kind enough to walk with me for a short while?"

"Yes, that would be an honor, Ty." They walked together, a comfortable silence between them.

The portal door opened, and the two men stepped through. Once more, Andarean experienced the feeling of being instantaneously transported to another place in time. Turning around, attempting to take in the Dome visually, he saw only a vast, flowing landscape.

"Ty, how is all this possible?" he asked.

"Some things we, even with all our knowledge, are unable to explain. The portal was found several millennia past by an adventurer named Duhcat. That is another long story. I will see to it that you have a full record of Duhcat's life, or at least what we know of him, archived aboard your vessel. You will find the mystery and legend of Enricco Duhcat unbelievable, yet the story is true, I assure you.

"Duhcat gave the portal to our society in return for the promise that a select group, carefully chosen, would protect it and keep its mystery within our grasp. The Fifteen are sworn to uphold that promise made long ago to our benefactor. You see, Duhcat has been, and is, our protector. Many past and present souls who have passed through the Dome of Wisdom would say that he is the patriarch and provider, the primary catalyst that enables the Seven Galaxies realm to expand and govern so large a portion of the universe. Without his technological advances, benevolence, and moral discernment, we would be a much more backward people and culture, I'm afraid."

The admiral fell silent, apparently enjoying the scenery, in particular the mountains, which seemed rooted in the sparkling water. He took a few deep breaths, obviously consuming the scents. His eyes roamed the gardens and finally, after a heartfelt silence, he turned and spoke softly to Andarean once more. "I regret leaving this place every time duty forces me to. I dream of it. When sleeping, I often find myself walking here. It is a surreal and soulful experience. Andarean, in my mind's eye, I see the Virgin as being like this place. Will you promise me one more thing?"

"Of course!"

"Will you make a place on the new planet similar to this? It would mean a great deal to me."

Andarean felt kinship to this man, a feeling that he could not understand since they had just met. "It will be my absolute pleasure, and I will consider it one of my life's greatest projects. Perhaps one day you will visit us there?"

"I am sorry to say, it is not in the cards. You will understand more of the whys and why nots in the future. Safe journey, my friend; good fortune to you and yours."

The admiral turned and walked back the way they had come. This time Andarean did not watch him walk away. A feeling that he would never see Ty again pervaded his mind, bringing an unexplained sadness that left him contemplating his future and the adventure that would take him away from the planet of his birth, a world that he loved dearly.

He shook off the unsubstantiated thought and walked downhill towards the shimmering estuary of blue water.

TWELVE

TAYGOR ran with his grandfather up the steep, winding trail towards their favorite spot. They had been coming since Tay was old enough to walk. In the years gone by, his grandfather had always been the first one to the top, but not today.

They reached the cliff edge and sat side by side as always, panting. His grandpa looked him square in the eyes. The old man's eyes were twinkling. "Every time we have run this path in the past, I've always managed to win!"

"I never knew it was a contest, Grandpa."

"Yes you did, you little liar!" Ty smiled. "Today is the first time I have not won. Is it that I am finally getting old, or is it that you are now so long-legged and so fast, I may never have a chance again?"

"Dear Grandfather, you will never be old. Wiser, a teensy bit slower, but never old."

"You have a way about you, son, a fluid grasp of words with which you can salve an old man's ego or smooth the ruffled feathers in most any group. It's a talent I am fond of, for in all my years and travels I've still not learned what comes to you so naturally. How are your languages? How many are you fluent in?"

"Four, Pa, not counting my native."

"The gift of easy communication *and* the art of diplomacy both come naturally to you. I must say that I'm slightly envious. Command came naturally to me, but I always found social graces a tedious process to learn. This forced me to practice regularly, and to learn the ever-frustrating art of patience." He looked at Tay sitting beside him and said, "I am so happy to see you. You have grown so tall, as tall as I at your age."

"Pa, it has been many years since you saw me last. Surely you did not think I would still be licking milk from peach fuzz on my upper lip?"

The old man laughed. "No, surely I did not picture you doing that. However, I did wonder if the handsome and charming young rake you have become would be overburdened with so much feminine company, you would not have time for your feeble old grandfather!"

"Now you are the jester. I will always have time for you. Besides, my studies are important. I will not become distracted by overzealous interest in young ladies. I see it already happening with many of the young men I know. Sacrificing dreams once held above all else for the warmth of feminine companionship and the ever-present ring through their noses."

"Well put!" The old man began to laugh and Tay laughed along with him, but when his laughter faded, he found the old man still rolling.

"It must have been pretty boring shipboard for you to find such extended humor in my last comments. I fear you will die of a cardiac arrest if you don't calm yourself!"

THE SEEDING SEVEN'S VISION

Tay was only adding more levity to the situation, but his grandfather calmed himself and became serious for the first time since his arrival.

"I must talk to you, son, of serious things, situations which cannot go un-discussed between us. I am here for a short while only."

"But you've been gone for more than three years! Surely High Command will give you more days on-planet!"

"I have been on-planet for ten days—nine of them under official duties of a high level. I was not allowed contact with you until meetings at the Dome were complete."

"The Dome of Wisdom? You were there for nine days?"

"Yes."

Tay's mind raced. No common commander went to the Dome—no one but the Fifteen and their discreetly selected staff went there; few of those ever left once they were honored with admittance.

"You are not kidding? This is surely one of your jokes. You are really on leave and will be spending the majority of your next six weeks bantering with me?"

"I am sorry to say that I cannot stay longer than I have already informed you," Ty said, shaking his head. "I said I had to speak of serious things. I changed the channel then; will you do the same?"

"Of course! Of course I will, if you require it."

"I require it," he said.

The young man became serious, a sponge willing to absorb all his grandfather wished to impart.

"As you know, I have dedicated my life to upholding the moral standards and spiritual values our society holds dear. The precepts of which I speak are the foundation of our civilization. Without their governing morals and decency, we would eventually find ourselves back in caves, scratching for firewood with which to cook our raw meat."

"Yes, Grandfather."

"An imminent danger pervades our worlds. All that I and many of my respected peers have worked our entire lives to build and uphold could come toppling down."

"What is this danger of which you speak?" asked the young man, alarmed.

"You must swear to me on our blood that you will speak of this to no one."

"No one! I swear!" said Tay.

"The Nesdians."

"But how could they possibly be a threat? We are taught that our technology, sheer mental superiority, and moral conduct all render the Nesdians effectively impotent to act against us. If they were a threat, it would change many of the teachings. They are brutal, cruel, and greedy, yes—but no match for the Fleet. They are savages, barbarians living in the darkness where their last acts of aggression left them. They would not approach a single colony under protection of Seven Galaxies. They wouldn't dare! Would they, Grandfather?"

His grandfather did not answer. This meant he was serious.

"Would they be so stupid as to dare to threaten Seven Galaxies?"

"The Nesdians have already burned two of the Fleet's cruisers, which were lulled by complacency and fell into a trap. They have also landed in three colonies in that patrolled sector and taken control of the ground."

"It is unbelievable, Grandfather. How can it be possible?"

"Calm yourself, Tay, and listen, for I will impart all I am able on the subject. I do not wish to cast a dark cloud over our reunion; however, it is not I who blackens the thought-waves in our sectors with the minds of conquest."

"What do you mean?" asked Tay. "I need to understand. Are you going away to war?"

"Yes," Ty said, nodding solemnly.

"But we have lived in peace for over two centuries—peace forever! That is what we are taught in school. Now it has all changed?"

"Where I go and what I do cannot be taught in school, Tay."

"Please, dear Grandfather, I only question to understand."

"I take no offence, son. This burden I am carrying should not be unloaded on you."

"You must tell me! I swear, I will never forgive you if you leave without sharing the troubles you carry. Maybe I can help."

TyGor brightened at the prospect of having a trusted confidant. "While residing in the Dome, I was given permission to speak of certain things to you."

"I was mentioned in the Dome?"

"Yes," Ty said, smiling briefly. "Do not let it go to your head!"

"I swear I will not."

The admiral continued. "An alliance that we do not understand has been formed between the Nesdians and an advanced race about which we know little. They hail from a sector deep in areas of the universe that we have never explored. We know they exist. They are surely aware of our civilization, but both our races have kept to themselves, in communication and sector."

"What has changed? What do we call this advanced race? You must mean that they are equally as advanced as we are? Why have they embraced the Nesdians? What does it mean for the Fleet and all the progressive worlds we have settled?"

"Tay, you ask questions, many questions. Some of the answers you seek, I hold; some, I do not; and some we may seek together. Other answers may never be known. Will you accompany me on this quest for understanding? I desire your help."

"Grandfather, I have dreamed of having such an opportunity once I am out of Academy. You know, of course, that I have been accepted and begin my studies there in the fall. Once I graduate, I would be capable of your request. However, with my meager knowledge of tactics, physics, creative design, and space-drive theory, or of officer's responsibility and leadership, I would be of little help to you."

"You, my son, have already helped me."

"How?"

"First, by showing me that I am not as young as I once was. Then you made me laugh harder than I have in years. I am in council with a person I truly trust, a person I know from personal experience to be unselfish, honorable, diplomatic, fearless, and extremely intelligent. Do I need more?"

"Experience!" Tay said. "You need someone with much more of that. It is a critical element that I do not yet possess."

"How, my dear son? How does one gain experience in the art and tactics of war and diplomacy?"

"Life and the path one chooses teaches these things over time. I am not familiar with another way."

Ty nodded, pleased. "A good answer, and before you is a choice: two paths confront you, and only one can be explored. Each route is different, yet similar. Each will impress you with knowledge, one through books and theories, and the other through the realities of life aboard the vessels of the Fleet."

"But, Grandfather, with all due respect, I desire to be an officer of the Fleet. That requires certification from the Academy."

"You are correct."

"Then by leaving without finishing my studies, I would in all senses vanquish a life goal very dear to me."

"There is a solution, if you will listen carefully," the admiral said. "Hold your inquiries until I am finished imparting my thoughts. Can you do this, son?"

"Of course."

"I would not ask that you vanquish your dreams, only to think in a more creative manner of how a path different from the one you have anticipated might bring you to your goals more rapidly. Your time aboard the ship would not be easy, and your studies would continue—not this fall, months away, but within a week. All education aboard the Fleet's most prestigious vessel will count towards your Academy certification. Also, credit for active service will trim one-half from the usual four-year term at Academy. Your certification would be possible in a mere two years.

"In your time on the ship, you would gain knowledge of tactical strategies and application, shipboard diplomacy, and potentially a diverse range of actual experience—non-theoretical. If you accept my proposal, I intend to appoint you as my special advisor and liaison for all language needs aboard ship." TyGor stopped, apparently finished.

"Grandfather, what vessel do you mean by the Fleet's most prestigious vessel? Do you mean *Independence*?"

"The same."

"*Independence*! But how? Admiral Vestige commands *Independence*. No one boards her without being thoroughly scrutinized by the admirals special twenty-four, and they test you on security, psychology, history, mathematics, physics, and other fields. They are regarded as the best in their specialized fields, and no one is cleared for boarding without unanimous approval. Only one in a million is admitted to the review roster and approved to sail. How could I possibly qualify? I have no experience, no credentials!"

"You have your experiences, and you have your credentials. Just because you are young does not mean that you lack these things."

"I don't understand. How could it possibly be? This is cruel, and, I might add, not in the least bit funny."

"I told you we were speaking of serious matters!" Ty said, growing impatient. "I do not apply levity to situations such as this. The rule of the twenty-four was instituted by the Dome not only for *Independence* but also for all other craft of war heading into Deep Space. I fully understand the rigorous testing applied to persons seeking acceptance and entrance into the Fleet's Strategic Arsenal. What do you think, Tay?"

"I don't know," Tay said, shaking his head. "I think these are an aging grandfather's dreams. You have created something in your mind, some unattainable fantasy, because you are leaving me so soon."

"In my mind, you say?"

"Yes, Grandfather. Only the Fleet's Admiral determines the final selection for staffing *Independence*. You, with all due respect, do not possess that authority. Why would you ask me to join such mental folly? You know that every student of the Academy dreams of serving on *Independence*. Why would you raise my hopes when surely it is impossible?"

"First and foremost, Tay, from this moment on, when in official capacity, you must address me as Admiral Gor."

"I am sorry, Grandfather; I do not understand you."

"Admiral Vestige has retired, citing age, family, and a challenge in which failure could literally unseat the entire High Command. To retire with a perfect record, citing age, health, and long-neglected family ties, is well."

"Vestige has retired?"

"Yes. It has not yet been officially announced, but it will be shortly. I have consented to the appointment as Admiral of the Fleet on one condition."

"This is truly unbelievable. You put forth a condition to the Fifteen?"

"Yes."

"And what, pray tell, was that?"

"I informed them that unless my terms were met, I was not interested in the responsibility."

"Grandfather, there are many who would gladly give all that they possess to acquire that position."

"Yes, I understand. Many yearn and lust for power for selfish reasons. Will you let me answer your last question?"

"I am sorry, Admiral. This is overwhelming!"

"My condition was that you accompany me as my special advisor."

"You did what?!"

"Do you need to clean your ears, young man? I spoke clearly and plainly."

Tay was speechless. His eyes glazed, and TyGor thought the kid was going into shock. Finally, Tay composed himself a little and could only say, "*Independence… Independence*, and with you as commander. This is a dream. Surely I will wake and be sadly disappointed."

TyGor punched his grandson in the fleshy part of the thigh.

"Does that feel like a dream, son?"

They sat silently for a time, looking out over the small valley, which had been their family's home for over three centuries. The sun had risen high, casting the fields in golden green. Tay saw Shadow down by the river, evidently coming back from a drink of cool water. He always preferred to drink there instead of from his water trough. Even from this distance, Tay could see him struggle to make it up the gentle slope leading to the current's edge.

The horse had grown old as Tay had grown into manhood. A chapter in Tay's life was closing, while another opened. Sadness gnawed at his heart—his beloved horse, his mother, this place that was one with his soul.

Tay had always felt as though his body had been made from the soil of this valley. The scent of it when he plowed reached deep into his being. The taste of the spring water, even as a small boy, had seemed familiar, as though he had lived here before, in another life. "I will miss this place, Admiral," he said.

"As I miss it when duty calls me away," Ty said, in understanding. "We have that and many other things in common. We go to make sure that when we return, it remains as it was when we left. In that calling, we honor our ancestors and all others who love their homes as we do ours."

Clouds moved across the sky, creating patterns of shadows that shifted on the valley floor. They stayed up on the cliff edge all afternoon, taking in the changes of color and light, watching—as they had many times in the past—the ever-altering display nature provided.

Over an hour passed while neither said a word. Finally, TyGor broke the comfortable silence. "You have not actually agreed to come."

"I haven't? In my thoughts, I made the decision, but I was so overwhelmed that I forgot to verbalize my willingness to leave the valley and come with you."

His grandfather placed a warm hand on Tay's back. "It is a good day. I am pleased with your choice. No one can forecast the future, yet in my heart I sense we will prevail."

"I, too, Grandfather, have that very feeling."

"Shall we walk down while we can still see the trail? It would be unforgivable if these two adventurers stumbled off a precipice in the dark without ever having searched for those Nesdian bastards! Let's go and see what your mother has made to eat. I am starving."

"Grandfather, why would the race of Unknowns help the Nesdians?" Tay asked, as they began the journey back home. "Why would they give the Nesdians technology and weapons that rival our own? Surely you have considered that, for the Fleet's cruisers to be burned, it would necessitate the Nesdian ships using stealth or cloaking technology."

"It is a fact I have not overlooked," said the admiral.

"They would also need a way—a trick or some weapon—to penetrate our shields. How is it possible they have acquired both?"

"I believe, based on the bits and pieces of evidence we have gathered, that they do have cloak; there is no other answer. As for the shields, it is textbook knowledge that the Fleet's warships must drop shield for a split second to transport people or cargo by particle acceleration or to launch a smaller rescue or exploratory vessel from the mother ship."

"I understand your conclusions, Grandfather."

"Many of us within the Fifteen believe, after analyzing the data, that areas populated by the Nesdians lie between the Unknown ones and our newest settlements in Deep Space. The Unknown ones may be attempting to create some form of buffer between their sectors and those that we control or are settling."

"Grandfather, how advanced could the Unknown ones be, allying themselves with an inferior race like the Nesdians? And you just said *us* within the Fifteen?"

"Tay, you ask some questions I am not at liberty to answer. Forget that I said '*us* within the Fifteen'!"

"I will forget, since you have ordered it, but I will always wonder whether you are one of them, one of the Fifteen."

Admiral Gor did not answer verbally, yet in his eyes, Tay could see the answer confirmed. *But how could it be?* he thought. His grandfather, one of the Fifteen, and Admiral of the Fleet as well?

The day had become surreal and now, walking down the ridge, Tay's legs felt a little rubbery, like he was walking on a bed of marshmallows. A couple of hours ago, he wouldn't have dreamed he would be boarding *Independence* inside of the week. His inquisitive spirit asked a tumbling torrent of questions, but many went unspoken.

Arriving at the house, Tay broke away from his grandfather. "I'm going to visit with Shadow for a while. I'll be in before long."

TyGor looked at the young man, understanding completely. Many years ago, he had departed this valley, saying goodbyes to some he had never seen again.

Walking into the barn, Tay took in scents with which he had grown up: sweet-smelling hay, Shadow's sweat, the aromatic cedar from which the barn was built, comfortably worn old leather, corn, oats, and barley. The river's rustling voice spoke in the distance. An owl cried out the familiar "whoo, whoo."

The young man took it all in as never before. An odd mist engulfed his thoughts.

Everything was just slightly out of focus; his eyes were watering. It was as though he were no longer part of this world, only visiting temporally.

"Hello, big fella. How ya doin?"

The old horse nuzzled his sleeve, anxious for some strokes. Tay rubbed the flat between Shadow's eyes, and the animal bounced his head up and down to the rhythm of his hand. "We've had a great friendship. I'm going to miss you, old boy. I'm leaving. I don't want to go away from you, but there is no other choice."

Taking up a brush so well worn that it fit his hand perfectly, he rubbed down his old and faithful companion. The great horse's beautiful dark color was now lightened by grey. Shadow swayed slightly into the pressure of the brush on each stroke. Tay felt a weight on his chest, knowing that in a few short hours he would be leaving this old friend behind.

Shadow nickered, and Tay broke from brushing him to fetch a few carrots. Shadow crunched them noisily while Tay finished grooming.

"I'll see you in the morning, big fella. Sweet dreams, green pastures, and cool water. Goodnight."

Entering the house, he could tell that his grandfather had already broken the news. Tay's mother looked at him in horror. The shock was quickly replaced with beseeching eyes.

"Tell me you two are not serious. Tell me it's not true."

"Mom, you know my dream, if not now then in four more years."

"But this was to be our last summer before you went away to Academy. I have my heart set on spending the next few months with you."

"I am truly sorry, Mother; it cannot be." Tay, the much-loved son and his mother's only remaining family member on Seven, went forward and took her in his arms. He felt her tremble.

"It will be okay, Mom. We are needed. There are important situations that cannot be left unattended. We go to make sure they are taken care of."

She straightened and broke away. Wiping away the tracks of her tears, she said, "Well then, if the matter is settled, we should celebrate!"

Opening a cupboard, she took out a bottle covered in dust. "Do you remember this, Father?"

"You are an angel, a dove, the child of my dreams... are you teasing me, or does that bottle actually contain Port?"

"Aye, Father," she said, smiling. "It has never been opened. It is the one you left on your last visit. I was saving it for a special occasion. Would you do the honors?"

The three ate, making small talk and sipping what TyGor referred to as "nectar from the heavens."

Before long, the young man became drowsy. Leaving his mother and grandfather to their visit, he dragged himself off to bed. The day's impact had left him drained to the core.

The mattress welcomed a fatigued body, which flopped down, not bothering to undress or cover up. Through Tay's mind flashed the events of the day, ending with him and Shadow in the barn, he grooming his beautiful old horse. Dreams of childhood haunted his sleep pleasantly.

THIRTEEN

Tay had always possessed an inherent and inexplicable deep love for horses ever since he could remember. As a toddling child, he begged his parents incessantly to give him one that would be his own. After years of persistent pleading, hounding, and profuse promises to care well for the animal, his father relented and they began searching out a horse for Tay.

The boy had books about conformation and equine training. Tay had learned to read at the age of three. He was fascinated by, and was widely read in the horse's integral participation in ancient warfare. Tay read every book he could get his hands on about Alexander the Great and about the feared and revered Mongolian horsemanship style of Genghis Kahn's time, along with many other classic writings. He consumed literature in reference to equines in prodigious amounts and was constantly asking his mother and father to explain sections of the books he did not understand. Many times in more complex writing styles, his mother read to him and explained as she went along.

Tay would search the local newspaper daily and drag his father to see any that sounded interesting, but none were good enough for the boy. Most of the horses, his father understood why Tay rejected; however, many others were beautiful animals, well-bred and with extensive training, yet repeatedly Tay rejected them.

"We have looked at over a hundred horses," his father said one day. "Why haven't you wanted to buy one of them?"

"Dad," Tay said, in a tone that suggested it were common knowledge, "when I find MY horse, the one for me, I will know; there will be no doubt. So far none of the animals we've seen spoke to me in that way."

The boy was six years old and made perfect sense. His father was tired of the search, but as horses were potentially dangerous animals, whatever happened and however long it took, he did not want to force a decision for the sake of expedience.

Tay had three more horses on his list for that Saturday. The next address was not rural farmland but in a light industrial area. They drove past scrap yards and run-down homes that had once been farmhouses. The city had encroached on this area; it was no longer farms and, at the same time, was not yet city. The transition taking place appeared painful.

They drove slowly so that they could read the addresses. Tay finally exclaimed, "Here!"

The facility before them was no horse farm but a junkyard dealing in used autocar parts.

"We must have the wrong address. Let's go."

"No, Father. The man I called described the fence and gate; it's the same."

Unbelievable, Tay's father thought.

The fence consisted of ancient roofing of the corrugated galvanized type, yet the roofing was so old that no galvanized coating showed; there was only rust. Tay climbed out of the autocar, and his father followed. A fierce-sounding dog was barking constantly somewhere nearby. Tay walked up and pushed a button next to the gate.

The gate was made of the same roofing material and was adorned at its apex with the figure of a miniature horse in full gallop. The figure reminded Tay of the mental picture he had formed of Beucephalus, Alexander the Great's renowned and lifelong mount.

A small doorway opened in the fence and a man—fat, unshaven, with the stub of a cigar protruding from purple lips—stepped out of the opening. The lips spoke around the cigar: "Whadya want?"

"We came to look at the horse," said Tay.

"Oh! You're the first. I got a lot of calls but nobody's come."

They entered the enclosure to a sight that Tay had never before seen. Wrecked autocars were stacked everywhere. Motor oil lay on puddles of water in sheens with all the colors of a sickened rainbow. Broken shards of glass littered the filthy ground. A dog of mixed breed, chained to a car bumper, strained, lunging against the chain and barking nonstop. When the dog hit the end of the constraint, his body would swing in a half-circle and his bark would become hoarse as the chain bit into his neck. The dog would then gain his footing and repeat the stunt.

"Shaduup, you mongrel!" the man screamed.

Tay's father gave him a look like *are you crazy?* The boy followed the man.

Passing row upon row of junked autocars, they finally came to an opening where there were none. A makeshift fence of wooden pallets formed an enclosure about ten meters square. The miserable horse stood in mud over the hocks. A hoard of flies harassed it without mercy, and there were thousands of bumps all over its skin, with open oozing spots in places. In those areas, the plentiful flies could be seen en masse.

My God, this poor creature! Tay's father thought.

Some dirty rags had been tied about the horse's rear left leg.

"Has he been injured?" Tay asked.

"Oh, that damned mongrel broke his chain yesterday and jumped in with this horse, see, and so the horse jumped over the fence with the dog chasing. Quite a circus, I'm telling you! The horse, he slid into one of the heaps and cut open his leg."

"Can I look at the injury?" Tay asked.

His father was astounded. Most of the animals they had seen, Tay barely glanced at; here he was about to inspect the injury of this most unfortunate creature. It was more than a mind could bear.

"Tay, I think we ought to be leaving!"

"No! Father, we will leave when I'm ready." The boy turned back to the owner. "Sir, what do you know about his breeding?"

"Breedin'? Nothin'. I know my daughter looked a long while before she found him, and I spent a hell of a lot more than I'm askin'. She said he was an appy, or something like that."

"An Appaloosa?" Tay asked, excitement in his voice.

"Yeah! Yeah! That's it! Then she went and got knocked up. She was keeping him at one of those fancy stables out in the country, but she lost interest in horses when she got interested in boys. Now I'm stuck with the beast, and I sure as hell ain't payin' no more boarding fees!"

Tay unwrapped the rags. The cut was not serious. Leading the horse around the enclosure, Tay saw there was no limp. He picked up one hoof and wiped the mud off with his shirttail. The contrasting vertical stripes of creamy white and charcoal stood out strikingly once the mud was clear.

Tay set the horse's leg back down and said, "I'll take him, mister. I'll pay you your asking price if you can deliver him now."

"Now?" the cigar-filled lips asked.

"Now!"

"Son, you got yourself a deal. Where do I have to take him?"

"Follow us. We have a farm about fifty kilometers from here."

"Okay. Say, why don't I just deliver him tomorrow? You can pay me now, and then I'll get started first thing in the morning, see. That would work better for me."

"Mister, I am going to lead this horse out of this junkyard and give him a bath while you hitch that horse trailer up. Then you follow us to the farm, and we'll pay when the animal is safely unloaded. If you have a problem with those terms, the deal is off!"

"No! No, you go on; there is a hose out front. I'll bring you some soap and some rags to wash and dry him with."

The disheveled man extended a hand, blackened by oil and grease. Tay took it firmly and gave it one quick shake before letting go.

As he led the horse towards the front gate, the owner asked his father, "That boy of yours, how old is he?"

"Six."

"You're kiddin'! I thought he was a midget or something. Drives a tough bargain, I'll tell you, and I've haggled with the best!"

Tay's father just shook his head, not really believing what had transpired. The man brought out a bucket with some hot, soapy water, and Tay began cleaning the animal. He was too short to scrub the horse's back, so his dad stepped in to help.

"Tay, I've got two questions: What on earth do you see in this horse? You're not just buying him because you feel sorry for him are you?"

"Dad, this horse looks pitiful, I know; but he has all the characteristics of ancient Appaloosa foundation stock, truly one of the greatest horse bloodlines in Earth's history. But more importantly, we connected. In his eyes, I see an honesty and intelligence I haven't seen in any of the others we've looked at. Trust me, he IS the one!"

The animal still appeared to be a miserable creature, even when clean, but the smile on Tay's face was priceless. The boy had finally found a horse that made him truly happy.

Tay named the horse Shadow because of his dark color. Whenever he was home from school, they were inseparable. Always, his mother was telling him to finish his homework before he could ride. Often as he walked home from school, he would find Shadow in the field, and so before going into the house, he would mount bareback and ride the forest trails encompassing the farm, out of his mother's sight.

As a boy, Tay loved—or thought he loved—that gelding even more than his parents. Most children took their folks for granted, and Tay, in his young adolescence, was no different.

The rain had been down pouring for days and finally let up. Sunlight shone through the clouds, steam wisped up from the saturated pastures. Tay was itching to take Shadow for a ride.

He took his .22 Caliber rifle out of the closet, knowing that grouse would be sunning themselves after the heavy rainfall. He walked to the barn and saddled his horse.

Soon, Tay was cantering Shadow across the field, the horse's hooves squish-squashing through the waterlogged grass. Reaching the tree line along the river, Tay removed the rifle from its leather sleeve and said, "Quiet walk, boy. Let's sneak up on them." He had trained Shadow to pick his hooves up high and to place them down ever so slowly so that the two of them would make hardly a sound.

Coming around a curve in the trail that paralleled the river, Tay spotted one of the birds high in a tree alongside the river. Taking aim, he whispered, "Steady boy." He fired.

The grouse was hit, yet it managed to jump from the limb, lock its wings, and glide across the river. It attempted to land on a tree limb but was mortally wounded and fell to the ground.

The river was running in a rampage with the water high on the banks, but Tay knew of a fallen tree he had used to cross many times before, so he rode down to it, intending to fetch the bird and take it home for dinner.

When Tay dismounted and stepped upon the log, Shadow became agitated, pawing the ground, snorting and nickering.

Tay said, "Don't worry, boy; I've crossed this old log a thousand times."

The water was white with speed from the massive rainfall of the past few days. Tay was about halfway across when Shadow went ballistic, screaming a shrill sound Tay had never before heard him make and rearing up on his hind legs.

"Settle! Settle!" he commanded the horse, unaware of the floating tree barreling downriver behind him.

The horse continued in a frantic attempt to warn the boy. Tay was perplexed; Shadow had seen him cross the log numerous times, he thought. What was wrong? At that moment, the hair on the back of his neck stood up, and he turned just in time to see the massive log, with root wad and limbs still attached, just seconds from impacting the log on which he stood.

A split second was all it took to size up the situation: if he stayed where he was, he would be hopelessly tangled in the mess of log and limb; the shore was too far; and there was no time to do anything else. Tay dove into the river, as far downstream and as fast as possible, thinking that he would simply swim to shore. Stroking downstream was easy, and he did this for a few moments to distance himself from the impending crash of timber. Hearing the impact above the river's roar, he turned and looked. The log he had been standing on was holding, but it was broken and bending, crackling under the tremendous pressure of water and floating wood behind. *I've got to get to the bank before it all comes down on top of me!* he thought.

Ferociously stroking for the farm-side shore, he was brutally dismayed to find he could make little or no progress; the raging current stole his strokes, and after fighting savagely for some headway, he was soon exhausted. His shoes had filled and his clothing, dragged by the current, rendered his efforts fruitless.

It was then that he heard thundering hooves. Shadow was a blur, jumping downed trees along the river's edge. He was coming, thought Tay; his horse was coming! At that moment, Shadow let out a shrill squeak before leaping from an overhanging bank. Tay saw Shadow soaring through the air, as if he were Pegasus, the flying horse. He landed in the water not more than a few meters upriver and then swam with a demon-possessed look in his eyes towards Tay, quickly closing the gap.

Tay grabbed hold of the saddle horn, and Shadow swam powerfully to shore. The horse gained footing on the bottom and, seconds later, leaped for dry land, nearly tearing the boy's arm from its socket. They were still hock and ankle deep in water when a thunderous crash engulfed their senses and tons of splintered logs and tree limbs swept by them.

They were both panting, and Tay thought his horse's breath never smelled so good! Shadow gave him a look as if silently reprimanding a child and made the odd, shrill squeak again before maternally nudging the boy up the bank with his nose.

By the time they reached the pasture, they were both shaking, not from the cold but from adrenalin and the realization of how close to them death had come. Tay stopped, and Shadow stopped with him.

"Thanks, big fella; you just saved my life. And where on Earth did you learn to squeak? I think that's your new nickname: Squeaks!"

The boy hugged Shadow around the neck, and the horse had never been happier.

One of Tay's responsibilities growing into young manhood was to take care of the farm. Some years before, his father and mother had divorced. Tay never remembered them arguing, but after they divorced his dad had quickly remarried a younger woman and began having children with the new wife. Tay rarely saw his father and was fine with the situation. When he did visit his dad's new home, it was uncomfortable with the young children and the unfamiliar new woman. He really didn't enjoy the visits. Besides, when he left for the weekend, he fell behind on his chores. So, things were just easier not visiting his dad on the weekends.

Tay had his horse, his schoolwork, and then his farm chores. His mom helped a bit, like by taking care of the milk cow, but when it came to haying the fields and planting their huge garden, he had full hands. Shadow didn't help; ever the playful prankster, the spunky horse loved to steal Tay's straw hats, among other things. Shadow would then run out into the field, letting out his unique short squeak, placing Tay on notice that the horse was in the middle of a practical joke. Shadow would then play keep-away with the hat, chewing and bobbing his big, dark head up and down. Tay would have to take a break from whatever chore he was attempting to accomplish so that he could go to the barn and fetch some grain, which Shadow would let him trade for the hat. Sometimes it was infuriating, but normally the big horse could soften Tay with a warm nudge or an embarrassed look, and the boy's mood would lighten into a laugh.

When Tay was busy with chores, Shadow never failed at finding a trick. Always he would find a distraction, often it was mischief that would force Tay into taking a break and paying attention to the big dark horse. Stealing silently up behind Tay, he would sometimes send him unexpectedly sprawling with a simple but powerful thrust of the head. He never hurt the boy, and Tay always felt that trick was an exclamation point to the horse's unspoken feeling of being ignored. One of his favorite tricks was to jump the garden fence, pull a single carrot, and stand inside the fence with it dangling from his lips, nodding his head up and down as if to say, "See what I got?" Tay swore that at these times he could see a smile in Shadow's coal-colored eyes. Tay would have to stop what he was doing and let the big troublemaker out by the gate. Shadow never ran in the garden, and never tore it up or did noticeable damage; he just stole that single carrot to get Tay's attention.

Tay figured he would fix that problem once and for all. He spent an entire weekend putting extensions on the fence and raised its height to nearly two meters. No sooner had he completed the grueling project, Shadow, in an apparently effortless jump, miraculously cleared the fence. Then he stood inside, looking back at Tay's exhausted countenance as if to say, "You see? That was unnecessary. We could have spent the weekend riding and having fun."

Tay gave up trying to keep the horse out of the garden. Instead, he concentrated on spending more time paying the pain-in-the-ass horse extra attention. Shadow seemed satisfied and became less trouble. So the horse had taught the boy a very valuable lesson.

Tay could never stay mad at Shadow. His extraordinary qualities more than made up for his pranks. One day, he and Shadow rode into the eastern hills, into hot, rocky country. They stopped to rest and have something to eat. Shadow was cropping grass growing on the banks of a little mountain stream, while Tay sat on the ground. The sun had become hot and Tay, daydreaming under the blue, blue sky above and listening to the whisper of the little creek in his ears, had completely forgotten that there were rattlesnakes in this area.

When he stood up after his rest, all of a sudden he heard the sound of several snakes warning him. A family of the poisonous reptiles confronted him; each of the three were coiled and ready to strike at his minutest movement. They had evidently come out of the ground seeking the sun's heat.

He remained anxiously frozen in place, not wanting to utter a sound for fear it would set them off. He was at his wit's end. Up here alone, a snake bite could mean death. He stood stock-still.

He heard the slightest footsteps and looked up to see that Shadow had silently come up behind the three snakes. Sizing the situation up in a nano, the horse reared up on his hindquarters and then came down quickly with one hoof on each of two snake's heads. The third was smashed in the same instant by a lightening quick stutter step of one front hoof—and the crisis was over.

Tay was overwhelmed. "I guess you really are worth all the trouble you cause me! Sometimes I was beginning to wonder." He hugged Shadow around the neck, just as he had the day his best friend had saved him from the rampaging river. He mounted up, and the two of them headed for home. Shadow let out his trademark squeak, and Tay patted him on the sides of his neck, saying, "Thanks, boy. I really needed you just then!"

FOURTEEN

When Tay turned ten, he decided to begin martial arts training. Upon informing his mother, she said he could not. When he asked her why, she responded by saying that it was not a method of conditioning she approved of, and she therefore forbid him to associate with the people at the club. She told him that violence was not the answer; love conquered all.

The next day at school, a group of teenage boys was picking on an unfortunate kid, calling him a geek and worse. The verbal insults soon became physical, and the boy's glasses were broken. Tay had seen enough. Marching up to the sorry group, he immediately spoke to the instigator and informed the bully that he had to stop harassing the poor kid.

Turning on Tay, the oaf said, "Are you looking for trouble? 'Cause if you don't mind your own business, I'll give you a belly full!"

Tay replied calmly that he was the victim's protector, and that if the violence didn't immediately stop he would be forced to intercede.

In classic Neanderthal logic, the bully responded by saying, "What you got to prove?"

"Only that your behavior is not socially acceptable, or lawful."

This brought the full wrath of the degenerate into Tay's face, and the fight began.

Punches were traded, blood flowed from both, and the big oaf grew exhausted. In the end, he gave up after a profuse pummeling. The younger boy, infused with adrenalin and determination, had won.

Tay found Shadow in the field. He rode to the river and cleaned himself up as best he could, hoping his mother wouldn't notice the damage. Upon entering the house later, she immediately confronted him.

"What happened to you?"

The interrogation began, and his explanations of the incident did nothing to calm her. She went on telling him that violence was not the answer and that she forbade him to fight or participate in any attempts to protect other unfortunate boys; it was not his responsibility, and so on.

He listened respectfully, without interrupting, and when she finished, he plainly told her his mind.

"I could not live with myself, to stand by and do nothing. If I am unable to stand up for what is right, to fight injustice when I see it, what kind of man will I become? Do you want me to grow into someone who turns a blind eye to the troubles of this world, who sticks my head in the sand and pretends bad things don't happen? Do you desire a son who runs from moral dilemmas because that is easier than making a choice, however painful, to uphold what is moral? Do you think I just did what was easy or fun for me? If so, you are mistaken; it was the most difficult choice I've ever made! I know there was honor in standing against the abuse of that boy. Nothing you say can take that from me."

She looked at him, sorrow in her heart. Her understanding eyes took in the boy she loved like no other, and she said, "When I was a child, your grandfather spoke similar words to me as a young girl when I beseeched him not to leave for war. I do not fully understand what drives a man to feel responsibility for these things. Wouldn't it be much easier to avoid the conflicts and live in peace?"

"Mother, dear mother, your view of the world and our obligations are over-simplified. We all have beliefs; I am not one to dictate yours. I would appreciate you understanding the dilemma I faced today. I believe the conflict tested my character, my morals, and my perception of right and wrong. I feel very good about what I did, even if it was mentally and physically painful. I hoped you would understand and approve of my actions."

"Oh! The thought never crossed my mind. I'm sorry; I have trouble accepting that you are now a fighter!"

"Mother, you are being overly emotional. I think we should discontinue this conversation before one of us says something regrettable."

His mother smiled and said, "Son, every time we debate a subject, I come away from the discussion with the intense feeling that you should pursue the field and science of diplomacy."

She stepped forward and embraced him. "I can only say that while I do not understand or approve, I am sincerely happy you are so sure of your path. Of course, you have always been gifted with that talent."

* * *

Tay felt fortunate to still possess all his teeth. He decided that if life necessitated fighting, he wanted an education that would allow him to be in complete control and not subject to the physical pounding he had just taken in the brawl. After re-living the fight of the previous day in his mind's eye, he was sure he needed instruction.

The next day after school, Tay went to the martial arts club he had been interested in joining. No classes were being held, and the rooms were empty except for the master.

"You are interested in studying here?" the old Chinese man asked.

"Yes, sir."

"You may call me Sifu. It looks as though you had a tough time yesterday."

"How do you know it happened yesterday?"

"The color of your injuries tells me. Did you lose the fight?"

"No, Sifu. I won, but not easily."

"Your adversary was older or larger?"

"Both."

"You may be a natural. Some people study here for years and will never be proficient martial artists; others absorb instruction like a sponge. Come, I will show you around. You must take three classes a week; no more, no less."

They walked through the rooms and arrived at a painting of a man dressed in the manner of the Chinese from ancient Earth. "Who is this person?" Tay asked.

"General Quan, a revered hero of my ancestors. He dedicated his life to truth and honor, and to protecting the weak. I keep his picture here to remember and to pay respect." The master bowed, looking up at the picture. Tay bowed as well.

"You wish to learn the art of fighting, or the more passive art of self-defense?"

"What is the difference, Sifu?"

"In one method, the opponent or attacker's inertia is used to thwart the offence. In another method, if you have made the decision and must fight, you are the arrow—the tiger attacking—and offence is your greatest advantage."

"I would choose the second method; it seems to fit into my philosophy better than the first."

"You are a philosopher?" Sifu smiled.

Tay blushed. "Well, no. I just meant, if I am forced into a situation where I must choose to fight, I desire to be on the offense and not have defense as my strategy."

"I believe there is, inside you, a philosopher waiting to be exposed," the old man said.

"I teach six days a week. You can practice Tuesday, Thursday, and Saturday; or Monday, Wednesday, and Friday. Classes begin at four thirty in the afternoon or six thirty in the evening. Which do you prefer?"

"The four thirty class will be good: Tuesday, Thursday, and Saturday."

"Okay. What is your name, young man?"

"TayGor."

"I had a young student with the same last name many years ago. You even look like him.... A relation, perhaps?"

"I don't know. What was his first name?"

"TyGor! I would never forget the name of the generation's most proficient in the art."

"My grandfather! I had no idea he studied here."

The old man looked the boy over more closely, a sparkle in his eyes. "I am happy you chose this school. There are many others. Why did you come here?"

"I did some research and felt the history of what you teach has good karma. Also, I believe in standing up for what is right and true, and in protecting the weak."

"Is that why you were fighting?"

"Yes."

"Another rule we must live by is no unnecessary fighting. Do you feel what you did yesterday was necessary?"

"Yes! It was absolutely necessary."

"I'm happy that you are sure. Indecision is an enemy. When a problem arises, it is important to act. Inaction creates a paralysis within the mind and body."

On the days of his lessons, after school, Tay would run instead of walk home. He would quickly finish his homework and then, not taking time to saddle Shadow, he would use a block of wood to mount and then gallop off towards town. Tay would hobble Shadow in an unfenced meadow close to the martial arts club and walk the rest of the way.

He did not want to ask permission to study under Sifu, for fear his mother would once again say no. Year after year, the ritual three lessons a week went on, and his mother never knew; or if she did, she never let on.

FIFTEEN

The morning after his grandfather's return and invitation to join him on *Independence* brought shafts of amber sunlight streaming through the bedroom window. Waking early and realizing he had been dreaming of childhood, Tay rose full of energy and took a quick shower. The house was quiet. Stealing to the door, he went out softly into a wonder of low-lying mist that draped the green-golden grass and trees. Sunlight broke above the forest along the river, and the chill of morning quickly disappeared.

Tay walked to the barn, intending to go with Shadow down to the river. Shadow was not in his stall, but he often went to drink first thing in the morning, so Tay followed the big horse's well-worn path down to the river.

When the trail broke out of the trees, he still could not see his old friend at the watering hole. Tay called out, and in response heard a weak whinny from up the bank.

Walking back uphill towards the sound, he found the beloved horse lying under a giant maple tree. The place was one of their favorites. Many a hot summer day had been spent here.

The river spun a wide arc, bending around the huge tree. Their favored swimming hole lay just beneath them.

Shadow made no attempt to rise, so the boy who still dwelt inside the young man sat down and leaned against the maple's trunk. Sunlight reflecting off the arc of water created what appeared to be thousands of shining crystals, shifting then trading places with one other.

Shadow turned his head slightly away from the river and took Tay in.

"I know, big fella. This is our best spot, isn't it?"

Shadow gave up a weak little puff of air, letting out a short squeak.

Tay moved and lay his head down next to Shadow's, saying, "Thanks for waiting on me, old friend. I could not have asked for a better companion.

"You saved me from the river that day, so long ago. I owe all that is before me to you. If there is any way possible, come to me in your next life, and I will know you again...I wish for you tall green grass; crystal-clear, cool water; and golden sunlight always on your back."

He laid a hand on the horse's head and said, "I love you, Squeaks."

With that, Shadow took in a deep pull of air, held it for a moment, and then let out a long, gentle sigh. He breathed no more.

Tay sat for a long while. When he finally got up and walked out into the open towards the house, the sun was high in the valley sky.

His grandfather came walking out to meet him. "I figured you and the horse were out for a stroll. Where is he?"

"He's down at the river, Grandpa."

Tay went into the barn and returned with a shovel. His eyes were red-rimmed.

Ty said only, "I'm sorry, son. Wouldn't it be easier to use the tractor?"

"I don't want it to be easy, Pa." Tay choked out the words.

TyGor went into the barn, grabbed another shovel, a digging bar, and an axe, and then followed his favorite person to the river.

SIXTEEN

A DISTANT consciousness, I Am That I Am, watched, interested in honor, reactions, spirituality, timing, diligence, morality, love, intelligence, and what technology can be applied to a crisis; but most of all watching key people who would be cast into the fray, waiting to see how absolute trauma could inspire positive qualities in each human's personality.

I Am That I Am also looked for the negative elements: greed, lust, selfishness, jealousy, hate, religious fanaticism, cruelty, and the desire to rule over others without benevolent regard.

The young man was much like his grandfather. The physical likeness showed clearly through the difference in age and through the thought processes within each mind—the young, questioning mind of youth, and the older seasoned and combat-hardened mind of an experienced leader.

I Am That I Am's ever-present curiosity observed love, honor, selflessness, loss, sorrow, excitement, wonder, appreciation of nature's ever-changing beauty, happiness, sadness, regret, and dedication to humanity's ethical, moral, and spiritual beliefs.

I Am That I Am, in profound circumspection, thought, *The human psyche is a bewildering plethora of emotion; so many feelings, mental pains, pleasures, and wonders— all possible within a few short minutes. It is well that we have mastered these tempestuous seas and sail smoothly over water without such crests, valleys, and mountainous surges.* Within the concert of combined thought that created I Am That I Am, a twinge of admiration was felt.

SEVENTEEN

Tay began dreaming of the foreign world and enchantress his first night aboard *Independence*. The schedule had been grueling. The crew, all three shifts working nonstop in concert, had taken twenty hours to check provisions and secure stows, preparing her for Deep Space.

When *Independence* finally broke Seven's orbit, heading towards Sector-I, Tay had slept less than six hours in the past thirty-four. First, it had been due to the excitement of being aboard the Fleet's most prestigious vessel: the heartfelt dream, once imagined, now being lived. Second, the loss of his dearest friend, Shadow, weighed heavy—an anchor that kept his excitement pulled down to minimum level. Sorrow for his loss had been consciously kept in check, lest he come off to the other crewmembers as morose.

Now, with the ship and its support vessels under way, a normal routine could be maintained, at least until they entered the zone defined as "Danger of War."

* * *

THE SEEDING SEVEN'S VISION

The dreams came most often when he, exhausted from studies and the rigors of his martial arts, fell into bed. He thought of the subconscious visions as dreams and not as nightmares, because while at times they were frightening, they never filled him with fear—only wonder.

The dreams haunted him in waking hours as well as in sleep. He dreamed of horses, magnificent horses, with fierce determination and spirit shining from their eyes; hot, steaming breath snorted into cold, dark evenings or sunlit winter air; pounding, flailing hooves; bucking, nipping, bodies catapulted by the herd's momentum and portraying a primeval culture's order and flight so clearly. The herd was always there; the setting was always the same: a world he had never visited physically and yet one that seemed completely familiar, as though he had lived there before.

The woman, the enchantress, was not always in the dream. Many times it was only the horses; the scent of their sweat; their language of nickers, whinnies, and snorts; their thundering hooves and clouds of dust when the stallion determined the herd should depart; and the longing that held Tay waiting, hoping to see their wildness return.

It had all started with a glimpse of the stallion. Tay had been on some kind of exploration, hiking, carrying a pack, spear, shield, and sword. This is how he knew every time that he was dreaming; swords and shields were only used in ancient forms of warfare, some fifty centuries ago on Earth, the planet of his civilization's origins. Back then, warfare had been conducted in a brutal and personal manner. Soldiers met face to face on a field and fought with weapons of the sort he carried in his dreams.

The dreams never included battles, only the horses—the horses, and *her*. In the first dream, he had come over the brow of a hill. Before him lay a lush valley cut through by a small river with myriads of glistening, sunlit crystals along its surface. It turned, bending and weaving along the lowest channels, flowing amongst the overhanging trees that embraced its meandering course.

The horses fed on grass that was bright green with the soil's richness and well-watered roots. He lay low on the earth, peeking over the edge of the shelf where he could hear the horses, concealed from sight, cropping the lush green anxiously, as though they were woodcutters storing away precious fiber that would hold their warmth over the brutal winter soon to come.

The lead-stallion was a magnificent beast, charcoal black with a cast of dark grey. In that instant, Tay knew the horse to be his. He connected to the beast and felt the pull of overwhelming deja vu flooding his senses. Examining the stallion closely, he saw that the big horse seemed to mirror Shadow's coloring, graceful movements, and intelligent eyes.

Sometimes in the dreams, she would come to him—the enchantress who haunted both his sleep and his wakeful hours. She would come in that instant between conscious thought, in the pauses between periods of speech and the involuntary yawn or stretch, her image so vivid, so familiar, and so heartfelt that Tay knew instinctively she would come to him in real life someday, not just in dreams.

For now, he was satisfied with seeing her in surreal glimpses through ethereal mists or with simply noticing her footprints in the sun-bleached sand alongside the blue-green sea. He would run down the beach, the sound of the surf roaring and his heart pounding, filling his ears with a melody unlike any other while he searched, anticipating the moment he would find her.

She could be gliding fluidly through a field of tall, waving, golden grass, her hair like strands of ebony and redwood, fluttering and whipping when the wind was high. She looked so familiar that his heart would stop beating for a stroke, as though she were, to him, his life's blood.

Always, she captured his heart by her first glance. How could he describe the presence she had in the dreams? She haunted him with those eyes; colors flew from them that Tay had never before imagined. They seemed cut from the thin curl of cresting ocean waves as the violet, amber light of setting sun shone through.

The slight swing of her hips as she moved fluidly towards him struck to his core, as though in times past he had felt those hips sway against him, touched her lips as she smiled, gazed closely into her hypnotizing eyes, felt the brush of her silken hair against his skin.

Most evenings he fell asleep hoping to see her, yet she seldom came. When she did, she spoke no words—just walked towards him, bewildering, mysterious, beautiful. Mostly the horses visited him in the dreams. He walked among them, feeling their defiance to his presence. Defiant or not, their curiosity and hunger forced them to come.

In many of the dreams, Tay would be cutting mature, golden-tasseled grass headed up with grain. He used an archaic hand held tool he believed was called a scythe, an implement he knew ancient cultures used to cut tall grass. The grass would then be stacked in conical shapes to dry in the sun and become hay for the sheep and other domestic animals in winter months.

One day, while Tay was busy scything the standing field of grass, the horses came. He didn't notice them at first. He was so absorbed in his work. The rhythm and sound of the sweeping, arcing scythe, and his labored breathing, masked the sounds of their movements. Apparently, he had homesteaded their desired winter-feeding grounds, the meadow that froze later in the winter than any others did. The surrounding ridges kept the biting North wind at bay. Tay was removing their forage and storing it in a barn built with his hands from trees hewn from the forest. The stallion was unhappy, seeing this intruder, this strange new creature, invading the sacred valley of his birth.

Walking silently, as if to outwit a mountain lion, the massive beast crept stealthily from behind, while the entire herd watched anxiously from a shelf overlooking the small valley.

The stallion approached Tay quietly and then, using all the strength of his neck, suddenly butted Tay with his nose, sending him sprawling forwards onto the ground. He let out an odd, shrill squeak and pawed the earth furiously.

Several times, the stallion reared over the prostrate Tay, flailing his front legs in the air. Then he spun slightly, dropped all his weight just a foot to the right of Tay's shoulder, squeaked again, and tore off in obvious frenzy, sending clumps of sod skyward.

All of it had happened so quickly. Tay stayed on the ground, heart pounding, listening to the thunder of hooves echoing in the distance.

Upon lying down each night, Tay hoped to dream of the foreign world, the horses, and her. When conscious desire threaded into subconscious experiences, and the dream came, Tay lived the beauty of the foreign world in his sleep.

EIGHTEEN

INDEPENDENCE had been heading into Deep Space for three and a half days. Tay, hungry, walked to the galley for something to eat. Sitting alone, absorbed in thought, he was approached by a young man who asked if he minded sharing a table.

"Not at all. You're most welcome," he answered.

The boyish man sat down and looked upon him as though he were familiar. "You don't recognize me, do you?" he asked.

Upon examination, there was something familiar but Tay couldn't place him.

"I knew you when we were both in the same school about eight years ago. You defended me when that brute assaulted me. Do you recall?"

"Of course! How are you? I've forgotten your name."

"I have been doing exceptionally well. Thanks for asking. I'm Alex. Alex Delanport."

"That's right! Well, I'm sorry I didn't remember," said Tay, perplexed at the unexpectedness of meeting a childhood acquaintance aboard *Independence*.

"I wouldn't have expected it of you. A long time has passed since fifth grade."

"Whatever happened to you, Alex? It wasn't long after that incident that I remember you no longer came to school."

"It's a long story, TayGor."

"Please, call me Tay."

"When those bullies used to beat on me daily, I was in constant fear. Not just walking to and from school, but all the time. I was living in a form of mental paralysis from the abuse. I couldn't sleep, my study habits disintegrated, and my grades went from perfect to atrocious.

"After you stood up to that group of Neanderthals on my behalf and they quit constantly assaulting me, my life returned to normal; actually, way above normal. I decided that if you thought enough of me to suffer a physical battering in a fight, to defend my rights, I must be extremely special. I threw myself into my studies, and within six months, I was selected for the Junior Prodigy Program's Creative Research department.

"I've always been a natural with computers and binary programming. My talent evolved during the next eight years to encompass a wide range of skills. I worked on things like advancing our ancient cloaking system to the new Full Stealth Cloak, mining strategic minerals from asteroids, and other things that were not possible ten years ago."

"Seriously? You've been involved in all those technological advances?"

"Intimately," said Alex, a look of satisfaction glowing on his youthful face.

"I've read of these emerging technologies and am astounded that we humans can do such things. You're telling me that your mind contributed to the accomplishments, and here we are, both on *Independence*, renewing old friendship."

"Many of the projects are still classified and can't be mentioned," Alex added, nodding and pushing his glasses up with a forefinger.

"I never thanked you. I want you to know that if you *hadn't* stepped in that day, I'm not sure where I would be right now. I do know I wouldn't be here on *Independence*, talking with you! So thanks; I'm in your debt."

"The incident was a test of character for me. I'm happy for us both, and with the way everything turned out," Tay answered modestly.

"Do you eat here often?" Alex asked.

"Quite a bit. Do you want to start having lunch together?"

"That would be great! Same time tomorrow?"

"Sure. Sounds great."

"I must ask, what are you doing here, Tay?"

"I'm special assistant to the admiral and liaison of language."

"No way! How did you manage that?"

"Long story, most of which can't be told."

"Where are we heading, and on what kind of mission? Some rumors say we're off to war, but no one really believes it possible."

"Alex, the only thing I can tell you is that I can't tell you anything. Admiral Gor will give us the information we need when we need it. He was a commander in the Twenty-Seven Years War and has an amazing record. If it weren't for him, we could very well be under Nesdian rule right now."

"Perish the thought!" Alex added.

"He's one of the few who saw the conflict from beginning to end, and he's the only officer on duty today with that experience. His active record, if you care to study it, is all archived, including details about his battles, strategies, victories—it's pretty interesting reading. Whatever happens, we're serving under the most experienced commander in the Fleet. I've studied his entire history; he's been an absolute inspiration to me. I privately consider myself to be one of the top authorities on his strategy and philosophy."

"What was it like growing up with him?"

"To be honest, Alex, I rarely saw him."

"It must be a wonderful feeling to be on board *Independence*, spending time working with him."

"This whole adventure is a dream come true for me," Tay admitted.

"That makes two of us then." Alex stood up, needing to return to his duties. "Hey, I'll see you tomorrow," he said.

After Tay got back to his desk, Admiral Gor came in and dropped off some papers. "How are you doing? We haven't had much time to talk lately, Tay."

"Great! Admiral, I met a young man at lunch today. I knew him from school about eight years ago. He's with the Creative Research unit, specializing in computer science. He was involved in developing the Full Stealth Cloak."

"Yes, I've met him. A brilliant young man. Delanport, isn't it?"

"Yes, sir. Alex Delanport."

Tay was surprised as always with the admiral's ability to recall crew names, from the lowest rank to the highest. His ability to remember names and specialties was nothing short of miraculous. Admiral Gor had previously explained to Tay his belief in showing a personal interest in every crewmember and its importance in melding the ship's personnel into a respect-filled and unified fighting force.

"Well, Admiral, my duties so far have not been too strenuous, and I'm ahead in my Academy studies. I was wondering if you would authorize the two of us to work on some special projects."

"I think the idea may have merit. What did you have in mind?"

"I have of course read on the basic concepts of stealth, yet I feel it necessary to have a full understanding of the system and how the new advances changed and revised it. You see, Admiral, if we are to have a strategic advantage in the coming conflict, we need to analyze the systems in place, compare them to what we believe the Nesdians possess, and look for potential weaknesses in each other's defense and offense."

"Tay, we are working on that as you speak. All resources within Seven Galaxies are dedicated to that end. I feel another intelligent young mind would be a beneficial addition to the group. If you wish to be involved in the process, I'll have your clearances drawn and ready this afternoon."

"Thank you, Admiral."

"Tay, you said there were two things that interested you. What is the other?"

"Space drive theory, Admiral."

"What are your thoughts?"

"Sir, it will take us over a month at our present velocity to reach Sector-I. In that time, the Nesdians could be attacking in sectors far and away. I know we have ships in the vicinity and are holding them in reserve, waiting on the rest of the Fleet. I have had flashes of inspiration, which could possibly be used to drastically increase our present velocity. Am I close to our present strategies, Admiral?"

"Yes. I have stationed the Fleet in sectors that are in immediate danger in defensive posture only. They are to maintain Full Stealth Cloak, observe the enemy, collect data, and report back. Some commanders are none too happy. They worry about other attacks. Even the Fifteen had some trouble accepting the strategy.

"However, if we rush in, we stand to risk losing many craft, so many in fact that the odds would definitely turn in the enemies' favor. Consider war a game of chess; strategy is everything. One must test one's opponent to understand his strengths and weaknesses. Fools rush in, while survivors are cautious. Sometimes judicious caution can be construed by critics as a weakness or even as cowardice, but I tell you this: in command, what the critics think or say is unimportant. Protecting your forces from senseless slaughter and prevailing in the final contests are the commander's responsibility and duty. All else pales under these obligations.

"If we move hastily, we may be doing exactly what the Nesdians want. Certainly, the brutal attacks on our settlements were meant to provoke an angry and rapid response. In haste and emotion, intelligent decisions are elusive. We must calm ourselves, gather data, and explore all possible actions, reactions, and potential technology the enemy may possess, as well as come to understand and respect the technology they have already brought to bear." The message base sounded and Gor took a moment to key in a response, then turned back to the conversation at hand.

"I also know the Nesdian mindset very well. They wait, anticipating our angry response. Each day that passes without us showing, their frustration grows. They have waited two hundred years, salivating for their moment to reconcile and avenge themselves. In the Nesdian mind, anything is justifiable if it promotes their realm's power and dominion. Their anxiousness could be the very downfall of their offence.

"We are at a distinct disadvantage; we do not know the enemy. It has been over two centuries since we last engaged them. We thought we had relegated them back to a time of primeval weapons and did not consider that they might acquire Deep Space craft and weapons capable of destroying entire civilizations. As unpopular as my strategy is, in it lies our only hope of understanding the enemy we face and prevailing in the future conflict, which is inevitable." Gor paused and took in the young man, his grandson with seasoned eyes.

"As my special liaison, I give you the task of monitoring the progress of the creative research team. I also pass to you the responsibility of studying all intelligence reports and compiling a brief yet detailed account of the information. My time is taken with many pressing responsibilities; you will help by sharing that load. The last few days, since we've been under way, I've given you a short respite. I know you were exhausted; however, that is over, and we must now throw ourselves, with frenzy, into the tasks at hand."

"Yes, Admiral!"

The admiral smiled. "It is good to have you aboard. I'll take care of the necessary clearances, and the documents will be in your hand this afternoon. Prepare to begin the additional responsibilities just enumerated, tomorrow morning."

"Yes, sir!"

"Good day, TayGor."

"Good day to you, sir!"

NINETEEN

ON board *Independence*, Tay and Alex were busy—Tay, learning all he could about stealth cloaking, and Alex, teaching him.

"You see, the old cloaking system mimics a piece of space," Alex said. "The simulation takes into account all factors of coloring, stars, planets, and space debris, including meteors and asteroids. The problem is that it is not a flawless generation. If an investigating ship has the sector mapped down to the nap, anomalies that do not correspond to the realities of the area in use can be found in the image.

"The vast distances a vessel covers in space drive make it nearly impossible to continually map, and the memory needed to catalog vast tracts of the universe would be enormous. A ship would need one massive computer system dedicated only to mapping, and this would need to feed to the cloak programs. In simplistic terms, the standard cloak is an imperfect camouflage-hologram of sorts."

"So," Tay said, "if we could pick the area in which we were to stand and fight the Nesdians, we could theoretically map it down to the nap. Then, when enemy ships under cloak came into the sector, we could see the anomalies in their camouflage and know their locations?"

"In theory, yes, but there are many more complications."

"Such as?" Tay asked.

"Suppose the Nesdians have good shielding capabilities. Their old ships were tough to crack two hundred years ago, so it would make sense that they would have equal or better protection now. Then it becomes a pounding battle: the side with the most ships, most prolonged firepower, and toughest shielding capabilities would have the advantage."

"Unless we can persuade them to drop shields!"

"And how are you going to do that? Say, 'Dear Mr. Nesdian commander, would you please drop your shields so I can blast you into a billion smoking particles?'" Alex laughed.

"I have some ideas," Tay said. "Maybe they'll work."

"Mind sharing them with me?"

"Not now. I have to work on them a bit. I think we have a good chance of picking the location of our stand," Tay said, obviously deep in thought. "If we can pull that off, it would give us several advantages. I will speak to the admiral and see if he has any ideas on the subject."

Tay was already in Admiral Gor's outer office when he arrived.

"Good morning, sir."

"Good morn to you."

"Can I have a few minutes with you, sir? I wanted to go over some ideas Alex and I are working on."

"Certainly. Come on in."

"Sir, if we could pick our ground so to speak and be waiting for the Nesdians when they enter Sector-I, it's possible we could accurately plot and map the area in detail. Alex believes it would be a great advantage. We could then be enabled to see miniscule flaws and inconsistencies in the Nesdian's cloaking, while at the same time enabling ours to be flawless."

"There is merit in your thinking, Tay; however, we don't know if we can actually get there before the Nesdians. We are waiting on data from the Stealth intel probes, which have been in the area for a few days. We should know the Nesdian's capabilities and speed shortly. I have instructed Intel to keep the drones in tracking mode, reporting regularly on the speed and plot of the enemy craft. There should be some sensitive data arriving in the afternoon. I'll let you two have a copy of the packet when we have it decrypted."

"That will be most helpful. Thank you. Sir, do we have any other Full Stealth intel drones that could do the mapping prior to our arrival? It might make more sense than waiting until we get into Sector-I."

"There are two in reserve. I haven't wished to risk placing them in play at this time."

"Are there any others that could be transferred into our care?"

"I'll see if it is possible," said TyGor.

"Sir, if we can free up two drones, the mapping would only take a couple of days, and the newest data could be logged into our systems before we arrive. If our ships were in strategic locations ready to spring the trap, with the new data in hand, the Nesdians would be at a distinct disadvantage."

"Tay, the variables in the plan consist of many things: fire power and the ability to sustain shielding and position, knowledge of the enemies' capabilities and their knowledge of ours. What we need is a good plan like the one you are working on, a fallback if the first plan fails, and a third option—barring retreat—if our fallback plan also fails. In the manner just described, we have made preparations for varying degrees of limited success without turning tail and running.

"You will learn that any competent commander plans for the worst, plans for the best, and hopefully plans for the middle. If all those bases are covered, a potential disaster can be impeded successfully. You are off to a great start. Continue to cover any possible contingency that could theoretically arise. For instance, what if the Nesdian's shields are impenetrable?"

"Sir, with all due respect, you ask a question straight from the textbook."

"I wish to know your answer, TayGor."

"I would answer that we hit them with everything we have when they drop shields."

"Why would the enemy drop shields?"

"Because they wish to attack our settlements in Sector-I. When they drop shields to fire or accelerate ground troops, we unleash and catch them by surprise, because we can see through their camouflage."

"Provided we can beat them to Sector-I, have the area accurately mapped within hours of our arrival, see the nuances and imperfections in their cloaks, catch them in that split second while the shields are down, and not have them prepared to fire on us as we drop armor, then yes, we may have a good chance."

"A good chance, sir? *Independence* is the most technologically advanced vessel known."

Ty nodded. "Ah yes, and what do you know of the Nesdian war ships?"

"Nothing at this time, sir."

"Correct! Why don't you figure out what kind of craft they are flying? It would be most helpful."

"Do you practice the art of sarcasm, sir?"

"No! I am utterly serious."

"But how would we go about it?" asked Tay.

"You and Alex are extremely bright young men. I have some ideas, but I don't want to serve them up with dinner; I expect you to find them yourself. Report to me in the morning, the hour of eight, here in my office. Come with Alex. I wish you to have a written proposal including all that we have just discussed."

"To be clear, sir, you said tomorrow morn at the hour of eight?"

"Correct, TayGor. That will be all."

The customary salute was forthcoming from the young man, accompanied by a look that was at the same time perplexed and determined. "Yes, sir!"

Tay went directly to Alex and laid out all the admiral had just requested.

"Are you sure he said tomorrow morn?"

"I am sure, Alex. I asked for clarification."

"The heat is on!" Alex said, grinning. "Let's get cookin!"

Tay smiled at his new friend and said, "Let's!"

The packet of intel collected by the Stealth drones was delivered to Alex's office at the hour of fourteen. The packet consisted of a micro-hard drive.

Alex opened it and said in mock amazement, "Oh my goodness! Seven trig! How are we to get through that by morning?"

"Let alone formulate and incorporate the data into our presentation?" Tay added, looking completely overwhelmed.

"Let me show you some magic." Alex plugged the packet in and stroked the keyboard deftly. The data was consumed by a soft hum. "While you were working on a series of responses to Admiral Gor's requests, I was programming them into my weed and feed system."

"What are you saying, Alex?"

"Years ago, I grew tired of reading tons of technical data to extricate a few pertinent facts. I built a system to sort the unnecessary intel and to add or feed the file with correlating data from other banks. In other words, weed and feed. What comes out the other end is a compressed and elucidated study of the documents and relevant information from other sources that do not overlap the information in the original data feed."

"Sounds simple."

"Hardly," he said, shaking his head. "I spent three years writing the software, and then it only made the file larger. I fine-tuned the program over another six months. You'll see the result in a few more minutes."

It appeared magical. Seven trig of data was sucked in by Alex's program and came out as less than a hundred gig of data, all pertinent to the present quandary. Contained in the information was unencrypted enemy vessel communications, ship's plots and speeds, personnel on board, estimated fire power, types of weaponry, sensor scan capabilities, and assessments and fingerprinting of the invisible ion trails each ship left in its wake.

Alex and Tay analyzed the data, and a picture began to form of the enemy's signature. The young men stayed up all night, brainstorming and hoping to formulate a plan that, when reviewed by the hardened commander, would be found exemplary.

Tay was exhausted, yet a single thought kept coming back to him. It had been playing over and over in his mind for almost twenty-four hours. Finally, the foundation pieces were coming together, yet one was missing. He spit out his previous conclusions, leaving the new flash out for emphasis: "We know their strength," he said. "We can map the sector they wish to attack with the help of Stealth recon drones, and we can be waiting—our entire battle group under flawless Full Stealth Cloak. They must drop shields, no matter whether they intend to shell the planet or accelerate a physical army of destruction groundside, as they did when attacking Sector-G. We will know them, the signature of each ship, their weaponry and shielding capabilities. When they drop shields, in that nano, we destroy them!"

"Tay, it makes perfect sense to me. It's so simple. Let's take it to the admiral and see what he thinks."

"Sounds good, but I need some sleep. How many hours till we reach Sector-I?"

"Sixteen," said Alex.

"Perfect. Lay the plan, get some rest, and slaughter those Nesdian bastards before they have a chance to know that our wave is crashing down upon their sick little plan. Let's go to the admiral as soon as you can write this up. We will need ships in reserve, and we'll need to identify moons or planets to hide behind. He will not trust our technology to be infallible; he will want several fallbacks, none of which will contain retreat."

"Tay, I have studied Admiral Gor's battle strategy, tactics, and personal philosophy in depth over many years, too. He has been my mentor as well as yours. I knew you were cut from the same bolt of cloth when you protected me so many years ago. I will write the plan, and it will meet his every criteria. Rest now. I will be finished in a few hours. I'll wake you with some strong coffee, and you can present the strategy to him."

"You mean it? You don't need me to help write it?"

"No. You will review it after a couple strong cups of java and some food, and then we will march up there and show the old war horse what technological wizardry can achieve!"

"Sounds good, Alex. Wake me when you're ready with the report."

Tay paused at the door. "Oh! I'm so tired, I almost forgot. Can we use a few sacrificial drones as decoys, and place an onboard program into their computer systems that would mimic a full-dress ship of war? We could cloak them imperfectly to attract Nesdian fire, and create a holographic image to take over once their light shielding fails."

"What would the holographic image represent?" Alex asked, intrigued.

"The appearance of three full-dress ships of war with flickering shielding—tasty bait for our trap."

Alex's eyes flickered brightly with understanding. "I love it! Suck them in with weakened shielding and imperfect cloaking, and all the while our actual ships will be waiting in ambush under immaculate Full Stealth Cloak. We can hit them while they are distracted by their own blood lust. The technical side should be a breeze. If you can convince the admiral to sacrifice the drones, consider it done!"

TWENTY

Tay happily lay down on the lab sofa and was shortly asleep, dreaming of wild horses. The tall, lush grass of a pristine valley danced in warm summer breezes. A river threaded its meandering course over ancient stones, timeworn and smooth. Golden and silver light reflected along the water's many bends. Sunshine falling from an azure sky warmed Tay's body and spirit. He was up on a ridge, lying along the edge of a limestone shelf, watching the herd.

The scents of tall golden grass, ripening grains, abundantly diverse wildflowers, and conifer forests filled his nostrils. He breathed in the fragrance quietly, not wanting to give away his presence to the stallion.

Some of the female horses were overburdened with foals about to be born. One, a large bay mare he had seen before, was in labor. The conformation of this horse struck home as familiar; he was drawn into watching her struggle. The stallion would occasionally canter towards the birthing mother, as if to check on her progress, and then snort as if satisfied and walk a short distance away with his head held high, chest puffed, tail straight in the air: a proud father.

The mother in labor squealed once, and Tay saw the head of the small baby emerging. He had never seen such a wonderful sight and lay looking over the shelf edge into the valley.

The foal at last lay on the ground, the mother licking it dry. Before long, the tiny horse began its first trembling attempt to stand. Tay was mesmerized. The little horse gained its front feet and made several attempts to rise onto its back haunches, yet each time it faltered, not making it all the way.

The bay mare nudged the little animal on the fourth attempt, and the foal stood, shaking. Before long, it took a few trembling steps, and then within minutes the newborn was trotting, gangly, wobbling, snorting at the new experience of air and scenting all the wonderful fragrances, all completely foreign. The mare got to her feet and kept close watch of the tiny creature.

The stallion took point positions for a few moments on the outskirts of the herd, bringing the group into a formation that was closer knit and easier to patrol. He made his way around his group, nudging some, nipping more independent others, urging all to fall in line with his plan.

Tay understood the stallion's strategy at once. Fresh blood from the birthing mare would no doubt bring predators, and the stallion was forming the herd into a defensive posture. He watched, undetected, and was surprised at how much the lead horse reminded him of a commander preparing for battle.

Two other mares were ready to foal, and they moved to the center of the herd. The stallion circled, making sure no holes were left in the herd's perimeter. He seemed confident, as if he had done this a thousand times. Tay felt that the animal could not be more than six or eight years of age and found himself wondering if the stallion's skill came from some primeval instinct or was learned as an adolescent, watching the herd's previous leader.

The foal rolled in the cropped grass. Tay noticed that the newest addition to the herd was a colt and that his beautiful dark coat was not black but gunmetal grey. No other mark of color could be seen except on the hooves; they were striped vertically with bands of creamy white and charcoal grey, which matched the color of the coat.

Tay took the liberty of naming the young horse Eclipse. He felt a particular fondness for the beautiful colt. Marveling, lost in thought, he remembered his old friend on his home planet. He wondered whether there was a link. He questioned the values instilled in him by his mother's religion, and then cast all learned formalities away. He saw in this newborn colt a horse that had saved his life as a young boy.

Tay reeled; the possibilities staggered his mind. Upon Shadow's faltering last breath, he had asked his beloved friend and companion to find him, if at all possible. Could it be? he thought. Tay was caught in the moment, enveloped in something so personal, so dear, so desperately wanted and longed for that a stabbing pain struck his heart. He did not notice the stallion depart the herd and approach silently from behind his prone position.

A loud snort startled Tay, and he rolled to the side just as the stallion's front hooves came crashing to earth where he had just been lying. Adrenalin rushed through him, allowing him to rise quickly, to gain his footing in a nano. The stallion, a crazed look in his eyes, was obviously challenging this strange intruder.

The man and horse sized each other up for a moment.

"Whoa boy! I mean no harm. Whoa, it's okay."

The monstrous beast made a short forward kick with his right front leg, as if to say, "Move! Be on your way and don't return." Tay grasped the meaning well. Not wanting to turn from facing the furious beast, he began to back away from the shelf edge, distancing himself from the herd. With each backwards step, the stallion made a forward one, keeping the space between them the same. It was a harrying experience for the man and a new one for the horse.

Tay found himself wondering how long the frightening beast would follow him. Every once in a while, the big animal would cock his ears to the side, turn his head for a nano, listen to his group, and then turn back towards Tay, as if to say, "You are distracting me. What is your purpose?"

Tay kept talking in a reassuring voice, yet nothing seemed to calm the wild horse.

The two of them had covered over a hundred meters, backwards for the man, forwards for the horse. Tay was sweating profusely. *This is the longest I've ever walked backwards!* he thought.

The stallion quickly sprang forward and butted him in the chest with his head, knocking him to the ground, and then rearing up in the same motion, flailing front hooves over Tay's grounded form. Once back on all fours, the horse stood and watched the fallen man again. They remained still for a moment, in a standoff.

Tay thought, *He does not want to harm me, for surely he could have easily just killed me.* But when he tried to rise, the brute took the dominant position of attack. Tay paused and then tried again, but every time he tried getting to his feet, the stallion became hostile. Clearly, the animal was asserting territorial control. He wondered how long this posturing would continue between himself and the clearly dominant horse.

Suddenly, he heard a melody drifting upon the swirling wind, soothing, like a lullaby. Tay had never before heard such a sound. It resembled singing birds and cascading water flowing together.

The huge male horse turned, looking upward in the direction of the voice, and then stood frozen, as if in a hypnotic trance.

A wisp of low-lying cloud moved across the face of a shelf-like cliff above the horse and man. Ghostlike, the figure of a woman could be seen through the vapor. She continued to sing. The cloud moved on, and Tay recognized the woman from previous dreams. Her eyes were whirlpools that tugged at his lonely soul. Her hair streamed in the breeze, filtering sunlight through long, fluttering strands of ebony and redwood. Tay felt it was all intensely familiar.

The woman motioned with her hands while singing. He knew she meant for him to depart, yet he could not. Tay desired to stay. He longed to hear her voice casting a melody across this valley.

Her eyes met his, and she motioned with them for him to leave, yet he was frozen in place, as was the fearsome beast of a horse before him.

***

"Tay, wake up!" Alex was shaking him. "Wake up, TayGor! The report is finished. We must go and meet the admiral."

Tay awoke, realizing he had drifted. The stallion, the foal, and the enchantress—all a dream. He wished he could return and sleep. He longed, as all do when disrupted from wonderful unconscious experiences, to see a little more; to pick up the threads and draw them back, closer to us, so that we might continue adventures held within our mind's eye, and the flight of our souls.

TWENTY-ONE

The battle group under Admiral Gor consisted of seven of the Fleet's best ships and commanders. They made their way at top velocity to Sector-I, where the Nesdian's were expected to attack the settlements scattered on two planets there. Intel drones had sent enough encrypted data to indicate that Nesdia's navy was approaching Sector-I, but the Seven's group would arrive, good-fortune holding, a few hours before the enemy.

Everyone was in a keyed up state of excited anticipation. The decoy drones had been programmed to project holographic images of ships of war dressed for battle once they had taken enough fire to weaken their shields, thanks to Alex's creative thought processes while programming Tay's ingenious ideas. The Nesdians, if sucked into the trap, would believe the Seven's shields and cloaking were faltering, and they would respond by dropping their own shields and firing full barrages instead of intermittent ones between shielding.

If all went according to plan, the battle would last less than a few minutes.

The admiral had read through Alex and Tay's written report of the proposed plan carefully. When he finished, he said simply, "It should work, yet we will not destroy every one of their vessels. We will leave one unscathed, as though we never even saw it."

"But why let any go? Shouldn't we destroy them all while we have them?" Tay asked, confused.

"Perhaps, but I'm thinking we let one little weasel flee home so we can place two Full Stealth intel drones on its tail. That way, we can find the exact location of the Nesdian's burrow. At this time, we have large areas to scour if we want to locate the new Nesdian planets. Leaving one enemy ship undead may save us a great amount of trouble.

"We'll follow behind and surprise-attack the armament fortifications, depots, and manufacturing facilities, as well as the energy production facilities and all government buildings. With that accomplished, all that will be left is mopping up and sanitizing."

"Admiral, it sounds like it should work. Do you have anything more to say on the basic plan of ambush?" Alex asked.

"You two have done excellent work drawing this up. The strategy seems like one I would implement, except that the flawless Cloak and sacrificial drones mimicking full-sized ships of war is a technical bit of wizardry I would not have thought possible."

"That was Alex's bit of mastery, Admiral," said Tay.

"I am working feverishly on one other surprise for the Nesdians, sir," Alex said.

"And what might that be, young man?"

"Sir, I have had a programming inspiration. I am calling the program Fluid Motion and Triple Overlap. It's working well in simulator, yet there are a few small problems still to be ironed out."

"Tell me more," the admiral said, showing genuine interest.

"Explained in short form, the program controls all three of the ships' weapon systems, synchronizing them under one gun station instead of the normal three. This would allow us to use the best triggermen among the crew. The program also allows dead-on tracking accuracy, even if we are traveling at considerable velocity. It compensates for guns doubling on a target, an age old problem with multiple gunners shooting at numerous targets."

"Alex, when you are ready, we will set some target drones on evasive maneuvers and see how well it works. We will also hold a few of our ships in reserve with normal tactical-weapons firing systems in case something goes wrong, if I decide to implement your new system."

"Yes, sir," answered Alex.

"You both look like you need rest," Gor said. "Go and get some. We have plenty of time between here and Sector-I. There is no need for you to be driving yourselves to exhaustion. Is that clear?"

"Yes, sir!" Alex and Tay responded in unison, pleased by the order.

"That will be all," said Gor.

TWENTY-TWO

Seven's warships coasted into Sector-I, all under Alex's pre-mapped and flawless Full Stealth Cloak system. The mapping data had been installed in the ship's dedicated hard drive a few hours prior to their scheduled arrival, after being received as encrypted transmission from the reconnaissance drones.

From the information sent by the drones, Admiral Gor had learned that the Nesdians would be arriving in a few short hours. Orders were sent out to all of Seven's ships to obey the complete silence directive. In other words, no talking and no tools clanking; communication by sign language only: as if they were ancient submarines being stalked by listening surface ships. All computer audio-talk was silenced and placed on video screen so that it could be read and not heard.

Then, they waited.

Gor placed ships strategically behind moons and planets that would shield them from incoming hostile warships. The plan was to rise above cover when the Nesdian ships began firing upon the decoy drones. All waited, hoping the plan could be executed as designed.

Some of the crew were caught tapping a foot, others a finger. Admiral Gor ordered anyone not capable of controlling involuntary noisemaking to be sedated and placed in soundproof cells where their intermittent snoring could not be heard. Anyone with an itchy throat or involuntary cough was placed in soundproof isolation as well. Not a foot or finger tap remained. All nervous twitches had been removed.

The ships were absolutely silent, stalking, lurking predators waiting for their prey to show themselves. Looks passed between crew, but they were upbeat; surely the admiral had been here before; surely he would pull them through.

Death in Deep Space is not pretty. It could come from a direct hit and be instantaneous—you might have no chance to speak to loved ones in your last few minutes of life. It could come from vacuum suction if the hull was breached. A body torn from the ship's protective envelope streams precious fluids from every pore and orifice. It could come from an enemy weapon's radiation days after battle. All of those aboard Seven's warships had learned of the risks in Academy, and they thought of them now. Imminent engagement was upon them. Nine Nesdian ships of war carrying that brutal and unmerciful race were streaking towards their positions at Deep Space velocity.

Some prayed. Some drafted the last letter, just in case. Many similar to the admiral listened to their inner voice and their moral courage, believing decency would prevail.

The video screen blinked, and the computer spoke its silent message: the enemy was here. Most aboard took slow, silent, deep breaths.

It had been over two hundred years since Gor had felt the rush of adrenalin as strongly as he did now. He was keyed into a state of intense concentration, feeling completely in control of the moment.

Nine Nesdian ships under inferior cloak came, unknowingly, into the snare and ambush. The decoy drones emanated a trace that would be visual to onboard scanners, something of a ripple, like heat waves rising off a scorching desert floor. To the naked and well-trained eye, it was barely perceptible: a disruption ever so subtle in the black of space yet enough to give away their presence.

The Nesdian warships were drawn in like a man dying of thirst is drawn to water. They rushed in, thirsting for the kill, nine against an outnumbered three. They were bold and careless, not spreading out intelligently for a wider field of fire. They believed, in that moment of hyper-emotion, of spoken prophesies to be fulfilled.

Xeries thought of his crown and of the imminent victory. Zuzahna watched, trembling, from the Machiavellian designs she had wrought upon the unsuspecting Xeries and the outnumbered ships of Seven's battle group. Salivating after her crown, under which she would rule all of Nesdia's worlds, old and new, she reveled in the secret control she exacted over Xeries.

One Nesdian ship held back from the others, settling just level with a distant planet's moon. Obviously the command vessel, Admiral Gor thought.

The Nesdian warships began firing, dropping shield for a nano while intermittent bursts pounded the three outclassed vessels. The vessels under fire were unable to heave fire back towards the Nesdian ships because they were under near continuous bombardment.

The Nesdian's timing is good, thought the admiral, *better than in the Twenty-Seven Years War.* They had at least learned to inundate a ship with alternate firing to ensure the attacked vessels had very few windows of opportunity to drop shield and return the heat, something they had obviously learned from their humiliating defeat two centuries before.

Shortly, the light shielding held by the sacrificial drones began to weaken, diverting power automatically from Stealth Cloak to strengthened shielding, and a flickering holographic image of three full-dress battleships could be seen.

The Nesdians fell for the mirage instantly. Scenting what appeared to be Seven Galaxies blood, and a sure and imminent victory, they dropped shielding and began firing full barrages, unhampered by shielding. Each Nesdian commander was hungry for the accolades that would fall upon the leaders responsible for the destruction of one or more Seven Galaxies war craft.

Their inherent competitiveness and over-bloated Nesdian ego will once again contribute to their demise, TyGor thought.

The sacrificial drones, posing with the assistance of Alex's holographic imagery, were suffering the continuous and merciless heat of blistering Nesdian firepower; their shielding would fail shortly.

While the Nesdians were preoccupied with an apparent victory shortly to be won, the computer screens aboard all Seven's ships not held in reserve flashed: FIRE AT WILL!

Deep Space was lit brightly by Seven's ships of war, all firing upon the unsuspecting Nesdians who possessed not a shred of shielding at that moment.

The Nesdians had cast caution to the wind. Battle lust, desire to seek revenge, and fanatic belief in false prophesy had driven them blind. In their frenzy, they had made a devastating and ultimate mistake, leaving the entire mass of their attacking force exposed without a shred of protection.

A scene, miraculous and awe-inspiring, played out before eyes that had only in dream-sleep imagined such a spectacle. A display of tactical wizardry that would live in each crew member's memory, undimmed by age, until their dying day, unfolded before them.

All had read of Admiral Gor's strategies and past victories, yet to be here, at this moment, with the man, spoke volumes within each pounding heart. Brilliant platinum trails appeared, threads that sent Seven's gift of death to the enemy ships.

Admiral Gor knew from his vast experience that the battle was won, even before the first Nesdian ship exploded into a color-filled starburst of streaking debris and twisting, trailing embers. Gor counted quickly, silently: one, two, three, four, five, six, seven, eight, in the course of three seconds.

The firefight was over nearly before it began: the swiftest victory in Gor's long and decorated career. The admiral thought of Tay first, and then of Alex and the brilliantly decisive technology and innovative ideas they had brought to bear. Gor thought also of all members of the ship's crew—not one had been injured or lost. He gave silent, heartfelt thanks.

The screen flashed words: "Enemy war craft fleeing!" Gor gave a silent signal, which set the Full Stealth tracking drones on the running enemy's tail. All aboard breathed a long, heavy sigh of relief. Each and every person in the battle group under Gor gave silent benedictions in a multitude of faiths. Thankfulness filled each mind for their revered leader, his fearless entry into the fray, and his unwavering military prowess.

TWENTY-THREE

THE Seven's ships waited a few hours, scouring Sector-I and making sure no more Nesdian ships were lurking. Settlements were scanned and shown to be safe—none had suffered from any previous attacks. The debris from the destroyed Nesdian warships was captured for analysis to determine more about their culture's capabilities. All these things accomplished, Gor gave orders for the group to set course, following the tracking drone's signal. The battle group followed at a distance that would allow verbal communication between vessels yet be safe from the ears of the fleeing Nesdian ship.

When things settled and everyone's excitement diminished a bit, the admiral called for Alex and Tay.

The young officers entered the admiral's office to find the old man smiling. "The fight we have just won is the beginning," he began. "Your ideas and technological improvements are responsible, in no small way, for our success. I am happy to have such enterprising young men on board. I am sure that when the Fifteen receive my report, commendations will be forthcoming. Now, if you young men have nothing further on your agendas, you are free to go."

All aboard were reconciled to the blatant fact that within a few short weeks, they would be entering Nesdian space and would need to deal with all their defensive and offensive positions, which were at this time unknown.

Most had confidence in Admiral Gor, yet within some, the fever of doubt nagged and grew. Were they doing the right thing? Should they continue? Was their fate sealed? Trepidation crept into the minds of a minority of the crew, yet even a minority with negative thoughts can have a larger adverse effect. Like a cancer, it grows, infecting others who had not thought negatively before. The thoughts of those who doubted the admiral's path or who were, more importantly, uncertain about their chosen vocation, began to affect the ship's morale.

Admiral Gor was the first to notice the furtive glances or whispers that stopped as he came near; this brought the unfortunate subject to his attention. He called upon Tay and Alex, requesting their presence in his private office to discuss the concerns held in his mind.

"Tay and Alex," he began, "we have aboard *Independence* a small group of disaffected crew members who question our mission's intent. Our goal is clear: we are to destroy Nesdia and all planets that are diversions from treaties and not ones assigned to the Nesdians after the Twenty-Seven Years War ended and Nesdia willingly capitulated. We have no other option available to our mission. Our direction is preordained; any that question the imperative must be removed from our vessels before we enter Nesdian Space!"

"Sir, we will carry out your directive to the letter, if you will only tell us how to identify the offending crew members."

"Any and all persons aboard our seven vessels within this battle group who express any form of doubt or trepidation shall be removed to one warship. That ship will then reverse direction and set course home for Seven Galaxies Seven. We will not have these disaffected crew members aboard, influencing the remaining crew with their negative speak and thought!"

"Admiral, how do you suggest we determine the afflicted ones?"

"I have already compiled a list of all crew members aboard the vessels in our battle group."

"How did you compile the list, sir?"

"A simple voice program that selects for certain words. I used it in the Twenty-Seven Years War because we were against the wall, and I did not need a minority of wishy-washy crew members seeding doubt and anxiety amongst the majority of the crew."

"Very well, sir!"

"Consider the problem taken care of," said Alex.

"Thank you, Alex. Thank you, Tay." Gor picked up some papers and said, "These things are not to be taken lightly. We must all be of like mind and purpose to prevail."

TWENTY-FOUR

"At last, dear Zuzahna, we are home! Perhaps the people are ready with my crown. The incompetence of those bumblers in High Command have cost nearly half our Navy. I mean to tell them so! If I had had full, unfettered authority to act against the Seven Galaxies Fleet, I would have used the entire Navy, half in the attack and the other half waiting as we were, in ambush. When the Galaxies Fleet opened fire, we would have easily destroyed them."

"You are right, Xeries. They should not have hamstrung you so. You must make clear to them the mistake," Zuzahna said.

"It is a tedious and temperamental business, bringing the fault to bear onto those who deserve it. Many powerful men on the council will want to push the blame off onto a scapegoat."

"Surely not you, my lord?" Zuzahna in one sentence baited him and planted the seed of doubt.

Xeries puffed up. "I am the great-grandson of Xeries Eight. I possess the golden eyes. I am the rightful leader. It is time the council recognizes and consents, and time I ascend to the throne!"

Toying with his ego, speaking demurely, she said only, "Yes, my lord. You were born to rule, but I understand your cousin Xrisen is very powerful and holds favor within the council. He also has the golden eyes."

"Enough! Enough!" Xeries was livid. "Do not mention Xrisen again. He is the bastard son of my grandfather's brother. He doesn't even carry the great name Xeries!"

Smiling, Zuzahna said simply, "There are many more things to a man than a name, my lord."

Xeries eyes turned black. "Your disrespect is a never-ending frustration to me!"

"Perhaps your frustration stems from the fact that I have not allowed you into my bed for over two weeks?" said Zuzahna, taunting him.

"A sore subject indeed. Why do you bring it up?"

"I would consider allowing you the pleasure if you kneel before me and beg. You hesitate, Xeries. Bend to my will. Kneel before me. Call me your master and beg for the privilege of my bed!" Zuzahna knew her power. She had first stirred his adrenalin. He was literally shaking, his eyes black with rage.

She exposed a leg, and he faltered. She opened her tunic, and he became clay in her hands. "Kneel, I said!"

Xeries, commander of the Nesdian Navy, collapsed to his knees.

"Now beg!"

"Please, I must have you."

"You have forgotten to address me properly." She turned as if to leave.

"My Queen!"

"What?" Zuzahna asked, knowing full well what was on Xeries' mind.

"Master!"

"Very good. You now have my ear. What is it you desire, dear Xeries?"

"I need to lie with you!"

"Tell me why your need is so great."

"You are everything to me! I would gladly die for you. You are more beautiful than any woman alive!" Xeries was trembling, hoping he had said everything correctly. He quickly added, "No woman has ever pleased me as you do."

"I am irreplaceable, am I not?"

"Yes, my Queen!"

"Very good. Your submission brings you my favor. Come!"

Xeries stood and followed Zuzahna.

Xeries believed that upon returning to Nesdia Six, his wisdom would be sorely needed in High Council; yet after stepping off the land craft, he was ushered rather briskly to a hearing, presided upon by the Military Tribunal.

The charges were read aloud. "Xeries Ten, you are hereby charged with dereliction of duty, cowardice, and acting without proper authority. Also, you are being held personally responsible for destroying half of Nesdia's magnificent new Navy. How do you plead?"

"I do not understand. I demand the ear of the High Council. There are necessary explanations that, when heard, will be understood. None of what you have said is true!"

"The council has made clear to us they will not be bothered with this matter. It will be decided here, in Hall, today."

"I demand legal representation at least! This is preposterous! I am the grandson of Xeries Eight. I shall be the rightful ruler of all our present worlds and those to come! You dare deny me council of my choice?"

"Council is only available to *traitors* if High Command consents. In the present case, your request has been denied."

"Traitors?! This is outrageous!" Xeries exclaimed.

"Outrageous or not, this is your trial. We are here to determine the outcome of a very serious matter. Our decision will determine whether you live or die at the whim of the ruling class. Xeries Ten, you are charged with being personally responsible for the destruction of nearly half of the Nesdian Navy's Ships of War. This alone is the biggest debacle in our culture's history. Do you think you are still qualified to rule the entirety of our worlds?"

"Yes!"

"You must bring yourself back to reality. You stand at trial today. Your very life is at stake. Forget what you think you are entitled to and simply answer the questions."

"Yes, my lord!"

"Good. Your respect for this court is duly noted in the record. Question number one: Why did you fail to communicate with High Command for nearly three weeks?"

"I received orders!"

"What kind of orders?"

"Orders from the High Command itself, instructing me to return with the surviving ship back to Nesdia Six at maximum speed and to black all communication for the duration of the return trip, no matter what orders were later received."

"Interesting. Very interesting. You successfully attacked three settlements of the Seven Galaxies, laid the trap as planned, then aborted that carefully planned ambush and led your battle group without orders into Sector-I, to their slaughter. Why?"

He could not say it was because Zuzahna had persuaded him; that would mean a sure and torturous death. "The Seven Galaxies Fleet commanded by fear-filled women did not come! I went on search and destroy orders, well within my right as commander. I was attempting to provoke them into showing themselves, as it is written in the *Book of Prophesy*."

"Does not the *Book of Prophesy* say that the future king would be victorious in that conflict?"

"Yes!"

"Then do you, Xeries, still feel that you deserve to be king?"

"Yes! There will be other chances, other battles! Other opportunities to prove I am worthy to rule!"

The Tribunal members glanced furtively between themselves; hooded eyes hid any emotion. Shortly, Xeries could see each of them writing. The written notes were then passed to the one questioning. He looked at all the papers and then stared solemnly at Xeries.

"Xeries Ten, you have been found guilty on all counts. You will be removed from the Hall and taken to the Arena, where the people will decide your fate."

Xeries knew better than to say more. He walked with the escort and was taken to the prisoner's entrance of the Arena. He noticed the people were all dressed in the manner of the citizens of ancient Rome. Jeweled goblets passed between many of the affluent in Nesdian society.

After being cast into the prisoner's box, he searched the faces in the seats above for Zuzahna's. He knew she would be here for him. Perhaps Zuzahna could use her persuasive powers to negotiate his release. Finally, finding her beautiful face in the royal box, he caught her eye and motioned to her, beseeching her with his desperate movements to use her talents of persuasion.

Zuzahna looked him square in the eyes for a moment or two and then turned her striking face away and towards his cousin Xrisen.

Yes! Xeries thought. Xrisen was powerful within the council. Xrisen could perhaps talk sense to the leaders and circumvent the proceedings.

After a time, Zuzahna looked back to him, smiling coyly, and then looked to the ground, shaking her head from side to side in a classic gesture of rebuff.

Xeries couldn't believe his eyes. She! He had taken her from the gutter, adorned her with treasures, wealth, and status, and now she would not even look upon him! Xeries wrung his hands with disbelief.

There was still a chance, he thought. A chance the people would want the pit. If he was afforded the pit instead of immediate execution, there was a chance he could prevail in the contest and redeem himself in the eyes of the people. The Nesdian people valued and respected strength above all else. If the people would allow him to fight, he could win, even though the odds were incredibly stacked against one who was about to be executed.

The announcer stood, and the horns sounded, silencing the audience. "Xeries Ten, you have been convicted of crimes against the people and lands of Nesdia. Your crimes include exceeding your authority, cowardice"—boos and hisses erupted from the crowd—"weakness, failure to follow orders, dereliction of duty, and most importantly, you are personally responsible for the destruction of eight Nesdian ships of war. Nearly half our Navy! Your punishment will be decided by your peers!"

The announcer then called out options. "Beheading!"

Some cheered and screamed, but surely this was not the crowd's desire.

"Hanging?"

The spectators were slightly more vocal, yet it was clear to Xeries that they wanted a contest. His heart raced. Adrenalin flowed. There was still a chance!

Xeries looked up to Zuzahna and saw her eyes wide with excitement. He would show her once and for all what he was made of, he thought.

Xeries screamed above the crowd's roar. "I am Xeries Ten!"

The people calmed themselves, letting Xeries be heard by all.

"I am the only grandson of the Great Xeries Eight! I possess the golden eyes, foretold in the *Book of Prophesy*, and I am your rightful king!"

The crowd stood and roared, a sound that made the ground tremble. Surely this was his destiny, Xeries thought.

"Show us, great Xeries. Slay the three beasts, and we may believe you!"

It was Xrisen who spoke, but in his look, Xeries could see only pity—not belief.

A contingent of guards took him to the edge of the pit and then picked him up bodily and threw him into it. Xeries tucked himself into a ball, rolled, and jumped to his feet.

The crowd roared and stomped, calling, "Xeries! Xeries! Xeries!"

Turning to meet his fate, Xeries saw a scarred door made of ancient riveted steel. Breathing deeply, he waited.

Behind the steel door, three life-prisoners waited, huge beasts, blindfolded and strapped to the wall by chains. A man carrying a leather handbag approached them and drew a small wooden box from his bag. He opened the box, drew out a syringe, and injected the first prisoner deftly in the neck. He put the syringe back in the box, drew out another, and repeated the process with the next prisoner, and the next. Afterwards, he put the box back into the bag and then hastily departed.

Soon, the huge beasts began to tremble and stomp the ground, their hearts racing involuntarily. They thrashed at their bindings, muscles rippling and bulging. Their eyes rolled behind the blindfolds.

The man with the leather bag walked into a room behind the prisoner's chamber and said, "The drug has taken full effect. Release them now!"

The steel pins that held the chains in place were pulled, and the beasts surged towards the steel door.

"Open it!"

A lever was released, and bright sunlight shone into the dark hole that had held the man-beasts captive.

THE SEEDING SEVEN'S VISION

The steel door opened, exposing a dark chamber. Xeries braced himself for the evil that would soon be seen. Out of the darkness came three devils. They were Nesdians, from the most brutal and bloodthirsty clan, huge man-beasts, prisoners for life, unless they could kill Xeries and earn their freedom.

Xeries leaped at them before their eyes adjusted to the bright light, slashing in a frenzy with his short claws. Moving with the speed and grace of a dancer, he harried them mercilessly. Xeries was confident in his great advantage: being much smaller and more agile.

The eyes of the beasts adjusted, taking in the damage already inflicted. The three charged, each a shoulder's width apart: a wall of death. Xeries crouched, waiting for the onslaught. Before they were within striking distance, he dove low to the ground between two of the attackers, slicing at their legs as he went by and then rolling again in a summersault, jumping back to his feet.

The people screamed, "Xeries! Xeries! Xeries!"

The beasts looked one another over and then back at the small man who was embarrassing them. Xeries was unscathed, but his opponents were bleeding from many wounds, mostly superficial, but some looking more serious. Xeries saw the eyes of the beasts turn from brown to black. He could smell the scent of adrenalin exuding from their pores. *Now,* he thought, *it gets serious. My only hope is for the Nesdian death-strike. There is no way I can overpower these monsters, and I cannot keep up this pace for much longer.*

The three charged again in unison, this time closer together, lower to the ground—an impenetrable net meant to ensnare him. Xeries spun backwards and sideways, and then made two spinning leaps as they rushed him, swinging a backhanded death-strike. He hit home. At the same instant, the sharpened two-inch claws of his victim ripped through his right hamstring. The brute fell in a heap, and Xeries fought, staggering under the impact and burning pain, to keep his feet.

The two remaining prisoners took in his injury. They began to pant and drool, sensing a kill was near. Xeries, limping, moved in a backwards circle so as not to be trapped in a corner. They kept coming. Gone was his speed and agility. All that remained was his intellect and the death-strike.

The crowd began to scream, "Cowards! Attack him! Are you afraid of one so small?! Yellow curs!" This was the ultimate Nesdian insult.

The two charged again. Xeries spun once more, throwing the death-strike in forward momentum this time. His hand was deflected slightly by the attacker's wrist and missed its intended mark, slicing open an eyeball instead. The injured beast charged again, wild with frenzy, using the classic Nesdian spiral flail. His hands and arms were a blur of sharpened claw and fur.

In the royal box, Zuzahna watched. The roar of the crowd was nothing compared with the beating of her heart. It pounded in her ears. Each blow that inflicted damage to Xeries made her lips quiver. She ran her tongue rapidly across her lips and swallowed her saliva to keep from drooling.

Most of the spectators were salivating heavily, drool running in streams from their chins as they screamed with crazed excitement. Xeries, her despised Xeries, she thought. Each injury he sustained excited her more. Zuzahna writhed in anticipation.

Xeries was bleeding profusely from the severed artery in his right leg. Zuzahna, breath short from the excitement, began to pant. Her body overheated as she watched the pack-like action.

The berserk attacker with one eye misjudged Xeries' feint as he sidestepped. Xeries administered the death-strike successfully for the second time. However, on his way to the ground, his victim managed to slash Xeries' right arm deeply.

Xeries staggered away, attempting to gain time and space from the remaining beast.

Xeries' enemy studied him. Xeries was becoming paler, his arms heavier, and his legs more difficult to control. Numbness began to set in, and he thought to himself, *No! I am the rightful king!*

The crowd, screaming, pressed for action. A whip from above struck the beast, spurring him to attack. The beast leaped upon the weakened Xeries and took him to the ground. The attacker sat astride Xeries' prone form, took each of his blood-starved arms, and pushed them laterally away from Xeries' body while lowering his bared teeth closer and closer to Xeries' throat. "You have been a worthy opponent! I will eat your heart and honor you in death!"

Xeries searched the crowd for Zuzahna. His glance caught her, wide-eyed in wonder. She was staring down upon the scene, saliva running down her classic chin. Even though weakened by Zuzahna's magnetic beauty, Xeries struck a slashing blow to the attacker's face with his serrated canine teeth. The wound was deep and cut through the beast's cheeks and lips entirely. The infuriated attacker savagely head-butted Xeries into unconsciousness, and then tore out his throat.

The contest now over, most of the audience roared in unanimous approval. Others within the royal box were unhappy at Xeries' failure to survive. With his death, their position on the High Council was weakened drastically.

Xrisen beamed, puffing himself and embracing his supporters.

Brevlan, the senior military strategist from High Command, missed nothing. Disgust rose like bile.

The victor, who had been released from bondage, was flocked upon by admiring Nesdian women. The huge man took two women, one under each arm, and two more jumped onto his back. He carried the four admirers off to the champion's bedchamber.

Xeries' cousin, the golden-eyed Xrisen, mopped saliva from his face with a cloth before moving towards Zuzahna.

Zuzahna sat, breathless, heart pounding drums in her ears. She had known such events took place but had never been invited to attend one. Only the elite of Nesdian society were usually allowed in the Arena for such spectacles. She hoped she could curry enough favor to become a regular attendee at future events.

She let herself absorb the memory of Xeries' last glance. Even facing imminent death, he had longed to look upon her beauty. She had controlled him to the very last moment. Zuzahna was exhilarated.

She didn't notice Xrisen standing next to her until he spoke. "Dear Zuzahna, you are even lovelier than the last time good fortune allowed me to lay eyes upon you. The excitement does your color well!"

"Xrisen! I am so happy that we meet once more. It is a pleasure, as always."

Wiping the remaining saliva from her chin with the fine dark hair on the back of her hand, she stood.

Xrisen took her hand, kissing it and sucking her sweet saliva from the silken hair. It was a primeval courting ritual. "Ancient Customs deem that we take food after one of these competitions," he said. "Will you be gracious enough to join me?"

"It would be my absolute pleasure! I am famished in the extreme!"

She took Xrisen in with her dark, golden-flecked eyes and then, taking his arm, she walked with him towards the rooftop skyport's lift.

Few others were taking the air tube up to the roof. *The death of Xeries has just raised my social standing,* Zuzahna thought. *Here is a man who sits as regent to the High Command. No king has been chosen for Nesdia's new and powerful realm, but Xrisen has become the leading contender since the demise of Xeries and his claim to the throne. The* Book of Prophesy *speaks of a powerful king who possesses the golden eyes and who will lead Nesdia to its rightful place, dominating a vast empire within the known universe and defeating and annihilating the Seven Galaxies civilization.*

Zuzahna's ambitious personality, combined with curiosity, made her wonder what deviously underhanded part Xrisen had played in the casting of Xeries into the pit. She smiled and thought of Xeries' last look again. Yes, even in death, he had been under her spell!

The man she stood with now had the ear and respect of the entire Nesdian High Command. Xrisen was older than Xeries and much better smelling. She was not repulsed by him at all. In fact, there was an attraction she could not deny.

Zuzahna could feel saliva building in her mouth once again as she considered her hunger for power and the opportunities this man might present at her feet. *I shall work the same magic on Xrisen as I used to capture Xeries,* she thought, *and soon he will bend willingly to my every wish.*

Zuzahna smiled provocatively at her newest conquest and said, "I am so enchanted by you, Xrisen. Do tell me all about your dreams and desires."

"I would be delighted to talk at length with you, Zuzahna. Will you come to my apartments after we devour our food, so that we can talk as long as you wish?"

"That would be my absolute dream come true, to spend a long, cozy, intimate evening alone with you, Xrisen."

As Xrisen handed her into the skycar, she faked a stumble. As he caught her, she brushed her breasts against his chest.

"How clumsy of me. And you, so strong and agile! What amazing reflexes, to catch me so quickly!"

Xrisen inflated from the obvious flattery. "I am your willing servant, Zuzahna!" Xrisen said, with a flourish and small bow.

"How kind." Stepping into the skycar, she thought, *Little do you know how true that will soon be, dear Xrisen!*

Xrisen was secretly gloating over his devious victory. The despised and pompous cousin Xeries was no more. *To the victor go the spoils,* he thought. Looking Zuzahna over in the skycar, Xrisen was abundantly pleased with his newest prize.

TWENTY-FIVE

Reports from the stealth-tracking drones were received every hour. Six Seven Galaxies ships of war followed behind Xeries' fleeing vessel. The Nesdian commander's breakship speed was equal to *Independence* without magvelenhan drive, so *Independence* and five other warships followed at a distance that Alex believed would be undetectable—one leading point, two protecting flank, one at port, and the other starboard.

Not far into the cat-and-mouse game, *Independence* intel teams picked up life and industry readings on several planets that were not part of Nesdia's three treaty worlds. Upon the close of the Twenty-Seven Years War, Nesdia's remaining survivors had been sequestered on remote planets easily capable of supporting simple farm life. From incoming data, it was evident that Nesdia had somehow expanded its territory completely outside of the confines of the treaty's designated zone.

The additional worlds possessed rich mineral deposits as well as plentiful ferrous and non-ferrous ore deposits, all easily crafted into a war machine. It seemed to Admiral Gor that history was repeating itself. He let out a sigh of frustration at the news. It had been made clear by Leandra that he was to show no mercy to the brutal marauding clans of Nesdia.

A sense of gloom settled upon him. The responsibility of protecting his people took precedence over the lives of the innocents on all of Nesdia's six known planets. There was no choice but to attack and destroy all Deep Space craft, armament factories, energy-producing facilities, and communication systems. The plan would leave Nesdia's culture with billions dead.

Admiral Gor thought how easy life might have been if he had chosen to become a simple farmer like his father. The need for service had chosen him instead. *The choices we make!* he thought, as he prepared himself mentally for the inevitable.

Alex and Tay finished preparations on the new weapons-tracking system. Alex had designed the software so that a continuous barrage could be kept firing while the Seven's ships moved at speed. The program also allowed for three separate weapons systems to be deployed at the same time, something previously dreamed of but never perfected. By collating the tracking systems of the ships' weaponry into one fluid program, an overlap became three layers, all controlled by a single gun crew. Instead of three sets of gun crews, one for each weapon type, it became one crew for all types. Alex had named the program Fluid Motion and Triple Overlap.

After finishing simulator tests on the program to descramble any glitches, they were ready for a demonstration. Tay went to visit the admiral and found him in a brooding mood.

"Sir, we have completed the new calibration of synced weapons systems and are ready for a test. Will you come to the bridge?"

"Of course, Tay. I'll be ready in just a few minutes. Will you wait here and walk with me?"

"I would be honored, sir."

"Tay, I know of late I have not been myself. I apologize for seeming to be somewhere else. It is only that our mission weighs heavily on my conscience."

"What bothers you, sir?"

"No man should have to play God with billions of lives. I have accepted the responsibility and will carry it through, but my morals are bruised by the decisions before me. Would that I could trade with another, change hats and be done with this mess without ever having to live it."

"Sir, with all due respect, the Nesdians attacked *our* settlements, killed innocent men, and carried away their families to a certain and atrocious death. Nesdia is at fault here; not Seven."

"What you say is true, TayGor; however, knowing such does not lighten my load." He sighed. "Meeting ships and men of war on the open field is a challenge that, in past years, I relished. Even today I find honor fighting to uphold decency and the safety of our worlds. But, when it comes to the destruction of entire planets and the civilians residing on them, my old heart is heavy with the burden."

"Grandfather, I would offer to relieve you of that burden, with your permission. I shall lead the raids on Nesdia's worlds. You win this final battle, and I will relieve you of the horror of destroying our next targets, Nesdia's weapon-producing planets."

Gor thought for a moment. "It would be good tactical experience," he said finally. "Do you feel up to the task, knowing our orders and what must be done?"

"Absolutely, Admiral!"

"Then so it shall be," said the admiral, looking more tired than Tay had ever seen him.

"I will command the battle of Nesdia's defensive force of warships. We will be attacking Nesdia's worlds a mere three hours later. Then this old man will claim fatigue, and you will be in command for the duration of the necessary onslaught."

"Yes, sir!"

The admiral added, "I will be available for consultation, but I do not need or want pictures of Nesdia's planets burning in the pages of my memory. I will be in my quarters at that time. If you have need of me, just call. Now, shall we depart to the bridge?"

"Yes, sir."

When they arrived, they found everyone in a state of excitement. Alex approached them.

"Good afternoon, sir. Are you ready for the demonstration?"

Tay noticed a distinct change in the admiral upon leaving his quarters. Gone was the tired look. The commanding presence Gor was renowned for had returned to inspire all.

"Yes, Lieutenant. Proceed."

An unmanned sacrificial drone was released, flying in an erratic pattern that simulated evasive flight. *Independence* arced at speed, and Tay could see the drone on screen, a small speck in the distance, cutting spirals and dodging behind moons and meteors when cover allowed. *Independence* followed, like a hound on the scent of the fox.

Alex manned the trigger controlling one of the gun ports. When the drone had disappeared behind cover of an asteroids trail, Gor shouted, "Fire!"

Alex squeezed, and a short burst of three separate weapons fired in unison. The small craft emerged from the asteroid dust just as the barrage met its hull. A bright light flashed, and all that remained was a vapor stream marking the nonexistent craft's trail.

Gor thought for a moment. "Will it work that way every time, Lieutenant?"

"It should, sir. I have simulated over sixty-two thousand possible variations with a degree of accuracy reaching ninety-eight point nine percent, sir."

"I am satisfied. Very impressive. However, I want seven drones in flight, all at the same time. Do you think one ship can take that many targets at one time?"

"Sir, the drones have no shielding. If you are testing only accuracy, I would answer affirmatively, but in a battlefield real-time situation, we would be hard pressed to make do with one ship against seven enemy warships."

"Understood; we are only testing reaction time and accuracy. We will be going into the fight with three craft, for heat. Three more under Full Stealth Cloak will stand hidden in reserve, with orders to fire only out of necessity if one or more of the heat ships is damaged or suffers weakened shielding."

"Very good, sir!"

"It is my intent to keep the Nesdians in the dark as to our actual strength until the Nesdian worlds are under full Fleet fire. Run the test again, Lieutenant. Seven targets, all exercising evasive maneuvers."

"Yes, sir."

Alex released the seven drones and waited for the command to fire. Admiral Gor waited again until three of the seven targets were out of sight behind visual obstructions before giving the order. Seven short bursts were loosed and seven targets were destroyed, all in a matter of a few seconds.

"Very good, Lieutenant. Your work will be commended."

Gor turned to address the crew. "Any and all who have witnessed this display or have been involved in the developmental phase are placed under order of secrecy. This strategic advantage will not be talked about on-ship or off, except when implementing the system in battle or by its design team needing to discuss potential improvements or problems. Understood?"

The entire bridge saluted crisply, saying, "Yes, sir!" in unison.

"Helmsman, make speed for Sector-I. We are ready for the hunt. All six of the group in full readiness, formed and dressed for battle."

"Sir!"

Seven's ships, under Admiral Gor's command, had been following at a safe distance behind the fleeing Nesdian command ship for two weeks. Full Stealth intel drones had arrived undetected at Nesdia Three, Four, and Five just two days earlier. The mapping was complete and had been relayed to the admiral's group. Alex had seen to the necessary in-feed, enabling the new weapons-control system to be fully operational. Nine enemy warships had been plotted, and their patrol loops mapped.

A more startling discovery was that in orbit around the three Nesdian armament planets were seventy-two war ships, almost complete. The news was staggering. It appeared that in a few short weeks, most of the ships would be ready enough to set into Deep Space and could be finished while on active duty. All were heavily armed vessels dressed for combat.

When Admiral Gor heard the news, he lowered his head, looked at his feet, and said humbly, "They have sealed their fate."

Ominous words spoken by the man who held Nesdia's fate in his hands.

The Nesdian warships on patrol, guarding the three armament planets Nesdia Four, Five, and Six, did not seem to be deviating from a predetermined pattern: enemy ships were making oval paths, which overlapped at the end of each loop. There were three loops forming a triangle, with each oval being one side of the pyramid's shape. The flight plan was three-dimensional and covered all three inhabited planets in the Sector with the security detail.

There was an obvious flaw in the Nesdian's patrol patterns. Tay and Alex spotted it immediately: at certain preordained times, all the Nesdian ships would be grouped within firing distance of strategic ambush points that afforded an abundance of cover.

THE SEEDING SEVEN'S VISION

Alex and Tay had chosen the locations of potential battles with care, giving the Fleet ample planets, asteroids, and space debris behind which to take cover. Running the proposed battle plan through simulator tests hundreds of times, Tay and Alex were both astounded. The results always came up the same, no matter what variables were thrown into the mix: the complete and utter destruction of all Nesdian vessels without a single casualty among the Seven's Fleet.

"Let's take it to the admiral," Tay said in excitement.

"Wait. Let's think of some more variables, run it a few more times, and then go."

They did as Alex wanted and the results remained the same.

"We haven't even deployed the Full Stealth reserve ships, and we waste the Nesdian's while being outnumbered, counting only our active vessels, three to one!" Alex said, in obvious amazement.

Tay was ecstatic. "The admiral has been uneasy about entering enemy territory without a full understanding of their true strength or capabilities. The simulator tests we have just spent the last twelve hours running should relax him a bit, don't you think?"

"I feel more relaxed. It's hard to say how the news will affect the admiral's mindset," answered Alex.

The results of the simulator battles made Alex's job a piece of cake. They chose three different locations for Seven's ambush. All had been run repeatedly on the simulator, and neither Alex nor Tay had a preference as to which would be more advantageous. The admiral would decide after all. They needed only to present the information so that he could make an educated choice.

Assembling a simulated map and battle plan that would place the Nesdians at the most severe disadvantage, restricting their field of fire while catching the enemy ships in a blistering crossfire, was the result of all three proposed scenarios.

Upon examining the plan, Gor smiled that mischievous grin, which was so rarely seen.

"Young men, I wish I could have had you as my strategy assistants in the Twenty-Seven Years War; we may have wrapped it in ten! Good work! I will study the three scenarios on the simulator for a few hours and give you my decision as to which of the options I feel will be the best choice.

"One more thing. Once we have effectively annihilated the Nesdian Navy, our orders are to completely destroy all life on the armament planets. The intel drones have reported irrefutable signs of deep burrows. Immense piles of tailings from tunneling projects are evident on the intel vids. We have no way of knowing how many miles the tunnels run towards the planets' cores, and I do not care! I will not send any ground forces. I want a plan that will exterminate all life on these three planets, above ground and below, under the oceans or under the mountains. All life must go, without completely destroying the mass of the planets themselves. It is my wish that someday in the distant future, a peaceful race of people may inhabit these worlds and prosper without thoughts of war and conquest. Is all I have said clear?"

"Yes, sir!" said both Alex and Tay in unison.

Tay and Alex left the admiral's office in a very positive frame of mind. "He liked the work we presented, no?" asked Alex.

"Yes, he seemed very pleased. Well, let's tackle the next problem: killing everything on and inside the planets, without completely disintegrating the worlds themselves."

"What do you think, Alex? Textbook strategy teaches that the only process for extermination of burrows, which could be miles deep, is to inundate them with fire until the planet becomes so hot, it crumbles into itself and comes apart, but the admiral is asking for another solution."

"Yes, Tay, and your old friend has some ideas. Would you like to hear them?"

Tay looked at the small young man who had become his best friend. Smiling and thinking of everything Alex had pulled off, against all odds, Tay said simply, "Yes, my friend, what did you have in mind?"

Alex was like a chipmunk gathering nuts for a cold winter. He quickstepped from one terminal to another punching commands, one after another, until all vid screens on the show wall were combined into one display.

"Watch this carefully," he said.

The wall displayed a planet with two moons. The moons miraculously split almost evenly in half, and the two pieces of each began spinning elliptically away from one another. Two of the halves, one from each moon, came closer and closer until they collided with an incredible impact, each half ricocheting off the other. The impact propelled each piece closer to the world's surface. Tay watched as the halves of each moon spiraled downward like an ill-thrown football. Awestruck at the show, it took little intelligence for one to know they would shortly affect the planet's surface.

One of the halves stuck an ocean and created a huge depression in the water, which shot upward in the shape of an upturned wine glass and then fell back to the surface, sending two huge waves of incredible height speeding in expanding twin circles, racing for shore.

The second half-moon struck dry forestland. The land imploded, as if a rock had been thrown through a plate glass window. Moments later, brilliant red-white cracks erupted, fracturing the planet's surface in a multitude of directions. Magma poured forth from the opening cracks. The world's crust folded in, and lava closed over the submerged portions. Immense clouds of steam rose from the ocean water running towards the low inland areas, which were sinking. Shortly, the entire planet was engulfed in steam clouds and obscured from view.

"What the hell was that?" Tay asked Alex.

"The simulation you just witnessed is actually possible in the real world."

"How?" was all Tay could muster.

"We split the moons with strategic timing, ricocheting them off one another so they crash into the planet's surface. If the plan is successful, and if the simulator's version threads out in the world of reality, well…you just saw the result."

"What odds do you give it? And do we possess the technology? How in the hell do you split a moon?"

"The same way an asteroid is split, only a moon is more brittle because most moons were formed from the same planet they orbit. Hence, if a planet has oceans, the moons will be inundated with veins of frozen water. If struck strategically, they easily shatter, unlike solid rock."

"And if a planet has only one moon?"

The process takes one more step. Explosive thrusters ignited on the surface of the halves, once split, would have the same basic effect." Alex pushed his glasses back on the bridge of his nose, and said, "So what do you think, Tay? Will this fit the admiral's request?"

Tay nodded in quiet amazement.

TWENTY-SIX

XRISEN woke to the sound of the com-call beeping urgently. Rubbing his forehead, groggy, he looked at Zuzahna, who remained sleeping. As Xrisen rose to take the call, his head throbbed. What a night it had been! She was the most astonishing female he had ever met. Xrisen had coveted her from the first moment he had seen her draped on the former Xeries' arm some two years ago.

Fancy footwork and shadowed payoffs had brought the council and the tribunal onto his side. It had been no small task to convince those loyal to Xeries' great-grandfather, Xeries Eight, to leave ancient alliances behind and sentence the bungling commander to death. Some still felt it an unwise decision, yet the people had approved. The frenzy of the ruling class at the Arena had sealed the unfortunate Xeries' fate.

Zuzahna seemed more beautiful in the early morning light than he remembered her the evening before. The soft rush of her breath in sleep made Xrisen long to stay, to watch her in slumber, to sup his prize, the trophy he had won. All these thoughts rushed through Xrisen's sleep-filled, hazy mind as he walked to the call-com.

"What is it? This had better be good, waking me at this hour!"

"Xrisen, this is High Command. We are assembled and require your presence immediately."

"Yes, well, I will have my morning meal and be there within the hour."

"No, Xrisen; you must come now. Do not eat, and waste no time. Show yourself within fifteen minutes, or we will be forced to make decisions without your ever-helpful input."

"What is this in regards to?" Xrisen asked.

"Red Level! Fifteen minutes—no more!" The com buzzed off.

What in God's creation could possibly be so important? he thought. Xrisen followed the command, rushed in dressing, and kissed Zuzahna on the cheek. She never stirred. Briskly, he left his apartments.

Entering the strategic planning hall, Xrisen noticed that most of the council members were as bleary-eyed as he was.

"Xrisen is present! The meeting will come to order!"

The chair instructed Brevlan, director of military strategy, to summarize a brief report. The man's hands shook uncontrollably. Clearing his throat, he began reading in a faltering voice.

"Early this morning, at approximately the third hour and twenty-seventh minute, a massive attack caught nine of our warships by complete surprise. All were destroyed. Loss of life on all vessels, total."

Gasps and murmurs arose. An anxious buzz enveloped the great hall.

"Silence!" the chair shouted, demanding order. "Continue, Brevlan."

"It appears the attack was promulgated by the notorious admiral of Seven's Fleet and three warships under his command. Two of our vessels located in another patrol sector escaped without damage. It seems three of the Seven's ships came in under some form of Stealth that our intel sensors were not able to detect until the enemy began firing. Shields held through the first few minutes of continuous fire, yet the intensity and coordination of enemy weaponry along with the accuracy and timing did not allow our ships opportunity to return fire."

"How is this possible?" Xrisen asked, his voice shaking with disbelief.

"Do you speak of the destruction, my lord, or the inability of our commanders to return fire?"

"How is it that we were not able to return fire? Our shields have always given us even odds against the Seven's."

"It appears, and I must say information is sketchy, that the concerted firepower of the Seven's warships engaging our own was staged to allow no interval for us to drop shield and return fire."

"How can this be? Never before have we seen an enemy continuously barrage ships that outnumber them more than three to one!"

"My lord, the only explanation must be some form of advanced assault programming that allows the enemy to not only continuously fire while moving at speed but also to see when our weapons are bearing on their targets and are ready to engage. Each time our commanders thought they had a break in the onslaught and were training weapons on the moving targets, their ships were inundated with incoming hostile weaponry of several descriptions."

Silence ensued in the great hall while the disastrous news was assimilated by the council.

"I must add," said Brevlan, "that while we were blindsided, the enemy seemed to have a tactical blueprint of our positions, number of ships, and possible evasive maneuvers. It was as though the Seven's admiral could read the minds of our commanders."

"Brevlan!" Xrisen began a tirade. "Are we to assume that textbook maneuvers and ancient strategy along with the finest technology available to ourselves is no match for Seven's Fleet?"

"With all due respect, my lord, this is the second major defeat we have experienced within a very short period of time. It does not bode well for our few remaining warships, which were built, as you well know, *exclusively* by your companies! The last battle lost was casually blamed on Xeries' incompetence—by you.

"As regent, your intelligence and experience might have directed us to investigate more deeply the happenings that were responsible for Xeries' failure. A full inquiry into the lost battle should have been made posthaste. Instead, you were personally gloating over Xeries' humiliation and subsequent death. Rather than execute Xeries so rapidly, it may have benefited our military to have *his* personal account of the battle. From past experience is gained new and better understandings of the nature of the enemy's strategy and the holes in their defense. In your rush to dispose of your only competitor for the throne, you may have allowed personal vendettas and desires to cloud your normally clear thinking."

"How dare you!" Xrisen shouted. You have spoken words that are fantasy. Stick to the facts and do not enter such baseless allegations into the record."

The hall broke into unrest, with many council members attempting to speak at once and none of the words being understandable over the commotion.

Brevlan shouted above the unrest, "I am not alone in these *fantasies*, as you call them, Xrisen! Many of my party have seen the conflict within you, the covetous looks towards Xeries' woman, and a lust for the throne that defies decency!"

"Brevlan, you have just earned my wrath," Xrisen fired back. "I invoke my right to challenge your groundless insults! I verbalize my right in front of these witnesses, forcing you to prove your fanciful allegations on the field of blood!"

"Order! Order!" the chair screamed.

The hall was divided into three: those loyal to Xrisen, primarily ones who had been bought by Xrisen's unequalled wealth; those loyal to the fallen Xeries and the legends and history of his great-grandfather, Xeries Eight, Warrior of all Nesdia; and those who were undecided. The chair continued, unsuccessfully, his attempt to establish order, while the three groups formulated separate stands.

The chair finally gained the attention of the council by banging the gavel so hard the handle broke and the head of the tool flew onto the floor. "We must come to order!" the chairman yelled above the din. "We gain no ground fighting amongst ourselves. It is up to us, the leaders of our great nation and God's vehicle, to formulate a plan and make some sense out of the debacle at hand!"

All quieted. Xrisen asked Brevlan, "Where are the Seven's warships now?"

"They are a mirage, first appearing then vanishing."

"You mean to tell me we don't have any reasonable data to fix their present location or course of plot?"

"None whatsoever! The sensor equipment your companies manufactured is obviously inferior to Seven's!"

There was a heavy silence in the great hall for the second time this morning, while all present considered the ramifications of their predicament.

Xrisen was first to break the silence. "With our Fleet nearly destroyed, the Seven's ships will waste no time in setting course for our most populous planets. Expect devastation unlike any experienced in our lifetimes. For all intents and purposes, we are fish in a barrel, waiting to be shot!"

"There must be some solution, Director. What thoughts do you have on the matter?" The chair placed inquiry upon the floor.

Brevlan's head rested in his hands. Perspiration dripped from his chin and onto the papers before him. Removing his hands from his head, every man in the room could see the tremors quaking his body. "I am afraid, gentlemen, I am at a complete loss. I wish to place on the historic record that I opposed unprovoked attacks on the Seven's settlements. I wish the record to be clear. I was outvoted. Members of this council, I address you formally as director of military strategy. The Book of Prophesy led us down a false path. None in this room may know our destiny until we are smashed in the head by it!

"We must immediately throw ourselves into surrender, knowing from these obvious examples that the technology produced by Xrisen's companies is *inferior* and no match for the Seven's fleet! We must beg for forgiveness from Seven's admiral and learn from our tragic mistakes to live in peace with our neighbors, understanding they are different and embracing them as friends!"

Xrisen grew purple with rage at the accusations cast upon the floor by Brevlan: that he, Xrisen, had been responsible for selling inferior hardware to Nesdia's military; it was an offence that would cost Xrisen his life if it were proven to be true.

"Brevlan speaks blasphemy against the *Book of Prophesy* and its wisdom, which our God has imparted!" Xrisen began with vehemence. "Do not listen to this coward! Faith in our God and his divine path is all that will save our worlds from complete and utter destruction. We may be at a severe disadvantage, yet faith in the *Book of Prophesy* and the teachings therein are our only hope for salvation!"

Mumbling agreement followed.

"We must invoke battle plan redirect. It is our only remaining chance," he added.

"Our remaining chance to *kill millions* more innocents?" Brevlan questioned, his face turning a brilliant red, his eyeshade blackening. "I have had enough of this madness! Do you think redirect will save us from the retribution soon knocking upon our door?"

"Weakness has no stomach for what must be done!" Xrisen said, goading Brevlan. "The prophesy must be fulfilled. Only then will God come to our salvation and destroy the infidels!"

Murmurs of accent prevailed. Brevlan was silent, shaking his head in disbelief.

"We must vote! All in favor of battle plan redirect, stand!" said Xrisen.

Brevlan sat, head in his hands. Eighteen of the twenty-six stood, a clear and decisive quorum.

"It is decided," Xrisen said, vindicated. "Battle plan redirect will be carried out. May God honor us with final victory over the infidel!"

Xrisen rushed back to his apartments. Storming in, he yelled, "Get up, Zuzahna; we must leave in fifteen minutes!"

In a sleep-filled voice, Zuzahna asked, "Where are we going, my lord?"

"On a little vacation, my dear."

"But I have no clothes. All my personal belongings are in transit from the ship and are yet to be delivered here," she said, sitting up.

"No matter; everything you need will be provided aboard my cruiser."

"We are going into Deep Space?"

"Yes!"

"Oh Xrisen, I have just spent the better part of a year on board a warship. I would rather stay here on-planet in the fresh air and sunshine. I have need to visit old friends and catch up on what is happening in current events."

"You will have plenty of time for that when we return," Xrisen lied, knowing that Nesdia as she knew it would shortly cease to exist.

"I cannot possibly be ready in fifteen minutes," she complained, pouting. "I must bathe, dress, and eat. Give me two hours to prepare, and then I will accompany you."

Xrisen's eyes blackened. "Did you not hear me, woman? We leave in twelve minutes!"

"Xrisen, if you plan on treating me this poorly when we have been together less than eight hours, I am loath to consider how you will treat me a year from now. I think, based upon this new side of yours, which I have never seen before this moment, I choose to stay here on-planet. We will take this little relationship slowly. I can see you need some extensive training therapy, dear, and I am just the doctor to cure your troubles." Zuzahna smiled most mischievously. She fluttered her eyelashes, attempting to charm the angry Nesdian regent.

Xrisen said nothing more, only grabbed Zuzahna's arm in a bruising grip and ushered her, without a stitch of clothing on her person, to the air tube.

"How dare you manhandle me!"

Xrisen backhanded Zuzahna with such force that her head bounced off the lift's bulkhead. She crumpled into unconsciousness.

Xrisen picked Zuzahna up, threw her naked bottom over his shoulder, and stepped out of the air tube. He entered his private yacht and strapped Zuzahna in. Moments later, a preordained flight plan was enacted. The small, sleek vessel blasted out of Nesdia Six's gravity and set course for a pre-chosen haven, far and away from the brewing storm.

TWENTY-SEVEN

WITH the second Nesdian war over in a short one and a half years, ship's time, the crew of *Independence* were given the unfettered right of extended leave. All were anxious to return to Seven Galaxies Seven. The nearness of Seven, the planet where many persons aboard *Independence* had been born, created a heightened sense of excitement aboard the ship.

The trip back home would be made in a record three and a half weeks, as the normal length of the jump would be shortened by nearly half due to Alex and Tay's innovative mag-grav drive.

Not long after the ship was given orders to set course for their home planet, Tay noticed a difference in his grandfather. First, it was his quietness; and second, his command presence—or his diminished state of command presence at least.

TyGor was two hundred forty-nine years of age. He was not an ancient, yet Tay felt that his grandfather had never wished to live so long and see so much. The old man seemed to be reflecting for large portions of the day, turning more of the shipboard responsibilities over to Tay and Alex, as well as to others.

One day, while in the admiral's office, Tay presented him with a direct question. "Pa, sir, may I ask what has been on your mind these past days? You don't seem your normal self."

"My dear son, may we speak informally, as family and as friends—off the record?"

"Of course!"

His grandfather began. "My life has been lived in the service of our people. There were many times in my life that I wished to be a simple farmer, as my father was—to live in the valley of my birth and not be concerned with affairs outside of my small and sheltered world. But events unfolded, destiny spoke, and certain choices decided my path. The road of service and necessity is often a long, lonely journey. I have been without my family and personal companionship of a meaningful nature for the better part of two hundred years. I believe that I tire of service. Reflecting on my life and the opportunities in front of me, I have come to some decisions."

"What decisions, Pa?"

"First, I have decided to retire. My important work on behalf of Seven Galaxies comes to a close. We will, of course, brave the celebration upon our arrival; and the forthcoming decorations, which are inevitable. When that circus ends, I desire my return to our valley, to watch the sunrise in the mornings, to hear the birds sing and the voice of the river, so familiar to me as a youngster. Most of all, I desire peace, and the ability to walk the forest and fields not disturbed by concern for Seven Galaxies. I have earned that place and have decided I will not be dissuaded."

Tay had not considered the possibility of his grandfather's retirement seriously; the idea took him totally by surprise. "You have earned the right, Grandfather, and I will not be one to attempt to change your wishes, yet others will not be so understanding. Others will prevail upon you to continue your command. They will, I'm sure, insist!"

"Their insistence will avail them of no change in my heart. My decision is made, and it brings me great happiness that you understand my feelings."

"Grandfather, changing the channel back to command of the Fleet, who do you think would be the best choice and most likely candidate for future command?"

"Son, there are many qualified, yet few who possess the most basic morals and ethics to deserve command. I have been thinking a great deal on the subject and have some ideas. I can say no more at this time. I have enjoyed our conversation. Will you come again later?"

"As often as you wish, Grandfather."

"It will be good for you to come often, as my son and not my official liaison, so that we may talk of old times and new. We have spent very little time together of a personal nature; let's spend the next few weeks catching up, shall we?"

"I would enjoy that immensely, Grandfather!"

"Tay, before you go, I must get back to responsibilities. I will be placing more of my duties upon you during our return trip. I desire more time alone, without all of the daily shipboard details, if you have no objection."

"Of course not, sir!"

"Very well then. I'll see you later." With those words, the old man smiled at his grandson, feeling honored to have him along.

"Son?"

"Yes, Grandfather?"

"I wish you to keep the content of our conversations strictly between you and me."

"Of course. I understand," Tay said.

On the third day of the return trip, the information officer came to Tay while he was on bridge. "Sir, we have detected an anomaly traveling at breakship speed, running approximately parallel to our present course. It appears to be a small vessel, fully cloaked."

"What readings are coming in? Is there any chance to determine the ship's origin?"

"Sir, we are at this time only detecting a disruption in the known space through which the anomaly is traveling. Nothing more can be determined unless the ship drops cloak."

"Then we must make it do so. Hail on all frequencies with all known languages and see if she responds."

"Sir, we have been hailing just as ordered for the past three minutes. The anomaly only picked up speed, sir. It seems she is trying to outdistance us."

"Is she widening the gap between us?"

"Slightly, sir, yet we are only applying seventy percent of our potential velocity drive."

"Bring the drive to ninety-eight percent and drop two hydrogen torpedoes in her forward path. Let's see how this little mystery craft responds." Tay smiled.

"Very good, sir. It should prove interesting."

"Alert the gunners that we may be firing to disable the craft."

"The gunners have been on constant alert for the duration of our mission, but I will apprise them of the immediate situation, sir."

"Very good! Gresham?"

"Yes, sir?"

"Good work. We cannot be too careful."

"No, sir, we cannot. Thank you, sir."

The torpedoes streamed out, invisible on the screen but detected by the subtle variation they caused in the picture, like heat waves rising from a desert floor. The torpedoes detonated and cast a sheen of hydrogen through space. Within the sheen was a small void, and then a flickering that finally presented itself as a ship. The craft was sleek, made for speed and obviously not for fighting.

Tay asked, "Shields, Lieutenant?"

"Light shielding, sir. Weapons are light as well. Nothing that could penetrate our armor."

"Drop quarterdeck gun shields for a nano and fire a disabling high-frequency burst. I don't want her damaged, only stopped in her tracks."

"Yes, sir."

Screaming tracers of electromagnetic disrupters became visible on the screen. When the tracers encompassed the little vessel, she shimmered slightly and then coasted to a stop.

"Interrupters successful, sir!"

"Hail her again and see if she responds."

"Yes, sir!" The lieutenant hailed the ship, and after a few moments said, "We are receiving a weak signal generated by the ancient vibratory method. It says, sir, that all her systems are down and they have life support for no more than an hour or two." He paused. "The decibel reading shows that the person communicating is screaming angrily—not speaking in normal tones."

"Is the speaker male or female?"

"Male, sir, but there appears to be another body on board the craft that is definitely female."

"What language is he speaking, Lieutenant?"

"Ancient Nesdian, sir! He claims the vessel is on a diplomatic mission and is carrying peace to the Seven Galaxies' highest authority."

"Inform our screaming diplomat that we are heading to Seven Galaxies Seven and would like nothing more than to tow their disabled ship along and give our Nesdian diplomat the finest quarters available in *Independence*'s brig."

"Yes, sir!"

"The disabled vessel responds that they would find the brig vile treatment for diplomats of the highest level."

"Ask the alleged diplomat why they were trying to evade us and why they refused to answer our hails. Why not speak, for that is what protocol deems diplomats must do."

The lieutenant followed his orders. "He says they thought we were an enemy sent to destroy them, and so they attempted to flee. It seems, sir, that the speaker is calming. The decibel range has reduced dramatically."

"Accelerate both persons aboard to isolation in the brig. I will inform the admiral to the presence of our new guests. Place the disabled craft in tow and proceed on our plotted course to Seven Galaxies Seven with haste. I will return shortly. You have the seat, Gresham."

"Yes, sir."

Tay hastened to inform the admiral.

"Nesdian diplomats you say, son?"

"Yes, sir, they allege to be."

"The ship—would it be the type of craft to carry high level diplomats?"

"Yes, sir, very fast, full cloak. She was trying to outdistance us, sir."

"And yet our mag-grav drive allowed us to close the gap and capture her undamaged?"

"Well, sir, every circuit interrupter on board was blown or fried, but otherwise undamaged, yes."

"Very good, Tay."

"Let me shower and dress. We will eat while our new guests do the same. Diplomacy, if I am correct, should not be hurried. Do you agree?"

"Absolutely, sir! It would not avail us to speak to them while they are so hot and fresh from being captured. I think it would be much better to let them eat and drink until such time as they feel more amicable."

"A good plan, son. It has been many years since I have had the undeniable pleasure of speaking with one of the enemy's diplomats within the safety of our brig!" The admiral began to chuckle, finding some humor in otherwise humorless duties.

TWENTY-EIGHT

ZUZAHNA was panting. She had to think quickly. The capture of Xrisen's cruiser had been completely unexpected. He had assured her that the ship possessed speed and cloaking technologies that would outwit the fools and infidels of the Fleet, yet here she sat in the brig of *Independence*, a vessel well known throughout all of Nesdia's worlds to be commanded by the admiral of the Seven Galaxies.

Her thoughts raced. Surely Xrisen would be brought before the war crimes tribunal and tried, just as all Nesdian politicians and commanders had been at the end of the Twenty-Seven Years War when Xeries Eight was defeated. Her fate could be the same, she thought. How would she survive?

The answer came in a flash, as if inspired by a higher power. If the Seven Galaxies thought she had been Xrisen's willing companion, a dark light would fall upon her. The Nesdian destruction of the Seven's settlements had been decided in council while Xrisen was regent to the council, so Zuzahna must distance herself from him somehow. Was not regent only one step below king? Surely, since the demise of Xeries Ten, Xrisen had risen in power, and was looked upon as the rightful heir to the Nesdian throne; therefore, logic spoke that Xrisen would field much of the blame for the atrocities waged upon Seven's settlements.

Prophesy foretold that the king would be crowned upon returning from a victorious battle against the Seven Galaxies. Now, however, Nesdia lay in ruins: punishment for the blatant aggressions, which were the result of arrogance, lust for power, and obvious false prophesy, all consented to and encouraged by the regent.

A plan formed in Zuzahna's quick mind. She would say that Xrisen had kidnapped her. She would tell those who asked questions that she had been forcefully taken as his mate, against her will, which was mostly true, as Xrisen had fled the Fleet's destruction of Nesdia's worlds. She would feign hatred for Nesdia's ruling class and for their aggression, compliment the Fleet's commanders on the Seven Galaxies victory, and befriend anyone aboard that she could.

Soon she would be accepted, possibly even honored as a potential diplomat. It could work. *It* will *work,* she thought. *It must! I am not a criminal! I will come out of this unscathed, if the game is played carefully. I must act distraught and cry my eyes out, even though ordinary Nesdian women do not cry.*

A door slid open in her cell, and two men stepped in. One was an older man of distinction, perhaps Admiral Gor himself, she thought; and the other, a young man whom she found very handsome. Zuzahna instantly liked these humans. They did not smell strongly and were interestingly void of the body hair so prevalent on Nesdian men.

Zuzahna made her large eyes wide and allowed tears to be seen. She cried out, "I have done nothing wrong!

I was kidnapped by that beast, Xrisen! I will cooperate and tell all I know of the council's treachery. I never approved of the Nesdian government's cruel and diabolical policies. Please, have mercy on me. I am just an innocent trapped in a situation beyond my control!"

"Calm yourself," the elder spoke. "We are not here to harm you."

Zuzanah's breathlessness subsided. "Thank you, kind masters. I am at your service. May I leave these awfully cramped quarters and be allowed freedom aboard your ship?"

The elder spoke again: "Not so fast, young lady. Innocent or not, you are a prisoner of war aboard this vessel. You will be confined to the brig until we arrive at our destination and can turn you over to the proper authorities for questioning."

"Will they torture me?" Zuzahna asked.

"Of course not," the younger man said. "Our culture does not allow that sort of treatment of prisoners."

Zuzahna considered all that was said and changed tactics. "Ever since I was a little girl, I have been afraid of confined spaces. I begin to pant; dizziness overtakes me. Surely you must have some secure place that is more spacious than this?"

"There is one cell much larger, but at this time it is occupied by your traveling companion. Do you wish to join him?" asked the elder.

"No! No! Perhaps he could be moved, and I could have his accommodations?"

"I will consider your request. For the moment, you must calm yourself. I am Admiral Gor. This is my special assistant, TayGor."

"I am Zuzahna. I am very pleased and honored to make your acquaintance," she said, curtsying ever so slightly and holding out her hand.

Tay was compelled to take her outstretched hand. She fluttered her long dark lashes lightly and noticed the reaction in the young man. Tay faltered, holding Zuzahna's hand a nano longer than appropriate.

Tay had seen pictures of Nesdian women, most of whom were short, squat, hairy, often very homely creatures. The woman before him stood tall and graceful. The hair on her face and hands was extremely fine, similar to peach fuzz yet dark in color. Her eyes, some of the largest eyes he had ever seen, were a dark brown with minute golden flecks. Her form radiated classic beauty in every sense of the word. Tay studied her with subdued interest. She exuded a scent that was an intriguing combination of adrenalin and perspiration. The result was a personalized perfume that engulfed Tay's senses and made him feel compassion. A slight longing for her in the pit of his stomach began to grow.

"Well, uhm, Zuzahna, we are honored to have you aboard," was all he could muster.

Zuzahna and TyGor both saw the reaction in Tay. His grandfather smiled inwardly and promised himself to sit the boy down later for a long talk about this type of Nesdian woman.

TyGor asked, "Your lineage name, what might it be, Zuzahna?"

"Duhcat, Admiral. Zuzahna Duhcat. I am pleased to finally meet you. Your reputation, dearest Admiral, precedes you far and wide throughout Nesdia!"

"Yes, I have read some excerpts about myself and interpretations of events documented by Nesdia's historians. I must say, they do not portray me as graciously as you do."

"Alas, my dear Admiral, none have had the pleasure of conversing with you, as I am fortunate enough to. It is my understanding that most Nesdian commanders who have been unfortunate enough to confront you in battle are no longer with us on the physical plane. The ill-fated attempts by our previous commanders speaks highly of your skills as a warrior. None of them had any success in bringing out the kindness and leniency you have bestowed upon me this moment."

"It is my pleasure to see to your comfort while on *Independence*," the admiral said. "I apologize for the inconvenience, but your traveling companion is under investigation for war crimes, disregard for ancient treaty rules between our civilizations, and many other things. You should, perhaps, choose your traveling companions more carefully."

"As I said, gracious Admiral, I was kidnapped."

TyGor smiled, not really believing the Duhcat's story.

Zuzahna picked up on his thought instantly and said, "Look at the huge bruise on my cheek and the egg on the back of my head!" She brushed her cheek with the back of a hand, wiping away a covering of makeup to expose a large bruise on her right cheekbone.

"I am sorry, miss, for doubting your story, yet in circumstances such as these, I have heard it all—every variation you could think of. I will send a doctor to examine your injuries and make sure you are not suffering from a concussion. I will also see what can be done about larger quarters for you."

"Thank you, Admiral, for that simple yet most appreciated kindness."

"We have not visited your traveling companion, or I should say your kidnapper. Would you care to share a little history and some of his background?" TyGor asked.

"Please, make no mistake, he is not my companion. I despise that evil brute. He was bragging just yesterday about his involvement in formulating the attacks on innocent civilians on your settlement planets. His arrogance sickens me!"

"What possessed him to take you prisoner?" asked Tay.

Zuzahna smiled sheepishly. "An honest answer may redden the ears of this charming young man," Zuzahna said, looking directly into Tay's eyes.

"On my ship we settle for nothing less. If it embarrasses the lad, so be it!" TyGor's curiosity was provoked. Secrets were normally respected and privacy kept foremost on ship, but the admiral was relishing this woman's show and wanted to enjoy more of it.

"Honestly, Admiral, Xrisen told me that he could not live without my—shall we say—talents, for lack of a more respectable word."

The admiral was in a playful mood. "Talents, you say. Does he have need of a good accountant?"

Zuzahna was up for a quick exchange of wits and replied, "I have tallied Xrisen's numbers on occasion."

Tay was left behind. It seemed the admiral and Zuzahna were speaking riddles. This was to be a very serious meeting, interviewing prisoners of war. Preordained protocols seemed to have dropped away and been quickly forgotten by the admiral.

"May I interrupt here, sir?" Tay said, breaking into the playful exchange. "It seems we are moving off track."

"Go on."

Admiral Gor let Tay begin. "Zuzahna, surely a common Nesdian doesn't have access to such a craft as your kidnapper was piloting?"

"There is nothing common about that beast! Xrisen is regent to the Nesdian High Council. Many believed him to be the rightful heir to the Nesdian throne after he plotted and killed my life-long love, Xeries Ten. My *dearest* Xeries was the unsurpassed choice as ruler of our worlds by the Nesdian people!

"I weep to this day thinking of poor Xeries' betrayal. He was one of the few compassionate commanders who spoke out—condemning aggressive movements against the Seven Galaxies. If he were alive today, perhaps things would be different. Possibly we would have met at the Diplomatic Peace Council instead of as enemies fleeing the destruction of what was once Xeries' great work. *Imagine*, a united Nesdia living in peace with the Seven Galaxies.

"You see, that is why Xrisen plotted to have Xeries killed, to usurp his peaceful control over the people of Nesdia. With Xeries out of the way, Xrisen could and did incite them to act out aggressions against the Seven Galaxies as written in the ancient prophesy and taught by the many evil shamans. Zuzahna wrung her hands, then looked up with imploring eyes.

"I cry myself to sleep most nights thinking of what might have been possible if Xrisen had not designed

Xeries' untimely death!" Tears welled once more in Zuzahna's striking brown eyes.

"Admiral, if I cooperate and tell you all I can about Xrisen, will you promise to set me free in the near future?" Zuzahna asked.

"It is not within my power to promise such a thing to you," Admiral Gor said. "But in my report, I will give you a glowing recommendation and speak highly of your behavior during your capture and subsequent time aboard this vessel—if you live up to my expectations, which I am sure a woman of your caliber shall have no difficulty doing."

"Caliber," Zuzahna responded. "An interesting choice of words, Admiral. I can assure you I will be on my *very best* behavior." Zuzahna smiled demurely at TyGor.

Showing nothing on his poker face, he thought, *Yes, my dear; that is what concerns me most.* TyGor looked at his grandson and noticed a doting look in the young man's eyes.

Zuzahna noticed the look as well and directed the focus of her feminine wiles towards the young man. "Dear Tay, I do hope we will become fast friends during our voyage together," she said. "You will come and see me often, won't you?"

"Of course! I mean, if it's okay with the admiral."

"Oh, dear Admiral, please *do* consent. I have so much to learn about your culture! I have been taught many lies by the atrocious Nesdian government and even more by the *Book of Prophesy*. I wish to learn the truth at last! You would not deny me this simple request for some honest and meaningful conversation to help me gain a true understanding of your history, culture, and philosophy, would you?" Zuzahna looked at Tay again. "I desire to have someone intelligent and well-informed to converse with for a change, as well as companionship and someone to enjoy the journey with."

Admiral Gor thought, *She is quite good: very persuasive, complimentary, graciously endearing, and positively alluring, all in the same breath—qualities I would expect from a Duhcat.* He knew he must warn Tay to be careful with this one. "I see nothing wrong in you two becoming associated while Tay is not busy with his normal duties," he answered.

"Wonderful!" Zuzahna said, beaming. "I am positively so thankful and happy that you, dear Admiral, rescued me from that beast Xrisen!"

"You must thank Tay for that service. I was not on the bridge when we spotted your vessel."

Zuzahna took in the young man once again, storing new information in the crypt of her intellect: Tay shared command with the admiral, she thought—an important piece of data. She smiled her most graciously seductive smile at Tay and said simply, "Thank you, my new and wonderful friends."

TWENTY-NINE

Admiral Gor and Tay left Zuzahna's cell, intending to see Xrisen for the first time. The cell door slid open, and they walked in abreast.

Xrisen glared. "You are Admiral Gor, I presume?"

The admiral only nodded, taking in the Nesdian's rage.

"I am the strategic diplomat on a mission of peace and extreme importance to the Seven Galaxies. I have diplomatic immunity under the flag of Nesdia!" said Xrisen. "I demand that you explain why you have commandeered my vessel and taken me hostage!"

"If you are on official diplomatic mission, then why did you ignore our hails?" asked the admiral.

"I am regent of all Nesdia's worlds. I am not in the habit of answering every hail from unidentified ships while on a mission of such great importance."

"We identified ourselves when asking you to respond, yet you refused to answer. What message do you carry?" asked Tay.

"I will share it only with the rulers of the Seven Galaxies, not some military men with limited intellect!"

Most men would bristle at the insult, but Admiral Gor took it all in stride. "Xrisen of Nesdia, I will clarify one *very* important point: you are not being held hostage; you are a prisoner of war. Nesdia, as you know it, no longer exists. Held by the Seven Galaxies, you are formally under investigation to determine what part, if any, you played in attacking our settlements and in the murder of innocent civilians. In our worlds, I am in complete control of war prisoners, their interrogations, and subsequent debriefings. Please share with me your message, and I will make sure it reaches the proper authority."

"And if I refuse?" challenged Xrisen.

The admiral answered, "If you choose, you may sit silently in the brig for the next three weeks and then share your alleged peace treaty with the War Tribunal when we arrive at our destination, or you may share it now. To me, it makes no difference."

Xrisen spoke. "Torture? Do you intend to extract my knowledge through pain? Your artisans of suffering will never be successful!"

"Xrisen…Nesdia is the only culture I have encountered in all my years traveling the stars that prides itself in the art of suffering. You are a backward and pitiful people with too much hate, arrogance, and secularism. Look where it has brought you."

"We of Nesdia have conquered three of your settlements!"

"Yes, you have attacked three of our outposts without provocation, killing unarmed farmers and taking their wives and children into bondage. Nesdia's military attacked unprotected innocents. How could your race justify such brutality?"

Xrisen faltered. His eyes danced between the admiral and Tay.

"Our *Book of Prophesy* tells us that we must suffer the innocents of the Seven Galaxies to draw the cowardly commander of the Fleet out and, as the prophesy predicts, defeat him and rule over Seven Galaxies' worlds!"

"And do you honestly believe that your world can progress at the expense of ours?" the admiral asked.

"It is the only way!" Xrisen shot back. "Our God's word is infallible! The *Book of Prophesy* has been passed down through the ages. It is the unadulterated word of the universe's only God! Nesdia's God! Nesdia is marching on God's mission. Through the millions of lives sacrificed, we are assured that the ancient prophesies will become reality!"

"Your *Book of Prophesy* was written by Nesdian men, evil religious fanatics with a grudge against all other races and religions. The *Book of Prophesy* is complete and utter crap. It lacks even a shred of rational decency." The admiral spoke calmly, yet he was goading Xrisen.

The Nesdian bristled. "It is in no way over! Fire shall engulf you! Our God, the only God, will rain death from the stars upon you. It is so written!"

"Meanwhile, Xrisen, you will sit here and stew for the next three weeks. I will waste no more reason upon your fanaticism," said the admiral tiredly.

"The paths of asteroids now plotted may change without warning!" Xrisen spewed angrily. Spittle flew and saliva dribbled down his long, hairy chin. His previously golden eyes turned black with his rage, and his body literally shook in anger. An unpleasant scent, similar to that of a wet dog, exuded from the fanatic Nesdian regent.

Admiral Gor said simply and unemotionally, "You call yourself a diplomat? You look to me like a rabid dog that should be put out of its misery."

Xrisen lunged as if to attack. Tay stepped forward quickly, administering a heart strike, in the ancient Chinese fighting style. Xrisen flew backwards, hit the bulkhead, and then crumpled to deck.

"Admiral, there is no use trying to converse with this cur. We should depart."

"Yes, Tay, it would be best if we took our leave now."

Xrisen gained his feet with some difficulty and went into a strange hypnotic trance, chanting in the ancient Nesdian language. "Take me. I come, oh God of war; oh God of the universe. Prepare my Virgins. Prepare my eternal kingdom, for I die in pursuit of your prophesy!"

With the smile of a madman etched into his ghastly face, he showed his large canine teeth and then bit down hard, grinding his jaw sideways. One of his incisor tips broke off, and his eyes gleamed, a wild animal, a crazed lunatic. Xrisen swallowed the broken particle of tooth. Immediately, a fit of seizure rent his body. He fell again to the deck, thrashing and writhing spastically.

Admiral Gor looked at Tay and said, without emotion, "Goodbye to stinking rubbish," and then he opened the slider and exited the cell.

Outside, he gave instructions to the security team. "Remove the body, straighten and sanitize the suite, and then move the woman prisoner into this cell. Transfer all the dead Nesdian's personal effects to the woman, including the jewelry, according to Maritime Law."

Admiral Gor then walked on without saying another word.

Tay stood silently, attempting to take it all in. There was, Tay thought, a warning riddle, a message for the Seven Galaxies in Xrisen's last words. He booted the recorder and sent the file to his computer. He and Alex would review both conversations, Xrisen's and Zuzahna's, as soon as Tay was back in the lab.

THIRTY

"Tay," the admiral began. "I called for you because I want to share an interesting story, or some would say a legend, with you. It concerns Zuzahna Duhcat, in a roundabout way. Do you have some time? It's a fairly long tale."

"Of course, Admiral!" Tay sat down on the sofa in Gor's personal quarters.

"There was, in our ancient history, a man who lived to be several thousand years old, a man who amassed wealth beyond that of kings and moguls. He would, in essence, become the patriarch of many planets across a wide spectrum of areas traveled in the universe. His name was Enricco Duhcat.

"Duhcat received doctorates in space drive theory, astral and quantum physics, and computer science, all on ancient Earth—and not through formal education but by challenging the university finals. He took the most acclaimed teachings of engineers and scientists of that time to an unprecedented level. No one, including the High Command, could believe a young man, a novice who was not trained at University, could come up with designs that would unseat the theories of the ruling class of physicists and scientists of the period.

"Some say Duhcat was walking in a park with a romantic companion that fine spring day when inspiration, the foundation of his theories, came upon him like a flash of lightening. Others say he sold his soul to the Devil for the power and wealth he would achieve.

"Earth's military powers took control of the technology and concepts, claiming reasons of planetary security. Duhcat's intellectual property was simply taken. They robbed him.

"Duhcat had invested everything, including his family's fortune, in seeing his experiments through to fruition. The opportunity to profit from what he claimed were inspired concepts, and his intellectual property—concepts that were, within two centuries, to become the standard of Deep Space travel—became dust in the wind. He was never paid a credit for his designs.

"Duhcat's years of informal education and his connection to a higher source of creative inspiration were washed away in the government's desire to control the power he had intentionally unleashed. He never received a penny from the government. His family lost everything to the banks because they could not repay the mortgages Duhcat had placed against their properties to fund the conclusions of his work."

"What happened to him?" asked Tay.

"He was not seen in public again for some three hundred forty-seven years; however, his business interests were well known throughout a large portion of the universe. His drive theories, implemented two centuries later by the military on ancient Earth, were quickly pirated by hackers and soon became the basis for the Great Diaspora of ancient Earth."

"Duhcat's technology made the Diaspora possible? How can this be?" Tay asked, confused. "We are taught in school that Earth's military leaders and their scientists came up with the theories that gave the people of ancient Earth the ability to Deep Space travel and settle other planets that were previously unattainable because of their incredible distance from Earth."

"If you will listen, all your questions will be answered," said the admiral, showing frustration at the interruptions. "The military leaders of the time called upon Duhcat and attempted to explain their decision regarding his intellectual property. They told Duhcat, in no uncertain terms, that credit for the discovery would be given to the government scientists who were working towards secret space technology that would allow for advances such as Deep Space jumps. If the public understood that such technology could come from the private sector, zillions of credits worth of funding would dry up overnight.

"Duhcat was offered a job, which he, in a rage, refused. You see, it had been Duhcat's intention to allow the private sector access to the technology for a price, yet the government and military agreed that would be a terrible mistake to allow private persons access to something so potentially powerful and dangerous.

"People who knew Duhcat personally spoke of a change in the man after that. Normally gregarious and friendly, he became instantly reclusive, keeping away from associates and friends he had enjoyed for years. It appears that the experience created something within

Duhcat that had never previously existed—a determined ruthlessness, born of the will to survive; or a deeper-seated primeval nature that was brought to the surface by the damage done to his dreams and to his family's wealth and health."

"How could the government of the time justify stealing his work and not paying him for it, and how could they take credit for the discovery while allowing his family to be ruined financially?" Tay asked.

Gor shook his head. "I regret to inform you that much of history is written by those who have, for thousands of years, stifled creativity and kept extraordinary and liberating technology from the common man. May I continue my story without your querulous interruptions?"

"Yes, of course, Admiral!" Tay said, smiling at the old man's impatience.

"Duhcat departed Earth, leaving behind a giant hubbub and, consequently, a strategic tumult, which the officials in power at the time tried to cover up. However, Duhcat had left behind a small group dedicated strictly to him. They were computer geniuses, his prodigies, who kept in constant contact with him through unbreakable encrypted communications.

"Duhcat had blasted out of Earth's orbital gravity on a ship he had secretly built, and he had completely disappeared within a nano. It was as if the ship had instantaneously jumped into another dimension—or perhaps something even more fantastic, according to the many imaginations that pondered his departure. A jump into Deep Space was inconceivable at the time, and completely unprecedented. He had obviously outfitted a ship built secretly with the new drive system before his unorthodox laboratory work was seized by the military of Earth's reigning power. All of this was kept completely hushed, including the fact that twelve of ancient Earth's military High Command vanished from a strategy meeting without a trace."

"They were never found?" asked Tay.

"No," Gor said, shaking his head. "Anyone privy to the situation knew that Duhcat had somehow particle-accelerated the twelve from a battle-hardened installation previously thought to be impregnable. The installation had shields in place, and no one at that time had even heard the term particle acceleration before.

"It seems Enricco Duhcat had a surprise or two up his sleeve that Earth's military leaders had not even conceived of. One piece of his mystery and legend, and one very important point to remember in terms of his strategy, is that Duhcat purposely left some critically necessary keys out of his seized work, without which the material was virtually worthless. At the same time, he was building the secret ship and a ghost computer system that has never been found. The confiscated work was only a decoy, a mirage created while he worked on the real project in a cavern on his family property that was unknown until the ship emerged."

"You said Duhcat lived for some three thousand years yet surfaced some three hundred years later. How is that possible? At that time on ancient Earth, life expectancy was no more than a hundred forty years, tops."

Gor smiled. "That is another thing that made Duhcat wealthier than everyone else."

"How so, Grandfather?"

"The ultra-rich from across the universe flocked to his clinics to be rejuvenated, not questioning the cost. Duhcat milked them like a mechanical machine, squeezing every last drop, taking them for all they were worth. Many a ruthless, grasping billionaire was happy to start fresh, penniless, with a young virile mind and body.

"His beliefs were clear. He distrusted governments with a passion and despised the moguls of ancient Earth who suppressed technology and enslaved the common man with an illusion of freedom, when in actuality they were worker bees gathering honey for the selfish few. Within Duhcat's lifetime, they were all groveling at his feet."

"So what happened to Duhcat?"

"No one knows. Some say they have seen him recently."

"That's impossible!" Tay said, frowning. "It has been what—several thousand years?"

"Yes. Duhcat founded a mining empire that utilized his technology to access regions within the universe previously unattainable. He proposed to begin catapulting shells full of refined ore to ancient Earth—namely, minerals and metals that had been depleted there. Those strategic commodities at the time were as valuable as diamonds, and that is what he demanded for payment.

"Scientists on the government payrolls laughed at the proposition and said it was impossible, that Duhcat was mad, twisted in the head. Yet the irrefutable fact remained that Duhcat had left Earth's orbit and had literally disappeared in the blink of an eye, something that would require a velocity thousands of times faster than the speed of light."

"Grandfather, why is all this ancient history so important?"

"The important fact to remember is that Duhcat delivered on his promises, and ancient Earth became an addict for the materials he could catapult. He became more powerful than kings, more influential than a thousand diplomats—you see, because he could deliver. Earth desperately needed the resources that he controlled, and offered at no small cost."

"Why didn't the military of the time just take the strategic resources from him, just as they took his space drive theory? Once they had the keys, or figured them out, then they would have the ability to utilize Duhcat's Deep Space drive."

"Remember, Duhcat was arguably the most brilliant mind of that era. He had thought the entire program through as if it were a chess game, and he was a master of chess. He effectively had a two-century jump on Earth and was operating far and away from the feeble forays that Earth's ships were making into Deep Space. He signed treaties with any worlds that had planets or moons he wished to extract from, for a percentage of the materials. He was virtually untouchable. Stopping Duhcat's operations would have been an act of war. He had a freedom of movement that is unrivaled to this day, and he had the protection of a vast and varied portion of the universe. He was a strategic resource, never to be threatened again."

"And so, dear Grandfather," Tay said, beginning to see the larger picture, "Zuzahna is a Duhcat! A genetic progeny of Enricco Duhcat?"

"No," Gor said, correcting him. "An adopted child of the Duhcat foundation."

"What do you mean, Grandfather?"

"I am attempting to explain!" TyGor looked at his grandson with the stern eye of a parent ready to rebuff a child's transgressions.

Tay received the look and fell silent.

"Duhcat realized that the most powerful force in our universe was not money or technology but the persuasive talents a few women possess. During the mining years, it was inevitable that race mixing would occur. Crews of Duhcat's men traveled the universe far and wide. Whenever exploration brings races of people together who have never before been in contact, the result is the same and has been throughout time. The mulatto or mixed-race children were often thrown to the wolves or simply ostracized and relegated to a lower caste, much like ancient Earth did to mixed-race people. Have you studied the mixing of blood on ancient Earth? The Native North Americans mixing with the white settlers, the black slaves mixing with the white races of the time: all these children were considered social outcasts, segregated by societies' unwritten and many times painful rules and snobbery."

"Yes, Grandfather, I have read of such ridiculous class distinctions."

"The same thing happened to the mixed-race children created by Duhcat's mining enterprises. Duhcat realized that his operations had contributed extensively to the problem, and so he dedicated his fortunes and himself towards a program of training that would come back to haunt the ruling classes that had cast out the children.

"Duhcat selected and enrolled the most desirable, beautiful, or handsome in extensive training in the love arts, bringing the once ostracized children back as powerful courtesans, male and female. Through their art in the bedchamber, they could extract knowledge that could then be used by Duhcat to navigate and influence the future.

"The rest, those who were not ultimately desirable, were trained to be ladies and men in waiting: dedicated servants, secretaries, and bodyguards to those who supplied Duhcat with strategic information and assisted him as a vast web of information gatherers. This allowed Duhcat to see from the inside out, in essence giving him a crystal ball with regard to the powers ruling a broad portion of the known universe."

Gor fell silent for a moment, then said, "Be careful of Zuzahna, son. She is a very powerful person. You could learn much from her, but if you do not watch yourself closely, she will happily work her magic on you. You are an exceptional and extremely intelligent young man, yet you are inexperienced in the dark ways and lack, I am afraid, the worldliness and hardened nature that would make it easier to deal with the likes of Zuzahna Duhcat. Goodness knows, any man would have difficulty keeping her from ruling him. I speak of these things only out of my love and concern for your wellbeing." The admiral laughed good-naturedly, yet his concern was obvious.

"Grandfather, if you wish that I should not befriend Zuzahna, just say the words, and I will follow your direction unerringly."

"Son, it is not that I wish to halt your friendship with the woman. I only wish you to carefully bridle it and restrain yourself consciously in her presence. I fear that if you are not always aware of her many and varied talents, you might succumb to them."

"Rest assured, Grandfather, I will tread as if on thin ice. Your words will be ever-present in the forefront of my impressionable and easily influenced mind." The young man smiled disarmingly. "On the subject of Enricco Duhcat, sir, I wish to find out more about him. I never learned anything of his life in history lessons."

"His history is classified. Governments not only deny his existence but also their alliances and dependence on his vast web of resources and human capital. You will only find him in the UIA files, but as yet you have no clearance for that system.

"I will rectify those clearances for you and for Alex, but you must swear to keep anything you learn of him strictly between yourselves, and keep me informed of all new data you turn up concerning his whereabouts or movements. Some say he is immortal, for what other entity could have passed through three and a half millenniums of our time?"

"I will keep you posted of anything that seems interesting, Admiral. Thanks for the clearances. I also appreciate you sharing the legend and mystery of Enricco Duhcat."

Tay left Admiral Gor's apartment and hurried to inform Alex of the new clearances and unbelievable tale of Enricco Duhcat—and Zuzahna's connection to him.

THIRTY-ONE

Tay entered the lab to find Alex sitting at his computer. He sat down next to his friend, and Alex asked, "So, what were the Nesdians like, Tay?"

"Night and day could be no closer."

"What do you mean?"

"You won't believe this, but the male just poisoned himself. He committed suicide while chanting something about Nesdia's God and a prophesy being fulfilled. The guy is dead. What a freaking lunatic. He was literally frothing at the mouth, spittle flying, when he spoke. I forwarded the recording so we could review it together. I think there is a hidden meaning in something he said, except I can't quite put my finger on what it is."

"What about the woman? You said they were night and day. What was she like? I've never met a Nesdian before."

"Alex, she was beautiful, charming, and, quite frankly, sexually stimulating. I was flabbergasted."

"You, stimulated by a Nesdian woman? You're joking!"

"I wish I was, Alex. It's a little disconcerting."

"How so?"

"Well, you know the Nesdians are considered humanoid, yet there is a primeval side to them that is clearly evident. Why Zuzahna affected me the way she did is a mystery to me."

"Oh! It's not 'the Nesdian woman' anymore but *Zuzahna*!" Alex batted his eyes and patted his heart, having fun at Tay's expense.

"Shut up, will you, and let's review the recordings!"

"Yes, sir!" Alex continued chuckling while the images loaded, but he halted abruptly when Zuzahna's image appeared on the screen. His mouth dropped open in disbelief. "She is the Nesdian?"

"Yes," answered Tay.

"I had no idea there were Nesdian women like *this*. In all the pics I've ever seen of them, they were hairy, stumpy, frumpy things that made me think of trolls or hobbits."

"I know. Isn't she something?"

They both sat, watching Zuzahna in action. Both young men fell silent, attempting to take in everything about her.

When the recording finished, Alex turned towards Tay, a bewildered look on his face.

"How could she be so alluring, Tay?"

"I'm not sure, yet in person it was even stronger. Her magnetism reached out and touched me. I could barely let go of her hand after she offered it."

"Whoa boy! Whoa! You got it bad, don't you? Tay, with the iron heart, finally gets bagged by an alien life form!" Alex began laughing.

"Shut up and boot the other interview!"

"Yes, sir. Of course, sir. Anything you say, sir." Alex was having too much fun at Tay's expense, but at the same time, he was a little concerned for the young man's mental health. He had never seen Tay look at anyone the way he looked at Zuzahna.

The next scenes were of an angry, hairy, golden-eyed creature dressed as if he were some sort of king. Fine jewels and silken cloth adorned most of Xrisen's body. His face was twisted in hate. Alex and Tay watched Xrisen's tirade without comment.

After the show was over, Alex said, "Whooee! What a nut case!"

"You know it!" Tay agreed.

"What do you think he meant by raining fire and asteroids, and plotted paths changing course?" asked Tay.

Alex shrugged. "I'm still processing. I'm having a hard time changing the channel from the picture of that crazed Nesdian to being back in the real world."

"Switch, Alex. I think this is very important! Look, we believe there are still some Nesdian war ships that have escaped our nets. Eighteen were destroyed in the battles, and the admiral feels they would have held a few more in reserve."

"That makes perfect sense to me. What command would risk every ship down to the last?"

"Would it be possible for an asteroid's path to be altered mechanically or with some sort of explosive weapon?"

Alex thought for a moment. "It *is* possible. One of the research projects I was involved with in mining technologies was to redirect moving 'stroids."

"Stroids?"

"Asteroids. The theory was that if a 'stroid rich in minerals or metallic ores could be maneuvered closer to a base that could refine the raw materials, a huge savings could be made by shortening the distance the bulk space-carriers had to haul material."

"How could it be done?" Tay asked.

"Several ways are feasible, but the most efficient was to plant a massive thruster, similar to those once used to launch large payloads out of a planet's gravitational pull."

"You mean like a rocket thruster?"

Alex nodded. "We were able to simulate a drastic change in direction, provided the subject 'stroid was already traveling in the general direction of an intended target. Another way would be to simply tow the rock with a very powerful ship or two."

"Do you think the Nesdians are capable of redirecting a 'stroid so that it would impact one of our worlds?"

"They certainly could produce the technology and the hatred to justify something so ominous."

"What sort of damage would the impact create?" asked Tay.

"That would depend on the size of the 'stroid. Damage could be planetary fatal if a big enough stone were cast. Even a relatively small one would create massive tsunamis and cause tremendous devastation along the seaboards if the world had vast oceans."

"A planet like Seven?"

"Yes, absolutely, my friend. You don't think the missing Nesdian ships could be plotting such a sick scheme, do you?"

"You saw the Nesdian regent. What do you think?"

Alex shivered. "I think we had better get to work!"

Tay stood abruptly. "Assemble a research team immediately. Create a search and tracking program. I want the moving location, direction, and distance from any of our inhabited worlds of any and all 'stroids that could be manipulated and cause catastrophic damage if they crashed a planet. I'll go and speak with the admiral on the subject now. Alex, this is top priority. I want the search done immediately!"

"Understood, sir!" This time, the sir was serious; Alex jumped into the problem. Within a few minutes, the team was chosen and buried in programming and tracking data. Alex crafted a simulator screen that would monitor and automatically report any directional changes in the many 'stroids traveling through Seven Galaxies sectors.

Tay found the admiral ruminating in his quarters.

"Sir!"

"Yes, Lieutenant?"

"May I interrupt? I have an important topic to discuss."

"Interrupting an old man's ponderings could be a good thing. What is on your mind?"

"It is about something the Nesdian regent said that left me feeling very uneasy, sir."

"Well, spit it out, Tay. I have always taught you to listen to your inner voice."

"Sir, you believe the Nesdians have at least a few warships that escaped our drag, do you not?"

"Most assuredly. They would never risk to the last. They always hold ships in reserve, if for nothing else than transporting the politicians and royals to safety when their gruesome designs fail."

"Suppose, sir, that some of those vessels possessed technology that could change an asteroid's path so that it became a weapon of destruction against our worlds?"

"I believe if the Nesdians had the technology, they would not hesitate to put it into use."

"Sir, Alex believes they do possess the necessary elements. We are tracking all 'stroids that could be manipulated at this time."

"What put you onto this possible Nesdian plan?"

"Xrisen. He said the paths of asteroids could change and that fire would rain down from the stars upon our worlds, fulfilling an ancient Nesdian legend spoken of in their *Book of Prophesy*."

Admiral Gor reflected and then said, "So, this old man missed the clue, and the riddle embodied within the threat."

"Sir, he was slathering, speaking as a fanatic. No wonder you didn't take his words seriously."

"Tay, what you have just imparted would be a worthy excuse for a man with less responsibilities than mine. In my younger years, I would have heard the threat and my mind would not have rested until I had sifted fantasy from fact, as you have just done. I thank you for your diligence. Now do you understand why it is time for my retirement?"

"Admiral, I don't believe for a minute that you would have gone many hours until you sorted the same uneasiness into its proper place."

"Son, you grace me with more aptitude than I have remaining. I am very thankful you have been aboard to assist me in the last years of my command. Had you not joined me as I requested, I fear worse things would have encompassed the Fleet."

"I am honored by your confidence in my abilities," Tay said. "Shall we track these Nesdian ships? I think I will know shortly where they work."

"You have carte blanche, Tay. Do whatever is necessary and keep me informed, day or night."

"Yes, sir!"

Tay returned to the lab. Alex had the tracking team in high gear. All asteroids were plotted and followed. None showed the slightest deviation in their travel paths.

"Do you think we are on a wild goose chase?" Tay asked.

"Tay, we cannot afford to let down our guard. We all believe the Nesdians have some warships in reserve. If they could pull something like this off, it would encourage the remaining Nesdian populous into believing that their wretched *Book of Prophesy* had some form of divine truth imbedded within its riddles. Fanaticism fulfilled could create a wave of hate that would ripple through the entire universe. What did the admiral have to say?"

"Carte blanche."

"You're shitting me?"

"No, absolutely not! The admiral believes the possibility is plausible; he has dedicated any and all Fleet resources to that end."

"Tay, I've been thinking: we could take our newest settlements out of the scope of our most intense search pattern due to lack of a large population base. We could agree that the Nesdians would desire a strategic target, one with billions of potential victims and vast oceans, so that even a smaller asteroid would have devastating impact. This would narrow our search for the Nesdian ships by a factor of ninety-seven percent."

"I agree. They would desire to strike the worlds that would have the greatest death toll, but we cannot disregard the possibilities of them attacking our lesser populated centers."

Alex nodded. "I am not advocating leaving the search to a few sectors. I am only thinking of focusing our most advanced technology on the sectors that would be primary choices for the Nesdian bastards."

"How would you go about determining where to search? Are you speaking of Full Stealth recon drones?"

"Absolutely. We have them spread around, keeping their ears open, yet we have had no data that would warrant us focusing their search on a limited area. If we both believe the Nesdian's plan to manipulate 'stroids that would impact our most populated and vulnerable worlds, we can diminish our search area by over ninety-seven percent. I admit, it's a gamble."

"Do it, Alex!"

Alex looked at Tay. "You want me to redirect all drones?"

"How many are available for use?"

"Full Stealth, there are fourteen close enough to be put into play within the next day and a half, within strategic areas which affect our largest population centers."

"Move all the other drones and focus the search into Nesdia's known sectors. We want to watch and make sure we have destroyed all their armament capabilities. They may still have a few hidden dens. We should keep a close eye on that possibility."

"Just to make sure I understand," said Alex. "We have carte blanche to cover Nesdia's sectors with, say, seven full stealth drones, and to dedicate all the others to the most susceptible targets."

"You've got it, Alex. See it through. I'll run the plan by the admiral and see if he has any further ideas or input."

"Tay."

"Yes?"

"I never thought when I boarded *Independence* that I would have the opportunity to direct one facet of our strategic Intel arsenal, let alone the entire network! Thanks for your confidence."

"You, my friend, have earned it!" Tay walked briskly out of the lab on his way to the admiral.

THIRTY-TWO

VOLTRANS sat at his desk, a clutter of thoughts flooding his mind. With the war won, everyone was ecstatic. Jubilant celebrations were erupting everywhere. Seven Galaxies culture had turned the event into one huge party.

Voltrans was unsettled. It had been too easy, he thought. Surely there were more Nesdian ships out there. Certainly, in the vast reaches of the known and unknown universe, there were many places to hide, dark corners that would remain hidden even to Seven's scans.

His planetary security chief, white-faced in shock, walked in, interrupting Voltran's troubled ruminations. The security chief began stumbling through words, but his broken delivery made little sense.

"Calm yourself, Dadian," Voltrans ordered. "Then spit out whatever it is you are attempting to impart."

"Sir! An asteroid's path changed just moments ago; it is heading straight towards Seven!"

"What do you mean changed?"

"Sir, we have been tracking this particular 'stroid carefully because its path showed it would pass very near to us, although it should have cleared all planets in this sector. As of a few minutes ago, a gentle arc in the 'stroids path placed Seven in harm's way."

"What size is this rock, and how much time before impact?"

"Approximately thirty-six hours, sir. The mass will be planetary fatal upon impact if we cannot split her with the boring drones."

"How many explosive boring drones do we possess on Seven?"

"Twenty-six, sir!"

"That should be more than double what we need."

"Sir, I suggest you key up the screen. All the pertinent info will be at your fingertips. This is not your average 'stroid. We call this category of rock 'mammoth' class. They are rare, yet 'stroids of this size do indeed exist."

Voltrans brought up the screen and let out an uncontrolled gasp. "How could a hurtling asteroid of this magnitude change course in the matter of a few hours?" he asked, searching for a sensible answer.

"I can't say, sir; we are delving into that question as we speak."

"Mobilize eight of the boring drones. I want them on their way within the hour. In the meantime, perhaps we can study the asteroid's character and shape—look for potential weak points, fissures, or cracks. Perhaps we can identify a vulnerable area that would make the drones' work faster."

"Yes, sir. We are gathering everything we can at present; however, there is an envelope of some sort around the 'stroid, which is making it difficult to extract clear pictures of the surface."

"A gas cloud?"

"It seems the only explanation, sir."

"Highly irregular. Aren't they normally free of such envelopes?"

"Normally, yes, sir."

"Give what intel you have, and inform High Command. We will meet in thirty minutes. Red directive under Black!"

"Yes, sir. Red under Black directive."

"You are excused. Thank you for your diligence."

"As always, sir, I am at your service!"

With that, Dadian spun and rushed from Voltran's private office.

Shock waves left him feeling uncertain. He shook off the feeling, knowing that he must keep them from infecting and rooting into his mind. Remembering his intensive studies when in the Academy, he reflected: a dark and dreadful pondering is, without fail, disastrous in the final judgment. Voltrans knew this from textbook study yet had never been placed in a situation where he was forced to keep his mind focused and clear of fear. Checking himself, his posture and demeanor, he put on the brave face of a commander who will not be defeated.

Gathering all available intel and stuffing it quickly into his briefcase, he walked briskly from his office towards Mick's.

Walking in without knocking, Voltrans found his old friend pouring over the same data. "Well, bud, what do you think?"

"Bud, is it?" Micky said, with a crooked grin. "I haven't seen hide nor hair of you in weeks. Now that your ass is between a hard place and a rock, and I do mean that literally, you need old Mick here—you grace me with your wonderful and all-powerful presence."

Voltrans broke into a genuine grin, thinking if any other person of lesser rank on base spoke to him like this, he would put them on ice for a day or two. "You're right, Mick; we need you and all that know-how you're always spouting off about!"

Mick turned serious; the play was over. "Eight won't do. Send ten minimum. I would prefer half of the twenty-six, but it's too risky. We must hold them back as a failsafe. Even if we manage to crack this monster, we may still have to split what's left again."

Voltrans picked up the secure phone and hit a couple of numbers. "Dadian, Voltrans. Send ten, not eight. Copy that?...Yes, ten."

Mick tapped him on the shoulder and asked, "When do they lift?"

Voltrans looked at his watch. "Fifty minutes."

"Volt, get them up now! Here, give me that phone." He jerked it from Voltrans' grip before his commander could object.

"Listen, Dadian, I want those ten boring drones in the air and out of planetary gravity, torqued to maximum velocity, within ten minutes! Do you understand? Here." Handing the phone back to Voltrans, Mick went back to the computer simulator.

"Yes, Dadian, do as he says: ten within ten, torqued to max velocity. Good. I'm counting on you!" Voltrans hung up.

"Let's go!" Mick was on his way out the door.

"Where?" asked Voltrans.

"Listen to me, Volt!" Mick didn't even slow his trot; he simply spoke over his shoulder.

"We're headed to the launch! You realize, if anything goes wrong, you and I will be the ones with our necks on the block. Do you want to trust every life on Seven and your cushy retirement to some snot-nosed kids seein' to this strategic launch?" They rushed down the stairs into the garage and were inside an autocar within a minute. "I mean, they are good," Mick continued. "But I am in charge of this operation. That is why you pay me the big bucks, to solve problems that no one else can. Do you think I'm going to sit in my office hoping all goes well?"

It was a rhetorical question, so Voltrans didn't bother answering as he strapped in.

Mick wove through the low-level traffic so quickly, everything was a blur. Voltrans closed his eyes; he didn't need a heart attack right now, and when Mick drove like this, he was always scared shitless.

They jerked to a stop, and before Voltrans could unbuckle his safety harness, Mick was out of the autocar at a dead run. He disappeared into an unmarked hangar.

Voltrans followed, and by the time he caught up, Mick was already beside the ten drones, checking each for velocity frequency, explosive load, and homing info. Mick looked over the young men who had prepared the drones, took a moment to make eye contact with each, and said curtly, "Good job, men. I see you learned what I taught."

The young men, some not much more than boys, smiled with satisfaction at the abbreviated compliment. Voltrans noticed that they all stood just a little taller.

"Let's get these little jewels up in the air and out into the blackness to meet their nemesis."

Mick pressed a hand to his lips, then placed it on one of the drones, closed his eyes, and appeared to say a short prayer. The young men copied his action. Then, they rolled the boring drones outside, hinged them upright on their launch sleds, and left them standing: ten mechanical soldiers off to war.

"Colby!" Mick said, as the hardened door closed. "Set fire to those little monsters and pray they get to the target safely."

"I have a meeting in nine minutes," Voltrans said. "I need you there, Mick. Good job, men." Voltrans turned and walked back to the autocar.

No sooner had they climbed in than Mick was accelerating. Voltrans was slammed back deep into his seat by the force. Sliding through traffic, Mick barely missed numerous obstructions in their path. Voltrans shut his eyes tightly again and said a few prayers.

His wireless rang. "Yes, Voltrans here. Yes, sir, we are engaged in the problem. No, at this time I do not have odds of success; I will talk with the specialist and call back momentarily."

The caller said, "Thank you," and the line went dead.

Mick looked at Voltrans with raised eyebrows. "Odds of success?"

"The chair of Fifteen would like to know."

"The Ancient just called you personally?"

Voltrans only nodded, saying nothing.

"Look, Volt, it's bad enough that we have this planetary fatal life crisis, but now they want odds?"

"Yes, Micky, odds."

"Shit! How does a guy calculate something like this? It has never been done before. Hell, we don't even know what the rock is made of. She could be solid nickel or steel, and then I'd tell you we are all truly screwed. It's like, stick your head up your ass so you don't see the explosion and just be glad it's someplace warm, if not comfortable. Hell, we got this freaking mammoth rock flyin' at us, threatening everything on the planet with sudden and instantaneous death, and they want odds of success?"

"I know there are variables," Voltrans interjected.

"Variables. I like the way you put that. It sounds as though we're choosing toilet paper at the Super Shopper, not balancing the lives of everyone on planet on the ability of some drones, which, by the way, have limitations as well."

"I know, Mick. Can you give me something?"

"Yeah! Yeah, I'll give it to you, but old Leandra ain't gonna like the answer much."

"Will I?"

"Shit, Volt, I don't like it, but this is how it lays: If the mammoth damn rock *is* a rock, our chances are good, say ninety percent, that we can split the monster. What happens after that, you had better start praying about. When we split it, if we can, provided it is not solid metal of some description, there is no plausible way to use a simulator to determine where the pieces will end up. We have saved sixteen drones because we must split the halves into quarters. If one of those pieces hits an ocean, we've got massive tsunamis like no one in our entire civilization has ever witnessed. If a piece hits land, we've got earthquakes up the ass, hitting nine to fourteen on the scale. If two pieces hit, one in the water and one on land, we have both."

Mick stopped the autocar abruptly. Voltrans could see sweat forming on Micky's brow. "You see, Volt, I think we can break this bastard, but what happens after that is anyone's guess. I would start by evacuating all those on seaboards to high ground, and I mean *high*, preferably above sixteen hundred meters, preferably behind mountain ranges."

"The odds, Mick…I must report them."

"Ninety percent in favor of breaking that bad boy, ninety percent in quartering it, and ninety percent that one or more quarters crash into Seven. Shit, Volt, what are we going to do?"

Voltrans saw clouds in Mick's eyes as he spoke the odds aloud for the first time. The ominous truth penetrated each man's brain.

"Mick, look at me! You have never let me down; you are the best man for this job. That is why I am asking you these difficult questions. You asked me what we are going to do, so I'll tell you straight up! You are going to bust that big bastard into as many little pieces as possible. I will know in my heart whatever happens afterwards that *our* part was done as well as it could have been. I am going to brief High Command on the situation and implement exactly what you just advised: evacuate and prepare for impact. If we are fortunate enough and Seven doesn't take a direct hit, all is well. If Seven is hit, we'll know we did all we could to protect our people. I need to call the chair of Fifteen."

Voltrans took a deep breath and punched a button on the wireless.

"Volt here. This is the way it stands: If the rock is solid metal—we have no idea at this time whether it is—then it can't be broken, not in the remaining time, and our situation is planetary fatal. If it is some form of rock, the odds are ninety percent in favor of us being able to break it in halves and again into quarters. Then there is a ninety percent chance that one or more quarters will impact. We need to evacuate everyone on seaboards to sixteen hundred meters altitude, preferably behind mountain ranges to protect the camps from the sea…. Yes, sir. Thank you, sir. Yes, it was Mick…. I will tell him." Voltrans signed off.

"She asked after you, Mick. It seems she knows you."

"That is unbelievable. How could she know of me?"

"The Ancient gave final approval when I wanted you on staff. Without her okay, you wouldn't have made it. She wishes you good fortune and says that you will be foremost on her mind."

"You're shittin' me."

Voltrans looked at Mick with a seriousness that matched the moment and the crisis at hand. "I would never joke about any of the Fifteen, I assure you."

Voltrans and Mick walked into High Command media center for the scheduled conference. One wall of the large room was taken up mostly with an ultra-high-res vid screen. It was showing a large mass of vapor traveling through space. The vapor cloud changed shape continuously, first looking like a ball and then becoming oblong and tubular.

"What do you make of this, Mick?" one of the officers asked. "We've been unable to get intel photos that would give us clues as to this monster's mass and elemental makeup. We can only pray that it is not a metallic alloy of some form or another. When the drones get closer, their ultrasonic scans will give us the outline and shape, but not much about its composition; however, we will know if she is rock or alloy."

"When will the drones be close enough to achieve some readings?"

"Approximately two hours and twenty minutes, sir."

"Voltrans, this is, of course, your baby. Please update the group on what has happened so far."

"Well, I'll start from the beginning," he said, "in case you have not had time to read the packet. Approximately forty-five minutes ago, we received the first warning that this mammoth asteroid, for some unknown or unexplained reason, began changing course in a broad swinging arc that lined its travel path up with Seven. Since that time, the 'stroid has resumed a path that is as straight as an arrow. If not diverted, it appears from every bit of intel to be aimed at our planet's equatorial center. In other words, a direct hit.

"Mick is in charge of the boring and blasting plan to abate the threat to Seven, so at this time, I transfer the meeting into his capable hands. Mick, would you be so kind as to impart the plan to us in understandable terminology?"

Mick stood up. He appeared to be slightly nervous to Voltrans, who knew the man closely. To the others in the room, Mick was cool and professional.

"Gentlemen, what we have here is a rare mammoth-class asteroid." Mick pointed to the vaporous object shown on screen. "It is unlikely that any of us will see another in our lifetimes. We have known them to exist, yet we have never, in all our years, had the opportunity to view a specimen like this closely. Ten explosive boring drones were launched about twelve minutes ago, torqued to maximum velocity and loaded for bear. It is our intent to send them eight hundred meters below the surface in a staged line, and then to blow this monster in two.

"If we are successful, we will most likely have only one of those halves, the larger of the two, still traveling towards our home. Half of this rock would, in my opinion, still be planetary fatal upon impact. Thus, we will then have reserve drones bore and blow the remaining half in a similar fashion. If good fortune prevails, if the mammoth is not some kind of metal, we should have enough time to accomplish the procedure.

"When the asteroid half is split again, we will be looking at two pieces, rough quarters of the original mass. I don't believe either of these fragments will have enough velocity or mass to be planetary fatal. However, we have never done this before, nor have we suffered a strike of this magnitude. Any questions?"

One young man nodded. "Sir, are you saying that if we are successful in quartering this thing, we could still expect one of the pieces to impact?"

"I will not mince words. The odds are ninety percent that one, possibly two, of the quarters will impact. Also, there is the likelihood of shards and falling fragments. The strike or strikes have the potential to create massive tsunamis. If the pieces hit the oceans, which is probable since our land mass is less than twenty-one percent of planetary surface area. If they strike solid land, they will trigger earthquakes of magnitude nine to fourteen on the scale. The eruption of many dormant and active volcanoes will likely be set off.

"Evacuation to safe areas must be accomplished quickly, and the sooner we begin, the better chance we have of finalizing that directive in a somewhat orderly fashion."

Voltrans spoke. "Gentlemen, the evacuation is beginning in stages. Our military and police are supervising a sectional movement, which is being directed to keep traffic congestion to a minimum. If everyone left at the same time, we would experience gridlock in the air and on surface, which would be catastrophic to the evacuation process. The populace is being educated at this time and being given their windows for safe departure to high ground.

"Let us take a small break at this time. I have had sandwiches and refreshments brought in for everyone. Let's eat and then resume in say fifteen?"

Heads nodded as everyone in the room attempted to assimilate the devastating news.

After the short break, everyone sat down and watched the looming threat as it rushed toward Seven. Some begged leave for short durations, no doubt calling loved ones, making preparations, attending to family and safety combined.

Three hours into the saga, the drones were nearing the target. Their ultrasonic scans would give the group the first clues as to this hurtling object's geological make-up, and hopefully its weaknesses.

A picture came on screen, hazy, as though taken through thick fog or mist. Mick, Voltrans, and the others gasped at the same moment. Against a backdrop image of the mammoth asteroid were two Nesdian battleships, hidden in plain view by the mysterious gaseous vapor that had perplexed everyone.

"What in hell's name?" someone exclaimed.

The enemy ships fired disrupters en mass. A split second later, the picture was nothing but static.

"The drones, Mick?" Voltrans asked, struggling to keep the panic from his voice.

"Destroyed, sir! Every one of the drones have been destroyed!"

The room broke into a shambles, with everyone talking and asking questions at the same time.

Mick crash-landed into his seat. His face was a mask of shock, enmeshed with fear and loathing. It made his countenance frightening to look upon. "The bastards! All along, towing! That explains the mysterious arc when the beast changed course!"

The realization hit everyone in the same instant: this was no errant 'stroid but a weapon of mass destruction, manipulated by a fearsome and brutal enemy motivated by vengeance—a dark grudge held for two centuries.

Mick was the first to speak. "Sir!"

Voltrans shook himself from thought and looked at Mick.

"We have to scramble everything we've got, get out there, and not rest until Nesdian blood is splattered through space. We can't do anything about the 'stroid until we take out those two ships. We have sixteen boring drones left. It may be enough, but we cannot risk one more to these bastards." Mick motioned to the static-filled screen.

A technician booted up wide space view. The gas cloud was gone, evidently dispersed by the enemy's disrupter blasts. They could see them clearly: two full-dress Nesdian battleships towing the mammoth asteroid. The room fell silent. The only sound was the sharp intake of breaths as all in the room took in the scene for the first time.

Voltrans picked up a phone, punched a number, and said, "This is Volt! Scramble anything we've got that can carry payload the distance; no mercy, caution to the wind. Search and destroy the Nesdian ships at all costs. Spearhead formation, lapped shielding, seven squadrons, seven angles of attack! Understood? I will be sending the signed order momentarily. Get the plan rolling, Dadian, and waste not a second!"

Voltrans stroked a keyboard deftly. A print page jumped from the machine. He cast his scrawl below the print and motioned for a runner. "Take this to Dadian. Place it in his hands, wait for him to read it, get his acknowledgement, and then bring the paper back to me."

The young man spun and was out the door in a blur.

Complete silence covered the room. All were attempting to absorb what had just been witnessed. The threat to Seven, the heart and soul of their culture, was severe. No one in the room would have dreamed, just a few short hours before, that the life of their entire planet could be snuffed out so easily. In school, all had been taught that the brutal warring and fanatically religious clans of Nesdia had been relegated to reservation planets and were no longer a threat, just a distant and very unpleasant memory.

Now, here were the Nesdian's ships, an ancient nightmare from the past, towing an asteroid the size of a small moon and threatening a fatal planetary impact upon Seven. The weapon was locked and loaded, and bearing down upon utopian life at ever-increasing velocity.

Voltrans broke the silence. "Mick, once the Nesdian ships are destroyed, which I might add is a foregone conclusion, how long will it take the explosive drones to land and penetrate deep enough to blow this monster into two pieces?"

"Sir, we just received information that shows the asteroid is made of rock, not an alloy of some form or another. The drones are our best in metallurgical engineering. We can expect two hundred fifty meters in depth per hour."

"Your original estimate was that we needed the drones to reach at least eight hundred fifty meters deep before detonation. Is that still your recommendation?"

"Sir, I would prefer to bore twelve hundred meters, but the drones will falter. Their cutting bits would become dulled between six-fifty and eight hundred meters. During the time it would take to go from six-fifty to eight hundred, there would be a forty percent mortality rate. I believe we should ignite them at six-fifty, sir."

Voltrans nodded. "Six-fifty it will be."

"Once our fighters have destroyed the Nesdian warships, the drones must land immediately and begin their work."

"Yes sir! I will time it so."

Several hours would pass before the Seven's attack force arrived. The mammoth was gaining speed with every hour that passed, hurtling towards Seven.

Eyes in the command center flashed to the screen, hands fidgeted; everyone in the room wondered at one time or another whether the mission would be successful. Did the Nesdian's possess some unknown advantage that would render Seven's desperate bid impotent?

Some could be seen praying to the god of their individual faith. In this room were a group of men and women not denied the freedom to follow the spiritual path of their choice; they were unfettered by ridicule, fear, or a blanket of cookie cutter dogma applied to an entire culture. Seven Galaxies' foundation was that all people of different beliefs could unite as one consciousness, believing in the right of their brothers and sisters to choose their spiritual preference. Strength was gained from a unified focus, which was their shared home, regardless of their societies' vast and varied religious beliefs.

Mick paced, sometimes picking up the phone and speaking in calm, quiet, and deliberate tones. He instilled in the group a belief that they would prevail—that the mammoth would be blown, and Seven would survive.

The screen showing the time left until engagement ticked away—mere minutes were left.

A technical analyst monitoring the sensor probes spoke. "Gentlemen, the Nesdian ships are moments from the point of our offense. They have activated no shielding. All energy aboard the two vessels is apparently dedicated to drive systems only."

"You mean they don't intend to protect themselves—to fight?" Voltrans asked. His disbelief was evident in the tone of his voice.

"Sir, they obviously realize the futility in attempting to defend against our massive offense. They prefer, it seems, to dedicate all energy resources towards increasing the mammoth's speed. They are obviously betting that time will run out for Seven, and that any miniscule velocity increase in the mammoth's speed will increase their odds of success. For the record, that is my official analysis of the situation, sir."

Voltrans spoke again. "We should all have realized, from the beginning, this is a suicide mission."

Someone gasped. "Freakin' fanatics!"

All eyes were on the screen as Seven's spearhead formations closed the gap. Four separate attack groups launched into firing. Streams of brightness filled the screen as hundreds of glowing lines streaked towards the oncoming enemy vessels. There was a massive flash of blinding light as the Nesdian ships were destroyed. Nervous cheers rose from the room as everyone rejoiced in the small, forgone conclusion.

Mick spoke next. "Sir, if I may have your ear."

"Speak your thoughts to the group, Mick; we all deserve the opportunity to digest any ideas you have."

"Sir, we didn't expect the Nesdians to go down without a fight. We still have several hundred heavily armed craft; we haven't lost one. Do you see the narrow spot on the asteroid? It looks a bit like a waistline?"

"Certainly."

"I believe we should focus all onboard firepower to that section and soften it, so when the drones arrive they will have a head start. If we concentrate the impacts on one side of the mammoth, the inertia of the detonations should have a small influence on the 'stroids trajectory. Perhaps we can change it enough so the thing is no longer heading for a direct hit but more of a glancing blow. Then, when she is split, the larger of the two halves should be well outside Seven's atmosphere and will pose no threat. We will then only have the smaller piece to deal with."

"Let's make it happen! Any objections?"

The room was silent.

"Mick, mark on the screen the spots you want targeted, and we will dump every last charge we have into those locations."

Mick quickly placed four strategic dots on the screen.

The technician spoke. "Drones fifteen minutes out."

"Direct all fire towards Mick's chosen targets, and let loose!" Voltrans commanded.

The screen lit again with the blinding barrage.

"Darken screen so we can watch."

The tech did so. All could see a vague outline of the mammoth being pounded relentlessly. The firing continued for nearly seven minutes.

Voltrans spoke again. "Signal them to come home immediately, re-arm, and head out towards the target again."

Mick asked, "Is there enough time, sir?"

"Yes, it appears we can get them back to the re-supply platforms. If things go well, they can meet this bastard for one more hot date."

"If they are ready when we quarter the small half, the ships could then target the most threatening chunks left and perhaps minimize the force of impact, or, with good fortune, remove the threat completely."

Voltrans nodded. "Sounds good, Mick. We will hold them until all boring drones have been expended. The offensive force will become our last line of defense."

The tech spoke again. "Boring drones four minutes out, sir. Target points?"

Mick searched for the asteroid on screen and then set ten dots in a perfect line between the craters of immense depth and breadth that had been created by the fleet's efforts. "Depth before ignition, six hundred fifty meters. All drones timed to ignite simultaneously. Am I clear?"

"Yes, sir. Six hundred fifty meters; simultaneous ignition. Go!"

It was now a waiting game. The drones were estimated to arrive at their target depth within two to three hours; until then, there was not much to do.

All watched as the minute machines on screen approached the surface of the hurtling rock. Anchoring in like ticks on a dog, they went to work. Moments later, they were unseen, already boring deep beneath the surface.

THIRTY-THREE

THE Nesdian commander of the battle ship *Xeries Eight* felt the concussions of the first tracers breaking the ship's envelope. In that nanosecond before his ship disintegrated into uncountable shreds and vapors, streaming all directions into space, he thought, *I come! Prepare my kingdom!*

Floating, weightless as it were, the Nesdian's soul expected bright light, jewels, and unheralded vistas of a kingdom bought with the ultimate sacrifice. Instead, there was only a passageway, a tunnel of sorts, which was ill-lit and damp. His spirit body became heavy, settling down at the cavernous mouth of the eerie passageway. Behind him was nothing but a deep precipice; fear of the unknown unbalanced him. He lunged forward so as not to fall into the blackness, which swept into a bottomless abyss.

He went forward cautiously, for no other avenue presented itself. Slipping upon the moist, slimy footing, he fell—not once but repeatedly, bruising his hopeful body on jagged, protruding obstacles.

Light was near nonexistent. He could not see his footing as he tread cautiously on, feeling his way, thinking, *This must be some final test of bravery and faith.* He continued. He fell again. He had lost count of his pain-filled, stumbling crashes. Sliding down a dark, slippery, and jagged slope, he felt his skin being shredded. At last, he tumbled down a black and rugged embankment. He landed, broken in many places: a miserable sobbing heap. Pain shot through his tortured ethereal body, weakening his sturdy resolve. But his fanatical faith held, giving him strength. Did not the *Book of Prophesy* promise his kingdom and his virgins if he paid the ultimate sacrifice, his life, to fulfill its prophesies?

He prayed out loud, a desperate quaking attempt to reach the god he had followed into this dreadful, frightening space.

The only sound in the blackness was the echoing of his desperate pleas—unheard.

THIRTY-FOUR

Excitement permeated the room. The asteroid had been split. Mick, furiously attempting a simulation on his computer, ran through the complex scenarios and possibilities of successfully breaking the monster again and saving Seven's people from certain annihilation. Mick was not in a celebratory mood. Fingers flying deftly on the keyboard, he attempted to locate the 'stroids weakest point and then calculate the speed, plot, and potential impact zones. His face was etched into a mask of fear as he worked against time.

The last wave of boring drones would arrive momentarily. If the second break were unsuccessful, human life on Seven would be extinguished—if not directly from impact, then in a new ice age that would quickly grip the planet. The dust and debris cloud caused by catastrophic impact of such magnitude would block sunlight for years to come, effectively dropping Seven's climate threshold into sub-zero freezing temperatures planet-wide.

The room quickly fell silent as Mick's fingers coaxed scenarios from the electronic genius at his command.

Voltrans, although not wanting to disturb him, felt compelled to ask, "Well, Mick, how does it look?"

"Not good, Volt."

"Elaborate. All in the room are cleared to hear this news. Do you have anything concrete?" Voltrans asked. "Anything that would play out accurately?"

"Right now, I have twenty-one scenarios. I'm weeding out the less probable and attempting to narrow the choices." Mick looked up from the screen, speaking softly so the others could not hear.

Voltrans leaned in closer to understand the message.

"You, my friend, are not helping. Give me some space, for God's sake, and I'll let you all know what I come up with when I have something sensible!" Not looking for a reaction or response, Mick focused his attention back where it had been before the interruption.

The energy in the room was taut with heightened emotion. Furtive glances cast back and forth between each person. Moments ago, they had been cheering. Now, all eyes were upon Mick, their magician, as he caressed his beloved keyboard, attempting to extract an answer that all in the room prayed would be positive.

"We have it! By God's hairy balls, we have it!"

"Mick! The news is good!?"

"As good as could be expected. Look, Volt," he said, pointing to the screen. "This bastard of a rock is dead set on taking out a piece or two of our asses, but if all threads out according to the simulator, those pieces will be small...very small, and insignificant, when stacked against the loss of life planet wide."

"What are you saying, Mick?"

"I'm saying it looks like the reserve drones will blast her in half once more, with one of the quarters shearing away and missing Seven completely. We will be looking at an impact less than twenty percent of the entire asteroid's original mass. It ain't going to be pretty, but Seven will survive, if these simulations work out in real time as they have on screen."

"What if we sent the attack force in one more time?"

"Where are they, and when could they engage the beast?"

"Looks like just before impact."

"How close to impact?"

"Very close."

"Those ships can't sustain themselves in G-force; they are space only marauders, not atmospheric fighters."

"But if we could bust off the corners, soften the thing. Maybe it would disintegrate from the heat of atmospheric friction on its way down."

"Volt, there is no doubt the attack force could lessen the mass of this thing somewhat. Is it worth the risk? The loss of so many lives, not to mention the ships? Is the cost worth the value? I can't say, Volt," he said, shaking his head. "These are our men we're talking about! To hell with the ships, what about the men? What about their mourning families?"

"Listen, Mick: I know these pilots. Each and every one would sacrifice themselves without second thoughts if they could make a difference—if their efforts would save lives on planet! By choosing careers in service to Seven, we have sworn that oath: our lives if necessary to protect our home. Mick, we have to weigh losses. Every megaton sheared off this hurtling stone could save tens of thousands of lives on planet. I must make the decision. I need to know if you believe one more run at this bastard would lessen the damage to Seven and our people."

"Absolutely," Mick said. "Every megaton shorn from the mass would drastically minimize damage within the impact zone, with many small shards being preferable to one large mass."

Voltrans turned, walked to his station, picked up a phone, and said. "Dadian, everyone loaded to the gunnels. No returns until everything is dumped on the final target after the second split, do you understand? Yes, I know there will be losses. Yes, I believe it worth the risk. I take full responsibility. I will send the written order momentarily."

Once again, the orders were printed and sent by runner with instructions to obtain Dadian's signed acknowledgement and then return the original written order to Voltrans.

Voltrans walked briskly from the command center towards his private office. Upon entering the seclusion afforded by his closed door, he fell to his knees.

"You know, I've never been much for praying," he said aloud, but softly. "I always felt I'd save it for something really important. This *is* important: our families, our children, the planet of our birth, the centerpiece of Seven Galaxies. If you're listening, you know what kind of predicament we're in. Please help us. Please, for mercy's sake; protect this planet so dear to us and our families. Allow us to survive. Place your hand on these pilots, the young soldiers that I've sent hurtling towards near certain death, hoping they can make a difference. I have no way of knowing whether the cost is worth the gain, yet I have made the desperate choice. Forgive me, please, if I'm wrong. Allow their families to understand. I only gave the order in an attempt to protect them. Please don't turn away from us now. Give us your shoulder. Let us take shelter in the lee of your strength and benevolence. Protect us, I pray for your mercy and love, for we all love you."

Tears flowed; his heart was fearful. In desperation, he humbled himself, reaching out as a child reaches toward a parent for a hand held out in protection. Voltrans was that child, looking for a power greater than all Seven Galaxies possessed, a Force that could miraculously intervene and allow Seven and all upon her to breathe on.

THIRTY-FIVE

I Am That I Am observed conflict, brutality, hope, religious zealotry, tolerance, brotherly love, and fearless sacrifice: a planetary culture whose resounding theme and group consciousness had been nurtured throughout three millenniums.

In a hyper self-critical moment, I Am That I Am's combined consciousness reached across the vastness of Deep Space, touching ethereally a tumbling torrent of emotions and desperate pleas emanating in many faiths from Seven Galaxies Seven. While not fully comprehending the emotional plethora, in a twinge of rare emotion long ago lost, I Am That I am desired ongoing and future understanding of the baffling sentient emanations shrieking from Seven this moment and travelling, through time and space.

THIRTY-SIX

ABOARD *Independence*, Tay stormed towards Admiral Gor's personal quarters. He knocked and then rushed in without waiting for the admiral's welcome. "Sir!" he said, breathless from the run.

"Yes, son? What is it?"

"Sir, for some reason neither Alex nor I understand, *Independence*'s speed just tripled!"

"Tay, what are you saying?"

"I'm saying, sir, that if our current velocity holds, we will arrive back at Seven moments before the mammoth 'stroid impacts the planet."

The admiral catapulted from his chair. "You are serious?" he said, confused.

"Absolutely! Alex and I can find no plausible explanation for the drastic increase in velocity. Some unexplained force is pushing us towards Seven, sir, as if someone or something wants us there at impact!"

"Could it be Duhcat somehow helping us?" Without giving Tay time to answer, the admiral continued, excited. "Tay, if we can make it in time, before impact, we can help! Alert the gun crews; tell them 'ice breaker.' This is no drill, son; we are going to unleash on that rock a show of firepower unprecedented in our history. Let's give those Nesdian bastard's weapon a real Seven Galaxies welcome!"

"Yes, sir, I will make it so!" Tay looked at his grandfather. Gone was the tired look. A challenge faced the warrior, and the old man was rising to meet it, salivating for the chance to gain one more victory over a ruthless and fanatical enemy—one more chance to open his umbrella of protection over the people he had loved and guarded his entire adult life.

THIRTY-SEVEN

VOLTRANS checked his appearance in the mirror, wiped the traces of tears from his eyes, straightened his posture, and then walked from his office back to the command center. Entering the bustling room, he went straight to Mick. "How's it looking?"

"The second set of boring drones have landed and will be at detonation depth in a few more minutes."

The room fell silent. Everyone waited upon the outcome, most saying silent prayers in varying faiths.

A few minutes later, the tech announced that the drones were at depth.

"Detonate now!" Voltrans gave the command, an order that could save all the life on the planet from certain destruction.

They watched the blast. Plumes of debris shot from the bored tunnels the drones had created straight towards the asteroid's core. In the same nano, the asteroid broke in two pieces. The smaller of the two catapulted rapidly away while the larger kept its trajectory, heading dead towards Seven.

Again, cheers went up. The second split had been successful. Volt looked to Mick. "Prognosis, Mick?"

"Give me a moment, Volt." Mick's fingers flew on the keypad, coaxing out the answer to a question that was reverberating through every mind in the room. "What we have here is approximately twenty-nine point eight percent of the original asteroid's mass. That's roughly ten percent more than our previous simulator calculation. We've done well. We better all pray it's enough."

Mick fell silent, letting everyone take in the ominous meaning: a crude yet effective weapon of death was hurtling towards their home. There wasn't much more that could be done. There were no more explosive boring drones.

Volt looked at Mick, seeing the frustration and fear, the disheveled hair and dark circles of stress beneath eyes not normally so troubled.

"Everyone!" Volt began with authority and confidence, exuding leadership and calm control. "We have managed success with this man's guidance and knowledge." Volt placed a hand on his friend's shoulder. "Let's give him a hand and show how thankful we all are for his irreplaceable assistance." The room broke into applause. Hoots, yips, and shrieks filled the air. The crowd swarmed Mick, shaking his hands, ruffling his hair. The women embraced him, some kissing him. Several of the men embraced him as well.

When the excitement settled, Mick looked healed. The frustration was gone, and his old confidence had returned.

The monster 'stroid had not broken the man, thought Volt. The man, his best friend, had broken the mammoth rock instead.

"All right, Mick, we need to know where to hit this bastard with our last offensive. Most of the space fighters will be in range before dangerous gravitational pull will be a factor. We will continue firing on the rock until it enters Seven's atmosphere. At that time, a barrage from the planet will be released, one final bid at shattering it. We need speed, trajectory, and an impact-countdown clock. We also need worst- and best-case estimates of the damage that could be caused by the impact. I will be formulating a brief report and forwarding it to the Dome. Let's get it done!"

A buzz in the room began and then increased. Volt watched. It was like a concert, he thought—a concert of determined human emotion, knowledge, and love, interlaced with digital brains to assist and speed the process. Voltrans sat down and began hammering into a keypad the abbreviated report the Dome of Wisdom would soon receive.

THIRTY-EIGHT

Seven squadrons received the news. They had been flying over eighteen hours straight without rest. Now the hammer dropped on all pilots: unless they could reload, regroup, and attack the remnant of the mammoth once more, all life on Seven could be lost. All the men had families and friends on-planet. Once the details of the final mission were laid out, all knew how desperate the situation had become. They were being asked to fly, if necessary, into Seven's gravity, pursuing the hurtling threat until their payloads were completely unleashed.

Each and every pilot looked at their timepiece, checking their velocity and the klicks to the reload platform, calculating where in the line of attack they would fall. Some would not return. Those late in being reloaded would be last to strike, and they would be sucked towards Seven like water down a drain. The ships had not been built to withstand that sort of gravitational pull.

Throttles forward, propulsion screaming past the safe redline, each pilot streaked forward, fighting against time to survive the mission. Those in the tail end bit their lips, sucked air, and prayed for a miracle, a divine gift that would let their beloved planet live and for them to be able to see it again, to see it as it had been in their youths.

All pilots were offered the chance to walk away without shame. There would be fresh replacement volunteer pilots standing by at the reload platform to slip into the warm seat of any who did not care to continue. Every mind considered the opportunity to step from the fray onto the sidelines, but not one of the nearly exhausted flight crew took the offer. All would see it to its end; none would back away from this challenge.

Many in front said prayers for their brothers behind. Those in the rear said prayers for themselves and the families they would likely never see again. Each screaming ship and pilot longed to chip just a piece, a fraction, off the asteroid—to know that no matter what happened in the end, they had personally made a difference.

All of Seven Galaxies watched. None could imagine the destruction that would soon rain upon the cultural, spiritual, and governmental center of their society. In desperation, men and ships were to be sacrificed. Families who had loved ones flying the mission prayed silently as they watched the drama unfold.

Then *Independence* appeared, flashing brilliantly into Seven's orbit, to the utter amazement of all. It was a fantastic, glistening example of Seven Galaxies' strength and firepower.

News media outlets announced the almost magical appearance of Admiral Gor's ships, and billions of hearts leapt. Their Admiral, the guardian and protector of their vast civilization, had somehow materialized when hope for his help had been dashed by all previous reports.

Many left the vid screens to which they had been glued and ran outside to watch the giant rock break up. They needed to see the final show without a screen, to look destruction in the eye, to face the enemy's desperate and final weapon in utter defiance.

Expectation seized every soul. They wanted to see the blinding firepower unleashed from Seven's most formidable piece of technology in the arsenal. None were immune to the excitement, the wonder, doubt, and fear. All prayed TyGor, the legendary protector of all Seven Galaxies, could accomplish an impossible feat once more.

The night sky lit, flashing multicolored streams as *Independence*'s fury was unleashed. It was as if the sun had risen during the black of night to illuminate a scene for everyone observing. Countless eyes squinted against the brilliant show.

Everyone had been prepared. The evacuation from lower altitudes was complete. All minds, from child to ancient, feared the Nesdian's weapon and what destruction would emanate from the asteroid's impact.

But now TyGor was here. Within each awestruck heart leapt a prayer for his power, his intellect, his ability to conquer the giant, unfeeling stone cast at them by a hateful and ultimately merciless enemy.

A dark, uneven shadow appeared in the center of the brilliant light that illuminated an unforgettable night. For a nano, it became larger, then the shadow split into fragments. Two large pieces remained. The rest flew elliptically away from *Independence*'s massive barrage. The night sky darkened again. Each watching set of eyes would remember till their dying day, red-hot rock raining in the ominous dark of night.

Smaller shards took out city blocks. Others sizzled into oceans and then exploded after being dowsed in frigid waters, creating concentric rings of massive tsunamis that raced for multiple shores. Many hit land, creating pockets in the earth and sending skyward great dust clouds that streamed in all directions. The largest chunk hit the Dome of Wisdom, and the structure collapsed in upon itself. The massive complex moaned as columns tumbled, roofing caved in, walls broke, crumbling into pieces.

All upon Seven knew the Fifteen and their support group could not have lived through the massive impact. Those respecting the Domes unparalleled importance, spiritual guidance, and leadership collapsed wherever they stood. Knees were bloodied as desperate prayers were uttered. No one knew who would govern the vastness of Seven Galaxies in their future.

THIRTY-NINE

A TALL, slim man with steely grey eyes watched the drama and destruction from a hardened bunker buried deep within a mountainside. The protected haven was reserved for top echelons of government personnel.

Instead of being dismayed by the Dome of Wisdom's destruction, his lean, wolf-like face broke into a large grin. His greedy, twisted mind calculated, pondering the vacuum of power created by the 'stroids impact. The Fifteen could not possibly have survived, Ventras thought darkly. No longer would they be the bit in his mouth, directing, controlling, and reining in his lust for power and wealth.

FORTY

The command center took a direct hit. None chose to run and take shelter in the hardened underground bunker. All who had fought the rock wished to stare it in the eye in those final moments.

Mick was buried under rubble, and others were injured when a massive steel beam had sheared and given way directly above Mick's workstation.

Voltrans staggered through the debris. Clouds of dust filled the air, choking his breath and clouding his vision. *I have to find Mick!* he thought in anguish. Disoriented, he searched desperately for his friend. The building had been broken into a scattered shambles. Momentarily, just as the dust began to settle and he began to regain his bearings amidst the devastating damage, Voltrans saw a hand, with the watch he had given Mick years before on the wrist. Scrambling over wreckage strewn about the floor, he attempted to reach the hand. "Mick! For God's sake, Mick? Can you hear me?"

No voice responded, but a finger twitched.

"Here! Help me here!" Volt waved his arms, attempting to alert the others who were wandering around the rubble, dazed and stumbling over the wreckage.

Before anyone had reached his side, he was next to Mick, taking the hand and feeling for a pulse. The thumpety-thump of his friend's weak heartbeat seemed to pound throughout his own body. He began frantically pawing at the wreckage covering him.

"I'm here, Mick! We'll get you out. Just hold on! Do you hear me? Hold on!"

Uncovering the fallen form, Volt saw a massive steel beam that had once supported the structure's roof lying across Mick's legs. Blood was squirting, spraying the beam with every beat of the heart. Voltrans grabbed his friend's arms and pulled, attempting to free him from the wreckage. He fought against shock when Mick's fallen form slid free easily, his legs still beneath the massive steel beam that had shorn clean his legs from his body; like a cleaver, it had cut them completely through.

Voltrans screamed at the top of his lungs, "Medic! Medic!" He stripped his belt from the waist and applied it as a tourniquet above the missing limb. When the others arrived, he quickly borrowed another belt and staunched the flow of blood from the other side.

Mick's eyes fluttered open weakly, and he smiled, seeing his friend. "We blew the shit out of those Nesdian bastard's rock, didn't we, Volt?"

"Yeah, old buddy, we sure as hell did!" Voltrans said, not showing anything but happiness to his severely wounded brother.

FORTY-ONE

THIRTY-SEVEN space fighters and pilots were in free fall. Seven's atmospheric friction had heated the shells of their spacecraft to near red-hot. Not one of the men and women who had willingly flown into certain death gravity had a chute. They were space pilots and ships, chasing an organic enemy that threatened their home into forbidden territory. No one had foreseen a mission of this importance or of such a bizarre nature: who could have known? Falling to their gruesome deaths, being cooked like sausage in a red-hot skillet, each pilot thought of their loved ones, their beautiful planet, and the lives that had been spared for as long as they were conscious. All wished to live yet knew the inherent hopelessness of their situation.

Aboard *Independence,* Admiral Gor, Alex, and Tay, along with the other crew members, watched the huge chunk of the mammoth 'stroid, which was hurtling towards impact on Seven, shatter into hundreds of pieces. Cheers and catcalls sounded.

Alex was busy at one of his screens. "Sir! We have thirty-seven space fighters and their pilots in gravity free fall. In moments, they will be cooked alive."

"Can you pull them out, Alex?"

"I'm not sure, sir! Their speed, the heat, the scattering of their ships…I'm trying, sir, but it's complicated."

Gor walked up and placed a hand on Alex's shoulder. "Son, if anyone I know can pull them out, it's you. Settle your thoughts and emotions, calmly solve the problems, and make this happen!"

Gor strode to his command seat and settled in, closing his eyes. All wondered where he was going and what he was asking, for he had momentarily left them, even while seated amongst his crew on the bridge.

"I've got a lock on them, all but one, sir!"

"Accelerate now! Track and pull the last man when you can!"

Alex bent closer to the screen, its picture reflecting in his glasses. Tay walked up beside him.

"One more, Alex. You can lock on him, I *know* you can."

The target showed as a brief flash on screen, and Alex locked on and then accelerated. "We got him, sir!"

"No, son; *you* got him! Let's all go down to the transfer deck and greet our living heroes. Get the EMT's there, ASAP!" Gor walked over the Alex.

"Alex, words are not appropriate. Just know as long as you live, and in all of your hearts, that I am deeply appreciative of *all* each and every one of *my* crew has done!"

Stepping between Alex and Tay, Admiral Gor put an arm over the shoulder of each in fatherly affection. "Well done! Utterly fantastic! We totally kicked those fanatical

Nesdian's asses!" Gor was overtaken by joy: the uplifting wave of euphoria a commander receives when a decisive confrontation is over; he had directed the victory, and his people had reached safety.

The admiral began laughing like Tay had not seen him do since the day so long ago on the cliff-top, when Tay sat looking over the valley of their birth—the day Gor had asked his beloved grandson to join him on a journey through the stars, entering space and the unknown; just as intrepid, fearless souls had throughout the eons of time past.

In hours, they would be on a planet beloved, and then home in their valley. Tay thought of his mother, and of Shadow's resting place by the river, then of Zuzahna in the ship's brig—and the yearning she created deep inside every time she was close. Tay vowed silently to see she was soon set free.

FORTY-TWO

I Am That I Am watched the destruction religious fanaticism had caused to Nesdia and Seven Galaxies. The two cultures had lost much. Spiritual tolerance undoubtedly spoke in the outcome, for the fanatical and sectarian Nesdian culture lay in ruins. The most spiritually awakened of the opposing had not hesitated to annihilate their enemy.

Interesting that a culture filled with love could be so extraordinarily violent when it thought it necessary to its survival. Even in the teachings of love, selflessness, and generosity, there still prevailed the primal instinct to protect a beloved home and all that it sheltered.

I Am That I Am melded previous understanding of Seven Galaxies Culture within this new light.

FORTY-THREE

Ventras was ecstatic. Instead of mourning the dead and being shattered psychologically by the asteroid's devastating impact, he was walking on air. The Fifteen were gone. The power vacuum created by their absence would take little manipulation to fill. Ventras was chair of the twelve special legislators, the highest position in Seven Galaxies' administrative government. With the Fifteen presumed dead beneath the Dome's rubble, taking control of Seven Galaxies' government would be a simple matter.

All twelve legislators had taken refuge from the incoming asteroid in a hardened military bunker deep inside a mountain. The facility was at a high enough altitude to be safe from the sweeping tidal waves, which were still inundating the coastal areas and running far inland on lower ground.

Gathering the group of twelve for an impromptu meeting in an intrusion free room, Ventras laid out his vision.

"Friends, we are here to organize a new administrative system for Seven Galaxies. With the tragic death of the Fifteen echoing painfully in our minds, we must take charge. We are all the people have. We must come to their aid.

"Soon there will be humanitarian assistance pouring in from all parts of our vast civilization. People across the expanses of Seven Galaxies will dig deep to help rebuild the centerpiece of our culture. Due to the extraordinary distances between here and other planets, this benevolent help will be in the form of credits to speed rebuilding. We are the stewards of this immense fortune. We have been placed in charge. If we play this disaster right, each and every one of us in this room will be rich beyond our wildest dreams. Nothing and no one must stand in our way."

Ventras risked much speaking these sentiments. The planet was in the throes of disaster. In the mayhem, anything might happen. His tack would single out the moralists in the room. They would be easily known once they made their positions clear to the rest of the group.

"All in this room must swear a bond," he said. "We must stick together, for there will be others who will wish to strip us of this right, this endowment. At any cost, we must make sure this golden opportunity does not pass us by."

Others in the room murmured among themselves. Ventras watched them closely for ones that would be trouble.

Verdanse, a woman who had a long track record of benevolence and honesty, spoke first. "Ventras, what are you saying? What do you mean we will be richer than our wildest dreams?"

Verdanse had never liked the grasping, overreaching Ventras. Unfortunately, most of her fellows in the special legislative hall were similar to him: slimy, greedy, dirty politicians who had been cookie-cutter stamped out since the dawning of time.

She had entered politics as a sheltered young woman, who believed she could make a difference. Fortunately, she had been elected from one of the largest population groupings. Many of her constituents were extraordinary examples of wealth coupled tightly with morality. They were people like herself, who longed to maintain the purity of Seven Galaxies. She had powerful friends and had been well protected from darker forces in government—up until this point.

Ventras shifted his eyes quickly around the room, taking in the reactions from others he knew to be in his camp. "I was simply saying that we should be *well* rewarded for the extraordinary work that will be needed to accomplish the rebuilding. All of us will have to work grueling hours above and beyond the call of duty and should be compensated for our efforts."

Ventras, like most conniving, crooked people, thought everyone was susceptible to the lure of great wealth and power. He had stuffed his foot far down his throat with regards to Verdanse, yet this conversation would place her on one side or the other.

"Ventras, we *are* well compensated," she said. "It is our duty based on our oath of office to serve the people, protect them, and provide for their needs in times of crisis. There is nothing in the charter that would allow extra compensation for overtime. Nor can any of us construe that out of this disaster we should line our pockets extraordinarily. As chair of the budget committee, all reconstruction project budgets will be reviewed by me and by an independent forensic accounting team of my choosing, as stipulated in the charter. I will be watching this humanitarian aid, as you called it, through a very clean and powerful magnifying glass."

Furtive glances skirted the room. Her opinion seemed to be the minority.

Ventras recovered graciously. "Perhaps, Verdanse, I was overtaken by the magnitude of the tragedy before us. Please forgive me if I sounded like I was more concerned for our own well being than for the public interest." Ventras imagined a time in the very near future when he would find Verdanse alone, with no one near to hear her muffled cries. He could dispose of her and the constant thorn she twisted into his side. With Verdanse out of the way, everything would go smoothly, according to his original plan.

Ventras, while smiling outwardly, thought of how the disappearance of a politician of such strategic importance would be investigated with vengeance in normal times, but in the chaos of this time, few would think much of her going missing. The Political Security Team had their hands overfull with the devastation already. Verdanse was unprotected, vunerably naked without her normal veil of protection. She stood alone.

FORTY-FOUR

INDEPENDENCE arrived back at Seven Galaxies Seven to an outpouring of gratitude. The asteroid impact had devastated large areas of the seaboards and caused earthquakes of great magnitude as well, but the people and politicians greeted the admiral and crew as if the planet was fine, and the ceremonial commendations for the crew took several hours.

A banquet served in honor of the *Independence* crew and of the swift defeat of Nesdia was attended by many prestigious persons of wealth, military, and political pomp. Tay could tell the admiral had tired of flattery early in the evening. Not renowned for his diplomatic skills, and exercising a bit of impatience with the Gala, he brought the discussion at dinner back to business and away from the flowery compliments and frivolous talk.

"We have much work to do," he stated. "In particular the rebuilding of cities, roads, and water systems. The tsunamis decimated seaports as well as the fishing industry. We must organize and implement a plan that covers the direst necessities first and works efficiently to that end."

All at the table nodded ascent or verbalized it.

Looking at Ventras, who was impromptu leader since the Dome of Wisdom had been leveled, Gor asked, "What provisions have been made to clear the wreckage of the Dome and to rebuild it?"

Ventras, all smiles during the regalia, now turned a sour look towards the admiral. "Surely, Admiral, we have many more important projects in front of us than rebuilding a haven to sequester some of our greatest thinkers from public view. I move that we go forward with the government as it exists now; things seem to be running smoothly. After all, the Fifteen at the Dome were more spiritual leaders than actual administrators of the people's affairs."

Tay saw the admiral redden slightly. The old man cleared his throat and said bluntly, "You, Ventras, would surely like to see the interim government remain in power, for you are its appointed head. However, the authority given to the legislative side of Seven Galaxies' government has, for over two hundred years, *always* been held in check by the Fifteen. Do you propose that we alter what has worked so well and brought our civilization out from the darkness of the Twenty-Seven Years War into a future that has been incomparable to any known society before us?"

It was Ventras' turn to shade darker. He cleared his throat, obviously gaining time to think. "Surely, Admiral, you do not intend on rebuilding the Dome? Who would fill it? The Fifteen were all killed in the destruction. Who could possibly replace them?"

"Ventras, with all respect due, you have not answered my question, only switched and asked me one instead."

Ventras looked uncomfortable. He fidgeted with his napkin, wiping his lips before speaking. Small beads of perspiration could be seen forming on his forehead. "Admiral, if you believe that clearing the wreckage and rebuilding the Dome is so important, perhaps you could spearhead the work. We are much too busy with other projects to tackle one that would seem a vain attempt to regain something I believe lost forever."

"Ventras, what you believe on this particular subject is not important," Gor said, frowning. "What the people believe is. I will speak to them tomorrow."

"How do you propose to accomplish that?" asked Ventras, suspicious.

"I have already made the necessary arrangements. Do not worry your head about the matter." With that, Gor fell silent.

Tay looked at Ventras, noticing that the man's eyes had narrowed. His perspiration was evident to all who cared enough to notice. Ventras was seething. Tay wondered why.

Tay saw the twelve, who temporarily had control of Seven Galaxies' government, glancing furtively at one another. He took it all in. They had much to lose: complete power over a civilization that covered the largest diaspora the known universe had ever experienced. The twelve would bear watching closely. So much power in the hands of a few without supervisory control was as dangerous as throwing a lit match into a barn full of dry hay.

Ventras was curious. He once again put on his false mask of sincerity. "Dearest Admiral, what are your plans now that the war is won and you, the victor, have earned long and well-deserved leave?"

"Ventras, it is premature for me to share my intent with this group. Also, I am not the victor; *Independence* won the decisive points in the confrontation. She is a unit, and all aboard her, as well as her numerous support vessels and their crews, share equal responsibility for her success. I will make my desires known tomorrow, no earlier; however, your interest in my personal affairs touches me deeply." Gor smiled, the renowned poker face showing nothing but the legend he had become. The old man took up his glass of port and began an intimate conversation with a woman sitting next to him.

Tay had not noticed the woman before. The admiral appeared to know her, for their conversation, while spoken low enough to not be heard by the table, seemed very personal. The woman had striking blue eyes. They were wide and very large, and colored as the depths of an ancient glacier as it shears off into the sea. She was much younger than the admiral yet looked at him fondly. *No,* Tay thought, *not fondly but sexily.*

Was it possible that the old man and this woman were more than just friends? Tay could not help but wonder. The woman was extremely attractive and was touching the admiral's arm—*caressing* his arm.

Oh my, thought Tay. Did the old man still have it? He laughed to himself and thought, *You don't need to know.*

The banquet finally done, the admiral thanked all present for the beautiful and heart-touching reception. He then begged off, citing fatigue from a day full of tragedy, wonder, and joy. Taking up Serene's arm, he escorted her to an autocar, helped her in, and then joined her. The door swished shut, and the vehicle was there one moment and gone the next. All eyes followed its streaking path.

Their departure was soon forgotten by most as the party began, but Tay still enjoyed the vision of his grandfather, an extreme example of personal control, sitting in the rear seat of an autocar, intimately entwined with a woman who he had not even introduced.

FORTY-FIVE

The summer evening in the valley was grand. Serene, in splendid form, first teased, then caressed TyGor. Finally, she fell silent, replacing her words with tender looks as they walked together, lightly touching, taking in the river trail. Moonlight shone off the murmuring water and cast a flickering silver light upon them both. For Ty, it was all a dream long held: to be here, finished with official duties, and to have this enchantingly beautiful and gracious woman by his side.

They came upon the bend in the river that wrapped around the giant maple tree. It was Shadow's resting spot. The admiral remembered the day he and Tay had dug the great horse's final resting place. He stopped, somber for a moment, thinking of his beloved grandson and all they had been through.

"This horse, Shadow, saved my Tay when he was a young boy from this very river at high water," he said, pointing out the grave to Serene. The day before we went to war on the Nesdians, Shadow died of old age. Tay and I dug his resting place by hand.

"If the beloved animal had not managed to save the boy on that day so long ago, I would not have had Tay to rely upon during the conflict, and I often wonder whether Seven Galaxies would have fared so well." He crouched down to touch the earth. "This spot is sacred to me. Here lies the guardian of my grandson, and quite possibly the savior of Seven Galaxies as well: all that in an animal who simply loved his charge."

Serene could detect the slightest hint of tears in his eyes. She felt sure this display of emotion was usually hidden from others.

"I will stay here," he said. "I no longer wish to be anywhere else. Will you join me here, Serene?" He stood up and took her hand. "Before you answer, I would say that your presence here makes this moment irreplaceably dear. Your friendship multiplies all that is good in my life. I wish for your company...I long for it when we are not together."

"Dearest Admiral," she said in a playful tone, addressing him lovingly in his official capacity while her eyes betrayed a passion that was anything but professional, "I will consider your proposal, yet the evening is young, and you are weary from the banquet and your long day. Surely you do not have the energy I would require to close this wonderful evening on a more *intimate* note."

"The warrior must often dig deep," Ty said, feigning seriousness, "bringing up through fatigue hidden reserves, kept as precious gems for moments when he, as a champion, cannot fail." He smiled when he saw how his words had pleased her.

Taking Serene in his arms he said, "Thank you for walking with me here this evening. It is a memory I will always hold close to my heart." Pulling her tightly to him, he pressed lips gently against the curve of her neck.

This is a man who is so hard, and yet so soft, Serene thought, her heart racing. Shivers ran through her, and she felt the prickle of goose bumps on her skin.

"Dearest Admiral," she said, her voice filled with longing, "surely we are too mature to cast our passions upon one another here on the forest floor. Do you have a place that might not be so wonderfully natural, yet would have a cozy bed?"

Buried in the warmth of her neck, Ty said only, "Soon, my love. Soon."

"I will stay with you in this valley," Serene whispered, stifling a moan. "I wish to be nowhere else."

FORTY-SIX

The banquet over, the party that had just begun did not interest Tay. Surely there were important persons to meet, he thought, yet the time away from Seven aboard *Independence* spoke to him of a need for something away from the press of humanity, something more personal and down to earth.

Finding Alex, who looked a bit lost amongst the social, military, and political powers of the day, he asked, "Enjoying the party?"

Alex shrugged. It was clear that he'd rather be keystroking his beloved computers.

"What are you up to, Tay?" Alex asked.

"I was thinking of checking on Zuzahna. She was taken into custody, you know."

"I have been so busy tidying up files and closing down and securing my office, I hadn't even thought of Zuzahna," Alex said.

"Would you accompany me?"

"Sure, I'm pretty wound up and more than a bit concerned for you, my friend. What is your connection with her anyway?"

Tay blushed slightly, embarrassment showing. "She's just a friend, and I feel more than a little responsible for her welfare. After all, I was on the bridge when she was captured, so in essence she is here in prison because of me."

"You can't go around beating yourself up over that. She is Nesdian, and she was caught with the regent; she has to be debriefed. Don't worry; you've said she's innocent. She'll be released before long, and you two will be off-duty, no regulations hanging over your head. Hey, you may finally get laid." Alex smirked, pushing his glasses up on his nose.

Tay punched him lightly in the arm. "Enough!" Tay said. "After all, you're just jealous because she has the hots for me."

"Hots is an understatement—my friend, that woman would like to eat you alive. That's what I'm worried about. I believe if you're not careful, she might literally do just that. I can see her licking her lips right now."

"Shut up, you little geek, before I hit you again."

"Bully!" Alex said with a smile. "Sure I'll go with you. Someone's got to protect you from yourself."

"Funny, very funny."

They both laughed and caught the tram over to the security complex.

Zuzahna sat fretting. She had been in captivity for over three weeks. Her cell aboard *Independence* had been a suite reserved for high-level prisoners of some prestige. It was quite large and consisted of three rooms. Her new cell on this foreign planet was one small room and an open toilet and shower, without any sort of enclosure for privacy. The guards, fortunately all female, could walk by and see her naked, showering, or sitting on the toilet.

Not since Zuzahna was a child had she felt so humbled. The bed was a mat with no springs. She sat upon it, head in her hands, and wondered how soon she might be released.

A voice coming over the speaker in the tiny cell said, "Duhcat, you have some visitors. Make yourself ready."

Zuzahna looked in the metal mirror at her image and was aghast; dark circles of worry showed beneath her enormous eyes, making her look tired and afraid. She straightened her hair and waited.

She heard footsteps coming down the corridor and wondered who it might be. Then the cell door swung open, and Tay stood framed in the doorway, looking a bit sheepish.

She rushed towards him in her most enchanting posture, smiling wide, attempting to take the worry and stress from her face. "Tay, my sweet, I am so happy you've come. I knew my favorite person in the whole of the Seven Galaxies would not leave me here alone for long. Thank you, my dear!" Zuzahna embraced Tay, brushing the fine, silky hair on her cheeks against his own. At that moment, she pulled him tight to her, pressing the warmth of her breast against him.

Tay was taken with her power, as always. Even when he was away from her, he often wished she would hold him like this.

Another person stepped into the cell, and the guard shut the door. Tay broke her grasp without seeming distant and said, "Zuzahna, I would like to present my very good friend, Alex. I have told him much about you, but he has been so wrapped up in his computer aboard *Independence*, he never could pry himself away so that the two of you could meet."

Zuzahna took in the young man with seasoned eyes, saying. "Any friend of Tay's is surely a friend of mine. It is a *very* great pleasure to meet you, Alex. Such a pity it could not have been sooner."

Zuzahna offered her hand to the young man, who took it readily and bent at the waist in ancient ceremony, kissing the back of it lightly. Alex forgot to let go as he stared into Zuzahna's huge eyes. They seemed to swirl—two deep whirlpools, depths of brown with golden flecks. Her irises dilated slightly and a bit of adrenalin flowed as she realized her pull on him. This young man found her compelling, she thought. She was fulfilled.

Alex was speechless.

Finally, Zuzahna shook his hand lightly in a subtle signal that he should free his grasp.

Alex stammered a bit and finally got out, "A pleasure to meet you, Zuzahna."

Zuzahna winked one eye lightly at Tay, the eye hidden behind the bridge of her nose so that Alex was unaware of the signal. Tay stifled a laugh. Alex had teased him incessantly over his infatuation with Zuzahna, and now Alex was tripping over his own tongue, wide-eyed in wonder of her. Tay felt vindicated that he alone was not subject to the spell of her magnetism, beauty, and grace.

He laughed, quipping comically, "Well, I see you two are going to hit it off."

Alex reluctantly pried his eyes off Zuzahna, looked at Tay, and said in a dreamlike voice, "Yes. Yes, I certainly hope so."

FORTY-SEVEN

VENTRAS left the banquet seething with rage. How dare this Admiral Gor, a mere military commander, publicly challenge his carefully laid plans for Seven Galaxies and for her future, he thought.

Ventras sent an encrypted signal to the survivors of the original twelve—those legislators trusted by the people; those who had taken control of Seven Galaxies in the absence of the Fifteen. Ventras called a top secret meeting.

Before the Dome collapsed, the job of the twelve legislators was to disseminate public opinion through a regulated vote and pass on to the Fifteen a digested version of the populace's mind and formulated policies, which would then be considered by the Fifteen.

Within the Dome of Wisdom, the Fifteen would modify policies to fall in line with reality, and then send them back to the administrative, legislative body to implement in such a way as to promote health, welfare, education, prosperity, creativity, and lawfulness within the vast realm that had become Seven Galaxies.

The eleven remaining members met. Most had come incognito. The secrecy of the meeting was imperative. Ventras felt that the return of Admiral Gor posed a threat to the twelve's designs, and he wanted a chance to share his fears with the group. All were seasoned politicians with dirty, greedy hands, hoping that the opportunity to rule Seven Galaxies and siphon off its incredible wealth would not pass them by. All were eager to hear Ventras' views and plan a strategic power grab that was not temporary but permanent.

"Thank you all for coming," he began. "We have before us an epoch. One in which we must choose to ally ourselves as a strong and cohesive force, or be destined to return from whence we came.

"We must first find a suitable replacement for Verdanse. I'm sure all of you are aware of her tragic and unexpected death. She seemed so vibrant, so full of life. What a pity," Ventras said, with mock sympathy.

Ventras continued after a meaningless pause. "There are those who wish Seven Galaxies could return to the rule of the so-called Fifteen. This is not possible. The Fifteen are dead, crushed by the devastating asteroid that impacted not only the Dome of Wisdom but also nearly destroyed our entire planet. We must not forget that the people are now in our hands. From the tragic death of the Fifteen rises a phoenix from the ashes. We are that phoenix! We are the people's choice. We are in power. Do any of you wish to relinquish what you have gained since the Fifteen's demise?"

Not a hand raised. No one offered to give up what had been usurped.

"Then we must take the necessary steps to prevail against those who wish to strip us of our newfound position, our high-ranking responsibility, and the obvious benefits we receive."

"Who would go against us? Who would dare?" Belvidius asked.

"The obvious is as always right under your nose. Gor, of course."

"But Gor is simply a military commander, albeit the admiral. What possible chance would he have as a diplomat or political rival?" Telthin asked.

"Gor has the people's ear. He is two times the victor against Nesdia, and the people will not likely forget so monumental an achievement."

"What do you propose, Ventras?" asked Derian, speaker of the legislature, a small, wiry man whose eyes flitted around the room, missing nothing.

"Some things are best left to those few who have the stomach for the necessary work. I suggest we pick a group of three who have served us well during a crisis like this in the past, three who are ready to take care of what needs doing. The rest of you can go home, back to your lavish lifestyle, which has improved so drastically of late, and then you forget this meeting occurred. The three will need consent of all twelve, minus Verdanse of course…" Ventras and a few of the others snickered. "No holdouts; we must all be in this together. Are we agreed?"

Consent was given by all.

Ventras continued. "I nominate Derian and Belvidius."

On cue, Derian stood and said, "I nominate Ventras."

"Any objections?" Ventras added.

None were forthcoming. "Voted, passed, all others may leave the room and go home." Ventras finished the meeting with a smile, humor that came to his lean, wolf-like features while he dreamed of the legendary admiral's demise.

FORTY-EIGHT

Admiral Gor began his public address the morning after the banquet: "My brothers and sisters within Seven Galaxies and beyond, I address you as your equal and ask only that you stop what you are doing and give me a few moments of your valuable time.

"As a young man, I was called to serve the needs of our fledgling society, which was threatened by an ominous and powerful enemy. Our worlds were at war. It was a war unparalleled in our history. It was a conflict that brought our great culture to its knees. It was a brutal machine, a beast that thrived and grew stronger for a time, by regularly consuming, in its seething furnace, some of the best and brightest people I have been honored to know.

"In the end, there were few of us. Few of us stood united, against many fearsome and belligerently hostile foes. We dug deep. Most in our society wanted truce at the expense of our freedom, and all—including me—desired the fighting to stop.

"The majority of politicians in that dark period and our populace would have unjustly given up elements of freedom and progress to attain peace at any cost.

"A handful of besieged leaders, under the critical scrutiny of the majority, put their heads down to the insults, the accusations, and the ever-present torment that was cast towards them. Those few perceived a dream that could not be wrong; they dreamed of a progressive society, unhampered by war, with people free to pursue the depths of creativity within an environment that would nurture such freedom. For that dream, those leaders were ridiculed and despised. That dream has become Seven Galaxies. That magnificent dream, a vision into what would soon be the future, could have been drowned in the catcalls of the multitudes. But those few resolute leaders kept their eyes on the goal through the ugliness, and the dream prevailed.

"Who among us today could imagine a universe without this vastness we lovingly name Seven Galaxies? Who in all honesty would choose to expatriate themselves from a society, culture, and home that is unparalleled in our history?" Gor paused momentarily, placing silence as an invisible exclamation point.

"I ask these things not to demean or cast dispersions but to bring reality crashing down upon you, to shine a startling light into your eyes and to feed and nurture a loving spirit within your hearts. We are all brothers and sisters, we and many who have passed from among us. We built Seven Galaxies on truth, self-sacrifice, and love, and we are blessed to call Seven Galaxies home.

"We have much work before us. The asteroid's impact has left many wanting, injured, or dead. We must band together. If you have a hand that is full, reach out to someone less fortunate. If you have a home, share it with someone whose home was destroyed. If you have no home, find others like yourselves, join together, and build. All resources at our disposal will be there for your needs. We have built from a scattered and weak settlement a vast society we call home. Surely just as we built Seven Galaxies, we will rebuild, repair, and heal the damage. We must do this together, each person giving of themselves all the extra they possess, whether it be money, muscle, mind, material, or garden. Share what you have with your sisters and brothers. Embrace them." Gor spread his arms out wide and then pulled them into an encircling embrace to signify his words.

"I must move on to new subjects: the Dome of Wisdom has been destroyed. The wreckage must be cleared and the Dome rebuilt. It is the cradle of our society. It is the birthplace of the positive visions that have formed our reality. It is the moral ground, which governs us all.

"Some would say, now that the Dome has been destroyed, that the Fifteen cannot be replaced. That the legislative body should assume—or I prefer the word *usurp*—the power of the Dome. Even though none of the politicians of our day have ever been accepted into the Dome—for good reason—these same politicians feel compelled to govern our vast society. I do not agree.

"When we rebuild the Dome of Wisdom, its power will draw, by some magnetism I cannot explain, those persons who possess the qualities needed to unselfishly lead our worlds. It must be done. Will you help me in this regard? This is my wish—my absolute desire. Will you, my brothers and sisters, swear to restore the Dome of Wisdom to its former presence?"

The billions watching Gor's address cheered and swore that they would.

"I must now speak of matters that affect my person and, with that understood, you as well. I have served you all for my entire adult life. I have sacrificed the life I desired to lead for the betterment of the dreams we all held. I have done so happily, with my heart feeling for you each step of the way. I have been your guardian and protector. I have fought two brutal wars in which many of my dearest friends were not as fortunate as myself and did not appear on this side of the conflict. In memory of them, I offer a brief silence."

Gor paused a moment before continuing. "It is time for me to pass the torch, which I have unfailingly carried for the past two centuries. I grow old and wish to spend my remaining years in the valley of my birth, practicing the simple pursuits of a farmer. I long to enjoy golden sunlight flickering through a green canopy of leaves. I long to rest my tired bones while listening to the river's voice. I wish to wake in the morning when I want to, not when duty calls. Most of all, I want to share my remaining years with the ones I love. And so embedded in any ending there is the seed of new beginnings. This is what I wish to speak of next.

"The recent victory over Nesdia was swift and absolute, not drawn out for nearly three decades, as was the previous conflict. I will now impart to *all* my understanding and belief in that strategic accomplishment.

"My first, TayGor, and his creative research officer, Alex Delanport, were responsible for adapting newly developed technology and stratagems aboard *Independence*. These two young men and their crew are responsible for our sudden and spectacular victory. TayGor and Alexus Delanport must be commended to the highest degree. I have promoted them to posts: TayGor as vice admiral until my retirement is official, at which point I recommend he be appointed as admiral, even at his apparent youthful age. His right hand, Alex Delanport, has been appointed as vice admiral in charge of creative research and new technologies.

"It is my fervent wish that these two selfless young men take their rightful places within the formation of a new guardianship for Seven Galaxies.

"I wish to thank you all for your trust and belief in me over all these years. I go to my new life fulfilled and happy in my heart that my brothers and sisters will be afforded many millennia of peace, prosperity, and progress in our future. Thank you all, and farewell."

Ventras watched and listened to the admiral's farewell address in disbelief. "That bastard!" he exclaimed, once the admiral was finished. "How dare he? How dare he undermine publicly the plans we've made for the people of Seven Galaxies." Ventras ground as would a gristmill, the kernels of hate stored for years. His chance to finally rule would not slip away. He swore an oath to himself. "Gor must be gone: not into retirement but somewhere where he will never again interfere."

FORTY-NINE

THREE men sat in a special soundproof room. Each of the men wore masks so as not to be recognized by the visitor soon arriving. The plan had been formed. Now all they needed was the specialist.

They had used the woman before during their rise to power. Discreet death was a formidable tool when someone more popular in the public eye stood in their way. Strokes and heart attacks were commonplace. The specialist drove the numbers a smidgen higher. Unexpected death from an undetectable foreign source was the black arts niche in which she excelled.

They waited, seasoned politicians well acquainted with intrigue, power grabs, under-the-table payoffs, and the sordid but common dirty dealings in which scum like them trafficked; all the self-enriching reasons they had chosen the field of public service. All three were nervous. Machiavellian moves on the political chessboard rarely called for the drastic action they were about to set in motion. It had been determined necessary. Still, few men have looked into the eyes of death, as they were about to.

Cloaked in the form of a graceful woman who looked like a runway model, she was, in reality, a flickering shadow carrying destruction. Her appearance was one of her more powerful weapons. Camouflaged by beauty, she could move unsuspected almost anywhere.

Denali moved from the autocar to the pavement, slipping out of the machine like a cat on the prowl, glancing in all directions. No furtiveness was evident. She had been summoned by Ventras, who thought she did not know who he was.

Long ago, she had learned to investigate her employers, to know their business, to understand the nuances of a job and how it affected the bigger picture. In her profession, knowledge was king. By being adequately informed, a higher price for the work could be negotiated, and nasty complications a less-diligent operator might overlook could be avoided.

The warehouse loomed ahead, a relic from earlier days before automated cargo transfer made the facility a dinosaur. Unused, aging, and decrepit, it was the meeting place a film director might have chosen for this scene.

Ventras was a bit melodramatic for her tastes. He liked setting the mood. Denali laughed to herself when she thought how ridiculous he could be at times, masquerading in the dank old warehouse, thinking she had no idea who he was when a simple bit of research showed the building to be owned indirectly by him.

The click-clack of her heels on the pavement struck the tempo of her long-legged stride. A rusty old door cracked open, signaling to her that the men were here. The play was about to unfold.

What could it be this time? she thought, curiosity tingling the back of her mind.

The path to the meeting room was familiar. Weaving through pallets of black-market commodities, she made her way through Ventras' horde of ill-gotten treasures. He never ceased to surprise her with his blatant thirst for power and wealth. This warehouse was a small sideline business of his—one of many ventures in which he had dirty fingers.

The three waiting men heard steady footsteps, and their hearts beat a bit faster. It was a rare thing, beholding a gorgeous woman and a lethal weapon in the same glance. Bracing themselves for her entrance, Belvidius was already sweating profusely.

Ventras took in the obscenely obese man and said, "Lose some weight, for shit sake. You look like you're having a freakin' heart attack just sitting there."

Belvidius looked ashamed. "It's my metabolism, Ventras. I truly eat like a bird."

"I can believe that, you pig; birds eat half their own weight every day." Derian chuckled, joining Ventras at the fat man's expense.

Denali walked through the open door, not stopping to knock. "Nice masks. You never said this was a costume party." She smiled coolly at her joke; the others obviously didn't find the humor.

Ventras said, "Please sit," as he closed the soundproof door.

Denali slid into the only chair available and took in the room. "Impressive office," she said facetiously. The room was covered in dust. A calendar, ten years old, was the only art adorning the grimy walls. The furniture could have come from any garbage dump. An old door on sawhorses was being used as a makeshift table.

Derian asked, "Are you always such a smart ass?"

Denali took him in without responding. The other two she knew; this one she had never seen before. Her cool, confident stare made the small, wiry man squirm in his threadbare chair.

"I guess that's enough of the small talk and social graces. What do you have?" She looked directly at Ventras. She would know those eyes anywhere—little good the mask did, she thought. The eyes were a steely blue grey, the type that on a kind, handsome man would be appealing, yet on Ventras took on the hardened, emotionless gaze of a psychopath. A twinge crept down Denali's spine but didn't show. Her face was impassive, ready for information.

"Admiral Gor. As you probably know, he's home from the Nesdian conflict. He's in my way...in *our* way."

Denali took in the eyes once more. They were serious. This was no sick joke. She was shocked by the implications, yet her face remained blank. "He's revered by the people, even by me," she said. "He's an Epic...Stellar freakin' Hero! He saved our asses from those bloodthirsty Nesdian fanatics twice, and you want him ditched?"

"Yes," Ventras said calmly.

"Look, this one's heavy," Denali said, leaning forward in her seat. "All the others, a few slimy dirty politicians, no big deal. Seven didn't even miss them, but Gor? He's some very serious shit! You know what I'm saying?"

"Yes." The steely eyes hardened.

Silence engulfed the room while Denali weighed her options. The fat one was sweating profusely. The wiry one had a sick smirk plastered to his face, and the tall one just kept up that chilling glare.

Ventras spoke. "Of course, if this task is too much for you, I can find another worker, although I would hate to end such a profitable relationship, one that has benefitted you as much as it has us."

His meaning was clear: the phrases that appeared innocuous on the surface veiled a threat. The twinge ran down her spine again. He was giving her two choices. She was privy to the plan, so if she didn't participate, she would simply disappear. "How much?"

"A million credits."

"Not enough," she said instantly, shaking her head. "Shit, that wouldn't carry me two years. This task is a golden parachute. You understand? You threaten *me?* You think I can't reach out to you? Touch you silently.... This is a two-way street, *Ventras!* I know where you live. I walk out of here without you accepting *my* terms, and we'll be hunting each other. Got it?"

He had visibly started when she used his name. The arrow had stuck deep enough that he would take her words to heart.

"I'm not finished!" she said, turning to the others. "*You*, Belvidius, you want a piece of me? You will be first! And you, you little fuck, wipe that smirk off your face! I don't know who you are at this moment, but I snapped your mug as you walked in here, *before* you put on that cute little mask! You guys want to run at me?"

"NO!" they said in unison.

"Here's the deal: five million credits. Three up front, and two when complete. Say yes now or I'm up out of this stinking hole, and you won't find me until I'm standing over you watching you breathe your last breath. Then you'll know I've blown you a sweet, hot kiss." She licked her lips and then said no more. The cool alloy barrels under the sleeves of her jacket were comforting. Her eyes stayed centered between the three, not focusing on anyone. Adrenalin gave her confidence and hypersensitive vision.

Breaking the tense silence, she changed her tone to something more predatory. "Don't anyone flinch. I'm in kind of a bad mood. I feel a little twitchy for some reason."

"You've made your point," Ventras said. "We agree. Usual payment arrangements?"

"Yes, usual. What's the deadline?"

"Day after tomorrow at the latest. He is home. Should be an easy piece."

"Yeah! Easy," Denali repeated, sickened in her heart.

"If you three would do me a favor and face the wall over there, I'm leaving. I just feel a little uneasy here, seeing as our conference was a tad heated."

Ventras moved towards the wall. The other two followed, with Belvidius straining to rise under his gargantuan weight.

They heard nothing. Finally, when they turned to look, she was gone.

"That bitch is one freaky piece! Did you hear her?" Belvidius asked.

"Of course we did, you idiot; we were right beside you."

"I mean figuratively. She threatened the shit out of us! I'm surprised you took it, Ventras."

"She didn't threaten us. She laid out her terms, and we accepted them. End of story."

"Was she serious about all that?" asked Derian.

Ventras nodded. "Serious as a heart attack."

FIFTY

DENALI left the meeting barefoot. She ran through Ventras' ill-kept warehouse towards fresh air, she had left the soundproof room with the three masked goons standing facing the wall. The rust-eaten and decrepit door swung, hinges complaining, and banged loudly behind her. Jumping seven steps to the street, Denali pulled fresh air into lungs squeezed tight from expelling the last bit in the musty, evil warehouse.

Sunlight dove down through a hazy sky of blue yet did nothing to console her. What had she just agreed to? she wondered in disbelief. The sanction of Admiral Gor? The people's first choice as hero extraordinaire, and she said she would do it?

Golden parachute my ass! she thought. The job stunk, like the unwashed hold of an overused fishing boat baking under the heat of full summer sun.

Ventras was a loon, for sure, and the others were just as creepy—and she had agreed to work for them to save her own skin. If all went well, she would be set for the rest of her days. On the surface, without Denali's ever-active mental microscope delving the quandary deeper, appearances—the illusions of Ventras' plan—might seem to make sense. Yet upon scrutiny, the sums did not add up. Her mind raced, attempting to ferret out potential traps.

How would she keep herself clear? She hadn't a clue, and time was running out. Only forty-eight hours remained to prepare, pull off the despicable project, and make sure she wasn't one of the convenient casualties herself.

Ventras was not to be trusted. He would sacrifice her in a heartbeat if it meant consolidating his power, safety, or both. If she did this job, she would become a loose end. If she didn't, she had more even odds and only fate and destiny would determine who survived.

Denali never left her life in the hands of intemperate gods or people. She was pragmatic to the core and believed destiny to be controlled by a person's actions. Preparation for something like this was ultimate. She had to think of the angles of angles, of back schemes and trade-offs, of pawns to be sacrificed and the winning pieces.

Sometimes she wore herself out thinking. Yet it was her overactive mind that had seen her through tormented labyrinths, the depths of dark jungles of the mind, and a hundred planets to survive the unspeakable past she had lived.

All this flashed as lightning in a stormy sky while she ran barefoot to the autocar. It self-started and unlocked as she neared. The driver's door opened before she cleared the front bumper. In a blur, she was in the saddle and leaving the scene ahead of a noxious black cloud of smoking stinking rubber, the turbo power pack within the Astral Bordini screaming sixteen grand.

Driving always soothed her when her frayed nerves were attempting to unravel. The Astral Bordini swung into mountain curves, mercilessly biting at pavement. The scenery became a blur; the winding road, a trial to conquer. She tortured the machine, challenging gravity's limits. The shrill whine of the power pack complained and screamed through the manual power-shifts as she wound her way towards her favorite freehand face.

Denali craved a challenge, something so completely engrossing and all-consuming that her momentary problems might be forgotten. She desired treacherous and unrelenting granite.

Power braking the machine, she slid it sideways onto a tiny blacktop mountain road that wound its way near the cliff's foot. Slowing to a speed few would consider sane, she watched for the ever-present fallen rock and sand that could appear suddenly from a hidden corner, unseating an unwary driver.

She parked, slid out fluidly, and dug out her pack from the rear storage compartment. Changing quickly into her well-worn gear, she locked the autocar and walked the little-used trail to the cliff.

The mid-day sunshine cast shadows upon the foreboding rock, outlining the seams, chutes, and chimneys that would allow her to scale eighteen hundred vertical feet without a single rope or piton.

FIFTY-ONE

The pulsating showerhead pounded her aching, throbbing muscles. They were wet noodles from the grueling, heart-throbbing climb and seven-mile run down the backside of the granite face. She had turned the water first to scalding hot, and then lowered the temperature just a smidgen. Stepping beneath the flow, it hurt terribly at first, but as her body acclimated, the heat soothed her. She stayed under the brutal heat until she was literally swaying, about to pass out.

Walking into her sleeping room, her mind still screamed. Her sixth sense was attempting to warn her of impending danger. In that moment, Denali made a fatal mistake. She ignored her subconscious trepidation. She assured herself consciously that with proper planning and footwork she would be safe. Yet in that instant, she forgot the black consequences that loomed. Powerful karmic forces were set drastically against her for the light she was about to extinguish.

Admiral Gor, the foundation of Seven's morality, would be sacrificed. Denali, in her disheveled mental state, and in her desire to grasp the incredible fortune that dangled before her, had left moral fiber behind. She became, in that instant, an automaton, destined to suffer greatly for the mistake. Like the *Titanic* on ancient Earth, she steamed headlong into disaster, believing she was wise enough, powerful enough, well equipped enough to circumvent the dark power that held her.

Exhausted but satisfied that the end justified the means, Denali flopped into bed and was soon asleep. Her sleep was anything but peaceful. She twitched, tossed and turned, and made sharp utterances that broke her rest into pieces. What came in her dreams was mostly past experiences, childhood trauma and adolescent turmoil. Some of her dreaming became subconscious conjecture, derived from scraps she had learned of her birth and subsequent abandonment.

FIFTY-TWO

The beautiful young woman in make-up too heavy walked quickly through streets emptied of the now-sleeping working class. Taverns were closed. The city was, for the most part, quiet. In her arms was a coat bundled over a package held with care. Making way to a large building with few lights on, she kissed the bundle tenderly before starting up the front steps. Setting the coat and its contents down on the porch mat, she beat loudly on the door and then turned quickly, running towards shadows and away from the sorrow tearing her heart.

Moments passed and the bundle began to first snuffle, and then to cry weakly, volume increasing until the shrieking wail woke the occupants of the building. Soon the door opened, and the bundle was carefully picked up and taken inside.

The woman watched through tear-studded eyes, imagining another place in time, away from the sordid life she was living, where the baby could have remained in her arms. Sobbing tiredly, she soon disappeared, walking away into oblivion.

FIFTY-THREE

A VIBRANT young girl ran through sun-soaked grass. Streaming red-blonde hair flew behind her. A group of other girls raced in the rear, each one unbelieving that a child much younger could outdistance them so quickly. They attempted to close the widening gap between them, but Denali was far ahead. Relishing her lead over the taller, older girls, her competitive spirit drove her on.

At the finish, she leaped into a cat spring, rolled a summersault, and then lay on her back, catching her breath. The August sun illuminated her exotic features—her blue eyes, the perfect lips, and an enchanting smile that revealed straight, well-formed teeth, white as snow. Her face was sweaty from exertion, and her red-blonde tresses fell back, exposing a forehead high with native intelligence. Her eyes portrayed flashing emotions: satisfaction, exhilaration, and fulfillment at conquering the others.

Denali lay gazing into an azure sky that trailed streaks of stratus clouds on lazy and gentle winds. Summer's soft warm breath breezed, whispered through the grass and the leaves of nearby trees, cooling her damp face, speaking to her like a dear close friend, soothing her racing mind and calming her excitement.

The other girls arrived momentarily, out of breath and unbelieving.

"You sure can run, you little imp," one said.

They laughed as a group, falling and staggering onto the grass, giggling at their sweatiness and short breath. Some complained of stitches in their sides.

One girl, silent and solemn, showed no joy or happiness. She watched Denali furtively. Jealousy consumed her. The others grouped around Denali affectionately, like sisters honored by her win, but the solemn one despised affection given to someone other than herself.

Denali felt the girl's unfriendly stare. Attempting to draw her into the fun, she said, "Miranda, are you okay? You're so quiet. I worry you are feeling unwell."

"Well enough, yet my head is pounding from the heat and torture of that infernal race. Let's go into the shade where it will be cooler."

"Oh, Miranda, the sun is wonderful. Feel its caress, the wonderful warmth, the gentleness of golden lips upon our eyes, and then you shall see it differently than just mean heat." Denali loved the music of words and how she could describe nature's moods.

"You speak gibberish, as usual, child. I'll not stay here baking in this hellish oven a minute longer! Who will break from this nonsense and come with me?" Miranda stood, and all others but one followed suit.

Miranda gave Denali a look that spoke of her feelings of superiority before she turned her nose to the sky and marched away, leading the others, for she was Alpha of the pack.

A small, mousy girl with large eyes, deep-brown and sad, smiled and said, "Denali, I love when you speak so beautifully. I only wish I were as gifted as you, with strength, and intellect so quick to turn a sweet phrase. Alas, I am just a weakling of mind and body who craves some gentle friendship. I love when we can be like this, the two of us, without Miranda's imperious ways. Speak of this August day some more. Will you turn a few more words of beauty into my ears, so that I may momentarily forget the dark loneliness, which pervades my mind so often?"

"Dear Issy," she began, for that is what Denali had affectionately nicknamed Issabell, "I would gladly speak a world of happiness for you, a true friend so dear, who, in her loyalty to that friendship, stays with this one romantic soul in the August sun when she could be enjoying the cool shade and the drinking fountain, as well as the camaraderie of a group so much more boundless than myself."

Issy smiled at Denali's words, looking deep into her eyes, as if seeing something there normally missing in herself.

Denali, seeing the girl's rapturous face, was driven to perform something top notch. "Would that I were a bird, a swallow, perhaps, the golden sun reflecting off the blues and teals of my back while the wind caressed my feathers. I would fly high, looking down upon all, gliding over cool, babbling streams and golden fields of wheat; through mountain canyons, high where the snow still brushes its chill upon my wings. I would see the glistening rivulets—tears of melting—and the disappearing icy grip upon sheer slopes of stone. Coasting, wings tired from the great task of flying so high, I dive to the blue-green sea and along the shore. The crashing, tumbling surf fills my ears with its roar as it foams and shoots high into the sky, dashing against the bluffs. Fishermen's boats dot the horizon and duck behind islets along my path. The great blue marlin's fin breaks the surface; from beneath the Ocean's depths he rises, casting a glistening form from ever-cold water into heat of summer air. For the briefest moment he is a flash of glistening dripping color. Sunlight illuminates his jeweled body. Then, splashing down into his world, I see him no more. I cruise above farmer's fields, watching them sweat, bringing their hard-won harvest in, while I—free to pluck my food from the summer sky—fly back and light on the ground next to you, dear Issy."

"How do you do it, Denali?"

"Do what?"

"How do you take me with you on such wonderful adventures, as though I am on your back, a miniature of myself, flying aboard the wondrous swallow, seeing in my mind's eye all you have so wonderfully described?"

"You, my dear, have a very vivid imagination, appreciating my verbal wanderings through the great blue as no other person."

"I love when you talk so gorgeously, Denali."

"I find it wondrous to have you listening, Issy. August brings the best of me forward. It's such a wonderful feeling, lazily lying on the grass, taking a momentary respite from the biting chill of winter. I must say, my heart saddens just a little when the sun drops lower in the sky with each passing day."

"I never see you sad, Denali. I am the one who is naturally morose. You cheer me out of it always."

"I have fun doing so."

The two girls looked upon each other with affection and then fell silent, moods bright with friendship.

FIFTY-FOUR

MIRANDA, while feigning interest in her group, watched Issabell and Denali from a distance. The dark cretin preferred the company of that redhead brat over her own group, she thought. Her mind wound its way through shadowed patterns of thought, considering the ways she could separate the two. Miranda had tried many times in the past to worm Issabell away from Denali, yet nothing so far had worked. Perhaps something more permanent was necessary, she thought, her eyes narrowing in contemplation.

The school matron came, rounding the girls up for their evening meal. In that instant, the short holiday of sunshine and play ended. They moved towards the looming building two blocks from the park. All were kept in double file and counted at regular intervals, watched diligently so none could slip secretly away.

After the evening meal, when it was time for bed, Miranda found Issy in the small, upper-floor bathroom. "Issabell, I wish to show you something absolutely magnificent on the roof! Jupiter is out, and it absolutely *glows*—it's like a peach-colored ball in the sky."

"We're not to be on the roof! You well know the rules, Miranda."

"Not a soul will know," she said. "We can be up and back in a few moments, before we are put to bed. Come, it will be fun: our own little secret."

"I don't know," Issabell said, doubtful. "We could get into trouble."

"You are such a little sniveler, such a chicken. Why don't you do something daring for once in your miserable life, Issabell?"

"Oh, all right," Issy said reluctantly, not understanding why Miranda had suddenly taken such an interest in her. She followed the much older, larger girl up the stairs to the roof.

"You see, just over that tree. What a beautiful sight!"

"I can't see anything."

"Oh! You are too short. Here, I'll lift you up and you can stand on top of the short rail wall. I'll hold onto you so you can't fall."

"I don't think so, Miranda. I'm afraid."

"You big sissy! How do you ever expect to grow up like me if you are so afraid all the time?"

"Okay, if you promise to hold on tight," Issy said reluctantly.

"Of course I promise. Don't you worry about a thing." She helped Issy up onto the three-foot wall that railed the roof edge.

Issy said, "I don't see anything over that tree."

"And you won't!"

"Miranda! Put me down, you're scaring me!"

"As you wish! Sniveling, scrawny brat!" With that, Miranda ripped her hands from Issy's waist and gave her a quick shove forward. Issabell let out a short, shrill shriek, and then thudded sickeningly onto the ground four stories below. Miranda ran quickly down two flights of steps and mixed with the other girls, who were milling about readying themselves for bed.

When the evening head count came, Issabell was missing. The search began, and after a long time, Issabell's body was found in the shrubbery alongside the building. The school matron believed that she had jumped to her death. "She always was a dark and morose little thing!" she said, shaking her head sadly.

Denali was in shock. It had been a wonderful day, and Issabell had been in fine form. Surely there was another explanation for her death. Although overcome by grief, she believed the tragedy could not be explained away so quickly or easily.

Lights were eventually turned out after the police had come and gone. All lay down to sleep, some fitfully and Denali not at all.

Sometime before sunrise, Denali heard movement beside her bed and then a slight whisper. It was so dark she could not see. The whisperer spoke quickly, voice shaking with fear.

"I was in the upstairs linen closet next to the bathroom, fetching a towel. I heard Miranda talking to Issabell in the bathroom, convincing her to go up on the roof. She keeps a key to the roof in her sock. She stole it from the janitor's ring. I then heard Miranda run quickly down stairs, as if she were being chased by the devil himself. I think she did that monstrous thing to Issy."

The black form moved away. "Wait!" Denali whispered. "Who are you?"

The form was gone.

Denali's mind raced. This must be a sick dream, she thought, and punched herself under the covers to check if she was indeed asleep. No! This was not a dream, and the mysterious whisperer had vanished without her knowing who it was. Miranda!

She couldn't possibly be so sick and cruel! Denali thought, filled with grief and torment. Or could she?

Denali slid out of bed silently and crawled along the floor to Miranda's bed. She felt inside the girl's shoes for her socks. Pulling the fabric out, she felt for the key. The small metal piece shocked her hand and her mind. She took the key and stole silently to the stairwell that led to the roof.

Upon reaching the locked door, she slid the key into the lock and turned. The bolt clicked free and the door opened easily. The cool night air did nothing to chill the heat of her anger. Throwing the key with vehemence into the blackness, she caught a fluttering movement near the far corner of the roof where a large oak tree grew. The figure had long, dark wavy hair and was wearing a nightdress with roses embroidered along the hem. The outline was thin and ethereal, barely visible in the darkness.

"Issy!" Denali cried, running towards the wisplike form. Nearing the roof's corner, she found nothing but a breeze rustling through the great tree's frame.

"Nothing," Denali cried, heartsick. The harsh, sharp-edged emotion cut into her, biting and tearing away at her youthful tenderness.

"Miranda! How could you?" she asked the evening's chill air. In that moment, in the absence of love, where any previous fear may have crept, Denali was forever changed. She walked back down the unlit stairwell, the darkness oozing into her stricken mind.

She crept back to her bed, reeling in sorrow for her dear, sweet little friend. A bond of sisterhood had been broken by a brutal, vengeful act of murder. In that moment of anguish, something inside Denali went missing. Her broken heart vowed to right the wrong done to her only love, now lost.

The vendetta in Denali's mind grew stronger each day. Miranda's cocky looks did nothing to dissuade the rising tide of anger she felt at the loss of her dear friend. She watched the older girl for weakness, searching for a fault that would expose an opportunity to even the score and avenge her beloved, her sweet and innocent little Issy.

Dear *Issy*, she often thought, *how troubled I am that you are no longer near me.*

One evening, late, after all were meant to be asleep, Denali lay awake, thinking. The night was oppressively humid, so the windows were open. A slight breeze moved through the old building. It was then that Denali heard the sound, something out of the ordinary, a slight scraping.

Looking down the room, she saw a form, lit by a sliver of moon, taking the screen off one of the windows.

It slipped out through the window and onto the ledge outside. Denali got up and peered outside just in time to see Miranda climbing down a nearby oak tree whose limbs grew close enough to the building to reach.

Denali quickly donned dark clothing and followed. She spotted Miranda trotting across the lawn towards the park. Denali melded into shadows, a fearless predator stalking, hunting. She soon realized Miranda, the vile creature, must be meeting a boy.

Denali followed her to the river where her quarry sat on a large boulder next to the water's edge, evidently waiting. No one else could be seen from Denali's hiding spot along the river trail. Miranda's secret visitor must be late, she thought. Slipping from the shadows, she grasped a large, smooth stone from the rocky shore and crept up silently behind the unsuspecting girl. Swinging the rock fiercely, she smashed it brutally into the side of the wicked girl's head. A sigh emanated from Miranda's mouth, and she slid limply into the water. Bubbles formed from the remaining air escaping her lungs.

Denali found a long driftwood stick and pushed the unconscious girl, soon to be a corpse, farther off the rocky beach. The river's current caught the floating form, moving it among the flickering ripples downstream.

Denali ran faster than her feet had ever carried her back to the orphanage. She climbed the tree silently and then crawled into bed after quietly undressing. "That was for you, dearest Issy!" she said, eyes filled with tears of loss. She had whispered it quietly, no more than a soft breath, yet in her mind she screamed the same words for hours, days, months, and years to come.

FIFTY-FIVE

A FEW times a month, a couple—two unfortunates who could not make a son or daughter from their union—would come to choose a daughter from among the girls. Denali, while not really liking her life at the orphanage school, wished to remain, as she preferred to be somewhere she knew rather than be cast into a questionable future.

Many girls returning from unsuccessful foster home placements spoke with abhorrence of the parents. Denali looked as mean as she could when the visitors arrived. Screwing her beautiful face into a countenance of darkness, she had avoided being chosen and placed for nine years.

Today, the couple was a slovenly looking woman with dark circles under the eyes and an unhealthy pallor. The man had eyes that seemed to be constantly sizing up the situation, searching like a shark for food.

Denali shrunk from the eyes, averting her gaze and trying to look mean, as usual. She hoped and prayed she would not be chosen by this disgusting couple. Where did these bottom feeders come from? she thought, and who in their right mind had cleared them as worthy to raise a young, impressionable waif?

The man said, "We'll have her. She's a cute little bundle. Let's be off with her tonight."

The Matron took Denali's hand, went to her bed and locker, and gathered up her things. She stuffed them into a cheap canvas bag and said to the couple, "The paperwork will take just a few minutes, and then she's yours."

The sound of their signatures scraping on the paper remained in her ears forever to come: her life, being signed away as some nearly worthless chattel. She shuddered to think where she was going and what the future had in store.

The autocar was expensive and the upholstery soft, yet this did nothing to calm the her racing mind. The man whisked them away into the dark of night and into the unknown.

The house was bigger than her school, well kept and luxurious. Denali was given a room that had its own bath and closets, a writing desk, and many interesting books on the shelves. Maybe, she thought, her feelings had been wrong. Perhaps she had misread these people. Was it possible that her tension was baseless?

She tried to relax after dinner in her room. Lying in the big, soft bed with the cute stuffed animals did nothing to make her sleepy. The night rolled on, and the moon's pale path through the bedroom window spoke of her sleepless hours.

She heard the uneven footsteps first, like those of a sailor on a heaving ship, unbalanced on a deck that was pitching up and down—yet the house stood still. Denali pulled the blankets tight around herself.

The door opened and the man stepped through. His eyes were red rimmed and glossy, not flitting, not searching, but looking intently at her as he moved towards her bed.

"I'm fine, mister. I don't need anything and am not scared."

"Oh, you are fine all right. That's why I'm here."

He reached under the covers towards her private places, and she screamed, "Help! Help, he's after me! Will you help me?"

In the distance, muffled by the walls of the house, she heard the woman, her foster mother, yell in a slurring angry voice, "Shut up, you little tramp! I'd rather he were pestering you than me!"

The man leered sickly and grabbed Denali with both hands, holding her down so she could not move.

When she was sure he had gone back to bed, Denali made her way to the kitchen, crying. She opened drawers until she came upon the knives. She chose one that cut her arm easily when she drew the blade lightly across her skin. Walking back upstairs, she opened the couple's bedroom door and went in.

The woman was snoring loudly in bed, and the man was passed out on a small sofa in the same room. She went to the woman first. Taking the knife in her strongest hand, she thrust it point-first through the disgusting sleeping creature's throat and then pulled hard, sawing upward. The woman bolted upright, excited hot breath shooting out of her severed throat. On attempting to inhale, she sucked blood. Her lungs gurgled and she fell over in bed, twitching and thrashing like a chicken with a severed head.

Denali walked to the man next. He lay with his robe open at the front, the grotesque appendage clearly visible. Denali stabbed his groin first, and when the drunken man woke and lurched forward, she stabbed his throat.

She stepped back and watched him claw futilely at the protruding weapon. When he tried to pull at it, his blood-covered hands only slipped on the handle. Soon he was on his knees, and then lying on the floor, face down, thrashing as his ugly wife had.

Denali walked to the bedside phone, called the emergency number printed on its face, and waited for an answer. "Are you experiencing an emergency?"

"Not anymore."

"Why have you called?"

"My foster father hurt me really badly, and my foster mother let him."

"Are you safe now?" asked the professional-sounding voice on the other end of the connection.

"Yes, I'm safe."

"Where are your parents?"

"Here in the bedroom with me. I've killed them both," she stated calmly.

"You've done what?" asked the startled operator.

"I've cut both their throats. I'll go unlock the front door so your officers can come in when they get here."

She hung up the phone and waited in the entry hall, wishing she were back in her old familiar bed and that, upon waking, she would find this all to be a very bad nightmare.

FIFTY-SIX

Denali was sixteen and had spent the past seven years in a large, inner-city reform school. Killing her foster parents when she was nine years old, even though the disgusting excuses for human beings had deserved to die, had not gone over well. She was still considered dangerous, although a series of psychiatrists she had seen over the past seven years had declared her completely sane. She was never allowed back in her orphanage school. She was actually happy not to have to return there, where she had to deal with dark memories of her dead friend.

Denali wondered often how life could be so cruelly unjust.

While being certifiably sane, the psychiatrists all also noted no remorse in the young girl for what they called the "emotionless slayings of both foster parents on her first night in their home."

Denali, of course, was never given access to the reports. She would have responded, "Emotionless my ass!" She had killed them both while tears of pain blurred her vision and violent shudders shook her body.

It was only after the adrenalin hit that she was conveyed into a state of utter clarity and experienced the complete lack of emotion. She had been there before. Right after dispatching wicked Miranda, and she felt no remorse for avenging brutality done unjustly to her dear and innocent friend.

So it was with Denali. Right and wrong were clear. If blood must be let and breath snuffed to right an insufferable wrong, she had no problem doing what was necessary.

She had grown from a beautiful child into a striking young woman. Her exotic features turned the heads of admiring men and jealous women. Denali was indifferent to the attention, whether it was good energy or bad. She had learned long ago that the world was unfair. Her feathers were nearly impossible to ruffle, unless someone attempted to damage her or someone she loved.

Denali excelled in track and became the triathlon champion of all Seven's female reform schools. She also mastered soccer, and her team was undefeated planet-wide. Gymnastics came naturally to her tight, steel-like frame, and she bested every boy in one-on-one, free-hand rock-climbing competitions for years. She, being a prodigy in physics and computers, was singled out and watched more closely than any other young girl in Seven Galaxies by Duhcat. He needed talent like hers for his plan to keep Seven's culture from becoming the sewer that ancient Earth had become.

At sixteen, the most important event of the year was the June graduation and dance. Several of the boys' and girls' schools were brought together under steadfast supervision and were allowed, one night in the year, to celebrate their achievements by mingling with the opposite sex.

Denali was not excited as all the other girls were. The others were practically frothing at the mouth, giggling and being absurd. Denali was only going because she had earned the right through her exemplary performance; girls that misbehaved were penalized and not allowed to attend. She had only a cool interest in the boys that would be there.

The hall was huge, the music wonderful, and the parade of young men interesting. All the boys pushed and shoved, mentally and physically, to be near Denali and to be honored by her hand in theirs.

She donned no make-up and wore a simple blue-green hand-me-down sweater dress. It set off her sparkling wide eyes. She was, to her utter surprise, an object of attraction. Never had she anticipated such attention.

Denali had always found herself odd looking with her red-blonde hair, so different from the norm, her pale complexion, and her frustrating freckles, which jumped onto her face in summer months like shotgun perforations on a target. Yet here all the boys were, wishing her to dance. She was demure and self-conscious, attempting to please all demands and cut-ins till she felt exhausted. After the first hour, she took leave and visited the restroom for some quiet space.

Coming out of the stall after relieving herself, she was confronted by four older girls, all inner-city gang members with arrests and prison sentences in their backgrounds. Talk in the joint was that they had crimes under their belts that included robbery, murder, prostitution, extortion, hard-drug distribution, and many others too numerous to list.

Denali took the glowering group in without emotion.

The leader of the four spoke. "Bitch, we gunna mess up that purty lil face a yours so them boyz ain't findin' ya sos special 'n atrativ."

"What 'bout the legs?" another of the wretches said in her street-mouth slime. "She beat us at all du matches. Don'ya thin' we ut to fix 'em, too?"

"Yeah, lez do her leg an' th' face. Mess her up sos non o' them boyz is gonna wan' her no mo, and she won' be makin' us look shit like on the track!"

"Yeah!" they all said, sure of their superiority over this much younger, smaller girl.

"You four against me?" Denali asked, surprised but not afraid.

"Thaz right! An' ifn ya tell who don ya, we be back on ya like stank, ya hea'?"

"Yea, I hea'!" Denali mimicked their street dialect. "Then if I put the shit on y'all, ya won tell a soul, juzza same?"

"You?" The most intelligent looking of the four actually spoke a word defined in *Webster's*. "Shit, girl, if I was you, I'd be runnin' my ass clean outa this barn sos we don' hafta mess up that Cinderella face. You get yo sorry ass on outa hea' an' promise comin' to no mo dances, and we let you walk gentle without too much pain."

"I won't concede to you."

"Wha'd red bitch say?"

"I dunno," echoed the other three.

"You four give your word that if you lose, we'll keep this little meeting strictly between us. You can make up some story like you slipped in the bathroom, all four on the same spot—is that clear?"

"Oh! Ya, we all promise, yo sass ass!"

"You *don't* keep your word, you cause me any trouble after this, and I will simply and efficiently take your lives. Do you four understand *my* terms?"

"Oh! Ya! We unstan' yo g'tting' tha wors' of us, tha's wha' yo gettin!"

They came, a wild hoard, jealousy shredding common sense, wishing to expend all the frustration they felt by beating Denali into an irreparable mess.

What they got, in a sequence based on the nearest assailant to the last, was a very painful enlightening. It manifested itself on the first girl as a broken elbow, compounded out of joint by backwards overextension from Denali's strike, and three broken ribs from a lightning-fast triple-punch combination, administered with precision to the tender, undefended spot, just below her assailant's armpit as she flew by.

The second aggressor ended up with a displaced kneecap and severely fractured skull, after Denali cast her falling head into the bathroom sink.

The other two shared temporary blindness and broken eardrums from a double tiger claw to the face and flat-handed double strikes to the ears of each. As they fell to their knees, first one and then the other, Denali came up with her knee under the downward chins, breaking many teeth.

Denali's whole defense had taken less than six seconds. She looked in the mirror before walking out, straightening a few misplaced strands of red hair, while thinking that all those Chinese martial arts movies she had watched had come in *very* handy after all.

She returned to the dance floor and took her place amongst the starving multitudes.

FIFTY-SEVEN

DENALI woke at daybreak the morning after the dance. She'd had a great time the night before, regardless of the bathroom encounter. She rose and stretched. The small, high windows afforded little view, but the colors of sunrise were evident. No sooner had she showered and dressed than four guards walked in, summoning her to a meeting with the warden.

Denali knew what was about to take place. She had been accused. The four gang bitches' egos could not live with her besting them. All the gangs bragged. They assumed, incorrectly, that she would also.

Denali had taken their oath of silence. She had given hers. They had broken their oath. So on this beautiful morning, after such a fun and exciting night, she was being escorted under heavier guard than she had ever seen used, to the warden's office.

Ushered into the stark concrete room, she took in the woman at the big steel desk. "Hello, ma'am," she addressed her ruler, hoping in the show of respect to gain a friendly ear.

The tirade began. "Denali, you are accused of assaulting four young girls in the bathroom last night while the dance was in full bloom. What do you have as an explanation?"

"They attacked me! I asked them to let me pass, but they were jealous of my athletic accomplishments, and the fact that all the boys wanted to dance with me.

"I tried to avoid conflict, ma'am, but the wretches would have none of my forays into peacefulness." Denali told a half-truth.

"Denali! Two of those excuses for girls have fathers who are quite wealthy and influential in local government. While I personally believe you were only protecting yourself, no one else does. No one believes that you could have beaten four attackers. Everyone but me believes—and I must say, this sentiment has been influenced by the girls' fathers—that you attacked them without warning in a brutal and unmerciful fashion. Even though I am skeptical of this, I have been forced by the political climate to discipline you. I am sentencing you to two months in solitary confinement. This is, for a juvenile facility, unheard of. However, my hands are tied. I can do nothing else! I am truly sorry, Denali."

"Ma'am, this is not your struggle but mine. Fret not. Solitary will give me time to study up on subjects that are as yet in my future. Can you assure me you will see to it that books will be made available to me as I request?"

"Denali, I will do what I can to make this terrible wrong right. If you submit a list of needed material, I assure you that you will have it, along with a computer and access to the planetary library."

"It is well with me, ma'am. Worry not. I am happy with the arrangements."

FIFTY-EIGHT

Two months of solitary confinement did nothing but further Denali's intense studies and cement her resolve to fulfill her word. Upon being returned to her original block, she was surprised to find the four who had broken their oaths at her disposal. Surely, Denali thought, the warden had read her psyche profile and could imagine what might happen. *Lambs to the warden's sacrifice,* she thought.

So it came to be: the four who had attacked Denali without provocation and who then accused her of ambushing them met their demise. One slipped on a bar of soap, striking her head so violently on the tiled concrete floor that some fractured tile had to be replaced. One hung herself in a bathroom stall with strips of bed sheets braided together. The other two had died of overdoses, although no one knew where they'd obtained the drugs. They all died within a twenty-four hour period, which, by any stretch of the imagination, was more than coincidental—particularly since this was the twenty-four hours immediately following Denali's release from solitary confinement.

The Duhcat Foundation called her file and her life. She was whisked away in utter secrecy, disappearing during a very black night, placed in training to hone her metal to a razor's edge—transforming her into a flickering mirage, a fleeting shadow that fell silently upon evil, extinguishing it person by person within Seven Galaxies.

At twenty years of age, after four years of training, Denali was lithe and gorgeous. She was adept at her secret, ultimate, and deadly black arts and also at computer science and quantum physics. She was contracted by the foundation for ten years. The contract expired when her reflexes, no longer primed, left her at risk. She was pensioned off and given freedom to move as she pleased, with memories haunting her constantly.

Denali woke drenched in sweat. Trepidation from the job in front of her stole the morning's joy, and she resolved to prepare, to pull the dark task together and evaporate from sight—along with five million credits, stowed away secretly for her future.

She drove her utility auto from its dark home in the garage and made her way toward the admiral's valley and their intertwined fate. In the hidden storage compartment, custom built into the rear floor, was the weapon and a stealth-cloaking suit. Her plan was to wait in the woods, unseen, and then do the despicable deed and put the tragedy quickly into her past.

FIFTY-NINE

"Serene, I would like to speak of the Dome and the Portal to the gardens," TyGor said. "I cannot believe the rest of the Fifteen are gone. The portal within the Dome of Wisdom, do you know where it leads? Could they have taken refuge there before the asteroid hit?"

"Dear Ty, the legend of the portal goes back to a time before the Dome was constructed. You know, the Dome was built as guardian of the gateways. The tranquility and the openings or threads leading to travel paths within the gardens will never be violated by persons unaccepted by the Dome. Only those possessing the qualities, which are required in a person's character to gain entrance, can be admitted. All others have been forever forbidden.

"Some believe the portal takes us into another dimension—a haven, if you will—and that it is a layer, not accessible, not even with the technology we possess. This place cannot be penetrated except through the portal, hence the complicated and necessary screening process.

"The screening process to enter that sacred place is one to which I am very familiar. You see, one of the many duties I had when working with the Ancient as personal assistant was to monitor all data collected on candidates being considered for entry to the Dome. Electronic programs gathered, sorted, and constructed the reports. There were many other ways to obtain information. I was personally responsible for engaging the services of a private firm that specialized in identity and background checks.

"You see, electronic information is only as verifiably good as the best hackers. Any identity or history can be constructed, even in the absence of actual matter. The firm I speak of was engaged to take the electronic data files and physically investigate the authenticity of each and every alleged fact, whether it had a positive or negative affect on the candidate's acceptance.

"Thus, in the final analysis, we considered not only the compiled electronic files, compressed to the essential criteria, but we also reviewed and meshed the firm's investigative report. A very expensive and time-consuming venture, I assure you. However, it was all necessary to keep the Dome pure, and the wonders of the portal secure.

"I could share many things of the portal with you. Some are fact, some myth or legend...but the realities are still a mystery. We do not know where the portal leads.

"Some of the Ancients who are no longer with us on the physical plane left riddles, which lead to clues. Those clues that we have deciphered suggest that Enricco Duhcat was responsible for the portal's discovery. It seems he felt it was so powerful that he alone formulated a plan, which was then implemented by our ancestors. His designs have protected the portal from evil.

"You of course know much of Enricco's involvement as our culture's benefactor.

"Some say that within the portal's gardens, other gateways lead to who knows where. Ancients of the past spoke of hidden doors in the gardens—hidden to keep unknowing persons from unintentionally straying through them and being lost in another dimension, or even another place in time, with small chance of returning."

"So the Ancients of the past credit Duhcat for the portal's discovery, as well as we, their more modern successors?"

"Yes, all the clues dropped and all the riddles solved lead to that conclusion."

"The man becomes a deeper mystery with each tidbit I learn of his life."

"Do you know, Ty, that Duhcat was actually accepted to be one of the Fifteen? That he declined the honor without offering an explanation?"

"Surely an adventurer like Duhcat would find life in the Dome a stifling bit of boredom."

"Nonetheless, he has been accepted and could take the post at any time. He could have seniority even over Leandra. Once a candidate is accepted, their tenure is determined by the date of acceptance, not the time of physical service within the Dome."

"Serene, I can't help but feel they are trapped by the wreckage of the Dome. If they sought refuge in the garden, they could still be alive!"

"Yes!" she said. "I believe they are safe. That they are waiting and wondering whether Seven suffered catastrophic destruction, and whether the wreckage will be cleared."

"Then it is imperative that we begin clearing the rubble. We must know for sure!"

"Ty, you have appealed to the people. What more can be done?"

"Perhaps Ventras was right. Maybe *I* should organize and spearhead the work. I could...at least until it gets well under way."

"My dear man, you are incorrigible! You have been retired for *one* day, and you're already talking about going back to work!"

"Would you mind so terribly?" Ty asked, playing his large, dark eyes as a puppy will when he misses the sweet taste of adoration.

"Not at all, love," she said, shaking her head. "I desire to see the other fourteen freed and back in their rightful places. To be truthful, Ventras gives me the willies. There is something reptilian in his eyes, something that chills me." Serene shivered involuntarily, thinking of Ventras and his icy, steel blue eyes.

"Then we are of like mind. I don't like the bastard either. Since he doesn't want the Dome of Wisdom rebuilt, we should take the project upon ourselves. There will be plenty of volunteers, I am sure."

"Sounds good to me, dear, but could we do it part-time? I was just really getting into this whole retirement thing," she said, wrapping her arms around him.

"How about I let you do the scheduling, lovely Serene."

"You...*my* admiral...delegate so naturally. I feel compelled to obey!"

"That's my girl. There are rewards for service *faithfully* rendered you know." Ty smiled that mischievous smile, which only meant that he was really after something more than perfunctory secretarial services.

SIXTY

Tay came alone, wishing to speak with Zuzahna regarding the unfounded charges brought against her. He was attempting to make sense of a quagmire into which she had been sucked.

Tay, of course, believed in the judiciary and its ability to sort fact from fiction, to weigh upon the scale of justice and rely on evidence stripped of hearsay and circumstantial drift.

What Tay did not realize was the power of a welling tide, a tide that was not controlled by the moon. It was as though Ventras could push it or pull it at will.

In Tay's naiveté, he failed to consider the events unfolding behind closed doors. From this sprung a weakness in his character that was otherwise unblemished.

A person knowledgeable of Ventras' dark side may have been more prepared. Tay, possibly taking Machiavellian methods in hand, would have exterminated the scourge named Ventras before his damage could be wrought. The universe would have been left a better place. Ventras' departure would leave in his absence less of the trauma that was about to unfold.

Tay knew nothing of Ventras' plans. He knew only that the man seemed dedicated to keeping his grip on his usurped power. As a very young man, Tay would soon painfully learn the depths of depravity into which a soul can sink when wealth and power becomes, for a twisted few, the ultimate aphrodisiac.

Tay shivered as he walked the corridor towards Zuzahna's cell. The prison was cool in temperature, but not enough to make him immediately cold. He wondered why the involuntary shudder had come over him. The feeling persisted, as premonitions often do. The subtle clues threaded, streaming through the ether, little understood or acknowledged, attempting to warn of potential dangers.

Zuzahna waited excitedly for Tay's arrival. She quickly took stock of her appearance and composure. She straightened her hair and patted her cheeks to bring a glowing blush forward.

The cell door opened. As Tay stepped through, Zuzahna rushed to him, smiling, forcing a cheerful countenance.

"Tay! Oh dear Tay!" Zuzahna faked her ever-practiced stumble, timed perfectly to be within his quick grasp. He reached out to catch her, and she became heavier in his arms than necessary. She was forcing him to hold her tightly.

"Darling Tay, I feel light in the head every time you come see me! I miss your company so! I only wish I were free from this awful, dreary place. I long for a time when we could truly know one another better, on a more physical level!" She breathed short, quaking breaths. Her chin wrinkled and wet, salty fluid welled in her eyes.

"There now, don't fret. Everything will work out."

Tay pulled Zuzahna in, embracing her tightly and feeling the warmth of her trembling, sweet, soft, and inspiring form.

She clung to him. She buried her face in the curve of his neck and shoulders. She held onto him, as if for dear life.

Time stood still for both—two pounding hearts, longing for better circumstances and happier moments, beat a chorus, one against the other.

At last Tay said reluctantly, "Zuzahna, I have engaged an attorney to take up your case. He assures me you *will* be set free, and that the circumstances of your capture do not give the prosecutor a foundation that will stand the judiciaries' scrutiny."

Zuzahna held onto him, not saying a word, preferring to meld herself with him, to exude her magnetism, to draw him in emotionally. She desired a deeper intimacy from this young man, whom she had every intention of mercilessly controlling.

She brought her face up from its comfortable resting place, speaking softly in his ear while she expelled breath, hot from being held deep in her lungs for a time.

"What I want desperately…just as I do my freedom… is you!"

She nuzzled his ear a moment before looking up at him with sensuous, imploring eyes. They were vast, dark, golden-flecked whirlpools of longing.

Tay took them in as never before. Zuzahna was here in his arms, so close…no one could come between them, he thought. Tay melted into her and began his first unfettered free fall into the unfathomable depths of her eyes.

He kissed her, and she pulled him tightly to herself, moving, swaying. Tay was swept away by the talisman of her touch.

SIXTY-ONE

Ventras smiled, watching them on the prison video monitor. Each cell had a hidden camera and audio pickup. The smile came not from joy or humor. Happiness, as a descriptive word, could be not used—unless it were seriously misconstrued and taken completely out of context. Subconscious jealousy and the lust for power within his sinister mind were twisted by the loathing he felt for the admiral and Tay.

His thoughts spiraled elliptically to black depths, depths that were morally out of bounds. To Ventras, they were enticingly unexplored.

All this brought the self-important smile—a smile of satisfaction for his manipulation of events past and unfolding, events that would cause the two much suffering. These thoughts created an outward appearance of happiness, yet true happiness evaded him. Haunted, he searched, yet his path was dark and without joy or love. Light is happiness, and so is love.

Ventras, caught in a web of self-created darkness, was about to perpetrate another action that would inevitably cast him deeper into the abyss. Reveling in his temporal power, the smile grew larger.

***

Tay and Zuzahna heard the rush of approaching footsteps. They broke from their momentary bliss in which their surroundings had been forgotten. They had been caught up in the surge of emotion and desire that had swept them to another dimension, to a window in time that was being slammed tightly shut between them. They looked at one another, and a pervading feeling of dread quickly evaporated the joy they had felt just moments ago.

The steps came closer. A moment later, Ventras was standing, smiling, outside the cell door with four guards.

Tay, obviously surprised, asked, "Ventras, has the tribunal found her innocent? Do you bring good news for Zuzahna?"

"I have no news for Zuzahna, only for you. TayGor, you are under arrest. The charges are treason, consorting with the enemy, and the unlawful transfer of wealth."

"What?"

"Zuzahna is the enemy. She is Nesdian! You have secured the deceased Nesdian regent Xrisen's property in her name. I also have in my possession a very touching video of you two lovers in acts of intimacy."

"The Nesdian regent's property was transferred to Zuzahna as the only living person from the regent's vessel. I assure you, Admiral Gor ordered the transfer in accordance with ancient maritime law. The orders are recorded. Zuzahna is not our enemy but our friend. She was simply an innocent passenger aboard the regent's private yacht. It was not a vessel of war!"

"TayGor, I will waste no time debating with you. I am a very busy man. Here is the warrant. Take the prisoner and place him in isolation."

With Ventras' words ringing in his brain, Tay watched him spin and leave the room. He listened to Ventras' footsteps as he walked briskly away.

"Don't worry, Zuzahna; the admiral will get to the bottom of this farce…I don't know what is going on, but I think Ventras has lost his mind! Everything will be okay. I'll see you soon."

SIXTY-TWO

Serene woke with the sunrise as usual. Respecting Ty's desire to wake at his leisure, she attempted to slip from bed silently and not disturb him. She felt first a warm hand, and then an arm, encircle her waist tightly.

"And where do you think you're sneaking off to, young lady?" he asked, in a voice gravelly from slumber.

"I didn't want to disturb you. I thought I would rise with the sun to enjoy the morning colors for a while, before fixing my man something warm and tasty to sustain him. You must be famished, working with such abandon so late into the night."

"You call my efforts work? I believe them to be the struggles of an artist, attempting to bring his creations—through loving toil and sweat—to the attention of his one and only admirer."

"Your only admirer?" she asked, her smile possessing a quality that escaped words. Serene had a way of bringing her features into a form that not only made her irresistibly charming and desirable but also funny in the same moment.

"I have ideas for breakfast," he said with a grin.

She looked upon him with questioning eyes, not uttering a word. Her silence was a powerful tool, giving her undeniable mystique and a healthy charge of electricity.

Wrapping his other arm around her and squeezing tightly, Ty said playfully, "You smell rather tasty. Perhaps I shall devour you without mercy and satisfy the hunger gnawing at my heart!"

"You cannot possibly have the energy," she said, laughing. "I thought after your valiant and lengthy effort last night, as well as the banquet and awards ceremony, exhaustion would take hold and you would sleep till noon."

"Perhaps I will, when I have finished with you once more. Then I shall sleep the heavenly sleep of a babe suckled at his mother's breast, loved, nurtured, and tucked in with doting hands."

"Ooh! I like the sound of being ravished before breakfast, but I'm not sure my body could handle another thrashing like last night. You see, my dear man, I am completely out of practice. I am unconditioned for the rigors through which you have put me. Anyway, don't you think we should brush our teeth first?" Serene asked.

"Is my breath revolting?" Ty asked, looking sheepish and turning his face so that the words spoken would not flow straight into her face.

"No, not at all. I was thinking of my own," she said, placing a hand to one of his cheeks and gently pulling his face back so that she could look directly into his eyes.

"It has been my experience, Serene, that sweet and gentle people wake without the proverbial morning breath. Yours is reminiscent of fresh cut flowers, and I long to take in the fragrance for a time. Will you be so gracious, so compassionate and willing to give of your love to me again this morning? To one so desperate for your affections, so needy, I am a man dying of thirst in a vast desert. To me, you are the elixir, the cure; your tender touch restores me to my former strength and abates all the demons within me."

"Oh! You are so full of it! Do you really think these tactics will weaken my resolve to rise with the morning sun?" Serene asked, toying affectionately with him, not giving in too easily, wondering whether he would stoop to begging, as some men were known to.

"Alas, my dear, you are already too late. With our bantering, the sun has risen. What other excuse might you find to leave me alone?"

"I *am* tempted; however, I fear I will be rubbed raw if you go at me with the fortitude you showed last night," she said, only half-teasing. Ty was a consummate lover. The thought astounded her; quite simply she would never have believed a man his age could possibly be so randy.

"If I promised to be quick?" he asked, the look of a scolded schoolboy on his face. "Would that change your mind?" He donned bedroom eyes that made her weak in the knees.

"You, Admiral Gor, are incorrigible! Don't you dare try those puppy eyes on me! I'm serious. Don't you hear anything I'm saying?!"

"For your information, I am retired. I have heard everything you have said. I have listened patiently. The last words you uttered were that you are serious."

With that, Ty began softly tickling her in various places.

"Stop! Stop, I said!"

Serene was weakening, breathing in quick, short bursts between the heaves of laughter.

"Stop! I said I am being serious!"

"At this moment in time, you look anything but serious, my dear." He continued the light tickling.

"I swear!" she said, between gasps and fits of laughter. "If you don't stop, I'm going to wet the bed! Then you will be the one changing the sheets you—you meanie! Okay! Okay! I'll give in. If you make it quick. And if you promise to get up and hike to the cliff top with me, after we eat breakfast. You obviously have no problem getting all your exercise in a horizontal position! I need to stretch and walk, or I'll feel like I've been run over by a truck tomorrow morning. You bully!"

She tickled him back and was surprised to see him jump at the slightest touch like a young child.

"Ah! Your Achilles' heel!"

She went at him unmercifully. Every time he blocked her hands, she moved to another sensitive spot, reveling in making him writhe.

The great, unconquered Admiral Gor was at the mercy of a woman nearly half his weight.

"No! Don't! No!" he pleaded, desperate to end her affectionate torture.

"Do you promise?" Serene asked, giggling.

"Yes! Yes!"

Serene relented from the tickling.

Ty was short of breath yet quickly regained his composure.

"How quick?" he asked, humor and love's light showing in his eyes. He nuzzled her neck and pressed himself against her tightly as she pondered her answer.

"Don't!… Stop!" she exclaimed. "Please don't…stop! Please don't stop!" She melted into his embrace.

Leaving the house and stepping out into the fresh, cool morning, Ty took Serene's hand. They set out across the field towards the ridge trail. Frost lay upon patches of shade, telling of autumn's approach and the change of seasons: one of youthful greenery and abundantly colorful brilliance ending. The next beginning with the fading of wildflowers turned brown by the previous evening's chill.

The rainbow colors of dying leaves struck their appreciating eyes. The brisk morning brought with it an azure sky, which seemed to swallow their speech. They walked in silence, except for their footfalls, taking in the morning sounds. A formation of wild geese heading south called to one another, creating curiosity in Ty and Serene as they both wondered about a destination unknown.

Dew on the grass sparkled, reflecting golden sunlight. The river, low from so little rain fall, spoke the voice of fall, quietly caressing the stones worn smooth; so unlike the rushing torrent it would soon become when inevitable rainstorms hit. Small songbirds clustered in the forest along the meadow and created mixed choruses, each species singing its own melody as it readied itself for the journey towards warmer climes. The music of nature combined, serenading them while walking, removed from them the necessity of speech.

As they entered the forest trail, golden-red leaves fluttered, spiraling downward from the canopy above. Their footsteps became loud, reverberating as they crunched over foliage once live and singing in warm summer breezes.

The standing timber, stretching up the sheer hillside, created patterns of dark parallel shadows contrasted by the bright sunlit colors between. The trail was overgrown since Shadow, Tay's horse, no longer used the path. Ty and his grandson had been off planet over two years, and in that time the path had evidently been little used. They threaded their way over and through fallen limbs and walked below overhanging underbrush and the ever-present webs of mother spiders, some pregnant and ready to drop huge egg sacks in hideaways unapparent to passersby.

After a time, they made their way to the cliff top. They stopped and peered over the edge, breathlessly taking in what lay below. Serene had only seen the valley from a lower angle, viewed from the house, the field, and river.

"Oh! My!" she exclaimed. "It is heart-stopping… gorgeous!"

The foothills flowing downward to the valley floor were draped in colors: a collage of nature's creation. The orange, yellow, and red patches of scattered hardwoods commingled within a forest predominately evergreens. Distant mountains rose abruptly, thrusting broken fingered peaks into the sky. Snow clung in shadowed canyons and a glacier of aquamarine snaked down one mountain's sheer slope. Serene took in the scene in silence.

The river wound its course through the valley floor. In sweeping bends, sunlight shone upward, cast at a slant, illuminating the near naked limbs of trees stretched out over its course. It threaded glistening curves, disappearing upstream into foothills where it met a golden, green and brown valley floor.

Serene looked at Ty. He was as enraptured as she was, as though this were the first time he had seen the view. He was full of appreciation for the place that had nurtured him as a boy. A home and farm left so many years ago to go to war, a war which, if not won, could have taken this irreplaceable place, changed it, stolen its natural beauty and grace.

Finally, Serene spoke. "Thank you for sharing your beloved valley with me, Ty. I see now why this place is so much a part of you."

Stepping back, he took her in, saying, "I am, as always, in awe of my home. Through some of my darkest moments, I have been sustained by the never-faltering belief that my final days would be spent here. Now, with your beauty and grace added to a scene that has always been precious, two centuries of risk and toil seem an insignificant price to pay for the happiness I find in sharing my home with you.

"Winter will set in very soon. Sometimes we are snowed in here, with little to do but curl up before the fire, snuggle, and read. Those days have been some of the finest." Ty smiled, thinking of the long winter nights they would be spending together.

They sat for a couple of hours before setting off down the hill for lunch.

Serene was ready for a nap after eating and had no trouble coaxing Ty back to bed. They slept peacefully, naïve of Ventras' plot. In their slumber, they were unaware of the figure nearby, stealthily approaching the rustic home. A cloaking suit concealed the intruder's form as they drew nearer and waited in the woods by the house.

Serene woke with a start. A feeling of dread unnatural to her pervaded her normal tranquility. In an effort to shake off the mood, she rose and went into the kitchen, where she put some water on the stove for tea.

Ty followed her into the kitchen, rubbing his chest hair and wearing only his pajama bottoms. "I'm going out on the patio to listen to the river for a while. Will you join me shortly?" He wrapped his arms around her from behind, waiting for an answer.

"I would love to. It will be getting chilly though. You should put a shirt on or you'll catch your death."

Cold shivers ran down her spine, and Ty asked, "What is wrong? You seem so tense?"

"I woke with an odd feeling—nothing I can put my finger on, but perhaps there is a cougar out in the woods."

"In my entire life, I have only ever seen two of the super predators here, and never were they any threat; they fear us, as we fear them. It's a fair bargain. Besides, I am with you; you need not be afraid."

Serene relaxed in his arms, enjoying the way he held her.

The wireless sounded an incoming call and Ty said, "Yes?"

"Sir, this is Alex. Have you heard?"

"Heard what, Alex?"

"Tay has been arrested!"

"What are the charges?"

"Treason, and consorting with the enemy—a long list."

"Absolutely ridiculous!" Ty said with disbelief.

"I know! You must come!"

"I will be there as quickly as possible."

At that moment, the sound of an explosion echoed over the wireless.

"They're here! They've blasted my door." A click sounded and the signal disappeared.

"Bring me some green tea, will you, Serene? I need to collect my thoughts."

Ty ran his hands quickly through his hair and Serene could feel his tension building, the sensation struck her like a static electrical charge, except it was ominous and foreboding to her.

Serene nodded, shock leaving her at a loss for words.

Ty walked out to the patio, which had a good view of a bend in the river. Sitting down, an uneasy foreboding came over him. He discounted it, thinking, *How absurd. I will go immediately and sort out this farce! Too many years on watch.*

The near-invisible intruder took careful aim. Her emotions were intentionally suppressed. She squeezed the trigger, sending a silent and highly concentrated microwave beam deep into Ty's brain.

Ty felt searing heat and then shooting pain. He thought it must be a migraine, although he had never before been afflicted with one.

Serene walked out onto the patio with two teacups in hand. Ty was rubbing his forehead with both hands.

"What is it, dearest?" Serene asked, concern evident in her voice.

"I'm not sure…a pain in my head."

Attempting to brush it off, he picked up the cup and raised it to his lips. His hand suddenly went numb, and the cup dropped to the stone floor, shattering into pieces. The sound reverberated, echoing in his crippled mind.

"My darling!" Serene cried in alarm, rising to comfort just as he toppled from his chair to the stone floor.

"Ty! Oh my God, I'm calling for help!"

"No! Stay with me! Don't go, I beg you."

She obeyed, against her strong will, and sat down, cradling his head in her lap.

"There is not much time." Ty spoke with obvious effort.

"Don't be silly, love, it's probably just the news that has upset you. You'll be fine after the shock wears off."

"Listen, Serene! My soul hovers above us, it is attached by a gossamer thread…I am leaving you!"

"No!" she wailed. "Don't go!"

"You must promise me something," he said with difficulty.

"Anything!"

"Promise me you will do everything within your power to free Tay and end the injustice that has landed him in prison."

"I promise, dearest. Rest now," she said, her voice broken by fear and mourning.

"There are dark forces; I can feel them now. Those who take life from me are the same who have turned on Tay; I see it clearly. Tell Tay he must seek the Virgin!

Promise me you will tell him: the Virgin. He must seek her for his safety."

"I promise, I will tell him!" Serene said, not understanding but recognizing the importance of the request. "Don't go, Ty, please. I cannot stand to think of my life without you. My darling, please don't!"

"I'm sorry. The short hours we've shared together have brought me joy of an entire lifetime. Dearest Serene, thank you."

"No! NO!" she screamed in anguish.

"Ty, my darling, my soul mate, do you believe in past, present, and future lives?"

"Surely!" he answered with difficulty, his voice slurring.

"Then find me. Come to me, darling. If you believe we are soul mates then we will undoubtedly meet again." Flowing tears dripped from her nose and landed on his ashen face.

"I believe. I will come," was all he could say.

Looking into his eyes, she could see his tears of remorse; a new life only just begun had been stolen. Then the wisp of filament connecting soul to body frayed, and Ty was gone.

In her disbelief, she wept. Her body was wracked with convulsions. Her soul shuddered on the edge of a dark precipice as the pain engulfed her, swallowing her alive, crushing her former joy and wringing her until tears came no more. Hours passed. A wreck of grief and emotion, she mourned her loss, his loss, and the loss of the life they would have lived together.

* * *

THE SEEDING SEVEN'S VISION

On an otherwise gorgeous autumn day, with his soul mate at his side, Gor, the legendary warrior, fell.

Slain was the guardian and protector of Seven Galaxies, who had, for two centuries, blocked the path of an evil that held nothing sacred and that desecrated honor, spirituality, morality, and justice.

For consciousless greed, which consumed a handful of minor politicians who had usurped an authority, vast in its infancy, and grown immensely larger in the passing years, Gor's life was taken. He fell not on the field of battle, facing a known opponent; instead, his life had been stolen: a theft, blackened by cowardice, and perpetrated by a person fearful of direct challenges. The dark deed was done in the light of day.

The plan—spawned in shadowed labyrinths within musty corners of a devious mind—moved forward.

Tay was left alone, imprisoned for life under false pretenses, and now with no powerful advocate to bargain for his release.

SIXTY-THREE

DENALI walked through the woods, returning from her abysmal task. Through her infrared glasses, she saw a camouflaged form waiting on the hill in the woods above her vehicle. *A trap!* she thought. It was one she had anticipated. She skirted silently behind the waiting figure.

She threw her knife with precision, and it struck deep into the back of the would-be assassin, piercing the heart. The impact from the carbon fiber weapon knocked her ambusher from a crouch, flat onto the ground.

Denali walked slowly towards the unmoving form. Curiosity drove her to see who it was. Reaching the body, she rolled it over. Its weight seemed too light to be a person, and the face! The face was a mannequin's. The bee sting in her neck made her slap at the insect, but her hand made contact with a dart. *What in the hell?* she thought, her knees buckling. She fell onto her back on the forest floor.

Trees swayed above her, their limbs waving. She heard footsteps approaching.

"Well, Denali, not such the bad little warrior now, are we? Don't answer. Oh, that's right you can't speak, the paralysis has already set in." Ventras laughed. "You are awake but cannot move a muscle. Perfect! This is what I have desired of you for years." Ventras began unfastening the front of his stealth-cloaked cool suit. Denali had not picked up his lurking form with the infrared glasses because he had covered his body's heat.

"No, Denali, I am not going to kill you. You were always so hard. I've never seen your soft side. But today I will. Today, you are completely mine. When I've finished, you'll be found by a patrol, with your weapon and your gear. Your crime, the assassination of Admiral Gor, will bring you life in the penal moon. A lifetime to think of the mistakes you've made and to remember how nice I was to you, not taking your life—only some of your sweet tenderness."

Denali's eyes, wide in shock, welled full of tears.

SIXTY-FOUR

Ventras chuckled to himself as he walked towards Tay's holding cell, thinking that a game of chess is not really a game of skill if one cheats. That's the problem with honorable men, he thought, they do not calculate in the ways of Machiavelli. Ventras did. For in the maze of his twisted mind, he compared himself to that ancient scholar of darkness, the oracle of chaos and doom, the prognosticator of evil cause and effect.

Ventras gloated as his stride struck a dull chorus upon the concrete floors of the prison.

Stopping in front of the cell he had devised for Tay-Gor, he reveled in the fact that the young man never even looked up. Clearly, he must be depressed.

"Splendid!" Ventras said out loud.

The handsome and intelligent face of the young commander lifted. Ventras studied the features, seeing a young Admiral Gor.

"Do you have something for me? Some news I would find heartening, Ventras?"

"Aye, you are scheduled to depart Seven in the morning for the penal moon; good news for me, bad for you."

"What? I have appealed!" Tay said, shocked. "Surely my case will be reconsidered before I am shipped to the prison?"

"I am afraid, young man, that in your instance an appeal will not be considered."

"What do you mean? Tell me!"

"In cases of treason and terrorism, the tribunal's verdict is final. I'm afraid that you no longer have a *future* to look forward to, other than rotting for the rest of your previously amazing life, in a very small, isolated, and ultimately depressing cell."

"You cannot be serious! Admiral Gor will take up this farce with the High Court and not the assembly of kangaroos you appointed tribunal to funnel me through so quickly. I have rights under Seven Galaxies' Constitution! Who are you to deprive me?"

"Haven't you heard, Tay? Oh, that's right, you haven't been allowed near a paper or the news. Seven is under martial law. I am attempting, through the use of restrained force, to end the chaos that ensued after the asteroid hit. You know…looting…riots…murders. You should know, being a military man, that under martial law, the constitution and all the rights it guarantees have been suspended.

"Oh! And I almost forgot to break the other devastating news to you: I regret to inform you that the late Admiral Gor died two evenings ago. That is why you've received no news. Being the sentimental person I am, I wanted to inform you personally, not have you read it in unfeeling black and white. How do you feel about that? Do you understand now why he never came to your trial?"

The younger Gor's astonishment was evident by his speechlessness and the flush on his face. "This is all some sick joke! Tell me it is not true!"

"It *is* true, Tay!" he said, smiling cheerfully. "You are shipping out tomorrow, convicted as an enemy sympathizer, a spy, and a traitor. With Admiral Gor dead, there is no one to speak on your behalf."

Ventras flashed his long teeth, shiny with drool formed by his hunger to conquer this obstacle, this hindrance to his plan of rule.

Tay shrank away from the mastermind who had created the debacle consuming him.

After thinking a moment, he said, "And what of Alex?"

"Oh, your partner in the conspiracy? He has been convicted as well. Perhaps you will see each other once in a while. I have arranged separate quarters for you both. You see, we really don't need you two geniuses putting your heads together, do we?" Ventras' eyes shone, alight with the victory held in hand.

Tay glared back. "You really don't believe you can pull this off, do you?"

Ventras' voice was mocking, sweet. "You are an intelligent young man. Surely you can see that I stand out here while you are locked in there. I have *already* pulled it off!

"I have won! You are the loser! Perhaps if you weren't so upright, so naïve, and so gullible you might have seen the storm approaching. Yet you were so preoccupied, your star-filled eyes only seeing that *tart*, Zuzahna, and so you overlooked the mire I was creating, into which you are now hopelessly sunk!"

Tay had worked up a large, green mouthful of bile.

He stood and spit the mass upon Ventras.

Ventras boiled, literally shaking, his face darkened purple with rage. Bulging blood vessels pounded at his temples and on his forehead.

"How dare you! You should be groveling, pleading, offering to kiss my feet or other sensitive body parts, begging me to free you!"

"What did you expect, you scurvy, slithering slime?" Tay said, with barely contained fury. "That I should thank you for all you've done? That I should actually believe your sick little plan will prevail?"

Tay had approached the steel bars. Ventras quickly reached out and grasped the miniature porcelain Virgin Mary that hung around Tay's neck. He ripped it from the chain.

"What is this?" he asked in mock interest, inspecting it.

"It was my grandfathers. It is dear to me." The dream flashed—his grandfather saying, "Seek the Virgin,"—and then faded away again as if swallowed in heavy mist. The dream was baffling.

Ventras looked at the young man, gaining satisfaction from the fact that he had taken something held dear by the former Admiral Gor and his grandson. "More's the pity," he said, looking very pleased. He wound his arm back quickly and threw the piece against the concrete wall inside Tay's cell. The Virgin, the embodiment of Admiral Gor's riddle, shattered into uncountable pieces and fell to the floor, hopeless remnants of what was once whole.

"You are allowed no personal property in this prison, no matter how dear it may be to your heart!" Ventras said. Then he calmed himself and pulled a piece of fabric from his pocket. He began wiping the nasty residue from his face and front of his garments. In a falsely calm voice that oozed hate, he said, "TayGor, you might like to know that Zuzahna will be joining the penal moon's roster of life prisoners shortly. Her trial will be two moons from your own. I *was* considering allowing the two of you a shared cell, but after your despicable act against me, I have changed my mind. You will know she is there, near you, but I will make sure you *never* set eyes upon her, nor will you be allowed to write or speak to her. For you, from this moment on, she is as good as dead!"

"She is innocent!" Tay screamed.

"So are you, young man, but do you think that really matters in the darkest scheme of things?" Ventras began laughing, a mad, uncontrolled laugh that echoed down the concrete corridors in a reverberation Tay would hear in nightmares for years to come.

Tay closed his eyes to the madman before him. He swore a sacred oath upon all that Seven Galaxies stood for—for the admiral, his beloved grandfather; for Zuzahna; for Alex, who would be imprisoned only because of him; and for the freedom stolen from them all. He spoke a silent oath that this was not finished, that morality and light would prevail.

Once Ventras was gone, Tay began brushing up the pieces of the shattered Virgin with his hands, for lack of a better tool, and not caring that the sharp shards might cut into them. He wondered hopelessly how the pieces could be mended. He wished that he could salvage this thing that had been dear to him.

It was then that Tay found the small slip of white paper that was folded so tightly it resembled the small pieces of broken porcelain. Unfolding the message that had obviously been hidden inside the miniature Virgin Mary, he immediately recognized his grandfather's distinct script.

The mystery hidden within his grandfather's last message to him was revealed. The Virgin was *not* Mary, the mother of Christ, but a pristine planet far away, years travel from Seven Galaxies and Ventras' reign of terror. It was a lost gem to be found, a lee from Ventras' brewing storm.

Tay began to form a plan. It was desperately bold and ingeniously conceived. It was backed by all that is good and worthy, and opposed only by evil in the twisted minds of a few power hungry politicians—a group that had been elected as Stewards of Seven Galaxies. A group whose selfish desire to become emperors over the vast realm of worlds conveniently negated the sacred oath they had all sworn: to protect the citizens of Seven Galaxies and uphold, above all, freedom within the vast society.

Over the short term, Ventras' plan prevailed: Tay and Alex were shipped to the penal colony. Zuzahna was tried by the same farcical tribunal that had found Tay and Alex guilty of crimes they could not possible have committed. Zuzahna was shipped to the penal moon as well.

I Am That I Am, astounded and awakened by powerful sentient feelings, wept.

SIXTY-FIVE

VENTRAS was busy carrying out a plan that had been darkly conceived deep within the slippery recesses of his ever-calculating mind.

This evening, he sat in an unlit alcove in the bedroom of a prominent attorney who was respected throughout Seven Galaxies Seven. Ventras waited, knowing the man's routine, stalking his prey silently, searching for weakness and planning how to use such information. He knew even before their unscheduled meeting took place what the outcome would be.

The footsteps came right on time. The bedroom door opened, and the light in the main chamber flashed on, sending a shaft onto the alcove's floor but not illuminating where Ventras sat, unnoticed. Ventras had chosen his position well. His body was barely discernible in shadows.

The attorney began to undress, throwing soiled clothes into a hamper. His body showed signs of too much work at the desk: his middle-age abdominal paunch sagged, and his curved and sloping shoulders suggested thousands of hours spent toiling over precedents of law and archived cases that inevitably affected outcomes of future battles to be fought. Exhausted, he shuffled into the bathroom, hoping a hot shower would invigorate him.

The water ran a long time, allowing Ventras to mentally rehearse his part.

The attorney was unaware. He knew nothing of Zuzahna's wealth or her connection to TayGor. That suited Ventras well, for complete surprise was often the most powerful offensive weapon. He readied himself as a viper coils to strike, although his venom came not from within but from without. He prepared for delivery.

The attorney exited the bathroom, walked across the bedroom, and pulled back the covers. He climbed into bed. As so many mundane professionals do when the day is done and their tired bodies are finally at rest, he let out a long sigh, as if this were the most enjoyable part of his entire day.

Ventras let him lie still and enjoy the moment for a while, preferring that his adversary's sharp intellect be dulled by oncoming sleep. He would strike in that moment when consciousness and dream state intertwine, when reality and fantasy combine.

Soon, the attorney's breathing became measured, and Ventras knew his time was at hand. He called him by his first name. "Malcolm!"

The man sat bolt upright in bed said, fearfully, "Who is there?"

"Do not be alarmed. I come in friendship to talk about important matters that may only be discussed in private."

"How did you get in here? I demand to know!"

"The director of Secret Services needs no key, no warrant, and no permission to sit in your bedroom at any hour of the day or night, as you well know, Malcolm."

"Ventras!" His name emerged in a hiss of fear. Certainly the old attorney's mind was reeling, attempting to sort out the reasons for this unfortunate encounter.

"You, Malcolm, have a client charged with treason. You are defending her against Seven Galaxies."

The statement took Malcolm completely by surprise. "Yes," was all he could muster.

"You must take a fall on this one. I am well aware of your record as a trial lawyer, and I cannot have you winning this contest."

"What you ask would be an absolute breach of ethics, an abomination to my oath!"

"Frig the oath and your abominations. Just make sure you don't win this one. Zuzahna must go away!"

"What you ask is beyond my power. Zuzahna is an innocent caught in a web of intrigue and violence that she had nothing to do with. I will defend her to the best of my ability! I ask that you leave my house immediately, and do not come back!" The old man was livid.

Ventras expected such a show and now pulled an ace. "You have been seeing someone, Malcolm...someone other than your wife. How do you think she will respond to the news?"

"Friendship only!"

Ventras tossed a packet to the indignant attorney. "You might want to take a look at those."

The aging man tore the packet open, looking dismayed. Upon flipping through the neat compact portfolio of photos that Ventras had cunningly acquired, Malcolm's shoulders slumped. "How?" he asked.

"I hired her. Do you really believe you are—what did Ursulla call you? Your pet name?—the Superman of love?"

Malcolm flushed in embarrassment.

"The facts here are simple. I want you to do something; you don't want me to do something; and so we help each other and remain friends—not enemies." Ventras' eyes narrowed.

A cold shiver ran down Malcolm's spine, and small beads of perspiration rose on his forehead. "Friends?" Malcolm asked suspiciously.

"Certainly! I can be of great help to you and you to me. Isn't that what friendship is all about?" Ventras grinned, feigning a personality that did not actually exist.

"I assume you are holding copies of these photos?" asked Malcolm.

"Of course."

"And if I agree to 'take the fall,' as you have implied I should; then all traces of them will be destroyed and my wife will be left out of your little scheme?"

"You catch on quick! I like that. Nothing worse than a lot of wasted words explaining the eccentricities of an arrangement like ours."

"We have no arrangement! I don't give a damn if my wife finds out! We've been talking divorce for years. So you see, Ventras, your well thought out tactics have no power over me. I will not sell out and give up everything I hold dear—my word, my honor, my life's work—to help you accomplish whatever agenda you have." Malcolm was pleased, priding himself in always negotiating from a foundation of strength.

Ventras more than expected this sort of response. He switched to his second ace. "Gee, Malcolm, I didn't know you felt so strongly about things like your word, your *honor,* and morals."

Ventras had made a complete study of Malcolm's life. He loved the play unfolding, knowing that Malcolm would turn his arrogant nose up at his next offer. That's what made the game so challenging and fun. He liked to give his victim some hope, to play them by hooking them, letting some line out, wearing them down, and inevitably reeling them in, spent and helpless.

"Are you aware of Zuzahna's immense wealth?" Ventras asked.

"No," Malcom said, shaking his head. "She paid my retainer and assured me that the fees I quoted her for handling the case were no problem."

"Well then, I will enlighten you, Malcolm. When Zuzahna was captured, I am sure you are aware she was caught aboard the Nesdian regent's private yacht."

"Yes, I am aware of the circumstances of her capture and that the regent committed suicide rather than be tried as a war criminal."

"Did you also know that Admiral Gor transferred all the regent's personal belongings to Zuzahna after the suicide?"

"No, I was not aware."

"And did you know that the jewels that were aboard the regent's yacht are equal to a kingdom's fortune?"

"I was not aware. What does Zuzahna's inherited wealth have to do with you sitting in my bedroom keeping me from sleep at this late hour?"

"Very simple, Malcolm. You tell Zuzahna that the political leaders pushing her prosecution are out for blood, as are all the people of Seven Galaxies. Why, if Zuzahna were let out on the street and not kept in protective custody, if the people were aware of her true identity, she wouldn't last five minutes before some crackpot hater of Nesdia burned her.

"Tell her that crooked politicians need to be paid off, and that a new identity must be established for her. Tell her you can take care of all these things and invest her remaining wealth so that when she is freed she can live her remaining years in ultimate comfort. Get power of attorney from her. She trusts you. We will split her vast fortune when she is sent to the penal moon as an enemy of Seven Galaxies. Then, you and I can enjoy the bounty my little plan has reaped!"

"Ventras," Malcolm said, shaking his head in disgust, "I understand that you are a very powerful and influential person, not only in government but also in shadowed realms that are only whispered of. But I will take no part in your scheme. You will have to find another pawn to help you harvest the sickening fruit you cultivate!"

"I thought you would say something like that, Malcolm," Ventras said, releasing an exaggerated sigh. "Only I couldn't have dreamed up such a colorful description of my designs. You *really* don't like me, do you?"

"*Whatever* gave you that idea?" Malcolm barked, full of disgust.

"I see," said Ventras, his lips curling over teeth that were shiny with saliva. A smile formed on his face. It was the smile of a killer.

Ventras reached into a pocket and took out a wireless. He punched one button, waited a moment, and then said, "It is necessary. Yes, I expected as much." Then he put the device back into his pocket.

"What is necessary?" asked Malcolm, growing alarmed.

Ventras only smiled at the attorney, who just moments ago had been so sure of himself, so arrogant, so condescending.

"I said, what is necessary?"

Ventras sat in silence, watching Malcolm's self-confidence crumble. This was the part Ventras loved. He enjoyed the cave-in, when resolve dissipated and his personal efforts made broken wrecks of the previously robust.

Malcolm raised his voice. "*What is necessary*, Ventras?"

Ventras spoke calmly, as though he were commenting on the weather outside. "That you murder your wife."

"What in God's name are you rambling about, man?"

"God has *nothing* to do with this situation, Malcolm," Ventras said icily, his steely blue eyes taking on the focused glare of a psychopath. "This is entirely between you and me." Ventras once again let silence do its unearthly work.

Malcolm was now sweating profusely. "What is this nonsense you are spouting about my wife?"

Ventras only glared through slitted eyes.

"What is this about my wife!" Malcolm asked frantically, his forehead damp with the sweat of fear.

"No nonsense. The fact is, she is dead. You killed her with your own weapon. Not very smart, Malcolm; you could have used a black-market piece, which would not be so easily traced back to you."

"You are crazy! My wife is in the country at our cabin.... My weapon...is here in the night stand beside the bed." Malcolm reached for the drawer and opened it, and then removed his trembling hand. "What...? It's gone!"

"What is gone, Malcolm?" Ventras asked, enjoying the moment.

"My weapon, it's not here, where I keep it."

"I know. It was left at the scene of the crime, along with your DNA and fingerprints."

"You are a madman! You are trying to confuse me, trying to make me emotional so I will agree to help you with your ugly schemes."

"I am not trying, Malcolm. *You* will do as I say! Otherwise, you will be arrested in the morning for murder! She is dead. Right here on your estate, in the barn, in her car. Your weapon is on the seat next to her, your footprints are in the muck, the barn crud is tracked into the house.

"You see, I've left nothing out. The prosecutor, who as you know is a good friend of mine, has a bulletproof case. You are with no alibi except for me, your devoted friend who has been with you this last hour, sharing old stories over a few drinks. I'm the one person who can extricate you from suspicion."

"I don't believe any of this! This is a nightmare! I'll soon wake and realize it is over!"

"The only way it will be over is if you do exactly as I say. Make sure Zuzahna is convicted. I will make sure she gets life, nothing worse. She can join TayGor on the penal moon."

"You were responsible for the admiral's son?" Malcolm asked.

"Who else?"

"But why, Ventras? He was a brilliantly skilled leader. Why would you lay waste to such an asset to Seven Galaxies?"

"I do not feel threatened by many people. The Gor's were a problem for me. They had to go."

"You mean the admiral's death was not natural?"

"That is a question I will leave you pondering. Now, on to the positive attributes of our friendship." Ventras smiled at Malcolm, who was now white as snow and quickly going into shock. The man crumbled, his head drooped onto his chest, and his shoulders shuddered with silent sobs.

Ventras stood. "You will see to the power of attorney. We will split the fortune in half. I will take care of your wife's unfortunate murder. It will be blamed on a desperado, a vagrant, and a robbery gone wrong. Ursella is yours, I will see to that. With your wife out of the way, you can begin living—maybe not a moral life filled with honor, but one that with a bit of practice, you will come to enjoy."

The broken man lying in bed heard soft footfalls growing softer and then the click of the entry door followed by the swishing sound of a departing autocar. Malcolm was alone, in the dark.

SIXTY-SIX

The attorney walked with his head held high, though inside he was a crumpled heap. All the things he had held dear for a lifetime had been swept away by Ventras' scheming. Now he walked the lonely concrete corridor lined with patchworks of steel bars, preparing his delivery.

Zuzahna would be deceived into signing power of attorney over to Malcolm, enabling him to seize her wealth and then share it with the loathsome Ventras. He walked on, knowing well that his only avenues were suicide, disgracing his children and career; accepting a conviction for murdering his wife; or going along with this vile plan.

There were no other options, he told himself once more. Hadn't he been over this ugly predicament a thousand times in the sleepless nights he had spent since Ventras' clandestine visit and his wife's brutal murder? He would go through with it, he knew. He had no desire to become an unknown martyr for a noble yet secret cause. He braced himself for the meeting.

Zuzahna's cell loomed ahead. Malcolm swallowed his disgust and went to her.

"Oh! Malcolm!" she said. "I am so happy you've come. Do you bring good news? Am I to be released soon?" She stood before him, innocent of all the charges that would soon lock her beauty away from public view. She would remain hidden, robbed of her youth and wealth, with no hope of reprieve.

"I hope so, Zuzahna. How are you?"

"I fret, as you know, living here—if you could call it that—in limbo, wondering when I shall see sunlight once more. Oh how I dream of taking a long, deep breath of fresh air!"

"Zuzahna, I have some news. How you react could mean the difference between freedom and this place."

"Tell me at once!"

Malcolm began his persuasion, the words he had rehearsed, the pitch that would free him from Ventras' threats by trading Zuzahna's future for the safety of his own. "First, you must understand I believe you are innocent of the charges levied against you. However, public and political sentiment at this time is extremely hostile towards Nesdia, and you *are* Nesdian.

"Your incarceration has been kept secret from the public's eye. Just remember, politicians want to stay in office. If Seven Galaxies' populace were to gain the knowledge and understand that politicians in power released you without taking this case to trial, they would be forced from office. In fact, some of them wish to figuratively burn you as an enemy of the people, hence gaining popularity with the voters."

Zuzahna took on a hunted look. Deep creases formed on her normally smooth forehead, and her hands visibly trembled. *Good,* thought Malcolm. *What I have said has been received, stabbing the dagger home.*

"What am I to do?" she asked, fraught with worry.

"I have taken the liberty of meeting with a few of the most prominent leaders in, shall we say, a series of unrecorded settlement meetings." Malcolm paused for effect, building Zuzahna's apprehension. "I have posed a simple question to them all, when I was alone with each one separate from the others."

"What was the question?"

"How much? That is the question, Zuzahna."

"I don't understand, Malcolm. How much what?"

"Money, Zuzahna, the oil that makes greedy gears spin and brings about fast change in a system that is otherwise mired in long, drawn-out legal proceedings."

"Am I to understand that I can buy my way out of here? Will I have anything left after the politicians' pockets are filled?"

"Yes, to both questions. If you would allow me to invest your remaining fortune, you will be free and financially comfortable the rest of your days," Malcolm lied, straight faced.

"You are sure of this?" she asked, quickened by hope that had left her until now.

"I have an agreement. As long as we hold up your end financially, they will hold up theirs and set you free, with the voters being no wiser to the gambit."

"You trust these people?"

"Trust is not the issue. Sealing the transaction so that they cannot back out, that is my job, that is what you pay me for, Zuzahna: to be your fiduciary, to look out for your interests, to protect you. I assure you I will do all these things."

Malcolm despised himself for leading this poor wretch on, giving her hope and the belief she would soon be free when it was not possible. Malcolm was, in simple terms, trading her freedom for his own while enriching Ventras and himself at her expense. Life was unfair, he thought, feeling heavy in his heart and yet not willing to trade places with the sacrificial lamb.

"What must I do to make this plan a reality?" she asked, excited.

"Simply sign a power of attorney giving me control of your financial wealth, and then sit back and be patient a little longer," Malcolm answered confidently, as though he intended to act upon the plan.

"All right. Tay told me I could trust you implicitly, that you are an old, well-loved family friend. I will do it!"

Malcolm's eyes flickered at the mention of Tay and his long friendship with the family. He was struck by a feeling of overwhelming guilt. He busied himself with paperwork, not wishing to look Zuzahna in the eyes.

"Just sign here at the bottom, and then I'll sign and stamp it as your witness," he said, showing her the papers.

Zuzahna embraced the pen as if it were the key to her cell and freedom from imprisonment, when actually it was the mirror image. The simple act of signing away her wealth would leave her destitute and alone.

Paperwork finished, Malcolm stood to leave.

"Thank you for all that you've done for me." Zuzahna stood on her toes to kiss the taller man's cheek in thanks.

Perspiration from Malcolm's hair dripped onto her nose. She had not noticed him perspiring before, as she had been concentrating on the decision at hand. The little voice in her head spoke, telling her all was not what it seemed.

"Yes, Zuzahna. Well, I'll be going." He left the cell and walked rapidly away.

A sinking feeling came over her. She called out desperately, "What of Tay? What news do you have from him?"

Malcolm didn't turn back, nor did he acknowledge that she had uttered a word. His stride increased, carrying him away from the embarrassment of his treachery.

Preview the next book in the series:

The Seeding II
Virgin Landfall

Now available in paperback and eBook formats

ONE

Tay rose early. The warmth of his blankets called to him as his feet touched the cool wooden floor, but his resolve pried him away from the bed's promise of comfort, despite his aching muscles.

He had been cutting hay for days. The weather was sunny and hot, so the drying would go well if the monumental task could be finished before the rain came. With good fortune and sixteen grueling hour's labor a day, the barn would soon be full of hay—that valuable winter commodity.

Tay had no intention of selling the tall, golden grass once it was dry. His plan was, instead, to trade it to the herd of wild horses, to strike a bargain with them in midwinter, when empty bellies would lend more patience to their temperamental and often flighty personalities.

He made a coffee and fried some eggs. Then, holding the coffee in one hand as he scarfed an egg sandwich, he walked to the barn.

The scythe, to which he was enslaved for a few more days, was hanging inside the door. He stuffed the final bite of sandwich into his mouth and grabbed the tool from the wall in the same motion.

The day was cool, and sun-up was still an hour away. Hanging his straw hat on the garden fence he walked through the entered field, which was nearly half-cut.

Tay had planted twelve acres of high-grade orchard grass along a sweeping bend in the river where the dark, loamy soil ran deep. It had headed up with grain. The tops danced lazily in morning breeze. The sweet scent of it drying soothed the aching muscles in his arms and back.

As he lay into the standing grass with long, sweeping motions of his scythe, he quickly lost track of time. Fluid strokes back and forth flattened the tall grass. To someone watching Tay's smooth motion, it might have appeared an effortless task, yet it strained the limits of his endurance.

After a time, he stopped for a short rest and a drink of water. He wiped beads of sweat off his forehead with a shirtsleeve, looked down river, and saw him: the striking young stallion he had named Eclipse.

The elusive charcoal-grey horse was making his way down the far side of the field, not looking towards the sweating man. Something else was on his mind.

Tay took the beast in visually, remembering a dear friend he had left back on Seven. Seeing this horse was a trip back in time, to the days of his youth before Shadow had grown grey, to a time when Shadow had been full of himself and had legs like loaded steel springs.

Tay was surprised to see the dark horse heading towards the cabin and barn. Normally the animal was skittish and unapproachable, but now he was clearly headed for Tay's home—while Tay was far away, out in the middle of the field.

What is he doing? he thought.

Not taking his eyes from the animal, he watched the horse's flawless movement, a motion filled with graceful power. The young beast was poetry in motion, Tay thought, as the horse approached the garden fence, grabbed the straw hat in his mouth, and ran straight back out into the field, towards him.

Stopping a hundred feet away, Eclipse began bobbing his head up and down, his large, dark eyes filled with intelligent humor.

"Give me that, you bugger!"

Tay began walking towards the horse, hoping to save the hat before it was ruined.

As soon as he was near, Eclipse skirted him and ran a bit farther away, letting out a shrill, short squeak.

Tay experienced a stunning sense of déjà vu. Shadow had always made a game of eating his hats, to the point where Tay had quit setting them down and instead wore them on a string, so they could be taken off and rested against his back when not in use. Even then, Shadow would still sometimes make off with them, always letting out the shrill squeak and then playing his humorously frustrating game of keep-away, just as Eclipse was doing now.

Eclipse squeaked again, obviously enjoying the man's frustration. They were close to the river. Mist curled up from the water and rolled ethereally towards them. The horse kept eating the hat. He wasn't actually swallowing, Tay saw, just chewing and bobbing his head up and down, taunting the man as if this were some immense and very funny practical joke.

Tay said, "Wait till this winter when you're starving. I'll remember this!"

The horse turned suddenly, as if spooked, and ran to the water's edge, where it stood hip-deep in a surreal white mist that ebbed between them.

Then he saw her. She was walking upslope from the river's bend, appearing ghostlike out of the mist, gliding through the waves of tall, golden grass. Her haunting eyes—like violet, green, and blue pools—drew upon his soul, compelling his steps to falter so that he stood frozen in place, hypnotized.

She moved towards him and paused next to the horse, which stood still as she took the hat from his mouth. When she moved toward Tay again, Eclipse followed her. Her long, multicolored hair swung with the fluid movement of her hips.

She was here, he thought.

She had come to him before, just as she was walking to him now. The look in her eyes drew his heart into a knot. It beat so loudly Tay feared it might burst.

The horse and the enchantress were steps away. She reached out her arm, offering the hat. The scent of Eclipse's sweat, the aromatic smell of freshly cut hay, and her mystic presence so close he could almost touch her: it was all so familiar. *I have seen her before, in my dreams,* Tay thought. Then, in that moment, Tay started awake.

The shadows of the steel bars cast a familiar, depressing pattern of stripes onto the walls of his cell. Tay counted down. *Four days,* he thought silently. *Four more days.* It was the promise that allowed him to hang on.